"Stop Fighting Me!"
He Muttered against Her Lips

"No!" She twisted her head from side to side. Her fingernails were digging into his arms, but she couldn't help it. "You don't understand!"

"You don't understand."

He recaptured her mouth, smothering her protests roughly. Until finally, with his hands pinning her shoulders, his head lowered to the curve of her throat.

Mandy gasped. Then she gasped again, whispering half-words that didn't make any sense. The tiny explosions tingling down her limbs made her shiver.

She didn't want him to stop, and he knew it. Still, Mandy summoned what will she had left. She reached out, clasping his head in both hands.

"I'm not what you think," she choked, and squeezed her eyes tightly shut. The seconds spun out into infinity.

"You're not honest is what you're not," he said at last, with a depth of insight which chilled her. "You feel it, too. Don't lie and say you don't. . . ."

Dear Reader:

We trust you will enjoy this Richard Gallen romance. We plan to bring you more of the best in both contemporary and historical romantic fiction with four exciting new titles each month.

We'd like your help.

We value your suggestions and opinions. They will help us to publish the kind of romances you want to read. Please send us your comments, or just let us know which Richard Gallen romances you have especially enjoyed. Write to the address below. We're looking forward to hearing from you!

Happy reading!

Judy Sullivan
Richard Gallen Books
8-10 West 36th St.
New York, N.Y. 10018

An Innocent Deception

LINDA SHAW

PUBLISHED BY RICHARD GALLEN BOOKS
Distributed by POCKET BOOKS

Books by Linda Shaw

The Satin Vixen
An Innocent Deception

 A RICHARD GALLEN BOOKS *Original* publication

Distributed by
POCKET BOOKS, a Simon & Schuster division of
GULF & WESTERN CORPORATION
1230 Avenue of the Americas, New York, N.Y. 10020

ISBN: 0-671-43928-6

First Pocket Books printing December, 1981

10 9 8 7 6 5 4 3 2 1

RICHARD GALLEN and colophon are trademarks of Simon & Schuster and Richard Gallen & Co., Inc.

Printed in the U.S.A.

To Mary Lynn

An Innocent Deception

Chapter One

Two telephones of Dulick, Hanlin and Hanlin in downtown New Orleans jangled at once. As the delivery man from Land-Air Express tossed three parcels on the front desk to be signed for, an inner office door opened and a woman peered around the doorframe.

Amanda Phillips scribbled her name on the delivery receipts and closed slender fingers about the nearest telephone. Shoulder-length blond hair shimmered softly about her face. The gold chain about her throat was noticeably simple, delicate like her makeup. Her only other jewelry was a tiny diamond, a ring which had belonged to her mother. She presented a casual portrait—a smart, yet unstudied beauty.

"Miss McKinney was supposed to be upstairs fifteen minutes ago," complained the worried legal stenographer in the doorway.

"She's still in a meeting," Mandy explained. She and Julie Deasy, the other receptionist, scowled, daring the secretary to object. The door clicked shut.

"I'll take the other phones, Mandy," offered Julie. "You get him." Julie flicked a weary hand toward a tall, assertive figure filling the outer office doorway.

When the former receptionist had married, Julie had suggested Mandy to fill in temporarily. They were both Loyola University graduate students. Mandy, an honor student in journalism, had worked here one month—only since her life had abruptly fallen apart at the seams on the fourteenth of June. On her twenty-third birthday, when they had buried her father.

Glancing halfheartedly at the man striding toward the reception desk, Mandy snapped off her typewriter. She pressed the hold button for at least the twentieth time that morning and grabbed a note pad.

He must be well into his thirties, she thought. Really good-looking men were not easy to pinpoint. From the pinstriped Armani suit to the casually styled hair grazing his collar, he radiated the confidence of an urbane executive.

Another telephone buzzed. "I'm sorry, sir," Mandy apologized with a self-assured smile.

But her smile faded as he braced long fingers upon the counter. His hands were lean and capable, unquestionably controlled, like the line of his jaw. He would be difficult.

"Mandy, this is Bergman," came the voice in her ear. "I've got depressing news."

With the receiver resting in the hollow between her jaw and shoulder, Mandy averted her gaze just in time to glimpse a leisurely inspection being made of herself.

New Orleans had suffered temperatures hovering near the hundred-degree mark for a week. Blue haze drifted up from the Mississippi River, promising much-needed rain. But until the clouds burst open, the oppressive humidity was wearing nerves razor sharp.

Today she had dressed for the weather, wearing the thinnest of underwear. Cool, trim slacks brushed against her and her blouse fell free and sensuously. The stranger's expert brown eyes, moving over the curve of her hips and across her waist, paused at the low scoop of her neckline.

When Mandy caught him looking, he didn't pretend it was an accident. The frank quirk of his brows was undisguised. "Don't pretend you don't know how sexy you are," it said.

"Oh?" she sighed into the receiver.

Trying to follow Bergman's train of thought grew increasingly difficult. She kept repeating "Really?" With a cool reserve, which usually discouraged men, she forced an excessively polite smile. It did not seem to affect the visitor.

Admiration was never hard to take, especially from a man as cosmopolitan as this one. But years ago she had learned that flattering eyes was a lethal game her father's friends played with gullible young women . . . especially pretty ones. After having her heart broken over a married man when she was eighteen, she rapidly learned that flirting games were rigged in favor of men and stopped playing them. Amanda dressed well on her father's money and enjoyed her beauty in an uncomplicated way. And she kept almost every man at arm's length.

Now, in spite of herself, Mandy felt a hot flush creeping up her neck. For several seconds she hoped to outlast him in this unpremeditated skirmish of the sexes. He could not help but see he was embarrassing her.

But in the end he won. Resentful of any man so egotistical, she glanced downward, positive that he smiled. In a small gesture of satisfaction, he tossed an expensive Carrano case upon the desk.

` "Ahh . . . everything's a mess here today, Bergman," she explained irritably into the receiver. "One of the elevators has broken down, and we're shorthanded."

"Everybody's got troubles," was the lighthearted reply. "Come by my office during your lunch break. I'll take care of you . . . like I always do." Bergman Reeves loved to feel he was the most important thing in Mandy's life.

"Can't it wait?" she inquired.

"Not if you want to unsnarl your father's affairs anytime in the foreseeable future."

Mandy impatiently slid a tiny heart back and forth on the gold chain about her throat. The probating of Preston Phillips's will was acutely distressing. Bergman actually did take care of her. He was working himself silly to keep Amanda and her stepmother from selling personal belongings while he untangled a nasty legal hassle. Everything was time consuming. Already they had been forced to take two small loans at the bank, simply to keep the huge Phillips estate running.

"Be here, darling." From his plush attorney's suite in the Pontalba Building, he laughed softly.

Amanda hardly heard him; she was forming a strategy directed at the man who had just bested her in a silent war of eyes.

"All right," she agreed.

Fishing through her desk drawer, she took an inordinate amount of time to find a ballpoint pen. When the stranger cleared his throat, indicating his impatience, she smothered a smile. They were even now—rudeness for rudeness.

With the most unapproachable professionalism she could assume, Mandy faced him. "What may we do for you today, sir?"

He caught the edge of his lower lip in perfect white teeth. "I don't think you really want to know, do you?"

Mandy pretended his remark didn't bother her. She shouldn't have met his challenge. His attempt not to laugh was worse than if he had blatantly called her a liar.

Before she could speak, he did. "I need to see John Dulick."

"Do you have an appointment?"

"No."

Mandy felt the low boil of anger. "Your name, sir."

The pen she was holding trembled. They both stared at it, and she wanted to slam the traitorous thing down on the desk.

"Russell C. Gregory."

"Your *full* name please, Mr. Gregory."

"Russell *Cyrus* Gregory, miss."

Mandy printed it neatly on a memo form. "Well, Mr. Gregory," she said, "if you'll please be seated, I will try to work you in. It will be a while."

He blinked, as if he weren't used to women speaking to him in an I-dare-you-to-do-that-again tone. Mandy wasn't certain if the twitch at the corner of his mouth was a hint of amusement or an attempt to check his temper. The latter, she guessed.

"My plane for Zurich leaves at six o'clock," he objected. "I prefer to see Mr. Dulick right away."

"I'm sorry. He's in a meeting, sir. Mr. Hanlin, perhaps?"

"John Dulick," he repeated with soft authority. "This morning. Immediately."

Mandy shook her head. "Three o'clock this afternoon."

She had him and she knew it. Perspiration drizzled down the backs of her knees, and she set her mouth in a serenity she did not feel. Whoever Russell Cyrus Gregory was, he obviously was not accustomed to being denied or delayed. She was probably the first woman who had ever dared to challenge his stare.

When he walked behind the counter into the interior of the

office, striding between the desks as if they belonged to him, two pairs of feminine eyes followed him with stunned disbelief.

"I'm sorry, sir," Mandy began, her hand gesturing in protest. As her glance darted to Julie, Russell Gregory stepped to her telephone, removed his wallet from his hip pocket, dialed the operator and rattled off a credit-card number. He concluded with "please, dear."

"You can't come in here!" objected Mandy, stepping in front of him with what she hoped was the heavy-handed authority of her absent superior, Helen McKinney. Clutching her pen and some forms to her chest, as if they were a shield, she braced one hand on her hip and glared at him as he waited for the operator to put through his call.

"Your pen please, miss?" he said lightly.

Before Mandy could proffer it or refuse it, he deliberately removed it from her fingers, opening them one by one. Ignoring her slackened jaw, he scribbled some figures on a pad lying on the desk. Mandy jerked back her hand as if stung. Julie, hanging up her telephone in stunned slow motion, met Mandy's eyes behind his back. Mandy's helpless shrug said she had never seen such insolence before, and Julie's wave warned her to let Gregory have his way.

Mandy could not sit at her desk. Russell Gregory hooked his lean hips on the edge of it and crossed his ankles as if he belonged there, had always belonged there. Mandy shakenly found her way to the file cabinet. She motioned Julie nearer.

"Have you *ever* seen such nerve?" she whispered, opening a drawer stealthily and removing a file without looking at it.

"Who's he talking to?"

"I don't know. Someone in New York. Why, he just can't walk in here like that. Miss McKinney will have my head."

As far back as Mandy could remember she had gone out of her way to please people. To see someone as brashly demanding as the man now monopolizing her phone was intolerable. The sound of his step behind her gave Mandy the seconds she needed to disguise her dislike of his behavior.

As Mandy turned to protest politely, the scream of splitting metal spun them all about. Shearing rivets echoed through the hallway like some screeching demon. The impact of weight plummeting against concrete shook the floor. But that didn't send Julie dashing breathlessly for the doorway; it was the masculine cry of pain.

"Terry?" Julie cried, flying toward the hall.

The silence was as sudden and as sinister as the noise had been. For one horrible second Mandy froze, her blue eyes wide, instinctively meeting those of the man.

Terry and Julie had been engaged for two years. For the past week he and three other maintenance employees had worked on the building's old elevator. Tenants had been complaining that it jerked in mid-descent and refused to stop at floor level. A contract for a new one had already been signed, but meanwhile maintenance was making do.

Before Mandy could collect her bearings, Russell Gregory slung his case onto the leather couch near the door. He sprinted after Julie.

By the time Mandy reached the hall, curious occupants of the building were already pouring from offices on the upper floors. Stairways became congested with people yelling questions about what had happened. Several pale office clerks, not knowing what else to do, were unsuccessfully attempting to fight back the pressing crowd.

"Get back!" Russell shouted over the pandemonium.

Disagreeable or not, he seemed to be the only one retaining enough presence of mind to be effective. Julie was hysterical—frozen stiff, shaking her head and repeating "No, no, no," over and over. Mandy grabbed her in a tight hug.

"It's all right, Julie," she said. "It's all right." Steeling herself against lumbering bodies and shoulders which nearly knocked her down, she pulled Julie to a wall and gestured to some stunned secretaries.

"Take care of her!" she ordered. She pushed Julie toward them. Motioning to curious onlookers in the building on business, Mandy drew them out of the way. She grasped a small boy's arm and steered him toward his mother. "Don't let these children near the elevator!"

The clatter of men's boots rang loudly upon the tile stairwell above their heads, forcing a path to be made. After fighting her way to the shaft, with desperation thickening in her throat, Mandy peered down into the dim opening. Terry O'Connor knelt on the top of the aging conveyance. The cables obscured most of her view, but even from her poor position she could see that his whole arm was pinned in a network of lines and pulleys dropping from the center of the shaft itself.

Peeling out of his jacket and at the same time assessing the best way to get down to the man, Russell thrust his jacket into Mandy's hands. He tested the cables, squinting upward at the shaft.

He swung his arm in a wide gesture and spoke to a blank-eyed cashier. "Call the police. Keep everyone back."

"Yes," he said and elbowed his way to a telephone.

"I'm in maintenance!" shouted a drawn college youth. The crowd let him through.

"What about acetylene?" someone suggested. "We could cut through the cables."

"I don't think so," Russell replied.

"We were going to switch to an auxiliary unit," began the young man.

"Get some hydraulic jacks set up in the basement," said Russell. He ignored the ruinous black grease as he tested the secondary pulleys. After pausing to kick off his shoes, he grasped the steel cables.

Then his eyes scoured the onlookers for Mandy. She stood helplessly, holding his jacket. "Get some paramedics in here."

"Oh, God!" she breathed as he swung over into the dark opening. Hand over hand, his muscles straining as everyone above him held their breath, he began a labored descent to Terry's side.

Mandy gaped in awe. Gregory's agility was incredible—the skill one expected of mountain climbers in the movies. With hair tousled about his face, his feet carefully groping for a hold, his weight set the pulleys groaning.

Threading her way through the people, Mandy rushed to the office phone and dialed. Tossing his jacket aside, she drew over a note pad. As she supplied the necessary information to a paramedic dispatcher downtown, she scribbled abstract marks. Unconsciously flicking the fine lapel with the top of her pen, she realized that his pants were hopelessly ruined.

Mandy didn't search through Russell Gregory's jacket purposely. In her distraction, it simply fell open and spilled his passport onto the desk. Gregory's handsome face looked back at her from his photograph.

Ports of entry read Sweden, Denmark, England, West Germany. Recently stamped. And the passport was issued to Benjamin Hamilton.

"Good Lord!" she whispered, totally immersed in her own disbelief. Now she was oblivious to the emergency going on outside.

Her next action was no more planned than the first; it was reflexive, like grabbing for her nose before a sneeze. She looked into the pocket of the jacket.

Another passport with a different picture of him, as attractive as the other. People's Republic of China, South Korea, Japan. And issued two years earlier to Russell Cyrus Gregory. What had she found here?

Astounded, her eyes darted to his pigskin suede case resting innocently on the divan near the wall. As angry as she had been at Mr. Russell Gregory a few moments ago—or was it Benjamin Hamilton?—he certainly hadn't struck her as being a criminal. But what earthly reason could a man have for owning two passports if he weren't involved in something illegal?

Mandy's better judgment warned her to call Helen McKinney. Instead, she replaced the passports inside Gregory's jacket where she had found them.

Why? Because she sensed this was more than what it appeared to be? Or, even more honestly, was it because he was a man who refused to avert his eyes when she erected her wall of defense?

Mandy refused to accept that. She reacted because she was an aggressive journalist. The first piece she ever wrote, at sixteen, had won her four hundred dollars. The twentieth had landed her a full scholarship. "She shows promise," her father's friends in New York had complimented. Yet she knew what she wrote—safe, well-polished pieces that came much too easily.

"You're afraid to go out on a limb, girl!" yelled Ken Hagan, a grumpy retired editor, a friend who never complimented her. He ripped to pieces everything she submitted. "Go with your gut," he always said. "Don't try to write pretty. Trust your instincts."

And now Mandy's sixth sense riveted her eyes on the attaché case. Somewhere in this bizarre moment of chance was a crucial factor. She could not explain it logically, but she knew it was there. A man could not be admirably courageous and dishonest at the same time. Could he?

A uniformed policeman stepped into the office, startling

her. She noticed several more in the hall. Three units emptied into the building, one outside for traffic control.

"I'm all right," she said quickly, tossing Russell Gregory's jacket aside casually.

Static from the officer's two-way radio crackled. As he backed into the crowded hall, she heard him give a code number. Hasty commands bounced back and forth—crisp, staccato orders of men accustomed to working together.

Her hands were wet. Feeling like a character in a James Bond movie, her fingers nervously smoothed the brass clasps on the case. Then, with an intake of breath, she released one clasp. After a moment, the other.

When she laid open the case, finding it neatly arranged with what appeared to be financial reports from foreign industrial conglomerates, she slumped in disappointment. Aeronautics design, electronic systems manufacture, half a dozen computer printouts that meant nothing to her. A sheaf of letters in languages she couldn't read.

What was the man covering up?

The siren of the paramedic ambulance wailed outside. Mandy's head jerked up with skittish guilt. The snaps of the shutting case made incriminating, frightening sounds much like the furious pounding of her own heart.

Julie's voice directly behind her sent Mandy spinning around with a harsh gasp, the damning case in her hand.

"You scared the life out of me!" she choked. She tried not to, but she stood at the doomed attention of a convict and slipped the case behind her.

"Terry?" Mandy choked. "Is he—"

"He's all right. I'm all right," Julie told her with a relieved sigh. She braced herself on the desk, exhausted. "His arm's not even broken, thanks to that man. Mandy, what in heaven's name are you doing?"

"Listen to me, Julie," Mandy hesitated. "This . . . isn't what it looks like. You'll never believe it."

Explaining about the phony passport took less effort than describing the thoughts struggling to crystallize in her mind. The more she explained, the wider Julie's eyes grew behind her thick horn-rimmed glasses.

"Julie, do you know what constitutes success? Journalistically speaking?"

"I don't even know what you're talking about."

Mandy pondered for a moment. "How can I say this without sounding insane? You know, being in the right place at the right time?"

Julie's confusion did not set well on her frail shoulders. Julie was a creature of habit. She would never think in terms of risks and venturing into the unknown.

"More than that," Mandy continued, wanting her friend to understand, "having the nerve to follow through on a hunch. Look at it this way. What if someone hadn't been alert enough to notice some masking tape on a door of the Watergate Hotel? What if two *Washington Post* reporters hadn't grown insatiably curious about some campaign money?"

"But how do you know this is worth anything, Mandy?"

"I *don't* know. But neither did Bob Woodward when he picked up the telephone and started asking questions about laundered money."

Mandy swept her hand outward with a flourish, as if lettering huge headlines. "Investigation of the Corporate Conscience. Tactics of Big Business Illegalities Conducted Under the Table."

Julie frowned. "Illegalities? Not that man out there!"

"I'd stake almost anything on it. His false passport is a crime. It intrigues me. It doesn't fit the man somehow."

Mandy placed Russell Gregory's attaché case on her desk like an icon. For a moment both girls paid homage to the possible importance of its contents, until the commotion outside jolted them back to reality.

"You'd be taking an awful chance," Julie shook her head. "Snooping into that man's business. You could get sued."

Julie made sense, yet Mandy could not shrug off her drive to know. A good journalist lived by his nose, they said. Gregory was a contradiction. Her instincts warned her—he was no ordinary contradiction.

"Getting sued doesn't worry me. It's scraping up cash. Probating Daddy's will is taking so much longer than we figured. I'm wealthy and flat broke."

Julie fondly touched her cheek. "I've got to go to the hospital with Terry. He's on the stretcher. Will I see you again if you ride off on your charger?"

"I need to take off now." Mandy made a small sound of urgency. "I have to call an editor friend of mine. But if he says what I think he will, I won't be back for a few days. Don't think I'm mad. Hope I become famous."

They hugged each other, almost like accepting condolences. Mandy kissed her friend's cheek.

"Will you do me a favor when you get back from the hospital?" she asked.

"Sure."

"See that Gregory gets worked in to see Mr. Dulick. Getting money out of Bergman will be a royal battle, so I'd better get on it. Don't look so worried."

Julie's eyes lifted upward in wonder. "Aren't you even scared?"

Shrugging, Mandy moistened her lips. "Well," she admitted slowly, "I guess a little. I never investigated a person before, only humane societies and highway spending. Those safe little features they assign to women. Yes, I'm scared."

The commotion of the paramedics sobered them both. The police sealed off the shaft, and Mandy dashed to the divan. She replaced the case in the exact position she had found it. In a last-moment urgency, the two girls clutched each other.

"Be careful, Mandy. Even *Newsweek* isn't worth getting a contract put out on you by the Mafia."

Mandy wailed. *"Ju*-lie, the man is not the Mafia. Will you cover me with Miss McKinney? Tell her anything but the truth."

"Yes, yes! Now you better get out of here if you don't want to meet up with your 'suspect'."

Opening her desk, Mandy scooped up several items and crammed them into her bag. Julie, her immediate thoughts already focused upon her injured fiancé, blew her friend a breathy kiss.

"Be careful," she whispered.

"I will," Mandy assured her.

When Mandy slipped swiftly through the inner office she felt light-headed, as if she were on some insane emotional high. Preston Phillips had been dead one month. This was the first energy she had felt since they had buried him. She *was* frightened; she was uncertain about how to handle herself. No one deliberately made a fool of himself, and prying into people's business was a risky affair.

But taking the first step in anything was hard, especially

beginning to live again. Should she settle back on her father's money and play it safe? Should she be the predictable society debutante everyone expected?

Probably, she thought, opening a door onto the side stairway. But then, the Phillips family had never taken the safe way out.

As Mandy stepped through double swinging doors of the Pontalba Building a while later, she immediately searched for a pay phone. From the sunken cocktail lounge across the lobby, men sipped martinis and watched her take Ken Hagan's number from her purse. Waiting for the call to connect, she flicked burnished wisps of hair off her forehead and smoothed the ribbed neckline of her blouse.

Ken Hagan was a retired editor for *Today's World*—a gruff, frazzle-haired veteran who had taken the time to pencil-edit her work since she was a child. If Preston Phillips had not died, she would probably be at Ken's remote summer cottage in Connecticut again this year, laboring over mundane writing chores for his suburban newspaper.

"Hello, Ken?" she laughed brightly.

"Mandy! Where are you, girl? Are you in New York?"

"No, silly. Listen, I've got a tale for you, and I don't have all day to tell it."

Mandy related her impressions of Russell Gregory in rushed, eager chunks, stopping only to insert reasons why she could conduct this investigation even though she was "only a woman." She finished rather lamely, wondering if she had been convincing.

"Well," Ken responded with his usual biting caution, "it's a curious bit of circumstance."

"Bit of circumstance?" Mandy scolded him fondly. "What does it take to tempt you?"

He laughed. "I didn't say a man like this character wouldn't tempt me, but what if he's mixed up in drug traffic, or black-market babies?"

Mandy shook her head prettily, as if he could see. "He's not the type, Ken. He's intelligent, cultured, fashionable. That's what hooked me in the first place. Not drugs. No."

"Jewel smuggling, perhaps," Ken came back, "or even something so simple as a murdered wife."

"Wait a minute! Wait a minute, Ken. This man is special. If

he's a thief, he's one who steals with his wits, not a gun. Harold Phelps at *Business Today* would go crazy for a story like this, and you know it. He loves to catch those big business moguls with dirty hands."

Ken's voice boomed in her ear. "You've got a good head, kiddo. I've always told you that. But Switzerland? Let me call Arnold Keller and have him go with you. He's a friend. He'll do it."

Pinching the bridge of her narrow nose, loving his experienced knowledge and hating his common sense, Mandy finally yielded. "Okay, call Arnold. But just tell him to stay close to the phone. If I see I'm in over my head, I'll contact him immediately."

Ken chuckled. "Never call me a chauvinist, baby. Now, you listen to me. You do your homework on this story. Don't go bringing me back high-finance hearsay or what you *think*. And don't get yourself thrown in jail for invasion of privacy, either. In the meantime, *I'll* go out on a limb and see what I can dig up about this man's professional life in the States."

Mandy triumphantly rubbed the tip of her tongue along the edge of her upper teeth. Her blue eyes swept over the lounge, and when one man lifted a glass in a toast, she flashed him a smile.

"I'll stay out of his private affairs, I promise," she said. Her manner changed then, the seriousness being much more typical of her. "Ken, if I do this story well, do you think it has enough of a kick to get me noticed as a serious reporter?"

The pause on the other end was one of the things she respected Ken Hagan for; he rarely spoke lightly or off the top of his head.

"It's possible, Amanda. Exposé features are popular now, have been since the mid-seventies. The apathy of the modern business conscience is a good handle, but only if you have enough dynamite to build a bomb. Check it out. We'll see."

"All right," she said, ending the call. "We'll see."

When Mandy stepped off the elevator and glanced about the outer office of Bergman Reeves's law firm, its luxury sent an irrational anger surging into her stomach. It didn't seem quite fair that he should live so comfortably while he took his time sorting out her own confusing financial affairs.

There was no shortage of Preston Phillips's money, but the

bulk of it was being reinvested in his real property and
businesses. Spiraling inflation had necessitated some major
adjustments in his estate planning, and while in the process
of making them, Preston had died. That left hardly a penny
for Mandy's personal needs. Felice Phillips, Mandy's stepmother, was in no better shape.

"Sentimentality!" Bergman had raged when he began
probating the will. "Taking a wife at his age messed things up
badly enough. The rest of Preston's beneficiaries are heaven
knows where!"

In the meantime, the two women were nearly broke.

Bergman's secretary wore her competence in thinly
plucked brows which could wither people instantly. She
smiled her normal thin smile at Mandy and pushed a button
on the intercom panel. After a moment, Mandy was motioned to the rear suite of offices.

As she swept through the doors, Mandy hardly looked at
the consistent blue decor which had cost Bergman a fortune.
He was a careful man—a calculating one who planned years
in advance. He would scream when he learned what she
planned to do. Mandy decided she would be implacable; she
would be like her father.

Bergman did scream. *"Are you mad, Amanda?"*

Jumping from behind his desk only accentuated his short-
ness. But Bergman tried to compensate for his stocky frame
with the most expensive clothes money could buy, like the
black silk shirt opened at the throat and tucked into gray
slacks. His charisma was his volatile impulsiveness and his
ability to flatter—when he chose to. But he didn't choose to
now.

"You've always had everything given to you," he argued.
"You've never been denied a solitary thing in your whole
life!"

At Mandy's pained expression, Bergman tempered his
criticism.

"You're panicking, honey," he cajoled. "I know you think
you need to make a little money, but—"

"It's not the money, Bergman."

"Well, some damned academic achievement, then. But
this—whatever-his-name-is could have a dozen good reasons
for having two passports. This is the worst possible time to go
tearing off to Switzerland on a screwball chase."

Mandy's jaw had always been an accurate weathervane. Telling her not to do something she thought she could handle was Bergman's fatal tactic. He should have realized that after working for Preston Phillips for seven years.

"Serious reporting is a tightly dominated field," Bergman added lamely.

"You wouldn't say that if I were a man," Mandy said acidly.

"Dan Rather can do it." He spat his words.

Her face flushed hotly. "Barbara Walters can do it. That environmental piece I did for *Reader's Digest* got an honorable mention. And this has much more potential."

Bergman roared with laughter. *"Reader's Digest?* Look, baby, you're pretty good with a camera. Take a few pictures, and I'll get someone to help you publish a small book. But writing for the big time? Forget it!"

"You can't stop me, Bergman."

"You've got stars in your eyes, dammit!"

"They're my eyes!"

The attorney stood exactly level with Mandy, not wanting to press her farther. He reached a hand to touch her, thought better of it, and dropped it. She didn't trust Bergman when he mellowed. She stared at her sandals.

"Mandy," he said, a soft urging in his voice, "why do you keep putting me off? Hey, I know you don't hear bells when you're with me. But believe me, honey, that's all a stupid figment novelists write about. You're twenty-three. You should be married."

"I will get married, Bergman, when the time is right. *If* it ever is."

Bergman tipped up her chin and gazed into her eyes. They seemed much older to him than twenty-three. He could recall Mandy's mother, who had looked to Preston Phillips for the solution to all her problems. Mandy had very little of her mother in her and far too much of her father.

A strand of hair lay across her cheek like a thread of spun gold. When he brushed it aside, she tolerated it without flinching. Then, because she did not repulse him, Bergman closed her into his arms with a protective embrace.

"I wish you wouldn't do that," she said tonelessly.

Embarrassed, Bergman stiffened and thrust her from him. When his eyes narrowed, Amanda forced down a shiver. "I need to borrow some money against my trust fund," she said. Before he could begin arguing, she added, "I'll let you hold the title to my car."

Bergman's laugh was short and unbelieving. "That decrepit Datsun?"

"I'll go to the bank," she threatened.

Bergman clenched his jaw. "You're not going to *any* bank. You're in deep enough as it is. How much do you need?"

He could hardly hear her answer.

"A *thousand!*" he yelled, throwing a hand toward the ceiling.

More like her father than the attorney liked to admit, Mandy walked deliberately across the room and patiently positioned herself upon one of his plush leather chairs. When she crossed her legs with that intent gesture of tolerating no nonsense, Bergman knew he had already lost the battle. As she threaded her fingers and waited, she did not have to remind him that it was her money.

Reaching into his desk, Bergman withdrew a large spiral checkbook. As his pen began moving across the paper, Mandy rose to lean over his shoulder.

"You'll take the car as collateral?" she urged.

He grinned and noticed that if he turned his face, her breast would almost touch his cheek. Mandy noticed too. She shifted her weight.

"Forget it," he said, grinning. "If you can't pay it back . . . well, we'll work something out."

Mandy refused to rise to the bait. "You said you had depressing news," she reminded him and moved across the room, pausing, slender and brooding, before an oil portrait.

As if irked at the sight of her calm, oval face, he lifted his head. "Two of your father's beneficiaries are laying bricks in British Honduras. Another delay, I'm afraid."

"You could have told me that on the telephone."

He waved the detached check toward a small sheaf of authorizations. "Sign those papers over there." When she finished the last one and bent to place his pen back in its holder he pushed the check beneath her nose. She reached, and he held it a hand's breadth away.

"Don't play games," she said quietly.

He arched an eyebrow. "Make it count, love," he drawled. "I'm a shrewd businessman."

She moistened her lips. "That's not all you are, Bergman."

Mandy did not look at the check, but thrust it deep into her shoulder bag. She had one more stop before she fought this same battle with Felice, and that appointment would consume at least two hours of her precious time. She would pay a visit to her stepmother's extravagantly expensive hairstylist.

Chapter Two

The Boeing 747 coasted down the runway of New Orleans International Airport. Like a man filling his lungs with air, the plane gathered strength and thrust into the air. People around her relaxed and began talking again. Mandy positioned herself comfortably for the long flight to Zurich.

She had really done it. The exhilaration she felt must be like a gambler's when the stakes were ruinous. Here she sat, hastily jotted items in a spiral notebook, a textbook on corporate law bulging in her tote, and a rough draft of a feature outlined in her mind.

For the first time since her father's funeral, she was happy. A vague disloyalty washed through her.

Oh, Daddy, she thought, closing her eyes. Please don't think I've stopped missing you. But he would be the first to demand that she get on with her life.

Evidently she had been more clever in disguising her appearance than she thought. Her target sat only four seats beyond her, his head bent in conversation with a younger man—probably a secretary of some sort.

For one nerve-racking moment, as the stewardesses were seating the passengers prior to takeoff, Russell Gregory had fastened his dark, perceptive eyes upon her. She pretended she didn't notice him pause, then turn back to look at her the second time. Watching him now as he flipped open his case, Mandy discarded her gnawing dread that he recognized her. If he had realized who she was, he wouldn't have let it pass.

Mandy adjusted her large-framed glasses, grateful that the seat beside her was empty. She ruffled the mass of darkened ringlets capping her head. The hairstylist had been so clever: streaking Mandy's hair with brown, curling the straight locks and then suggesting subtle accents of makeup.

The tight designer jeans had been an afterthought—like the hand-painted silk blouse and no bra. Mandy appeared to be exactly what she wasn't—an experienced young woman who didn't give a hang about anything except herself. Russell Gregory would have been astounded to know that her head was usually in a textbook, that her sexual expertise consisted of a couple of close calls her freshman year of college and an abortive infatuation with a married man.

An hour past midnight, while many of the passengers dozed or listened to music through their headsets, Mandy made her way to the lav and refreshed herself. To her dismay, as she prepared to return to her aisle seat, Russell's lanky form blocked her path.

Leaning against her seat, his head inclined toward the passenger occupying the seat directly behind, she would be forced to pass within touching distance of him. It was possible that he even realized it. As confident as Mandy was that even her own friends would have to look twice at her, she wasn't ready to give her disguise the acid test yet.

She pivoted quickly. While pretending to rummage in her bag, she watched him obliquely. He shifted his weight. He removed his wallet from his hip pocket leisurely, drawing the coat of his suit aside. The flat stomach branching into muscular thighs, lean buttocks in pleasantly alluring trousers —his whole appeal troubled her.

Mandy could not deny his charm. It was powerful and had affected her the first moment she laid eyes on him. But why *him*, whom she did not trust one iota? Of all the men in the world who could make her look twice, why him? Please go back to your seat, Russell Gregory, she prayed fervently.

As if he heard her thoughts, Russell lifted his head. You interest me, his eyes said upon impact. She could have returned the same message, except for a different reason.

There was no way to avoid turning herself sideways and

squeezing past him. As she tried, Mandy thought she heard a small suggestive sound in his throat. And she wasn't at all certain if he bumped her purposely or not. She rather guessed that he did.

"I'm terribly sorry," he murmured.

But she knew he wasn't by the purposeful way his fingers circled about her wrist, pretending to steady her.

Mandy kept her voice husky and suffered horrors that he would recognize her. "Certainly."

She was attuned to the slightest change in him, any sign of recognition—a breath, a pause, an inflection in his voice. But if he noticed anything familiar about her, he hid it well.

Russell's fingers, clasped about her wrist for one second too long, sent the same odd sensation rippling through Mandy as before. But this time she knew it for what it was—a trick of the erotic senses.

It was dangerous to think that chemical attraction to a person meant anything in and of itself. To disguise her uneasiness, Mandy assumed an exaggerated boredom. Her smile was worldly and cool, as if men touched her all the time. She could handle him, her chin boasted.

Russell's inspection made no pretenses. It roamed over her chic haircut, the discreet curves of her breasts moving against the flowing silk, her jeans, her shoes, her bare, peeping toes. He moistened his lips. Obviously, he liked what he saw. And Mandy realized that she didn't find it entirely offensive.

"Are you having a pleasant flight?" he asked.

"I invited the lady to share a glass of wine with me," the man behind her seat interrupted. "But she declined. Perhaps I could coax you, Mr. Hamilton."

Mandy mentally recorded it: Gregory was using his other name.

"Not now, thanks. Another time, perhaps." His refusal was what Mandy expected, the practiced blandness of disinterested courtesy.

When she slid down into her seat, she swore she had left her intelligence somewhere in the vicinity of the restroom. Now that she was actually in the process of doing it, she doubted her courage to observe someone covertly. Perhaps it really was a "men only" occupation. Perhaps she should just come right out with it, place all her cards on the table. Perhaps she could worry the truth out of him. But honest confrontation would only send her home empty-handed.

"Here's the telephone number of the embassy," the man's voice continued behind her. "I'm sure we'll be able to throw some additional light on the problem if we put our heads together."

Another mental note: Russell knew people at the American embassy.

If Mandy expected Russell to resume his own seat, she was disappointed. Not after the wordless challenge which had passed between them. He merely braced an elbow on the seat above her head and waited.

Mandy fumbled in her bag, craving something to hold in her hands. What should she do? His next move would be to sit by her.

"Do you mind?" His words weren't a request.

"Of course not," she lied.

When he stepped across her legs, then bent his body to sit, Mandy did not have the impression of any awkwardness. The absent tug he gave to the creases in his pants was one of athletic grace. Russell Gregory could have stepped across the legs of Queen Elizabeth; it would not have mattered.

"Most people go to sleep by now. Are you nervous?"

"No!" she answered too abruptly. "I mean . . . yes. I don't know."

The impulse to crumple his shirt in her hands was almost overwhelming. She wanted to cry out, "You're not trying to make a fool of me, are you? You can't know who I am!"

"I get insomnia when I travel," she said smoothly, pretending a refined cough.

His eyebrows lifted, as if he didn't know quite how to take her. "May I get you something? A bit of cognac might make you drowsy. Flying can play the devil with nerves."

"No. No, thank you. I've already had something." Mandy placed her thumbnail between her teeth then snatched it away. "I'm afraid my tolerance isn't the greatest."

He smiled.

She smiled.

Then she sighed raggedly.

"You haven't had a drink with me," he said, smiling as if there were things she had yet to learn. He motioned to the stewardess with a passing flick of his fingers. "Could we have a small glass of cognac for Miss—"

Oh, clever! Very clever!

"Phillips," she supplied with a vexed sigh.

"A glass of cognac for Miss Phillips. I don't think I care for anything."

His strategy was perfectly clear—loosening her tongue and discovering why she had gone to such lengths to follow him. She became aware that she was snapping the cap of her pen off and on repeatedly. Russell was aware of it too. When he arched an interested brow, she stopped immediately.

"You're not married," he said.

"You're quite positive of that."

"You're not wearing a ring." He shrugged. "However, not every woman does."

Her blue eyes narrowed. Was he calculating how easy she would be?

"You don't look married."

She grimaced. "Why, do married women have a used look?"

He laughed. "You have freedom in your eyes."

She wasn't interested in his opinions, she informed him with a disrespectful sound between her teeth. Though she pretended to watch for the stewardess, Mandy wasn't watching at all. She was wondering how difficult it would be later, to keep from thinking about him. Russell was conceited and dishonest. Yet, she guessed she would close her eyes and picture what it would be like to be held in the arms of a man like him. Why? The lure of a virgin to an outlaw? Whatever, Mandy didn't think it would be quite the same as being kissed by David Rutherman in a deserted room of the Student Union Building.

She sat unmoving, withdrawn into a moody fantasy which Russell found intriguing. Her prickly barrier wasn't up, and he allowed his eyes to linger on the trim feminine foot dangling its spike-heeled sandal. When the stewardess arrived, she took him by surprise. He was too absorbed by the seductive line of Mandy's straight jeans, and the way her upper thigh swelled to fill them as she sat.

She reached for the glass, the silk stretching smoothly across her breasts. They were fuller than Russell had first imagined them to be. She didn't notice him loosen his tie uneasily, nor the grim expression on his face as he casually crossed his legs and shifted the crotch of his pants from her chance observation.

"Is Miss Phillips all the name you have?" His words were low.

Mandy lurched from her daydream, grabbing at the glass with both hands. Some sultry intimacy in his voice made her want to cover her curls and hide her face. But her jaw dropped at the sight of cognac spreading in a slow circle on the leg of her jeans. Tiny droplets slid down her hands.

"Oh!" she gasped.

Before she could decide where to set the glass or rummage for a tissue, Russell laughingly removed the drink from her hands. Sympathy would have been out of character, but she did think he could have the good grace not to smile. Instantly, Russell was using his handkerchief to blot her dripping hand. She suspected the touch was practiced.

"I think," he drawled, after she was dry, "that Scarlett O'Hara kept Rhett Butler's handkerchief."

"You're not Rhett Butler, and you may have it back."

Mandy jammed the handkerchief into his hand. Russell felt her temper and leaned back, openly amused. As she sipped, much too hastily, what remained of her brandy, neither of them spoke. The silence grew acute as most of the passengers drifted off to sleep around them.

Russell's voice was hushed and teasing. "If I'd known that asking your name would produce such a reaction, I'd have inquired about something less traumatic. Like your shoe size or where you were born."

Mandy shifted slightly so that she faced him a bit more. She attributed the growing ease with which she studied his impudence to the cognac. Everything was warm and delightfully pleasant.

When Russell smiled, the grooves deepened about his mouth and his eyes, and they were delightful. He shifted his shoulders. Mandy shifted hers. She sighed. This whole trip was just . . . delightful.

"I'm Benjamin Hamilton," he said. "I live in New York most of the time and make this trip several times a year."

Mandy's brows puckered. Like hell he was Benjamin Hamilton! Or perhaps he was. Perhaps he was neither. She leaned her cheek against the seat, unaware of her lips parting, moist and rosy.

"My name is Amanda." Her voice was lazy. "I'm an only child. I attended a parochial school and graduated with a three-point-nine average. My father died exactly one month ago. He still had his natural teeth. My shoe size is six-A. My favorite food is broccoli, and I hate only one thing more than the color chartreuse."

Chuckling, he tipped back his head at her ineffectual effort at sarcasm.

"And that thing is?" he prompted.

"Forward, talkative men."

"Touché! And I only hate one thing more than shag carpeting."

Mandy knew she musn't smile. "And what is that?"

"Beautiful, scheming women."

Scheming! Quickly draining the last drops of the cognac, her words tumbled over one another. Silence now would be intolerable.

"Do you meet many beautiful, scheming women, Mr. Hamilton?"

"The only woman I deal with on a permanent basis is fifty-four years old. Her code of human behavior has the inflexibility of someone just off the *Mayflower*. Does that answer your questions?"

"And her puritanism cramps your style?"

He grinned wryly. "Let's say it makes me extremely careful."

Mandy drew one leg beneath her and nestled into the seat more comfortably. "Many people depend upon your genius, and you sacrifice your own personal interest for their common welfare."

He lifted his brows. "Something like that."

His eyes traveled down the column of her throat and flicked upward for a reaction. When she gave none, they studied the shape of her mouth, her shoulders, the bend of her knee which was only inches from his arm. As she watched his silent approval, she wondered if this were a ritual he went through with every new woman he met.

"Unlike yourself, Amanda," he added after a moment. "You please yourself and like it that way."

"Why—" Mandy stiffened at his tactlessness. If he hadn't grasped her shoulder, she would have left her seat. Ignoring her impulse to lash out at him, Russell kept his voice low and insistently drew her back down. But instead of releasing her arm, he traced an impertinent finger across her collar, down the pointed "V" and hesitated like a ticking time-bomb on the top button of her blouse.

Mandy stared at it, her jaw slack, as if it were incomprehensible that she could brush it aside.

"Don't play games," Russell said huskily.

"Games?"

"Look at yourself, sweetheart. You didn't dress that way by accident." He could have trapped her face in his hands: she was completely incapable of moving.

Speechless, stunned by his blunt perception, for she actually did dress this way on purpose, Mandy could not protest as his face drew nearer. His lips were barely two inches from her own. And when he gently slid her glasses down the slender bridge of her nose, as if that were what he meant to do all along, he dropped them lightly into her lap.

"I beg your—"

"I didn't say I didn't like it, Amanda," he whispered.

Unbelievably, his long limbs shifted to make it easier to slip his free hand to the base of her spine. His lips hesitated, almost touching her throat. When she offered no resistance, they found the warm pulse. "I love it," he murmured. "You turn me on. You know you turn me on."

"Please," she begged. She would surely faint. She would die on this airplane. She was a dazed baby sparrow trembling in the path of this hungry tomcat.

Before Mandy could vow that she didn't believe a single word he said, his parted lips caressed her cheek. She caught his wrist with both hands, resisting his hypnotizing intimacy as he fit one large hand about her jaws. He only tightened his fingers.

"Why did you come on to me?" he demanded thickly, almost taking her lips with his kiss.

"I didn't," she protested.

"You did."

Mandy's eyes flew wide. Was he talking about Dulick's office? She had the fleeting impression that Russell was staring hard through his thickly furled lashes.

"Forget it," he said.

All she would have to do would be to relax her grip and he'd kiss her. As much as she wanted to yield, if only to satisfy the curiosity of what it would really be like to be kissed by a man like him, Mandy's pride rebelled.

She also felt guilt. Mandy suspected him of operating outside the law, and she had not immediately thrown up her guard. His lips, firm and warmly moist, continued to coax, gently moving upon her throat. Everyone fools around on airplanes, they seemed to say. Come on.

Russell took her resistance as rejection. He released her abruptly. He dropped his dark head back against his seat and closed his eyes. For several minutes, neither spoke. His gaze cut sharply and found her studying his profile.

"You don't do much for my ego," he admitted grimly.

Shattered, praying that he couldn't tell how badly, Mandy realized it would take a long time to understand what she felt at this moment.

"You shouldn't have done that." Her words came breathlessly.

Russell looked at her with something closer to mockery than passion. He wiped a hand across his face as if clearing his mind of her.

The man was cocky, actually encouraging resentment. He was so convinced of his own charm that he was insufferable.

"Nice men don't behave like you do," she accused, regretting her words instantly. They were the banter of a child. He knew that and chuckled as he rose and stood over her.

With an indulgent, paternal gesture, he slipped the glasses back onto her nose and tweaked it. The blaze of embarrassment scalded her. It was one thing to make overtures without being encouraged; it was unforgivable to behave as if she were a juvenile!

Mandy felt helplessly exposed. You'll pay for this one, mister, she promised deep in her private self. For whatever the reason or who's at fault, you'll pay.

It wasn't until Mandy stepped through the bustling terminal of *Zürich-Kloten* at one in the afternoon that she knew her first moment of genuine panic.

Zurich was not only the largest, but also the busiest, wealthiest, and most industrialized of all Swiss cities. Its role in international finance was striking. Cosmopolitan, it catered to one of the largest tourist trades in the world.

From the Grossmünster thrusting its twin towers into the Zurich skyline, Zwingli had preached a series of sermons which initiated the Swiss Reformation. During the Counter-Reformation, Italians and French had poured into the country, bringing their cultures and languages. Germany, to the north, also added her customs.

All these Continental influences combined to fashion a city which overwhelmed her now. She was unfamiliar with the currency. She could not understand any of the three national languages. And here she stood—Amanda Devon Phillips—having no hotel reservation, not a single friend anywhere, and a sum of money in her purse which could easily prove to be insufficient.

During the last month Preston Phillips's checkbook had protected her. Even so, she wasn't her father's daughter for nothing. Russell Gregory had underestimated her—if he had estimated her at all. With typical Phillips resolution, Mandy lifted her chin, even if her smile was rather bleak.

Switzerland, here I am!

It seemed like it took forever for her luggage to be unloaded. The sight of Russell's capable shoulders comforted her, and Mandy caught herself stealing glances at him. A pass from a man like him meant nothing—one of those insulting little advances men made when time lay heavy on their hands.

As Mandy retrieved her baggage, she turned instinctively. She searched for the security of Russell's dark head several inches above the others. Losing sight of him, even for a moment, wasn't something she wished to consider. That proposition, whether she accepted it or not, linked them together like an invisible chain.

Several times, keeping as far behind Russell as she dared, Mandy almost lost him. Strange masculine faces smiled with interest, telegraphing invitations to help her with her bags. But she only shifted the tote bag onto her other shoulder and carried her suitcases and raincoat with vexed stoicism.

Trailing Russell about Zurich for several days seemed the logical thing to do at first. Learning as much as she could before she was forced to tell him the truth was important. If she made friends with him enough that he would tell her things about himself, so much the better.

Once Mandy stepped outside the airport, glimpsing all the small European cars in the early afternoon sunlight, her confidence shattered. Rushing people bumped against her. They never looked at her face. A sick disappointment gripped her.

Bergman and Ken Hagan had been right. Being a woman was too much of a handicap. She could learn where he ate his meals and the company he kept. If he conducted business, she could ferret out what kind and even with whom, if she were lucky.

But what happened when he found out she suspected him of covering up something criminal? Obviously, he was a man of some importance. His friends would be important. And they would threaten to ruin her if she didn't leave them alone. She had no powerful editors to back her up. She could not say, "I'm a member of the press. I'm not alone in this."

With the wind ruffling her curls and blowing against her face, Mandy became fully awake. She felt she had suddenly grown up in the space of two minutes. She would be forced to call Arnold Keller.

When a sleek limousine hugged the pavement and swooped into the restricted parking area, she hung back. Her chin burrowed into the lapel of her raincoat.

The driver swung open the trunk and tossed in expensive masculine luggage. Efficiently. As if he had done it many times before. Another man in an undistinguished suit opened the back door and exchanged brief words with Russell. The limousine seemed to swallow Russell and his companion safely into its interior.

Then there was no one—in the whole city of Zurich—who knew of Amanda Phillips's existence.

She made a small sound of desperation in her throat. Now what? Turn around and go back into the terminal? Reserve a seat on the first plane back to the States? She could hear Bergman's sarcasm already.

"A car, *Fräulein?*"

Mandy whirled and saw a short-legged young man in baggy pants. He was remarkably homely, his only outstanding feature being a moustache which curled importantly at its ends. He seemed immensely proud of it, twirling it as he waited for her answer.

Then he gestured with a charming grin toward an old, but immaculately polished, sedan almost two blocks away.

Mandy hesitated. At least she could follow Russell and check into the same hotel. The next morning she would call Arnold or go home. She didn't owe Bergman or Felice an explanation about anything.

"Do you think you could possibly . . . follow that limousine?" she asked, pointing to the swiftly receding car.

"I can follow anything."

He grabbed her luggage with eager expertise. She wanted

to collapse with relief, though she could almost hear him thinking she was a vindictive wife trailing a philandering husband. But everyone abroad probably thought all Americans were lunatics anyway, zipping about Europe chasing people and strewing dollar bills like confetti. It was just as well.

"Where's it going?" he asked from the front seat, glancing back as he drove.

"A hotel. Just follow it."

His apprehension could be heard in his breath.

"I can pay," Mandy said wearily.

Cheerfully, the driver announced that his name was Erik and that he was happy to be at her service. And he didn't hint that he thought she was crazy. He didn't have to. After nearly an hour of driving, as Mandy caught occasional glimpses of the long car taking hairpin curves northward out of Zurich, she was positive she was crazy.

Mandy caught hulking glimpses of St. Peter's church thrusting up behind her. Shadows of a proud fourteenth-century castle reared above the city, calling her a fool. But the countryside blurred. Rain began to splatter against the windshield. She couldn't cope with the intricacy of gables and oriels. She was exhausted.

Where was Russell Gregory going? Would he travel all afternoon? And would she wind up giving the remainder of her money to this moustached driver with baggy pants?

Depleted with jet lag and frustration, Mandy hugged her tote bag against her chest. Resting her head against the sweet-smelling leather upholstery, she surrendered to her weariness. As the purr of the German car blended seductively with the sound of the rain, she slowly slid into the escape of slumber.

When the car whined to a smooth stop some time later, Mandy jerked up with a start.

"Where are we?" she demanded without pause, blinking in shock.

"We're almost at the border of Switzerland and Germany. A few miles this side."

Erik's face expressed unmasked concern when he turned to look at her. He was obviously worrying if he would get his money.

"Why didn't you wake me?" Mandy asked fretfully.

"I stopped for fuel. You were sleeping so good, I—"

"But I never dreamed—"

She clamped her mouth shut. It wasn't his problem. Erik gestured toward the limousine only two short blocks beyond, its length stretched before The Staad Hotel.

Myriad shuttered windows paraded across its width and up its four stories; it was no typical tourist accommodation. From the stone-chipped sidewalk in front to the sprawling grounds behind, it spoke of quiet dignity. Probably a family-owned business catering to only the ultra-wealthy who could afford their costly seclusion.

"Isn't there another hotel in this town?" Mandy questioned.

"This is the only one. Mattenaugst's a small place. Not tourist. Vineyards, mostly."

Bracing herself for the shock, so distressed that she could hardly organize two thoughts together, she asked the crucial question.

"Oh," she sighed. "How much do I owe you?"

Erik hesitated, fingering his moustache. He calculated for a moment, then grinned.

"One hundred American dollars. I will also get you a room." His teeth were very white when he nodded approval of his generous fee and suggestion.

"I can get my own room," she protested. Parting with that much money would strap her.

He sucked in a short sound of reproof, and Mandy didn't have the heart to bargain. As she fumbled about for her wallet tucked in the bottom of her tote bag, Erik got out of the car and swung open her door to reach for her bags. Impulsively, Mandy clapped her hand on his arm. He looked up in surprise.

"Erik, I—"

Tense seconds hung between them. Revealing human weaknesses to a stranger had always been some kind of profanation—a direct violation of the code the Phillipses had lived by.

"You don't want a room," he prompted.

"You'd charge me another fare to take me back to Zurich?"

His face fell. Of course he would. She had no right to ask him to do it without charge.

"Where's the nearest airport?" was her inevitable question.

"Not too far. There is a very small private one in Schaff-hausen."

Mandy's sigh didn't express half the distress she felt. Yet she did take a small comfort in the fact that Erik halfway understood. He wanted very much to please her. When she made a small grimace, he broke into an eager smile.

Before Erik could speak, however, Russell Gregory stepped through the swinging glass doors of The Staad. Framed against the elegance of the hotel, he looked master-ful, magnificently rugged and confident—everything that she wasn't. For that alone, Mandy almost hated him. She was exhausted. After the strain of travel, he stood with more grace than ever.

Taking the steps two at a time, Russell preceded his taciturn companion. There was another man close on his heels whom she had never seen before.

Didn't Russell ever tire? Didn't he sleep?

She felt Erik's unasked question as the trio climbed into a car: Was this the man she wanted so badly? The black machine paused for what seemed interminable minutes, growled to life, and whipped away from the building.

"Now!" Mandy said quickly.

"A single room?" he wanted to know.

She nodded, secretly blessing his parents, his grandparents, and everything else she could think of for his incredible discretion. With any luck at all she could register at the hotel, compose herself, and escape before Russell knew she had even come and gone.

"Hurry! And take the cheapest room they have!" she whispered loudly after the stocky form swaggering across the street.

If she could only get some sleep and some food in her stomach, she could hire a car to Schaffhausen. Then she would get back to the States if she had to swallow every shred of pride and cable Bergman for more money. Mandy laced her fingers tightly together and cursed her impulsiveness for beginning this thing in the first place.

The little town, located northeast of Zurich, was not as she had pictured Switzerland. Everything had a medieval appear-ance; some buildings in the valley looked like castle strong-holds. The countryside didn't jut with craggy mountains but rolled in gentle hills.

What seemed like hours was actually only eight or nine

minutes before Erik returned. When he opened the door and braced a knee on the edge of her seat, she waited impatiently.

"Well?" Mandy urged, gesturing with her hand, as if she could pull the words out of him. "Did you get one? Oh, disgust! They're not all booked up, are they?"

"In a way," he hedged, lifting his palms upward.

"Are you going to tell me or not?"

Erik waved his arms broadly as he explained, as if it would somehow make her view his difficulty with a bit more sympathy.

"There's an important meeting here. Every room is reserved for days." He traced messages in the air with a scrawny finger. "Hamilton party. Hamilton party. Hamilton party."

Mandy had the distinct impression she was about to be destroyed.

"I told them my fare needed a room for only one night. The man looked at me like I was—"

"Crazy," she finished.

"Yes. So-o, I told him you were part of the Hamilton party."

"Erik!"

"Well, he wrote you down," Erik explained innocently, as if that made his deceit perfectly acceptable. "You pick up your key at the desk. Everything's arranged."

Enormously pleased with his accomplishment, Erik extended his hand. Mandy was so tired of it all that she didn't bother to look at how much of a tip she was giving him. She placed a bill in his hand without even looking. He blinked at the twenty-dollar bill and strode importantly toward the hotel.

All Mandy did was stumble after him. She couldn't think; she needed to sleep; she had to eat. None of this could possibly be happening. And when the hotel clerk looked at her, Mandy decided she-positively-must-not-cry.

She didn't cry. Mandy felt she should have been congratulated for that. Pausing before the glass doors, she adjusted the shoulder strap of her bag and yanked the belt of her raincoat tightly.

With her first step inside the lobby, she received many impressions—priceless antiques, fresh wax, floating laughter of gentility, the subdued movement of the bell crew from lobby to stairway to mezzanine to stairway to lobby. Old money. Aristocratic money backed by decades of dedicated service and good breeding.

With a calculated shrug at the approaching desk supervisor, Mandy steadied her nerves. Taking a huge breath, which she feared might be her last for a while, she swooped toward the upright baroque desk like a curly-headed Marlene Dietrich.

The austere day supervisor, whose long face reminded Mandy of an American bald eagle, bowed graciously and stepped behind his desk. He personified protocol. His rimless spectacles were worn with impeccable demeanor. Amanda didn't look at his shoes, but she knew intuitively they were black and shined to a gloss.

Staad employees floated placidly about her like fluid wind-up toys—tending her luggage, waiting for the flick of the supervisor's wrist or the lift of his eyebrows. Mandy obliquely caught the glimpse of Erik deserting her through the glass doors.

When the supervisor placed the guest register before her, he did so with the same precision with which he ordered his staff. He lined the edge of its crisp pages exactly horizontal with the polished edge of the desk.

"So pleased," he murmured in guttural English. "So pleased."

Mandy returned his tiny pursed smile with one she hoped was brilliant and patrician.

"We've been expecting you, Mrs. Hamilton." His bow was almost reverent.

Preston Phillips would have been proud of her, Mandy thought. Not for one second did her smile falter. Not for one second did her hand tremble.

When the man proffered the pen, taking care to meticulously wipe the excess ink into its priceless well, she grasped it briskly. Half a dozen clerks waited behind her in orderly silence. He gestured to the register. She couldn't die, she reasoned numbly; she was already dead.

Mandy signed with a flourish and replaced the pen with as much care as he had offered it. The fingers snapped, and the supervisor twirled the register around.

"Mrs. Benjamin Hamilton."

He smiled in staid approval. As his newest guest approached the stairs with as much dignity as he had expected of her, Johann Gustave thanked his lucky stars. If Opal Patterson hadn't telephoned him two days earlier and told him, in the closest secrecy, he might not have known to warn his staff. Mr. Hamilton, one of the hotel's most prestigious guests, was spending a private rendezvous at The Staad with his new wife from the United States.

Chapter Three

With each carpeted step, Mandy visualized the forged name flashing before her eyes like a garish neon sign. How could she have done it? Life had contrived to back her into a corner. Now she was no different from Russell Gregory. She had little room to blame him for using a name which wasn't his.

Running away from her own actions was not something Mandy ordinarily did. She had *never* run before. But then she had never done anything like pretending to be someone's wife before, either. Was it possible, she wondered bleakly, to even yet salvage something, to extricate herself?

The bellboy, who said his name was Proctor, guided her down a long carpeted wing whose walls were covered with splendid frescoes. The ceiling was high and heavily ornamented. Mandy barely glanced at the craftsmanship. She wished instead that she were in a sleazy motel under her very own name.

"The queen of Prussia once stayed in the suite you will occupy, Frau Hamilton," he commented politely.

"Really? How nice."

With a movement of his key, he threw back leather-padded

doors. The Silver Suite was as large as a house. The broad-loom of the spacious living room was rich brown, like Swiss chocolate, and the walls were covered with silver moiré. Doorways led off from either end of the room—one to a partially visible kitchen, the other to a pair of bedrooms.

"Proctor?" she asked cautiously, walking immediately to the floor-to-ceiling windows. She drew back the inner sheer and gazed down upon manicured lawns and strolling guests. Tennis courts and a large swimming pool were set into the grounds like expertly cut jewels.

"Yes?"

"Are there side stairs? If I should want to enjoy a walk without going through the main lobby?"

Mandy made her smile beautiful and looked directly into his shy eyes. He flushed slightly.

"I'm afraid not, Frau Hamilton. Only the fire escape. Will that be all?"

"Yes," she sighed, placing a tip into his hand. "Thank you."

Dear God, what was she to do? Only a matter of moments stood between her and the inevitable. Russell *would* return. Well, let him suffer the results of his entanglements! What was she thinking? His wife, whom the hotel staff obviously had never met, would ultimately make her appearance. What then? Gregory could ruin her. She must get out of this hotel as soon as possible, if she had to walk every mile of the way to Schaffhausen alone!

"She's definitely not what I imagined," Johann Gustave announced to his hurriedly gathered day staff. "See that she's treated as suits her name."

A thin, balding man, every bit of seventy years old and who suffered from a bad case of sinusitis, snuffled loudly. "Bit of a thing, isn't she? Doesn't look old enough to have a seven-year-old. Women grow up so quickly these days."

"It's none of your affair, Biggens," clipped Gustave. "Simply see that she's comfortable. If she wants her meals in her room, see to it."

Biggens tugged at his white mess-jacket trimmed in blue. "I always do. I always do."

Proctor chuckled loudly, looked at his superior and swallowed it. He knew, as every other bell clerk knew, that Biggens's seniority of two decades carried weight. Gustave might not tolerate insubordination from anyone else, but when Biggens spoke, he listened.

"Mrs. Hamilton probably won't be seen much for the next few days," the old man muttered under his breath.

"Not if Hamilton has any sense," laughed Proctor in spite of Gustave's disapproving forehead.

"Not one breath that she arrived alone, with that . . . clown," ordered Gustave protectively. "The Pattersons are fastidious about such things. Send some flowers up, Proctor, and before lunch. On behalf of The Staad."

He smiled and adjusted his glasses. His skill at handling the delicate standards of protocol for old American families was unsurpassed, and he knew it. Large sums of money rested upon clientele like Opal and Reginald Patterson. A single breath of impropriety or indiscretion would never be tolerated.

"Perhaps the new Hamiltons have had a quarrel already," observed Biggens, shuffling about with poker-faced solemnity.

"I wouldn't let my wife arrive in a hired car from Zurich. Not if she looked like that!" Proctor laughed.

"If Mr. Hamilton wanted your advice, Proctor, he would have taken you into his counsel. Not a breath of it! One word of displeasure from a man like Hamilton, and we'd take years to recover. Take her order for lunch, Biggens."

He moved off. "Such a lot of trouble for such a little American."

"Biggens!"

But Johann Gustave didn't press it. He knew if anyone could be trusted to see that things ran smoothly for the new Mrs. Hamilton, Biggens could. It was going to be a very busy two weeks.

Mandy washed her face and applied fresh makeup sparingly. She looked tired, but better. She brushed her hair and fluffed the curls about her face. She should have been born a light brunette. She rather liked it.

She gazed longingly at the antique tub, but a bath was out of the question. While she waited for the menu she would change clothes. Then she would spare only the time necessary to eat. She could not afford to leave tomorrow if she wanted to avoid Russell Gregory.

Fresh flowers welcomed her from the bedside table where

the telephone was. At the moment she found their cheerfulness virtually obscene. And the flowers weren't set in an ordinary vase—not at The Staad. Sterling silver rimmed the cut-glass border. The bathroom fixtures had that desirable age—use by generations of the silent elite.

Feeling slightly better, even after a superficial repair job to her appearance, Mandy tossed her glasses to the coffee table. She sank into a chair and dragged her weary feet to a needlepointed footstool. A sound outside the door straightened her. The menu.

That presented a small problem. Her bill. How could she escape and still pay it? Of course, her luggage would simply have to be left behind with a letter explaining she would send for it. Smuggling it out was impossible. What a mess!

Food *had* to change her outlook. She had barely eaten on the plane. Mandy walked to the door and reached for the handle. When the knob turned beneath her palm, she jerked back in surprise. If she hadn't jumped from the heavy door's path, it would have bowled her over.

Catching her balance, Mandy stood face to face with the smoldering anger of Russell Gregory.

"God help us!" she choked, retreating backward.

"God doesn't protect liars from the fruits of their own folly, my darling Mrs. Hamilton."

If she had felt vulnerable beneath the penetrating inspection of those brown eyes in New Orleans, now they stripped her not only of clothes, they divested her of pride. She had no defense. She was clearly in the wrong.

The slam of the door behind him was earnest and ear-splitting. Mandy flinched.

"Please let me explain," she began. "I never intended any of this. It's been madness. I don't blame you for being upset—"

"Upset!" he thundered. His outrage drew the handsomeness of his features even more cleanly—thinning the delicate flesh about his nose, accentuating the arch of his black brows.

"What are you, an industrial spy? You've been following me ever since I left the States. I put up with that, though I wanted to turn you over my knee. But my wife? I intend to damn well find out what's going on here. By force if I have to. The choice is yours!"

"Spy?" Mandy gasped, stumbling, feeling faint from shock. "No, you—"

He stepped toward her with purpose in every movement of his body. Mandy could no more move from his path than she could extricate herself from the tangle of circumstances which placed them both where they were. Surely he could see she was no spy! She could hardly breathe before the vibrance of his wrath.

He boldly reached long fingers to thread through her curly ringlets. She jerked her head to one side.

"It was better blond. Did you have to go to such lengths, Amanda? If you wanted to get me in bed, all you had to do was ask."

Russell's eyes narrowed at the irate defiance spreading across Mandy's face. Then, as if he relished a good fight, he grinned. Even though the wide smile came easily, the intensity of his perception drilled through her.

"You've got everything all wrong," she pulled herself taller. "I was just going to write a small . . . feature. A master's thesis, maybe. Everything got all . . . out of hand."

"Feature story?" His laugh was short and unbelieving. "My God, child! For what? *Penthouse* magazine?"

Facing the door, he ran his fingers through his hair and twisted back to scrutinize her, to weigh her honesty. Then his laughter rang richly across the room. Mandy's cheeks flooded with fury.

"Well, it wasn't so insane at the time, Mr. *Russell Gregory Benjamin Hamilton.*"

"Ah," he reflected soberly.

His brows lifted and the corners of his mouth turned downward as a certain amount of respect flitted across his face. With an easy dismissal, he tossed the room key to the coffee table beside her glasses.

"You really were a spy, then." As he strode toward the bathroom Mandy followed him, hotly blurting her words to his back.

"You haven't exactly been honest either, you know. Oh . . . forget it! I'm leaving immediately. I'm flying back to the States as soon as I can get on an airplane. Whether you believe it or not, I really am sorry." Her voice hardened earnestly as he stopped walking. Russell did not turn around. "And I hope to heaven I never see you again!"

"You stay where you are, Amanda!" he shouted. He spun about to rivet his determined eyes with her blurring blue ones.

For the space of a second, something passed between them. Fingertips touching over a black void? Saying "please understand me"?

Before either of them could respond to it, the moment was gone. Things were as before. Mandy made a movement to leave.

"Do you realize I could sue the britches right off your lovely little behind?" he threatened.

"I—"

"As far as this hotel's concerned, I have a wife."

"B—But your real wife," Mandy objected, gesturing backward, as if to the desk in the lobby. "I mean, *they* may have mistaken me for her, but when she comes, there'll be two of us."

For one second his eyelids closed, and she guessed he was envisioning horrible repercussions. "There is no Mrs. Benjamin Hamilton."

Mandy made a small sound of protest.

"There was going to be. But"—he waved his fingers lightly—"things changed at the last minute. Opal Patterson's efficiency overdid itself, I think. Well, that's beside the point. The fact is, you now have the honor whether you want it or not."

"Tell them it was all a mistake," she sputtered. "I—I'll tell them myself."

Russell battled visibly for the final shreds of his patience. "That is not so easily corrected, I'm afraid. By the time the hotel grapevine dispenses with lunch, over a dozen countries will think I'm here with my wife, too."

"Who are you?" she breathed.

"Not who you figured, obviously." His eyes pierced her as if he would enjoy putting a gag into her mouth. "Now, I shouldn't have to tell you my work is sensitive. And until I can figure out a way of getting out of this mess without looking like an idiot, you will remain my wife. A very quiet, well-behaved wife. Do you understand?"

Close to twenty-four hours without food was a long time, even without stress. Mandy felt her knees buckling, and she flailed behind herself, groping for somewhere to sit. The man was mad! They were both mad! Tiny black specks swam into her vision. Before she could actually stumble, he reached her and swept her off the floor.

"Put me down!" Mandy protested, slumping against the flexing muscles of his chest as he pushed open a bedroom door with one knee.

"Shut up," he said and lowered her to the bed. Before she could object, Russell pulled off one slender sandal, sending it sailing across the foot of the kingsize bed. The other followed just as quickly.

"When did you last eat, Amanda?" He towered above her, loosening his tie with a relaxed movement that belied the swift aggression she knew he was capable of.

In spite of the foolish ease with which Mandy had bumbled her way into this mess, she was a good judge of character. Russell would not go out of his way to injure her. But if it came to a point of choices, he would not hesitate to protect his own interests. Whatever those were. If one of them had to suffer, it would positively be her. She entertained no doubts whatsoever that he had toppled stronger people than her.

"I'm all right, Mr. Gregory," she declared carefully.

"As long as we're here, call me Ben."

"But—"

He jabbed an index finger beneath her nose and she grimaced. "Do it!"

"Absolutely!"

For a brief second he dared her to push him any farther. Then he sauntered to the door to answer room service.

"I adore agreeable women," he said smoothly.

"I'll just bet you do, *Ben*," she agreed nastily once he was well out of earshot.

With some of the most delicious food in her stomach that she had ever eaten, much of Mandy's vigor returned. And so did a fresh determination to logically work out a plan to free them both from this catastrophe.

For long minutes she stood before the windows, staring down at nothing, her thoughts getting nowhere. With her fingertips absently caught in her back pockets, her breasts straining against her blouse, her bare feet slightly spread, she looked like a piece of booty on the cover of a paperback novel.

"I hope you brought something with you besides jeans," Russell remarked casually from the divan where he lounged. "I'll have to buy you clothes our first day here."

His right foot hooked over the back of the sofa in what Mandy had thought was an improper informality, considering the fragility of their circumstances.

She jumped when he spoke. "What? Oh, of course I did. Listen, Mr. Gregory, I was just think—"

"Ben," he reminded gently.

"Okay. Ben."

Mandy rotated, realizing then he had been studying her, his eyes dark and brooding. When he looked at her like that, with a lazy wonder teasing about his mouth, unwelcome sensations fluttered in the pit of her stomach. They weren't awe, and they weren't fright; they were sexual attraction. Russell was an extremely virile man. That virility not only suited his driving personality, it gave him a certain magnetism far too strong to ignore.

Mandy wasn't ashamed of being attracted to a man she didn't know, not even to him. But under different circumstances, surely. Having trailed him halfway around the world made her look like a sex-crazed idiot. She had never been the aggressor in any relationship. And in this one, no matter what she did or said to Russell, she would ultimately seem like a hungry female.

At twenty-three, Mandy had long since outgrown the selfish concept of "if it feels good, do it." Some relationships simply were inadvisable. And having to fight this one, to guard every word and every emotion, to resist the attraction which only grew more acute with every hour, would be ridiculous.

"Take a bath and get dressed in something nice, then," he said coolly. Swinging his foot off the divan, Russell began unbuttoning his shirt as he strolled to the master bedroom.

Mandy stiffened in disbelief at his overbearing confidence. "I beg your pardon."

He turned, the tails of his shirt flapping about his hips. His chest was deeply tanned and broad, but then, she'd already guessed that it was. He was smoother, too, than she had imagined. A smattering of dark curls crept down the center of his chest and tapered into a thin line to disappear beneath his belt. Moistening her lips, she felt too warm and frighteningly tense inside.

Russell saw it happen—her lapse of discipline. He saw the hopeless attempt she made to steady herself. One way or another, she had to get out of here!

The flash of a white grin streaked across his face, as if he knew everything she felt. He disappeared for a moment, only to reappear with a shaving kit, minus his shirt. He opened the bathroom door and talked to her over the sound of running water as she stood quietly near the divan. His lack of inhibition amazed her. She was about to shatter into pieces.

"You've stumbled into an extremely delicate situation here, Amanda Phillips," he said, appearing at the doorway of the bathroom with his face covered with shaving foam.

"I've offered to stumble out of it," she countered, directing her words at the safe vicinity of his hairline. "You can't blame me for everything. My share, yes. But you violated the law."

"It's only a misdemeanor," he said as if it were nothing.

"*You* say," Mandy retorted with a doubtful lift of her eyebrows. "What did you expect someone to do if he found out?"

He pointed his razor at her face. "Not to palm herself off as my wife!"

Mandy braced her fists on her hips. "I told you that was a mistake!" she practically yelled at him.

"Like the mistake that I was a criminal?"

"Yes."

"You make a lot of mistakes," he mumbled.

Russell's shoulders squared as he saw he could not badger her into being a manageable, docile female. As if he were reluctant to reveal his motives, as if explaining somehow weakened him, he chose his words carefully.

"I assume you're aware by now that the American dollar is in a bit of a difficulty." Mandy smirked at him. "I represent one of the largest banking houses in the United States. I'm what you'd call a . . . a troubleshooter of foreign investments."

He paused and chuckled with his razor poised. "This is one trouble I'm going to have the devil of a time shooting."

He lifted his head. "Anyway, Amanda, if you can, imagine what would happen to the American economy if foreign investors pulled their money out of American banks. Can you fathom that?"

"The American economy is still the greatest in the world," Mandy countered.

Russell corrected her. "American *industry* is the greatest in the world. But our dollar is no longer backed by gold, my dear. If you represented a huge foreign investor, would you

put funds into a country with a gold standard or one that has a
devalued currency?"

Mandy's mouth twisted. "Well . . . gold, I suppose."

"Exactly. And when the bank I represent holds these
meetings, which it does several times a year in different parts
of the world, it's my job to convince investors to leave their
money where it is. Not only that, but to invest more."

Mandy coughed uneasily. If what he said were true, Russell
Gregory held awesome power in his hands. He knew it, of
course. But still, it was frightening. He must be laughing at
her naïve attempts to write about his immoralities. She felt
embarrassed and foolish, and very much at a disadvantage.

"Investors are as skittish as virgins. I keep them happy," he
added in a final, deflating thrust. "Everything is based upon
their ability to trust *me* and my reliability. I *don't* do crazy
things to make them hysterical."

Dabbing at the remaining flecks of foam, Russell stood in
the doorway. Half-hypnotized, she observed the ritual men
went through—the splash of aftershave in the palm, the quick
pat of each hand upon the jaw, the final inspection in the
mirror.

From where she stood, the bathroom mirror was just inside
her line of vision. He was gorgeous. Images flitted through
her mind—the two of them in embraces too intimate to place
names upon. She was helpless to make them stop coming. His
body wanting her body—foreign, blistering heat which
scorched her. When his eyes met hers in the mirror, Russell
held them locked, challenging her with a smile.

"What's on your mind, Mrs. Hamilton?" he asked softly.
She whirled from his knowing taunt.

As Mandy paced the living room, spinning just as he
loosened his belt buckle, something in her snapped. This was
too much, she thought wildly. Something she couldn't handle
at all.

She darted for the bedroom where he had pulled off her
shoes. By the time he reached her, she had one on and was
slipping on the other. He braced his tall frame in the space of
the doorway with outstretched hands. Her raincoat and tote
bag still lay on a chair where Proctor had placed them.

Blinking back stinging tears, Mandy slung the tote over her
shoulder. In one hand she grabbed her coat and a suitcase.
Then the other. She defied his barring of the doorway by
trying to edge past him with her shoulders.

"Move," she demanded. "You're self-serving and immoral. I'm not staying here. You can yell or hit me or have me arrested."

Russell laughed down at her, removing his hands from the facings and crossing his arms across his bare chest like Mr. Clean. She wished she had the nerve to kick his shins!

"And if you try to leave, I'll do it," he promised.

"What? Have me arrested?"

"You bet!"

"No, you won't. You're too worried about protecting a false indentity. Do your investors know that Mr. Benjamin Hamilton is a fraud? Do they?" she railed at him.

"It's necessary. And they won't ever know. Not from you, anyway. Now turn around and put that junk down and take your bath."

Undoubtedly, Russell was the stronger by far. Not only in physical strength, but in willpower as well. Amanda was at the end of her wits and was grasping at the final shreds of her pride. At this point she felt she had nothing to lose.

She did drop the suitcases. But as she turned, she slammed the tote bag into his chest. Russell nearly doubled over.

Scrambling past, ignoring the dazed oath behind her, Mandy darted into the living room, toward the hall doors. Russell moved as rapidly as she did and caught her back pocket just as she reached the divan.

When he jerked hard, they both fell, nearly missing the divan. Mandy struggled upward, fighting her way onto it to escape the trap of his arms that were near to twisting her in half. They were both gasping for breath.

"Leave me alone!" she yelled, striking at him and missing.

"I said no, you hellion!" panted Russell. She was slithering out of his grasp, and he reacted instinctively. He grabbed a handful of the frilly curls and hung on.

Mandy wailed in pain. She stopped struggling immediately. And he released her hair as swiftly, resting one uncertain hand upon her thigh.

"You're horrible," she choked. Determined that she would not further degrade herself by openly weeping, she swallowed hard and blinked the tears from her lashes. Angrily, she knocked his hand aside.

Russell's face was grim. "I didn't mean to hurt you."

He replaced the hand deliberately. Mandy glared at it.

"Don't—touch—me."

"Listen, Mandy—"

"And don't call me that!"

"I'll call you anything I damn well please!" he said through gritted teeth, replacing the hand with a stinging slap. "You come into my life like a tornado, screw things up and tell me what to do. I'm not some high-school punk who has to take it and like it."

Mandy dropped her head until her chin nearly touched her chest. When Russell's erring hand trespassed higher on her leg, her eyes flared wide. She gaped at the fingers purposefully closing themselves into the softness of her thigh. He knew only too well what he was doing. And she knew.

Mandy started once to ask him nicely. But when she glanced upward and saw the deepening burn of his gaze, the flushed warmth creeping up the sides of his neck, the intent set of his mouth, she only shook her head. Her memory of his pass on the airplane was extremely acute.

"No," she whispered, tilting her head as if stunned.

"I'm just going to kiss you," he said thickly. "Good Lord! You've been parading around in here all afternoon, barefooted and no bra. You asked for it."

As her eyes searched Russell's face for the slightest sign of recognition of her true self, Mandy could not find it. All she read was half-aroused masculinity. If she surrendered now to the lips which swept across her cheek, searching for her mouth, he would never see her: not her pride, not her integrity. And she did not know if she even cared.

The weight of Russell's body lying sprawled half upon hers had forced her back against the brocaded satin. He was not a man who relished force, she knew. As he cupped her face in one hand, he paused only a moment before he closed his fingers about her free wrist. And when he slanted his head, fitting his mouth firmly to hers, she was certain he would take the kiss.

Even as Mandy's mind had misgivings, his tongue gradually invaded her mouth. It began as a languorous exploration, a cautious curiosity to see if she tasted as delectable as she looked. She neither fought him nor responded.

In that extended moment of intimacy—the first seconds of shared sexual wonder, then awareness—she felt dazed. Quickly, her temples pounded with an unexpected blaze of conflict between unwelcome attraction and personal honor. Russell's taste was pleasant, shockingly erotic. And in splintered seconds Mandy's senses spiraled with smells and weight and small sounds and flooding heat. Driven then, with the fear of losing control, she wriggled beneath the insistent pulse of his stirring manhood. But resisting only made it worse, for then Russell no longer coaxed. He began to force what she did not offer and to plunder her mouth with the urgent need to dominate. It was all wrong. Everything was wrong!

Mandy's resistance began in earnest. Russell's fingers were frighteningly skilled, and they loosened the silk from between their bodies. Her attempts to get away only crushed the heat of his bare chest to her breasts. She felt herself slipping; she felt herself on fire!

"God, stop fighting me!" he muttered against her lips.

"No!" She twisted her head from side to side. Her fingernails were digging into his arms, but she couldn't help it. "You don't understand!"

"*You* don't understand."

He recaptured her mouth, smothering her protests roughly. Until finally, with his hands pinning her shoulders, his head lowered to the curve of her throat.

Mandy gasped. Then she gasped again, whispering garbled half-words that didn't make any sense. The tiny explosions tingling down her limbs made her shiver. He was thinking she was saying no and meaning yes.

Light, breathy kisses trailed across the bones of her shoulder. They moved lower, dominating her like a drug. When Russell closed his mouth upon her breast, it responded instantly, excitedly. Any pretense she could offer was wasted.

She didn't want him to stop, and he knew it. Still, Mandy summoned what will she had left. She reached out, clasping his head in both hands. Sick with the truth, she forced it from her breast.

"I'm not what you think," she choked and squeezed her eyes tightly shut. The seconds spun out into infinity.

"You're not honest is what you're not," he said at last, with a depth of insight which chilled her. "You feel it, too. Don't lie and say you don't."

As his face hovered over hers, his breath came in hoarse gasps. She felt him thinking, studying her distress with penetrating dark eyes. He was weighing the difference between what she appeared to be and what she was.

Finally, when she refused to admit the truth, he swung to his feet. Mandy jerked her blouse shut from his wandering gaze. Pulling herself into a huddle and drawing her legs toward her chest, she mumbled against her knees.

"I want to go home," she said.

"You can't."

"You could fix things."

"I said no. It would destroy more than I could fix."

Mandy's head wrenched up at that, her eyes brimming with sarcasm. "Use all that famous persuasion you say you're capable of."

"We're talking of millions of dollars here, Amanda."

"And any human being can be sacrificed for money."

"Oh, hell!"

With a savage slam of her feet to the floor, Mandy continued clutching her blouse and irately gathered her things. Russell called after her as she reached the bedroom door. The brittleness in his tone warned her that he wouldn't tolerate rebellion.

"There'll be a number of important people coming in here. Two of whom are Opal and Reginald Patterson. They're from the old school, and I'll have to tell them the truth. But to my clients you will be a smiling, cheerful wife. No mistakes."

"I won't give away your secret, *Ben*." His frown reminded her of her lack of bargaining power.

"If security gets too tight I'll just have to—"

"Have to what?" she prompted.

"Nothing. You take that bedroom: I'll take the other." At her glare, he held up his palms. "I won't touch you, not like that. But you're not leaving here. And for God's sake, wear some underwear!"

"You owe me an apology, I believe!"

Russell hadn't moved from beside the sofa where he stood brooding, one fist crammed deeply into his trouser pocket. Preventing his masculinity from being so obvious, she guessed drily. His face grew moody and impassive.

Twice now, she had refused him. He would not understand. He would only despise her. And somehow what he thought about her mattered. It mattered terribly. Their eyes, when they met, were narrowed and sullen.

"I don't give a bloody hang what you believe," he replied grimly.

Giving her the scorn of his back, he left her. Russell disappeared into the other bedroom, which for the time being, at least, separated them by a door whose key was on her side.

As she leaned against the door, cursing her knees which had amazingly turned to liquid, Mandy wondered if she had ever regretted anything as much as she did buying that plane ticket. And to think that she had promised Ken Hagan that she would keep out of Russell Gregory's private life!

Chapter Four

At least they both knew where the other stood now, Mandy told herself during the next day of solitary confinement. A good deal had passed between them. But too little truth was tangled with too much deception. Each of them was too clever and too capable of a con job on the other.

So after they had time to reflect upon the judgments they had made of one another, each grew carefully polite. The more suspicious they became, the more diplomatically charming they behaved. It was a standoff.

There were moments when Mandy thought she had glimpsed the real Russell Gregory. Even though he had misinterpreted her, he really had desired her. A man, when he was in the throes of physical need, wasn't capable of complete dishonesty. Was he? He couldn't pretend *everything*.

Then she doubted even that theory. Russell was a student of human nature. He was a chameleon—capable of adapting to people in an instant to suit his needs. If she were a psychology major, that would be thesis material!

For the entirety of the day he studied the contents of his attaché case. They took quiet meals in the suite. Several times

Mandy watched him secretly, from over the top of a book she was not reading, or during a trip through the living room to the kitchen that wasn't necessary.

He had a habit of crossing his ankles on the footstool and making notes on a legal pad. He would pick up the telephone for a transatlantic call, compare notes with a computer printout, then continue working. Twice he spoke in French, once in German.

At one point she cautiously interrupted with coffee she had brewed in the kitchenette. After a glance at the lovely tray—arranged with silver, linen napkins and Rosenthal china— his brown eyes met hers with approving surprise.

"You read minds as well," Russell said, inhaling the coffee's aroma.

"As well as what?"

She stood watching him cradle his coffee cup in his lap, nibbling the end of his pen, as if he were debating if her courtesies were double-edged or not.

"Writing a feature on financial consultants."

Her lips curled. "I didn't put arsenic in it. Perhaps I should have."

"Ah, I'm a pushover for a woman who can make decent coffee." His grin bespoke momentary trust. After he sipped, his brows lifted and he added more seriously, "If there's someone at home who'll worry about you, Amanda, put through a call."

She allowed his thoughtful inspection of her jeans and cotton knit shirt to pass by unprotested. But when he motioned for her to sit beside him, she shook her head.

"No one'll worry about me. Not for a few days, anyway."

He bent his head to his work again, appearing perfectly content with her quiet movements about the room. Mandy sighed with the first relaxed moment since she had met him. The way he resumed his concentration, they could actually be married.

What went on in that handsome head of his when he scrutinized her so closely? Was he realizing that her appearance on the plane was all an act? That she wasn't really capable of coming on to a man? Or was he devising a way to get her in bed as payment for his inconvenience and very possible embarrassment?

The telephone seldom rang in the suite. Messages generally

came through Russell's companion, Simon Capice. Mandy didn't take long to deduce that Capice wasn't a secretary at all, as she had first thought. He was a bodyguard. When Russell confirmed it, she was shocked. And whenever he left their room for a conference, she could depend on Simon's unobtrusive presence.

At the end of a second tedious day, after Mandy finally despaired of separating Russell from *The New York Times,* she threw him an irritable goodnight and went to bed. Moments later, certain that she heard voices, she inched toward the door. She was clad in a flimsy apricot tricot gown with deep slits up the sides reaching almost to her waist. She couldn't hear anything. And the sudden silence puzzled her. She threw the door wide. Russell had gone.

Disturbed that he had left without telling her, as if he should have taken his role as a husband a bit more seriously, Mandy marched across the carpet. A furtive peep outside the door revealed Simon, who pretended that he didn't hear her.

She was being unreasonable, Mandy thought with heavy, depressed sighs. Russell wasn't obligated to tell her when he was leaving. But she would have told him if she had left. Didn't he think she cared if he just took off? Did she care?

Yes, she supposed she did. As galling as it was to admit it, the suite was strangely empty without Russell—even under these circumstances. Yet being left alone wouldn't bother her so much if only she knew where he was. They would still be connected by that invisible—

Bond? Mandy came to herself with more jolting clarity than she wanted to see. What was she thinking? Bonds were for lovers or husbands, and wives and parents and children. Bonds were between people who shared everything, from the center of the soul out. She and Russell had none of these things.

Feeling slightly foolish, Mandy left her bedroom door open and told herself she would listen for Russell's return. Visions of him being struck by a speeding car persisted in keeping her awake. She imagined him being mugged. Cold fear made her sweat. With each passing hour, a hot anger surged through her that he could be so insensitive as to make her worry.

After tossing restlessly until one o'clock in the morning, thick-headed and miserable, Mandy finally exhausted her imagination enough to drift to sleep. Her last conscious thought was that she hated Russell Gregory for putting her through this.

Their meals were expertly served by Biggens. If the old man noticed anything strangely amiss between the newly-weds, he was far too discreet to let it show. Putting his slightly nervous assistant through the paces, Biggens showed him exactly where to place the heated trolley. The second trolley was set by his own adept hands—the starched tablecloth precisely centered and appointed with napkins, glittering silver, china and long-stemmed crystal.

"Etienne is new," Biggens explained confidentially over Mandy's shoulder as he spooned Eggs Benedict onto her plate.

He was making the new Mrs. Hamilton feel like one of the "regular" guests by such an intimate remark. Mandy smiled at him prettily much to the thoughtful interest of the man slumped lazily on his spine, studying her.

They had both dressed casually today. Russell wore blue silk slacks which she noticed immediately as being flatteringly tight. Their flare brushed the tops of his buff leather shoes, flowing smoothly upward to outline the trimness of his hips. He certainly didn't hesitate to display his best assets, she thought wryly.

Her dress was a cream-colored knit—soft and femininely clinging. Its swirling skirt reached the exact bottom of her knees, which always earned her a second glance at her legs. And though it was nowhere as exposing as the blouse she had worn on the plane, its neckline scooped daringly low. Her only accessory was the gold chain about her throat. Its tiny heart nestled into the soft hollow between her breasts. She hoped she passed for the type of experienced woman Russell Gregory would have married—expensive and understated.

"The *Ecole Hôtelière de la Société Suisse des Hôteliers* in Lausanne," Biggens murmured politely in her ear.

Mandy's face fell. She blinked at her husband-of-pretense as he tried to hide an amused smile. He leaned far over the table to place a bit of buttered biscuit in her mouth.

"Etienne's fresh out of the hotel school in Lausanne," he whispered out of the corner of his mouth.

"Etienne's doing beautifully," Mandy congratulated Biggens. "The Staad is so much different from any of our American hotels."

"Huge places in America." Biggens shook his head gravely and motioned for Etienne to pour coffee.

"So impersonal," Mandy added absently, as her eyes met Russell's. Thank you, hers telegraphed. You're welcome, his replied.

Then she flushed at his slow wink. She had won the old man over, and somehow that pleased Russell. What she didn't understand was why his pleasure should satisfy her so.

"Rested enough for a walk?" Russell made the casual suggestion after their late lunch had been cleared away. "Get your sweater. I'll show you the lake today."

With an undeclared truce existing between them, Mandy did not know what to expect. It was a new feeling for her, and unnerving. She wondered if he felt it, too. His face was impenetrable; he could have been thinking anything.

Shrugging slightly, Mandy glanced down at sunlight chasing across the lawns. The deep green etched a somber contrast with the brilliance of the sky. Thunderheads piled ponderously. She had been cooped up long enough.

"I need to show off my new wife," Russell said. "After two days everyone's dying of curiosity."

"That's such a sensible reason, Russell!" Mandy instantly regretted the bite of it. "Oh yes, well. I guess it can't hurt."

"Not everything hurts, Amanda," he said soberly. And he moved nearer to adjust the tiny heart on her chain.

His fingers brushed dangerously near her breasts. It was a slow touch, not suggesting any promises, and completely out of line. She found it offensive. At least, that was the excuse she made to herself for the heavy thudding that pounded at her temples and wrists.

The musk of his aftershave drifted faintly beneath her nose. Nuzzling her face beneath his jaw would have been so comforting. She missed her father. She missed being important to someone—even Bergman. She was lonely.

As if she had said the words, Russell's eyes narrowed and grew dark. She held her breath as his fingers reached and poised, almost touching her cheek. He dropped them to his side then, and smiled.

"I think we both need it," he said. "The walk, I mean."

"I . . . I know what you meant," Mandy stammered much too quickly. Her hand spread across her throat, touching the hot flesh where his fingers had been. Before he could say anything more, she moved to open the door.

"I like your dress," his voice floated behind her head. She almost didn't hear it over the shutting of the door.

"Thank you."

"You're very welcome."

Silence.

She coughed lightly. "This is ridiculous."

"Ridiculous? Kennedy and Khrushchev couldn't bridge it. I'd like to know why we think we can."

"Bridge what? Mistrust? I don't mistrust you," she replied.

"Yes you do. You think I'm an opportunist."

Mandy stopped suddenly, in the middle of the hall. Fearing someone would overhear them, she glanced about nervously. "Well, aren't you?"

When she accused him with the lift of her chin, she found him oddly open. As if he were curious of how she felt about him. Once again she sensed the fleeting need to be understood but it seemed even more impossible now.

"Sometimes," he said.

After a moment, Russell broke the tension. "Perhaps we should begin again. We not only got off to a bad start, we didn't get started."

Mandy's scrutiny, when it flicked from the top of his dark head to his toes, was full of disbelief.

"You presume too much, Russell. You take things without asking."

"New husbands are supposed to take things without asking," he retorted coolly, just as a door at the opposite end of the wing opened and shut. At the sound of it, Mandy jumped back from him, only to find herself trapped in an unyielding vise of his right arm. A smart-looking couple somewhere near Russell's age, in their late thirties, strolled toward them dressed in tennis whites.

"New husbands," he continued blithely, "are supposed to do outlandish, impulsive things. Like this."

Before Mandy realized what he was about, Russell drew her easily into his arms and gently lowered his lips to hers. It was all for show, of course, but his slightly parted lips stunned her. Once again he moved too fast: she didn't trust him again.

Thrusting at his chest did no good. His arms only tightened more. Brushing her mouth with a brief, parting caress, he placed a fleeting kiss on the tip of her nose.

"Russell!"

"*Ben*. And smile." Though his face teased, his voice was

serious. He drew his arm securely about her waist until both sides of their bodies melded together.

Mandy had alway considered herself a fairly liberated woman, though she had never been one to make a public display of caressing. Terry and Julie had always been scandalous touchers. They were always making her wish she weren't with them. Now, when Russell openly kissed her and embraced her, she knew they looked exactly like the comfortable married couple he intended. The subtleties of his bluff were so perfect that she halfway believed him herself.

"Jerry," called Russell. "There's someone I'd like you to meet."

"It's about time, old boy. No one's talking about anything else. All kinds of speculation about what's been going on in the Silver Suite." He grinned.

Possessively, Russell's fingers moved below the swell of her bosom, and Mandy stammered through the introductions. Immediately before her spread a splendid fresco of Napoleon at Waterloo; she felt a weird kinship to it.

Apparently, Jerry Whitehall and his wife were important people to Russell. As if he and Russell were picking up the thread of a previous conversation, they fell into shoptalk.

"Walther Braughm sent you a portfolio, Ben. It's nothing concrete—just a bunch of personal assessments. He's afraid to let you see any hard stuff until you agree to take him."

Russell's laugh said he'd been through this before. Jerry's wife patiently slapped her tennis racket off her thigh as if she, too, had been through this before.

"He afraid I'll memorize it and sell it, Jer? Come on," Russell objected pleasantly.

"Have a heart, Ben. He's only being cautious. A man might as well feed data into a computer as let you read something. Anyway, I said I'd ask and told him there were no guarantees."

"Bring it by yourself. I'll take a look at it tonight."

"Opal and Reggie phoned," Jerry continued. "They'll be in this evening for the big bash downstairs. Join us for drinks. How about bridge tomorrow? We'll entertain Amanda while you work."

Beginning to gather her wits, still frightened at Russell's amazing ease in the charade, Mandy smiled, then laughed timidly.

"Ben despises playing bridge with me, Jerry," she teased. "I'm really quite dreadful at it."

Jerry's eyes twinkled back at her. He thought she and Russell were perfect together, and he let her see his approval. Russell began enjoying himself.

"I keep telling Mandy there's no royal flush in bridge," he said with mock seriousness.

He looked down at her curving mouth with the unabashed approval of a man head over heels in love. Whether it was the stimulation of being watched or not, Mandy pressed a teasing knuckle to his ribs. Russell's breath caught almost imperceptibly, and she read its message all too clearly.

She already knew what he thought. Once again they were playing with fire. The teasing came much too easily, and it wasn't nearly the pretense it should have been.

Pat Whitehall's laugh was rich and affluently secure. She proceeded toward the stairway with a jaunty wriggle of her hips.

"The honeymoon ends at the bridge table, Amanda," she called back. "She sounds too much like Jerry for me, Ben. Pair those two with Opal and Reggie, and you and I'll take the house."

Jerry lunged two steps forward and gave his wife a thwack across her behind with his tennis racket. They scuffled, and something tugged at Mandy's heart. She didn't know what it was, but it was painful—some vague hunger that she had never identified before.

Her smile faded, and she studiously inspected the toes of her shoes. She and Russell walked slowly to the stairway. Something had cut her off from the world. She was alone again.

"When it's good, it's real good, isn't it?"

His voice startled her. How could he possibly know what she had felt? She didn't even know herself until this precise moment . . . that she was envious of the good marriage that Jerry shared with Pat.

"I don't know what you mean," Mandy lied.

His voice was husky. "Yes you do."

A clock built into the opposite wall read half past two when they reached the landing. The lobby of The Staad was alive with activity, some of which migrated to revolve about the two of them.

The deception was then in its full glory. In the seconds which remained, Mandy knew she couldn't look at Russell's face, even for moral support. She knew what it would say—that they had not imagined the vibrations between them, that they would be fools not to reach out and explore something wonderful while it was there for the taking. And Mandy wasn't, in her first moments as Mrs. Benjamin Hamilton, capable of telling him they shouldn't.

Nothing about the man whose palm cupped her elbow prepared Mandy for the volley of impressions which filled the next hour. From all directions they came at her—names and faces which she knew were tremendously significant to the world's economy but which she could not possibly remember.

The lobby of The Staad was surrounded by small niches perfect for private conferences. Johann Gustave was accustomed to anticipating the needs of people whose responsibilities depended upon the whim of a teletype message coming from around the world. His staff was best in situations where minutes made the difference between success and catastrophe.

Telephones were plugged near clusters of chairs whose occupants spoke Japanese and Arabic. Inconspicuous men with attaché cases were spirited into waiting limousines; and careful note was taken of everyone, male or female, who walked through The Staad's glass doors.

Urgency, Mandy thought, couldn't be disguised by tired smiles or flourished cigarettes or jackets draped casually over a shoulder. And Russell was a vital factor in all of this.

It hit her then—how far in over her head she was. She didn't have any idea of the kind of mind she was dealing with in her so-called husband. The composite of Russell Gregory consisted of much more than a passing fancy to take a grad student to bed.

The moment their feet touched the landing, she thought everyone who saw him formed an invisible line to have a word with him. Outwardly, nothing changed. But messages were relayed with fingers drawn across mouths and pens flicked and weight shifted.

The man who fell into step beside them first was a thickly set junior executive. He wore his six-hundred-dollar suit like a burlap sack, and the circles under his eyes hadn't gotten there in just one week. He removed the earplug from the transistor radio he carried to keep him current on the latest news and stuffed it into his pocket. Then he gave Mandy a look which seemed to catalog everything she had done or said since birth.

"Here're the FDIC reports for your seminar tomorrow. Austria's man won't reach Zurich until the day after tomorrow," he said, then paused for Russell's reaction.

"Damn!" Russell gnawed the inside of his lip for a moment then nodded his head.

"There's a reporter nosing about. Calls himself Daniel Benton."

"Get rid of him."

"Yes sir."

Before the stocky figure turned away, he recognized Mandy with a smiling nod. "Mrs. Hamilton."

She smiled politely and lost him among the mingling clientele before she could reply.

Russell introduced her only when a couple stopped him with a personal greeting. Even then, his remarks were not overly friendly nor lingering. Ever so methodically he maneuvered her through the hotel, giving attention to consultants or making spur-of-the-moment decisions.

Near the entrance of the dining hall, where cleaning crews finished up after lunch, a trio of golfers conversed privately. The tallest man detached himself and strode forward. White hair on a man who couldn't have been a day older than she was startled her. Mandy caught herself staring and jerked about. When Russell released her elbow, she hung back discreetly. Barely within her hearing, they stood with heads bowed together.

"They want another ninety-day maturity, Mr. Hamilton."

"Give it to 'em, Allen. What's the bottom line?"

The younger man removed a pocket calculator and ran some figures through it. "Thirty-six million."

"They'll default if we don't. Call New York and have nine million transferred to the London subsidiary."

"Yes sir. Chase Manhattan is rumored to be raising a quarter percent before the day is out," Allen added.

Russell thought a moment. "Does Reggie know?"

"I just put it on the teletype."

"Stay on top of this one, Allen."

"You got it."

When Russell returned to the other two men, they conferred briefly and left. During the last half hour, he had not spoken one word to Mandy directly. Now he bent his head and smiled.

"You okay?" he asked.

"I guess so." An overwhelming need for him to know she understood washed over her. His responsibilities were heavy. Her father had carried similar burdens, and in the end they had killed him. Like a lost child, Mandy caught the fingers of his right hand. His step paused a beat, and his eyes filled with a puzzled attempt to reconcile two opposing forces.

"I'm sorry," Mandy whispered and forced a smile that would hardly come.

At least a dozen men stood about them, wanting a word with him.

"It's all right," Russell said gruffly and propelled her quickly past a recreation room filled with plush leather decor. Wives sitting in red velvet chairs looked up as the pair passed and continued to sip their cocktails. Clients who wanted to speak with him and couldn't decided to try again later.

Chapter Five

In spite of the tension in her back and her sweating palms, Mandy felt a certain pride in walking beside Russell. He was not what he had appeared to be. He was a man's man, and she got the impression he did his work, not because the power exhilarated him, but because someone had to do it well.

Skirting the parking lot, they dodged puddles left from the morning's shower. The occasional horn of a bus on the strip of highway meandering through the distant hills attracted their attention. But mostly Mandy concentrated on the sounds of their shoes clicking on the sidewalk in unison. With unconscious symmetry, they matched their strides and left the sidewalk. They cut across the lawns toward the lake. Russell took her hand, and she resisted.

"Don't stop being my wife now, just because we've escaped them."

She bridled at the couched intimacy in his voice. "The pretense is over. At least for a few minutes."

"Is it?"

A fringe of evergreens glistening with clinging raindrops skirted the edge of the lake. Mandy never saw them. Nor the silver-capped waves dancing across the surface of the water.

She was staring at her shaking hand when Russell drew it to his waist and threaded his fingers through it.

She had never felt so aware of so much physical sensation before—his enticing male scent, the way he had of moving his hips, the heat radiating down the sides of her neck, the obscure ache filling her.

Russell stood her squarely before him without releasing her hand. It was her left hand, and he studied it for long thoughtful moments. She struggled to concentrate on the sailboats dotting the distance, but every nerve in her body seemed centered in the tips of her fingers as he touched each one.

"Russell," she began breathlessly.

"Don't say anything. Just feel what's happening."

Mandy started to say "feel what?" But she knew what he was talking about—the chemistry that was making her body hungry. It meant nothing, she warned herself; it was only a need. Only a physical need that would deceive her if she let it.

"There's something I want to give you," he said.

"What?"

Her eyes darted to his face to see if he were joking. He wasn't. A tiny groove formed in the space between his eyebrows. He squinted across the water as if debating with himself. Then he reached into his pocket.

When he slipped the ring on her finger, Mandy couldn't believe it. Russell released her hand, and she stared as she cradled it in her other palm. The wedding ring was a heavy gold band encircled by infinitely tiny diamonds set in engraved rosettes. It was not a new ring, but one with a history. She had never seen anything so beautiful.

"Oh no," Mandy shook her head vigorously, tossing the curls capping her head. "This is going too far, Russell."

Confused, torn, she began twisting it off. Russell closed his fingers over her hand, gripping hard.

"It's necessary. I understand your feelings, Mandy, but—"

"You couldn't possibly know how I feel!"

She dropped her head, not wanting him to see her cry. She truly hadn't meant to hurt anyone, and now she was putting him in this embarrassing position, to say nothing of hurting herself. For in spite of their angry words and hasty misjudgments, she did care. And caring was painful. Very.

"Give me a little credit, dammit!" As usual, his roughness spurred Mandy's determination.

"None of this should have been necessary, Russell! I would've left the first day, and you know it. But you *had* to have everything your way."

"Selfishness has always been my strong suit."

"Think about the woman you're engaged to," she countered.

"We're not engaged. We seriously considered marriage."

Incredulous, Mandy laughed. "You're so chauvinistic I can't believe it."

She walked toward the extreme edge of the water. Wetness oozed up through the pebbles and about the tops of her shoes. The wind whipped her skirt, sculpting the slenderness of her legs. Refusing to turn around when she heard him behind her, Mandy let him take her by the shoulders. He had to force her face upward.

"Look at me when I talk to you," Russell demanded.

Their mouths were set and purposeful. Both needed far more understanding than either was capable of giving, and the glittering tears which threatened to course down Mandy's face did not soften the resolution of his jaw.

"You will wear the ring."

So quietly did her words come, they seemed rehearsed. "When I first agreed to this pretense, I was so guilty. I created it all, and I didn't feel I had the right to say very much. But I never realized so many people were involved with you. I thought . . . I don't know what I thought."

When he closed his arms about her, Mandy still didn't relax. She felt like a poker, even though it seemed like his heartbeats were passing from his body into hers. She had wanted to be in his arms before, and now she was. She didn't think it mattered very much, one way or another. Without honest respect, touching meant nothing.

"You have the prettiest little fanny," he said over her shoulder. It was such a ridiculous thing to say she wanted to laugh and cry at the same time.

"You're decidedly immoral, Russell Gregory."

"Yes." The next words reverberated in his chest—softly, sincerely. "I wouldn't deliberately wound someone. I wouldn't ask you to wear the ring if it wasn't for a good reason. It can protect us a lot. If you like, you can give it back when we leave for the airport."

Without waiting for an answer he stepped several feet away. Sharing a name, even as absurdly as they did, changed people; it made them vulnerable. Mandy watched the strength in Russell's arms as he pulled his elbows toward the center of his back. As if she, added to all the decisions and persuasions he must offer, wearied him.

"I'll wear the ring," she said to his back. "Don't worry about it anymore." His shoulders slumped in a sigh. "Russell? Why do you have two passports? It's against the law."

"There's the law, and then there's the law. I'm what I tell people I am, and I deliver what I say I can deliver. It's no different than a stage name." His words were a monotone.

"But—"

"Financiers get jealous, Amanda, just like anyone else. Some don't take kindly to seeing great sums of money diverted from their control. Even indirectly."

"Are you telling me your life is in danger?" Apprehensive, her eyes widened.

"I see these people once, maybe twice a year. By using a different name, I'm a little more difficult to track down when I return to the States. Anyone who handles money is a potential victim. Any bank president in the U.S. will tell you that."

"Russell!"

"It's nothing to worry about. I've never worried about it until—"

"Until?" she prompted.

"Until you came into my life. Now I worry about it."

"And I'm complicating things by drawing more attention to you than ever."

Facing her, Russell deliberately forced the concern from his features. Acting was second nature to him. He would not say, You're blowing my cover, Amanda. Was she intuitive enough to know if he were performing if he really chose to deceive her? Could she see through beautiful, lying eyes?

"I'm taking you dancing tonight. Opal and Reggie will be in for dinner. Wear something pretty." His mood lightened.

"My, my." She feigned surprise. "I would have never pictured you as a dancer, Russell."

He grinned then, pulling her toward the furred branches of a huge evergreen. The moist smell of flowers and grass mingled with the scent of fallen pine needles, the lake, the breeze. The descending sun cast long and chilly shadows.

"You don't picture me as a lover, either," he chuckled as

they ducked beneath a low-hanging limb. "I do both extremely well."

"Find yourself another date." Mandy tossed aside his pass with a shake of her head. Though she pretended otherwise, she realized his words would tantalize her for many restless nights.

"Sit down."

Russell pushed her down to a cushion of dry needles. The tree drooped its branches about them like a green skirt.

"I want to stretch out and put my head in your lap and try to remember what it was like to be a college kid like you," he said.

"I'm not a kid." Mandy stretched her tanned legs straight in front of her. "How old are you?"

He shrugged. "Thirty-nine."

"Good grief, Russ, you're old enough to be my father!"

Narrowing, promising that any teasing would only provoke his aggression, Russell's eyes riveted on her. "I'll thank you to know my thoughts about you aren't in the least paternal. And," he watched her chest rise and fall unevenly, "no one has called me Russ in years."

When he lowered one knee to brace himself, Mandy suffered the most incredible loss of time. It could have been anytime, anywhere. Carefully he flexed the other leg to rest his arm across it. They both watched, entranced, as a roaming finger reached forward to draw a slow line from her ankle to her knee. It digressed to fashion a sultry circle on her skirt.

He could as easily have traced images in her mind. The strength of his body, the inherent power of his manhood, would teach her things if she would only say yes. Pausing, resting upon her thigh, the hand seemed to ask a dozen questions. Only one man in her past had dared to ask so much, and the scars of his deception warned her now.

"Don't try again to seduce me," she said with effort. Her sincerity was convincing, and Russell did not guess she was panicking. He removed the hand and bent his face nearer hers, his breath on her jaw.

"I don't think it would be very difficult," he said.

"It would be quite difficult."

"I want you."

His words hit her like a sledgehammer. She could have admitted she knew he wanted her, that knowing it exhilarated her. But old habits were not easily broken. She remained silent.

Russell turned at last and cradled his head in the nest of her lap. His jaw pressed firmly against her belly, and he moved his face against the gentle curve. His breath blowing through the knit grew blistering. She gasped.

"Mandy, Mandy," he murmured after a time, until she thought her heart would never slow down. "You've never been to bed with a man."

"Is that a flaw in my character?" She hardly heard herself.

He laughed. "No woman in this decade could be as nervous as you are unless they're demented or a virgin. I think the latter. Bergman must be a fool. Or maybe he's demented."

"How do you know about Bergman?" Mandy felt a swift spurt of outrage and shoved his head roughly from her lap.

"I have a file on you," Russell explained patiently, sitting up straight and inspecting his fingernails.

When Mandy began sputtering, he grabbed her wrist. "Will you cool it? I have a dossier on everyone I have dealings with. Security, nothing more. If you worked for the government, they would have the same thing. No big deal."

"I think it's detestable! What else do you know about me? Does my file say that David Rutherman once kissed me in the Student Union at the university? That I wash my underwear in the bathroom sink?"

Russell stood suddenly and drew her out into the sunlight.

"This isn't getting us anywhere. Get rid of those shoes," he commanded tersely. "Let's go wading."

"You're crazy," she objected.

The water blinked at them, innocently pervading everything with an aura of well-being. Taking no care whatsoever about his slacks, Russell rolled them up to his knees. His calves were firmly muscled. He reached for her.

"But I'll ruin my dress," she complained, dying to get her feet wet, yet pulling back in resistance.

"I'll buy you another one."

It never occurred to Mandy that all talk of the ring had been forgotten. She kicked her feet free of her shoes and lifted the hem of her skirt several inches. Finding herself being dragged to the water's pebbly edge, she squealed in protest.

"Wait a minute! It's cold, Russell!"

"You're a baby."

She choked as he pulled her into the water. It lapped eagerly at the hem of her skirt. For a moment she hugged herself, wriggling a bit to get used to the chill. Then they walked, hand in hand, sometimes slipping and grabbing for the other, sometimes pausing to curl their toes about the smooth stones.

Russell bent, wet his fingers and flicked them in her face.

"Oh!" she squeaked and lifted a foot to kick a spray of drops across his chest.

Carefree and lighthearted, they frittered the afternoon away. He ruffled her curls, and Mandy grabbed his belt, half-ruining his pants. They fished about on the bottom for pretty rocks and stood in the sunlight, examining them. His father had collected agates on the Oregon coast, he said, and their heads touched as he filled the palm of her hand with the prettiest rocks.

She noticed the ring then, and somehow the glow of their childish antics dimmed. Russell pointed at the gulls squawking crossly above their heads. As her face tipped upward, the dark furl of her lashes shading her eyes from the setting sun, Mandy felt his nearness deep in her body.

They stood in the water with their clothes wet and the quiet peacefulness made them forget, for a while, the craziness of the last few days.

"Mandy," he said quietly, not touching her with the persuasiveness of his hands.

They weren't a foot apart. And when his head slowly bent and his lips reached down for hers, Mandy didn't turn her head away. Her heart seemed to be in her throat, and she didn't close her eyes. She watched as his cheek filled her vision and felt his nose fit neatly beside her own.

Russell drew a quick breath against her mouth and fastened his lips more tenderly than she would have imagined. For the first time, she let him part her lips and taste her. The lapping of the waves, and the occasional cry of a gull were the only interruptions her conscious mind was aware of. Slowly his tongue possessed her. Mandy met it with her own and felt things changing in the dark reaches of her soul—old feelings shifting, turning to become new.

She felt greedy and selfish. She wanted to know everything about Russell there was to know. She wanted to share his taste, his body, his pain and his dreams and be the only one who did. It was impossible, she thought, that they were

standing in a Swiss lake—kissing each other, because it was
the only thing they could do.

"What's happening to me?" Mandy whimpered when she
dropped her forehead to his shoulder. He drew her tightly
into his arms. "I don't know what's happening to me any
more."

"Shh. You're becoming a woman, sweetheart."

She sighed. "I never felt like this before."

"I know."

Men had kissed her before. She had never felt this with
them. How could Russell know that?

He spoke his next words with such intensity that Mandy
sensed he had been saving them. She doubted he had ever
said them before to anyone, and she wanted to melt into him.

"All my life I've worked at concealing what I really feel.
It's what I do in my work, but I did it before. I remember my
mother trying to get me to open up. It's hard to break a habit
like that."

Mandy said nothing but understood.

"Her name is Carolyn Wrather," he said. "She was the
wife of a friend of mine. He was killed in Vietnam."

"I want to go back to the hotel," Mandy said quietly. But
Russell held her tightly.

"Just hear me out." He grew hoarse. "Carolyn . . . isn't
the only woman I've been . . . involved with."

A small sound of pain sounded in Mandy's throat. The
spell, whatever it had been, was broken. She didn't think this
moment would ever be recaptured again as long as she lived.
Clasping his arm about her waist, Russell guided her out of
the water. They gathered their shoes in silence, and only after
they walked back to The Staad did he resume his explanation.

"She was really the only woman I ever considered marrying. Mostly I think it was for Mickey. He's Findley's son, and
I was with them when he was born. In some ways he's like my
own son."

Picturing Russell with a small boy seemed contradictory.
Casual passes were one thing, but genuine tenderness was
something he had not shown her until they had kissed just
now.

"I think I felt I owed it to Findley to take care of them or
something. I don't know." He sighed at his memories.

"You would be married to her right now if I hadn't messed
things up."

"My mother accuses me of having been betrothed to a bank the day I was born. That's not far from the truth."

The impassive look on his face left Mandy feeling miserable. She would have given everything she had—all of the Phillips fortune—to change their circumstances. If she had met Russell before, under normal conditions she could have turned to face him and said, "I think I could love you."

Now, when he said, "Opal and Reggie are probably here by now," Mandy only smiled sadly. The most beautiful moment in her entire life was gone. She suffered a greater sense of loss than when they had buried her father. Happiness was such a fleeting thing—a moment here, an experience there. The rest was the routine of living—getting by. And that, she reflected grimly, was all she had ever done. Get by.

Before Mandy finished dressing for dinner, there was a knock at the door of the Silver Suite. In the process of buttoning his shirt, Russell strode across the living room with steps bordering on impatience.

As nervous as she was, Mandy would have given almost anything to escape meeting Opal and Reginald Patterson. They would be different from everyone else she had met at The Staad. They would know who she was—not Mrs. Benjamin Hamilton, only Amanda Phillips, graduate student from New Orleans. She peeped out the door.

"Russell, it's so good to see you!" Opal cooed. "I told Reggie he would have to call the police if he thought he could keep me in that suite 'til dinner. We bumped into Jerry and Pat in the lobby."

Reginald came straight to the point. "What's all this talk about, Russell? Keeping secrets, eh?"

Mandy shrank tightly against the wall. Not overhearing the conversation was impossible.

"It's not so very complicated," Russell drawled an out-and-out lie. "Care for a drink, Reggie?"

"I could use one," the older man replied. "Well? Do we get to meet the clever lady who caught the elusive boy from Hartford, Connecticut?"

Russell hesitated. "Let me explain a few things first, Reg."

Opal Patterson's height almost matched Russell's, and her girth well exceeded his. She was a perfect example of the expression "a handsome woman"—not pretty, but well-dressed and very wealthy. Reggie Patterson might be the controlling force behind the Patterson fortune, but in size he was smaller than anyone in the suite, Mandy included. Side by side, the Pattersons looked like a powerful lady ambassador and her male secretary.

With a feeling nearing panic, Mandy closed her door and glided to the dressing table where she leaned heavily upon her damp palms.

Time was running out. In only minutes Russell would knock on the door. Mandy fluffed at her curls with trembling fingers. Leaning closer, she inspected her mascara and the faint blue eyeshadow the color of her dress. She needed the discretion of the Pattersons. Her sigh was heavy and depressed.

Not quite certain why she had brought an evening gown to Switzerland, she was nonetheless dressed appropriately. It was a Halston creation, revealing one shoulder, leaving the arms bare, cutting daringly low in a diagonal across her chest, and with a side slit showing most of one leg. She favored this blue gown above her others, not only because it was flattering, but also because it moved exquisitely with her.

After glimpsing Opal Patterson's "old-school" staidness, however, Mandy wished it was a turtleneck with sleeves reaching to her wrists.

The voices outside dropped to a murmur. Russell's explanation was taking too long. Mandy had just decided to walk out on her own, and had even pushed the door open, when Russell stepped directly in front of her. His eyes widened, impudently moving down the natural curve of her breasts provocatively outlined by the soft silk. He grinned broadly and challenged her with a lift of his eyebrows. Afraid to go through with it? they taunted.

Mandy swept from the room with the poise of Princess Grace. "Mrs. Patterson, please forgive me for being late," she said, her chin high. "This confusion has me a little behind schedule."

Russell's amusement drilled into her back. He loved it when she performed, and she didn't wait for him to introduce Reginald Patterson.

"Mr. Patterson," she cooed. "Russell has spoken of you over and over. I hope this . . . inconvenience won't keep us from being good friends. Would anyone like coffee? There's some in the kitchen."

Reginald's eyes snapped like steel traps. Once again Amanda blessed the inherited strength of her father. Many times she had watched him run the diplomatic gantlet, just as she was doing. The admiration in Reginald's assessment was frank; the wiry white-haired man liked her. He was an ally.

"Russell doesn't usually keep secrets from us, Miss Phillips," Opal said, smiling. Her apprehension was written plainly on her face.

"Amanda," she corrected the older woman.

"We're just making the best of a silly misunderstanding, Opal," soothed Russell. "Mandy, is my tie straight?"

His tie was perfectly straight. Amazed at his coolness, Mandy met him, ploy for ploy. As if they had been intimate friends for years, and this arrangement were the most natural thing in the world, Mandy stepped toward him.

She met him with steady blue eyes and took the knot in her fingers. Pretending to adjust it, she then smoothed the stiff corners of his collar with a wifely concern.

"You're doing great, you foxy little hypocrite," he muttered, hardly moving his lips.

"Hush!" She spoke through her own congealed smile.

"This whole thing is awfully precarious, Russell," observed Reggie thoughtfully, as if he imagined well-laid plans going down the drain.

Mandy dropped to the divan beside the older man and crossed her legs with a brisk confidence. Her beige heels peeped from beneath her hem.

Talking in spurts between puffing attempts to light his cigar, Reggie continued. "If *we* were shocked, you can imagine what Carolyn is going to think. What happened between you two, anyway?"

"Reggie! That's hardly proper to discuss here!" his wife scolded. Her glance apologized for her husband's tactlessness.

"Why not? This young woman's no dunce." He paused, then laughed. "Well, you did get yourself into something of a pickle, didn't you, girl?"

"That I did, sir," she smiled back.

Russell turned his back. Mandy would have given a lot, at that moment, to have seen his face. "Carolyn and I talked everything over in New York," he said tonelessly. "We decided to wait. She and Mickey would come over here, and we would decide something then, that's all. How Mandy bounced into the picture is history."

"I didn't bounce," Mandy disputed, then clamped her mouth shut. Reggie and Opal weren't missing a single vibration passing between Mandy and Russell.

"You know how these investors get sometimes," Opal argued, breaking the tense silence. "If someone starts wondering about Miss Phillips and even writes an innocent letter—first one question, then another. Before you know it, we're faced with an explanation that makes us all look foolish. Or downright dishonest."

"I've thought of that." Russell poured himself a drink from the bar and swirled the clinking ice cubes. He was uncomfortable. This was the first drink Mandy had ever seen him take.

"Hell, bluff your way through! I've bluffed all my life," Reggie chewed on his cigar. "This'll last only a few days. Once you clear out of Switzerland, it'll die a natural death."

"You're discounting the human factor, Mr. Patterson." Opal pursed her mouth like a dowager queen. "Things may not be so simple when Carolyn Wrather steps onto the scene. Russell, you really should have telephoned her. She just can't walk in on this."

"I tried," Russell said, "but she's left New York. I don't know where she is. She could be in London. Anywhere."

"Carolyn has never been famous for her sweet disposition. You can expect trouble on a grand scale," warned the older woman.

Russell's quick smile sobered. "I think not. One of Carolyn's . . . gentleman acquaintances is attending this seminar. When I tell her, she'll behave like an angel."

Opal's look at Mandy was free of hostility, but the compassion she hoped for was missing. "I was young once, Miss Phillips," Opal said, slightly remote. "I won't say I didn't do a few crazy things myself. But in my day, when a woman said she was married to a man, she was married!"

No matter how distraught it made her look, Mandy could not remain seated any longer. She arose and walked to the bar. Compulsively, she blotted up the moisture ring from Russell's glass with a napkin. Even though his sympathy was reaching out to her from across the room, he would do nothing to bail her out of this one.

She defended herself with forced restraint. "I'm doing nothing immoral, Mrs. Patterson. It's true we're all a bit too human sometimes. And there seems no correct solution here.

I'm taking responsibility for my actions in the simplest way for everyone concerned. Except for myself, of course."

Before she got the words out, Russell shifted his weight—ill at ease, pacing a few steps back and forth without comment.

"Leave 'er alone, Opal," ordered Reginald. "She's doing a fine job." He crossed his ankles on the footstool and blew smoke at the ceiling in an unperturbed stream. "Now, back in the days when newspaper reporters *worked* for their stories, this girl would have gone places."

"They still do work for features, Mr. Patterson," Mandy could not refrain from saying. "Justice would have far less chance than it does if it weren't for the courage of some reporters to go out on a limb."

"Well," he chuckled and pointed the glowing end of his cigar at her. "You did go out on a limb, that's for sure."

Reggie clapped a hand down on his knee with finality. Her interrogation was over, at least for the present. What score she had made wasn't clear, but at least she had not failed the test. What happened when Carolyn Wrather arrived would be another story entirely.

"I'll get my jacket," Russell eagerly ended the conversation. "Opal, Reggie, will you excuse me a minute? There're a couple of dinner guests I need to brief Mandy about."

"By all means," Opal replied, doubt in her eyes.

"She'll do fine," Reggie comforted. Though Opal enjoyed her authority, in the final analysis Reginald's word was law, and his wife accepted it gracefully.

"They ought to get married," she whispered in one last criticism. "What if some idiot runs a security check, Reg?"

"Don't cross your bridges so fast, honeybabe."

What Opal replied, Mandy did not hear. She stumbled toward Russell's bed and dropped upon it, flopping onto her back and staring at the ceiling. "Who do you want to brief me about, Russell?"

He towered above her, his fists on his hips. "No one. Look at me."

When she did, her face wearily lacking its usual barriers, he sank down beside her, his weight on one hip, a muscled arm bracing on each side of her waist. No condescension stained his face, only understanding. He would do everything he could to protect them.

The chemistry blazed between them, almost savagely.

Mandy's first impulse was to turn herself into the length of his body, to mold against the masculine power of him. But her hand only fit its palm about the line of his jaw.

As Russell's mouth curved in almost painful self-mockery, Mandy was astounded to watch him lose a fraction of his control. He hesitated. Then, with a tear in his breath, he turned his head and pressed his lips against the soft palm. She thought, as his lashes fell darkly upon his cheeks, that she had never been so terribly drawn to another human being. If Reggie and Opal had not been waiting outside, the need burning between them would have soared into a fire impossible to extinguish.

"Russell?" Mandy breathed, begging him with a shake of her head to stop the flow which she could not control.

In the seconds that their eyes locked, both of them desperate for the other to do something, they both reacted. Mandy averted her gaze and snatched her hand away, unable to bear the distress in his eyes. Russell's concern for her anxiety straightened him upright, and he coughed uneasily into his collar.

"Mandy," he said, clearing the hoarseness from his voice, "listen carefully to everything I say tonight." She stared hard at the throbbing pulse in his temple. "If Carolyn shows up, we'll take it as it comes. Go with me, no matter what happens."

Nodding, she licked her dry lips. When she caught a long, ragged breath, he grinned. "I don't want any trouble with Carolyn," she said. "Just . . . no trouble."

He paused so long before he replied, Mandy wondered if he were remembering something he had shared with Carolyn. Irrational jealousy sent moisture sliding down Mandy's ribs, and she threw herself off the bed.

"You really did well in there," he offered at last. "I didn't think you had it in you."

Her reply was tight. "It was terrible. I thought I'd throw up."

Taking her hand in his, pulling her to face him, Russell studied the wedding band on her finger. He didn't smile. "It wouldn't be such a bad idea, you know."

She knew what he meant. "What wouldn't?" she asked numbly.

Deliberately he held her ringed hand between them, then dropped it. His face was drawn with too much compassion.

She thought his games were easier to deal with than his honesty.

"Forget it," he said shortly. "I don't beg women."

"It was nothing personal, Russ. You know I—"

"Don't call me Russ unless you mean it!"

"Well!" Her teeth gritted in embarrassment. "Don't call me Mandy, then! You're a bit human yourself, if you didn't know it."

"I never said I wasn't human. *God, you don't know how human I am.* All those nights I've lain awake in there, I could have shown you how human I am. Give me ten minutes and I'll show you right now!"

"I know . . ." she began, bitterly aware of his barely reined passion, "I know all about your masculine humanity, Russell." Her words softened to a whisper. "Can we go now before one of us makes a terrible mistake?"

For a second fierce pride erupted in his eyes. Calmly then, stiffly controlled, Russell took two steps until he was standing within inches of her. He searched her face, forcing her to drop her eyes. As if the sign of weakness pleased him, he reached for his jacket and shrugged into it.

"Baby, you don't know the first thing about my—" He paused, then chuckled to himself. "About my *masculinity.*"

When Mandy refused to contradict him, only standing pathetically still, he gentled. "Let's go. Smile a lot and don't discuss politics, money, or the President of the United States."

Giving a brazen whistle, he drew a finger down the length of her naked arm. When Mandy spun from his provoking intimacy they both knew why he had done it, why it had been necessary.

Even though she thanked him for the stability of his brashness, her eyes were a hard, icy blue. "If I live through this I'm going to show you a thing or two, Russell Gregory."

"God help us all!" he laughed. "My name is *Ben* tonight. Don't forget it."

She marched to the bedroom door. His words came softly behind her head.

"I live for the day you show me anything, my darling," he mocked, when he wanted to adore her.

"You chauvinist!" she hissed, hating the sound of her own words.

Russell was chuckling when he wrenched open the door.

Even his saunter was sexy, Mandy thought drily. She followed him into the living room as he took Opal's arm with an exaggerated bow. Reginald's understanding gray eyes felt like cool water on a hot day. When he gave Mandy's fingers a friendly squeeze, she blinked her thanks. He didn't doubt her ability to pull this off, and she slipped her hand through the fatherly loop of his arm.

"Well, Mr. Patterson," she murmured, "for whatever it's worth, we enter the arena."

Chapter Six

The first dinner at The Staad with all of the Hamilton party assembled together was a formal dance. The ballroom was set with forty tables. One end of the floor was left open, decorated with velvet streamers and flowers. Accoustical equipment and instruments for a twelve-piece dance band waited promisingly in place.

It would be a full-course banquet, with dancing until well after midnight. And during casual conversations around tables, in restrooms, leaning against walls, or dancing close, millions of dollars would change hands.

Red-coated waiters already darted in and out the service doors, stiff menus in hand, cocktails and refills coming and going. Russell seated Mandy at the Executive's table as the Pattersons greeted some of their guests.

Over the hum of milling people being seated, Russell sent signals of recognition to associates. Mandy never stopped smiling. When people bent over their chairs, she laughed the proper responses, and placed her fingers upon the proper forearms.

"She's a doll, isn't she?" a male voice remarked under his breath to Reggie, behind her chair. Mandy blushed, not knowing whether she was meant to overhear or not.

In spite of his social obligations, Russell's eyes persisted in returning to hers. If he left the table, he searched over shoulders for her face. And though the long-stemmed glass before her had scarcely been tasted, Mandy's head whirled giddily. As the waiter moved about their table with skilled inconspicuousness, she was only vaguely aware of soup, steamed trout served on hot, oval plates. Sacher torte disappeared from her dessert plate, and she didn't recall eating a bite.

Finally, tired of pretending, she allowed herself to drown in the depths of Russell's eyes. She smiled at the delightful curve of his mouth and the deep richness of his laughter, his efficient hands, the strength of the tanned muscles in his neck.

"Don't get drunk on me," he murmured in her ear as he returned from a brief conversation with an electronics expert from West Germany. Dropping into his chair, he leaned forward, leaving an unhurried trail of kisses down her nape.

Heads turned. "People are staring at us!" Mandy objected.

"Let them." He was deliberately making them the center of attention. Caught up in it, she flushed with pleasure. She was proud of him. Proud of them both.

"Do you do this all over the world?" she asked.

Russell shook his head and sipped his drink. Leisurely, he contented himself with an admiration of the sensual curve of her throat.

"And you couldn't care less. Admit it," he laughed, refusing to be distracted.

Mandy grimaced. "You make me nervous."

"You love it."

She had no answer, vividly aware of his growing desire. She glanced blindly at the dance floor. His breath falling upon the back of her neck was warm and sent a shivering weakness through her knees. Playing these games with Russell was so dangerous. His groan in her ear was not nearly as teasing as he pretended it was. She knew what he wanted.

"You're beautiful," he said thickly into her curls, inviting her honest response. He might as well have said, "Please let me make love to you tonight."

Too much was happening; she didn't have the experience to reply. If he had taken her hand that very moment and led her upstairs to his bed, she knew she would have followed.

In self-conscious protection, Mandy's hand touched her throat. Russell took it into his large brown one. He toyed with her fingers, each touch sending its drugging message until she could hardly breathe.

"This is such a lovely hotel," she gasped feebly.

"Shut up."

He drew her hand beneath the table and placed the flat of her palm upon the hard swell inside his thigh. Its strength sent tangled images spiraling into her mind. She could only imagine the heat of loving him—yearning flesh blending, limbs reaching to hold, whispered words fusing the spirit.

She tried unsuccessfully to free her hand. "I'm afraid," she said, her words almost inaudible.

"I wouldn't hurt you, little one."

"I know, but—"

"You want it as much as I do."

Mandy's reply was only a sound. Russell knew he couldn't press her any further. The dance band had been playing half an hour. The floor had filled. Russell, after pushing their drinks back, slid his hands about her waist. He stood her up and, pushing her chair back with a toe, laughed at her dazed expression.

"Come on, lazybones," he teased, the quirk of his eyebrow as disturbing as his seductive wheedling. He nodded in the direction of a tall, leggy female vocalist singing a heated Latin ballad.

"You're kidding," said Mandy, her eyes coming to life.

"Why, can't you do the rhumba?"

"Well, yes. But I didn't think you could."

Russell danced with a graceful rhythm. The flashing challenge of his smile prodded Mandy to match the subtle twist of his hips, the flex of his knee.

"Timid?" he teased.

Extending his arm, he guided her backward in a languorous twist. The beat pulsed on and on. It swirled her skirt about her legs sensuously. It flowed down through her head into her feet and into her blood. Then Mandy moved not only with him, but for him. And through her peripheral vision she caught signals passing through the band. It played for them, grinning at the sensual, throbbing effect they created.

Never did Russell release her eyes from his. They flirted and teased with her and sent disturbingly erotic messages about intimacies they had never talked about. Fire began melting Mandy's bones. And when it was over she could have collapsed in his arms.

The beat changed, mellowing to a dreamy smoothness.

"Waltz," Russell whispered into the shell of her ear. Possessively his arm tightened about her waist, and he twirled her about the outer edge of dancers.

She flirted with him. "Body-rubbing music."

Leaning her head back upon his arm, Mandy's body was captured tightly against his. She laughed up at him. Glowing intently brown, Russell's eyes dropped to the suggestive curve of her breasts.

"Don't say anything you don't mean," he warned, his voice hoarse.

The whole evening swept Mandy up in an Alice-in-Wonderland whirl of unreality—a beautiful young woman dancing in the arms of a virile husband who wore his power with understated dignity. They painted a lovely picture, even if it was a forgery.

"You're casting a potent spell, darling," he mused against her temple. "I don't know if I can stay decent."

Mandy felt her dress clinging to his legs, concealing the seductive aggression of his movement.

"Russell?" she asked softly. "Ben, I mean?"

"What?" Leaning his head back a few inches, he smiled down at her.

She did not return his smile. "About what you asked before?"

He sobered, too, and she could feel him adjusting things in his mind. A large hand slipped lower to the base of her spine, expertly guiding her through the spirals of dancers.

"Oh, Mandy," he moaned. "Let's get out of here."

Mandy shook her more practical head. Her words sounded strangled. "We can't."

"Yes we can."

Such frankness had not existed between them before. And now, when Russell took the risk, his own desires were undeniably vulnerable. "I know you're right," he said. "If I could just hear you say it."

"I—"

"Say, 'I want to love you, Russell.' Please."

"I want to love you, Russell."

"Oh, God!" he groaned, burying his face in her hair.

So caught up in their blistering passions, drifting somewhere in half-awareness, Mandy hardly realized when Jerry

Whitehall touched Russell's arm. At the private message he stilled, and Mandy was jerked harshly back into the real world—thwarted needs and unavoidable responsibilities.

Russell's expression, when he looked down at her, was swept clean of any emotion. Only his everlasting efficiency remained.

"Mandy, I have to leave you a few minutes," he said.

"What's wrong?"

"Nothing's wrong. Will you be all right with Opal and Reggie?"

His manner angered her after the sharing which had passed between them. He was treating her like a child. Though she could be taken to bed and deprived of her virginity, she was unable to cope with more serious problems.

"I can take care of myself," she said coldly. "Do whatever you have to. But don't ever speak about honesty to me again."

Russell wanted to argue with her. But there was no time. He smiled grimly and placed her into the arms of his friend. Whether her feelings were written all over her face or whether her defeat appealed to his sympathies, she didn't know. She realized only that he yielded to her wishes, a thing he had never done against his will before.

"Carolyn just arrived," he said simply.

Though Jerry Whitehall was not in Russell's confidence to the extent that he knew about the alias, he was still a close friend. When he danced Mandy to the edge of the floor, she couldn't remember being quite so grateful for a familiar face. As if his only purpose was to protect her from possible unpleasantness, Jerry kept his arm securely about her waist and fell into step as he walked her back to her table.

Some yards from it, he shielded Mandy with his back from the stream of guests moving to and from the floor. A speaker was mounted above their heads, intensifying the music, making it almost impossible to hear. It forced him to place his mouth against her ear.

"Pat will drop by your table in a few minutes, Mandy. You girls can go powder your noses."

When their eyes met, even in the dimmed light, she read his intentions. *Let me help you,* they pleaded.

"You think I may need to escape from 'the other woman'?"

she jokingly replied when he bent his head to catch her answer. She didn't feel the slightest bit humorous. Jerry smiled and shrugged his shoulders.

"With Carolyn, only God knows. I don't envy Ben telling her."

"Thank you, Jerry."

Mandy returned the comforting pressure of his fingers and allowed herself to be seated beside Opal. Jerry leaned forward between the two women and within hearing distance of Reginald's disturbed face.

"Carolyn Wrather is here, Mrs. Patterson," he warned. "Ben went to meet her."

"Oh, Lord!" Reggie groaned, stubbing out his cigar.

"Mr. Patterson," Opal's gray eyes glanced momentarily to question Mandy's composure, "do something."

"What, for crying out loud?" growled her husband.

Mandy winced at Opal Patterson's unspoken resentment toward her. Even though the woman lifted her head the genteel amount and pressed her mouth in well-bred resignation, she blamed Mandy.

The Pattersons' sympathies would lie with Carolyn. They had expected Russell to bring her to Switzerland as his wife. Carolyn Wrather was a stable commodity in the marriage market—not impulsive enough to pretend to be a man's wife to get a hotel room.

Mandy wished she were dead.

When Russell approached the table from behind her, she didn't need to turn. She felt his presence even before his hand rested upon her shoulder. She envisioned the apology that would be in his eyes. She suffered his disguised displeasure at being trapped in a situation he had not initiated and could not get out of.

Twisting her head about, Mandy's sight filled with swinging, shoulder-length red hair. She watched stiffly as Carolyn Wrather placed her rouged cheek against Opal's and laid long, beautifully polished nails upon Mandy's own arm. Carolyn's voice was deep and rich and full of sophisticated gaiety, free of condemnation.

"Oh, darling!" she laughed to Opal. "I was just congratulating Russell."

The embarrassed clap of her hand over her mouth was cleverly done, and all eyes riveted to Jerry Whitehall's back to see if he had overheard. Carolyn sighed in relief and straightened her face in mock soberness.

"I was just congratulating *Ben* on his good taste in women." They all smiled at Mandy except Russell who kept flexing the muscle in his jaw. "I'm Carolyn Wrather, Mrs. Hamilton. Ben explained to me in the lobby about your marvelous whirlwind courtship. Isn't it romantic, Opal? I adore romance."

"You adore everything, Carolyn," Reginald said. "Sit down."

Reginald pulled over an additional chair for Carolyn to squeeze in between him and his wife. She cuddled familiarly against his shoulder.

"Now tell me, Reggie," she began, loud enough so everyone could hear her. "What have you been doing with yourself besides fending off good-looking women?"

"Working myself into an early grave," answered the older man.

Carolyn gave his cheek a peck and Reggie, laughing, pretended to throw up a defensive arm. Opal lifted her brows. As if sharing a private joke, they bent their heads. Mandy wondered if Carolyn always behaved this aggressively and if Opal always took it so well.

Knowing what she did about Russell's taste, Mandy guessed that the woman's pushiness was more a show for her benefit than anything else. Staking her claim, perhaps? The evening abruptly seemed endless.

"Opal," Carolyn chattered, "I really *love* the color of your hair. I told my hairdresser what Kelvin had done for you, and she tried it on that . . . Jackie Burdette I was telling you about. She *loved* it!"

Unnoticed, Mandy leaned on her palms and studied Russell's reactions. He was unusually quiet, but behind those thick lashes it was hard to know if he were enjoying his friend's vivacity or not. Carolyn withdrew a fold of white paper from her glittering handbag.

"Mickey drew a picture of you at playschool, Reggie. His teacher put a star on it. Now, you will have to admit that he captured something of you. Don't you think so, Opal?"

A ripple of laughter over the crayon drawing caused Mandy to shift in her chair. Without realizing how nervous she appeared, she twisted to search for Pat's familiar face.

"Carolyn," interrupted Russell brusquely, "would you care to dance?"

"You know I'd love to, darling. If it's all right with your . . . wife."

The woman's hesitation sent Mandy's heart into her throat. Carolyn knew! Or she guessed enough of the truth!

If she had not glanced at Opal, Mandy would have wondered if she were imagining things. But their silent message agreed. Russell must be protected. The alliance between Opal and herself was immediate—born of necessity.

Opal laced her fingers together tensely, and occupied herself by frowning at the striking couple as they twirled about the dance floor.

The silence at the table was deadly. Mandy could hardly keep from wringing her hands. She and Opal couldn't talk about it. And whether Reginald guessed that Carolyn saw through everything was impossible to tell. A few minutes alone with his wife, Mandy thought drily, and he would be convinced that a catastrophe was impending.

The sight of Jerry and Pat almost sent Mandy spinning out of her chair. Outwardly, however, she arose with the coolness of a duchess.

"I'm going to the ladies' lounge, Amanda," Pat said. "Want to come?"

Mandy hoped her smile wasn't ecstatically relieved. "Yes!"

Jerry's next words were meant for her, Mandy knew, the moment he spoke them. "Carolyn brought Mickey with her. Isn't that nice? You wouldn't believe how that kid has grown."

Opal stiffened. Reggie muttered "Damn!" but Mandy was probably the only one who heard him. Predictably, he fished for a fresh cigar.

Opal sent Mandy a "how could you create such a compromising situation?" look. Pat's hand, when she drew Mandy from the table, was so welcome that Mandy stifled the urge to kiss it. She blindly followed Jerry's wife out to the lobby.

"Don't let Opal throw you," whispered Pat. She wore a crisp ballgown—raw silk with a diamond choker. It suited her straightforward personality. "Opal has planned a ten-thousand-dollar wedding for Ben ever since Jerry and I have known him."

That explained a few things. Opal Patterson knew absolutely nothing about her own family background. For all she knew, Russell had pretended to marry the daughter of a convict.

"Ben told me how fond he is of Mickey," said Mandy once they were in the lounge. "I hope nothing gets too awkward." She tried to make conversation while Pat repaired her makeup. The older woman was blessedly involved in what she was doing and didn't notice Mandy's distress.

"Awkward?" Pat talked around strokes of her lipstick. "Reggie will see to that, the sweet old billygoat. Ben's never been suited to Carolyn. I told Jerry the day we met you how relieved I was that Ben fell in love with someone like you."

If Mandy hadn't felt like a traitor before, she did now. She combed her curls furiously, then tried to cover her scarlet cheeks with powder.

"Carolyn's a human barracuda," Pat offered generously as Mandy swung open the door to the lobby.

"She didn't seem so bad to me," Mandy murmured, her eyes instinctly scouring the dance floor for a glimpse of Russell.

Pat turned to give her a long, serious look. "You must have been raised an innocent."

Mandy laughed. "My parents were gentle people. We had everything we wanted. But I did learn something of human nature. Still," she shrugged, "I hope Carolyn doesn't feel Ben . . . jilted her."

"Pooh! I wouldn't waste a minute's worry about what Carolyn feels. She has a string of men trailing behind her wherever she goes. She doesn't have anyone who loves her son, though. Ben and Findley were very close. When Mickey's dad got killed, we all thought Ben would lose his thread for a while."

Mandy drew into her own thoughts. She had imagined Russell doing many things, but grieving had not been one of them. Who did she think she was, disregarding the delicacy of a relationship between Russell and his best friend's child? The women wound their way across the crowded lobby, occasionally brushing arms and bumping shoulders.

"How did you and Ben meet, anyway?" Pat's question made her stumble. They grabbed each other, and Mandy disguised her chagrin by examining the heel on her shoe.

"Ah . . . in New Orleans, would you believe? I worked in an office there. We kind of . . . I don't know, caught each other's eyes, I guess you might say."

"You're perfect for Ben. He'd eat, live and breathe banking if someone didn't take him in hand. He's really brilliant, you know. Jerry says he has a photographic memory. Simply incredible. Without Ben, Reggie might as well go out and hang himself. Ben's kept that bank from going under during the interest-rate crunch. And that's not easy."

"Oh," was all Mandy could think of to say. She wished she had washed her hands. She suddenly felt sticky and soiled.

When they returned to the table Russell was standing, one hand in a pocket, his eyes roving tensely over the moving heads as if he had been searching for her. At the sight of them he stepped forward. Tossing Pat a smile of thanks for taking care of her, he drew Mandy aside.

Before he could say anything she clutched his arm. "Russell?"

Time didn't allow her any pretenses. She felt like getting down on her knees and begging him to spare her this ordeal. Though seemingly still remote, Russell's eyes probed. But Mandy was more attuned to his masks now, and his anxiety at being caught between two women was visible. Love was double-edged—a sword capable of great pain and miraculous ecstasy, one cutting as deeply as the other.

"Please, Russell," she said. "Is . . . is there a car available I could drive? I need to get away. Just for a little while. Please."

His expression accused her of cowardice. He didn't want her to leave him. "You owe it to me to see this through," he said flatly.

"I don't owe you anything!"

She could have wept at the viciousness in her words. Russell gave his full attention to her then—forgetting Carolyn, the Pattersons, the scores of people whose trust he bore.

Mandy fumbled to explain. "You know what almost happened to us on the dance floor."

"Don't tell me it wasn't right, dammit!" He looked as if he would liked to have thrashed her.

"I'm trying to. I need to get away and think. Can't you see? I don't want to hurt you."

His short laugh reflected helpless bitterness. "Then don't."

"You're going too fast, Russell," she choked. "Give me a chance."

"Don't-call-me-that-here." With a swift glance over his shoulder, Russell drew them nearer the lobby, into an alcove filled with plants nearly as tall as they were. His jaw set menacingly with objections she knew she couldn't refute.

"All you have to do is look at me. You know what happens," Mandy confessed, thinking as she did so that it was a grave error.

Standing very still, Russell behaved as if he didn't completely trust her. He didn't touch her but rubbed the muscles at the back of his neck.

"Okay. We're not flirting now," he said. "We're not caught up in the heat of the dance. Tell me, what happens when I look at you? I want to know."

Mandy had never said such words to a man. In the past, halfhearted flirtations had protected her—an armor to hide behind. "This is hard for me," she said, distressed.

He could be so deliberate; he could go straight to the heart of things, cut away pretenses. He didn't want to risk making a fool of himself. Well, neither did she, and she searched in her mind for something to hide behind.

"Go on," he said tightly. "I want to see if you know what you're dealing with here."

Blinking back the tears was almost an impossibility. "I don't enjoy fighting this attraction between us," Mandy hesitated. "But it wouldn't be a casual affair for me, Russell. You could live with it later. I don't know if I could."

Not once did Russell offer to make her admission easier. His eyes darted once to people who laughingly passed them, and she followed his gaze simply to avoid seeing the dissatisfaction with her answer.

"You think that giving yourself is a mistake? You have hang-ups about saving it until marriage?" He laughed, then ceased his feigned mirth. "We are married. Remember?"

She compressed her lips at his crude irony. "If I said something that tacky, you'd slap my face. That woman came here, expecting things to be like they were when you left her. There's her son, too."

"Leave Mickey out of this."

Mandy wanted to stamp her foot, to throw her hands in the air for his colossal double standard. "I can't leave Mickey out of this. He's important to you. I can't have a one-night stand. There! You wanted to hear the truth, now you have! Forget the car. I'll go for a walk."

Russell had lost. His hands closing about her shoulders were more painful than he realized.

"Wait here," he said after an awkward silence. "I'll be right back."

When he returned with Proctor, he dangled a set of keys before her. Then he took one hand and dropped them into it. He looked as if he would liked to have said much more. But in the presence of Proctor he only tightened the corners of his mouth.

"A white Mercedes," he said tersely. "Proctor will show you."

Mumbling incoherent thanks and some comment about being back later, Mandy clutched her handbag and threaded her way through the crowd.

Proctor cast an odd glance her way. "Watch the step, Frau Hamilton."

The fresh air outside was never more welcome. Proctor walked Mandy to a Mercedes parked at the far side of the lot. He unlocked the door. The night wind whipped at her dress and tossed her hair. Mandy wished, as she paused with her hand on the door handle, that she could look out across New Orleans and hear the growl of city buses moving along Canal Street. Or turn her face toward the Mississippi River and listen to the mournful whistle of a freighter leaving the port.

Slamming the car door shut her into a solitary cocoon of expensive leather. She flipped on the radio and backed out of the lot. The music drowned out everything for a while, even her thoughts.

Here she was, Amanda Phillips, driving along a winding road in north Switzerland. For the first time in her life she wanted something she could not have. Not only because of Carolyn. It was more than that—pride. Self-justification, too. Maybe even a little stubbornness.

Telling herself to be patient until things could be worked out didn't help at all. Everything between Russell and her kept taking wrong turns. And people could never really go back and begin again.

It seemed she drove for hours, with the windows down. The wind chapped her cheeks, but she didn't care. Her emotions had been through a shredder, and the only thing she was certain of was that she was miserable.

Carolyn Wrather was not some kind of witch. She was a beautiful, intelligent woman—the kind who would complement a man like Russell. She carried herself well. She was nearer Russell's age, which was an asset. And she possessed a trump card that Mandy could never beat. Carolyn's son was fused to Russell with deep, intangible bonds.

The hill country of Mattenaugst was so shrouded in darkness that Mandy could see very little of it. It occurred to her that this was the first time she had been off the grounds of The Staad since Erik had driven her up from Zurich.

Realizing that the speedometer sat on a hundred twenty-five kilometers an hour, Mandy slowed and took the hills more carefully. Oncoming headlights warned her from a distance when they flickered up and down the valleys. The purr of the powerful engine blurred with the music and her distractions.

When red taillights zoomed into view over the next hill, Mandy slammed on the brakes. The tires screamed and she made a terrified sound in her throat as the Mercedes swerved sideways, skidding broadside for at least a hundred feet.

Fighting her instinct to wrench the wheel in the other direction, she pressed the accelerator hard. With only inches to spare before the side of her car looked as though it would smash into the rear bumper of the other auto, she straightened the wheel and roared past.

So badly did she shake, that she could hardly keep her foot on the accelerator. Before Mandy drove another two miles, she slowed to a stop. Leaving her emergency lights blinking, she parked on the shoulder and climbed out of the car. Her legs could barely hold her up, but she walked a few steps and breathed deeply to stop her heart's racing.

Good Lord, she'd been driving close to eighty miles an hour! She could have killed someone! Mandy buried her face in her hands, too distraught to even weep. What was she doing? What was she doing *here*, in Switzerland? What was the confusion spinning in her head?

When the pair of headlights stabbed over the hill behind her and the car crept to a stop directly behind the Mercedes, Mandy snapped her head up. A very real, very cold fear slithered through her.

The door of the other car opened, and Mandy warily began inching to the passenger side of the Mercedes. A man stepped into the glare of the headlights. He was very tall and wore a light sports jacket and jeans.

"Was that you who nearly took us both to heaven back there?" he barked in English. The British man was so angry that he didn't bother to consider what language he spoke.

"It was my fault," Mandy agreed quickly, though she was still shaking.

"You were driving like a bat out of hell!"

He moved toward her. Mandy hugged her waist.

"I'm sorry," she muttered and reached a tentative hand to support herself against the Mercedes. He must have realized she was frightened, for he stopped once more and his voice was quite gentle when he spoke.

"My name is Richard Sanders."

By now Mandy could almost distinguish the features of his face. She squinted hard.

"Is there something the matter?" he inquired solicitously.

"Nothing's the matter!" she almost screamed at him. He probably thought she was drunk. She watched him bend to read the license plate on the car. He shrugged.

"If you say so. You'd better be careful. You're an American, aren't you?" he said, suddenly noting her accent.

"Yes." Mandy swallowed and laced her fingers so hard that the circulation was cut off. "I'm terribly sorry about what happened back there. Are you all right?"

"I'm fine, actually. I was simply startled," he said and gestured with his palm. "Are you quite certain you're all right? You look fairly shaken up to me."

Standing in the middle of a strange road, talking to a perfectly strange Englishman whom she had nearly killed, Mandy began to go to pieces. Shivering shook her body. Hardly able to stand, she listened to her own teeth chattering and clamped them hard.

At an obvious loss, the man cautiously took one step nearer. His voice softened, but he made no move to touch her in any way.

"I shouldn't have pounced on you like I did," he said. "I apologize, too. No harm done. I live near here so it would be no problem to drive you to where you're going. Someone can pick up your car later. It's not good to stay out here alone this late at night."

"Thank you," Mandy mumbled at last through her gritted teeth. "I'll be all right. Really. In just a minute."

She hated being under inspection by someone she didn't know, who probably thought by now that she had escaped from a mental hospital. Her words came jerkily, and she caught a deep breath.

"Are you in trouble, miss?" he inquired. She glanced at a

face nearly the age of hers. He was clean-shaven and wore dark-rimmed glasses. Perhaps he was a student.

"No," she shook her head. "Just a personal problem, that's all."

"Oh. They can be bad."

"Yes."

For a moment they didn't speak. Mandy watched tiny insects flying directly into the beam of the headlights.

"I went through a divorce last summer," he offered. "I came damnably close to chucking everything."

His gentleness reminded her very much of Terry's ready and sincere sympathy that was so easy to respond to. Thinking of Terry reminded her of Russell's rescue effort. Mandy sighed heavily.

"You must love him or hate him a great deal," he said with a hesitant grin.

Without pausing to realize what she said, Mandy replied, "I guess I do."

"What, hate him?"

"N—no."

She listened to her own words. Talking aloud to another person sometimes clarified clouded thoughts. They became facts, like seeing them in print for the first time.

"I . . . love him," she whispered. Her voice sounded as if it came from a long distance away, and she was surprised that this was the first time she had spoken it.

"Well," Richard shifted his weight, "that happens. Look, I need to be going now. If you're sure you're all right?"

"What?" she focused her eyes. "Oh, yes. I'll be fine. Thank you for the offer. I'm . . . okay now."

Mandy did not look up again, but she heard Richard Sanders's step in the gravel. He stopped briefly, then shut his car door. When the engine growled to life, and the lights swept onto the road, she finally lifted her head to stare at the fading taillights. Then, once again pitch blackness surrounded her.

David Rutherman, she recalled, had picked her up as usual at the university one freezing day in January. He had half-dragged her into the Student Union where it was warm. With flushed cheeks, he had stammered through his confession that he had not gone back to work at ITT as he had said. He had gone home to a wife and small son.

Mandy had thought that her life was over, ruined. She

would have given herself to David if he had asked, and as he kissed her and begged her forgiveness she could not believe the enormity of the pain. It took her four years to recover.

But she had not learned. For now she stood on a lonely Swiss road, marveling that she had allowed herself to be vulnerable again. This time love would surely kill her, for what she had felt for David was nothing compared to the depths of her feeling for Russell.

The truth was not welcome, for Mandy knew herself better by now. She might as well be in love with another married man. Russell was as committed to his carreer as David was to his wife, and she did not believe that it would turn out any better.

Chapter Seven

The clock in the lobby read two in the morning. A few guests straggled from the dance floor as the musicians packed up their gear. Women leaned heavily upon the arms of their escorts. Laughter and the too-loud talking of some who were drunk floated about.

Mandy slipped past Herr Gustave's eagle eye and kept her head down as she passed people on the stairs. It wasn't until she reached the locked doors of the suite that she realized she had no key.

"Oh, darn," she sighed, glancing about for the sight of anyone familiar—Biggens or Proctor. Not a soul was in sight. She was about to knock when the doors parted, and she was jerked into the living room. It was ablaze with light.

Reggie Patterson sat on the chair nursing a drink, his hair standing out where he had repeatedly run his fingers through it. Opal's legs were crossed. Her ankles were swollen, and her back was stiff with the undaunted resignation of one accustomed to trouble.

And Russell? He looked as if he had been in a boxing ring. His tie was off, his shirttail bunched untidily where he had attempted to stuff it back into his trousers. The dark shadow of his beard cast a menacing look about his face that made Mandy gasp in alarm.

"Where have you been?" he shouted, nearly dragging her inside the room and slamming the doors.

Mandy wrenched herself free and glanced from face to face in an attempt to figure what they were thinking. "I went for a drive. You know that!" she cried.

"I've been worried half out of my mind. Do you have any idea of what time it is?"

"It's a few minutes after two," she replied tersely.

When Russell's hand reached for her again, Mandy retreated from him, holding out both her own and cocking her head in an unspoken warning; if he manhandled her again he would regret it.

"Look, everyone!" she burst out, weary of being treated like a delinquent child. "I'm over twenty-one. I drove out in the country for a few hours so I could decide what to do. I'm leaving, first thing in the morning." Her decision was made in the split-second she said the words.

"You're leaving," Russell glanced at his watch, "in exactly three hours."

Half out of her senses from the tension of the last hours, feeling as if her brain had reached the bursting point, Mandy pulled herself up to defy the masterful figure. His eyes glittered darkly; his mouth was pinched and white; he looked anything but romantic. Behind her, Reggie coughed uncomfortably. Russell's hand, when it closed about Mandy's wrist, was unsteady.

"Let—me—go, Russell!" she demanded in a hissed whisper.

Before he could reply, Mandy's reasoning powers returned. She realized they were either overreacting or something had happened in her absence. Her outrage extinguished like a blaze under water.

"What's wrong?" she demanded.

She faced Opal. The woman wouldn't protect her from the truth. But Opal talked as if she were musing to herself. "I knew something would come of all this. 'A person never outruns his sins,' my daddy used to say."

As Opal grimaced cryptically, Mandy scoured Russell's face. She tugged at a lock of her hair; he walked the length of the room with carefully placed steps. And, Reginald created an enormous double chin as he pondered.

"You're going home. It's that simple," Russell said with an emphatic set of his shoulders.

"Don't insult me again," Mandy reminded him of his overprotective behavior at the dance. "I'm not made of china."

Russell jerked off his tie and threw it at the arm of the divan. It missed and lay in a twisted curl upon the floor. Not realizing the intimacy of her act, Mandy stooped and picked it up, smoothed it and placed it on the coffee table.

"There's no need to fly into a dither. Opal's going back with you," he said.

Shaking her head, Mandy tried to fit a puzzle together though the vital pieces were missing. "And?"

"There's been a crisis at the branch office in Zurich. Nothing that hasn't been tried in the past, in one form or another. We just want you women out of here. In case."

Her words were wooden. "In case of what?"

He shrugged. "Well, would-be thieves aren't ever predictable. What starts out as simple gets out of hand. They panic and do crazy things."

Reginald flicked ashes on the carpet. "We're having you two women driven to Schauffhausen before dawn. We've arranged for a flight out at seven o'clock. Absolutely nothing to worry about, of course. A simple precaution, that's all. Honeybabe, do you remember when one of our California branches was bombed we—"

"Bombed!" cried Mandy.

The room became so silent that Mandy heard the hiss of burning tobacco from Reginald's cigar. Russell's shift of weight seemed out of place. Feeling as if she were choking, Mandy moved to the window and flung one section wide. Crisp air brushed against her cheeks and ruffled her hair as she inhaled deeply. The stars seemed as remotely untouchable as reality.

Russell patiently began to explain, "The Swiss Mercantile just received a message on the computer. Some klutz plugged in on it. He says he's planted an explosive device in one of the lower offices. If we don't deliver three million dollars by noon tomorrow, it will be detonated by remote control. Of course, we've called in a bomb squad. It could all turn out to be a hoax."

"Sure, sure," nodded Reginald. "That's probably what it is. Some computer nut trying to get his name in the papers."

"Anyway, as a precaution, we want you and Opal safely home," Russell finished.

"Will you put that cigar out, Mr. Patterson, before we all succumb?" Opal's voice was shrill, and she apologetically gnawed at her lip the moment she blurted the words. "I'm sorry, dear. I know better."

Extinguishing his cigar, Reginald arose to comfort his wife, placing a thin arm about her ample waist. Opal sighed heavily. "This business has never been worth it, Reggie. You know I don't complain often."

"You've always been a pro, my darling." He bent to place a kiss upon her shoulder. "Let's go back to our own suite until it's time." He helped Opal get up, and she leaned against him.

"Russell, I don't mean to be difficult," Mandy began, tilting her head at an angle. "Why do we have to leave? Surely the problem in Zurich can't affect us here."

Russell's eyes narrowed at her naïvete. "Hostages are an order of business these days. Every thief, if he can't do it with a computer, charges in and grabs himself a hostage. Airplanes, banks, embassies."

Russell clamped his mouth shut abruptly, regretting that he had said so much. Mandy understood then, that he feared she or Opal was in danger of being an insurance policy for a would-be terrorist.

Her look at the frowning figure was not disbelieving. Yet she caught a swift breath before her final question.

"Will Carolyn Wrather be coming with us, too?"

Russell's face was a mask. "What Carolyn does is her own business. I don't tell her when to come and go."

The Pattersons looked from him to Mandy. Then, as if mutually agreeing they should not interfere, they wordlessly walked to the door, closing it quietly behind them.

"I'll be ready in fifteen minutes," Mandy said, already walking to her bedroom.

When Russell stepped to the hall door and motioned for Simon, Mandy stopped to watch. Even with Opal's distraught prattle, the talk hadn't seemed to be more than an overcautious gesture. The appearance of the tall, slender man sent a chilly thrill of danger slithering through Mandy. To watch Russell's dark head bend to confer with him put things on a shocking life-and-death basis.

The horror which swiftly rose in her throat was not for herself; it was for Russell. Reginald Patterson would never be allowed in the vicinity of such a volatile crisis. Russell would be the one who would take the risks, who would negotiate with heaven-only-knew what kind of lunatic criminal.

Though wrapped up in her own thoughts, she overheard Russell's instructions to locate Allen. The hurried dismissals and agreements to meet in the lobby at half-past five seemed like inconsequentials to her detached mood. She was in the way. Mandy felt like a mother must who was dragged away from an injured child—useless.

Unseen, she slipped into her room, leaned back against the closed door and turned the lock. She had loved him for only a speck of time, and already she hurt.

A kindred sympathy with women everywhere sent a stinging pain through her chest. How removed she'd been all her life to the wives of war dead or missing in action, to policemen's wives who never knew if some maniac would kill their husbands over a malfunctioning turn signal.

All these years Mandy had been in the world, but never a part of it. Until now. Now she loved a man who was about to walk into a situation that could cost him his life. How *could* Russell lay his life on the line when she loved him? She thought she hated him for being so thoughtlessly cruel.

"Amanda?"

Russell's low voice came from the other side of the door. She didn't think she could face him now. She was too out of control.

"What?" she mumbled.

"I want to talk to you."

Blotting at the tears drizzling down her cheeks with trembling fingers, Mandy swallowed hard to steady her voice.

"I'll be out in a minute, Russell. I'm . . . packing."

The doorknob turned, gently. Then once again not so gently. Mandy stiffened and felt the breathtaking beat of her own heart.

"Open this door, Amanda," Russell demanded quietly. "If you don't I'm going to bring the hotel down around your head."

"I'm all right. Leave me alone."

"I won't, dammit! Now open this door."

Mandy knew Russell wouldn't kick against the lock. He

wouldn't send his body crashing against it in a silly attempt to splinter it in pieces. He would simply find Johann Gustave who would provide a key.

"Please," she begged.

The evening had been a long one. It took almost more strength than she had to keep from sliding down to sit on the floor. Forcing her chin to a proud angle and bracing herself, Mandy threw the lock. Russell shoved open the door, compelling her to take a step backward as she met his glowing eyes.

"Don't you ever lock a door on me again." He gritted his words. His jaw clamped angrily.

He could have hit her. Russell's threatening height, making her look upward, almost sent Mandy over the brink. It was so terribly easy to wound someone you really cared about. With hardly any effort it could begin—the hating, the bitter words that never really healed.

"Don't look at me like that," he said. Mandy thought his composure crumbled a notch. Deep lines drew his face.

"You tell me you're shipping me home while you run down to Zurich like a sacrificial lamb. What do you expect?"

His fingers threaded through the hair at the back of his head in a distraught gesture. He almost turned away. "I expect—Hell, I don't know what I expect."

With a bitter shrug of his shoulders then, he moved. The compassion Mandy felt welling inside her nearly choked her. He had never intended to become so deeply involved with her, Mandy knew. Things had gone beyond his control, and he wasn't the kind of man who could take that easily.

"Let the police handle it, Russell. Don't go to Zurich," she pleaded after a long silence.

"It's my job. It won't amount to anything but a game of nerves."

"Then let Reggie play it."

"Reggie is good at other things. Not this. We have an . . . understanding about things like this."

"An *understanding?*" she cried. "That he'll pay for your funeral expenses?" Her lower lip began trembling violently. She clamped her fingers over it and pressed hard until she tasted the salt of blood.

"For God's sake, Amanda, I'm not going to run in and start looking under desks!"

She knew he wasn't yelling at her but at the critical

circumstances. Russell pushed her into the living room as if she were not capable of steering herself. When she stumbled to a stop, shaking her head, still holding her mouth, he pried off one hand, then the other.

"Drink this."

He would force it down her if she didn't. Taking a mouthful of the fiery liquid he placed in her hand, Mandy swallowed it down. Then she bent double in a strangling seizure. Several seconds elapsed before she could catch her breath. Rather ungently, Russell pushed her down on the sofa. He slumped down on his spine beside her in glum distraction.

"Lean your head back and close your eyes. You'll feel better in a minute."

Mandy obeyed him, but she didn't feel better. "I think I hate you as much as I hate myself."

"You're better already," he teased.

"Shut your mouth." Out of the corner of her eye she could see his fingertips pressing against his forehead.

"We're two adults," he said flatly, as if reassuring himself. "You're going home. I'm staying. There's no big deal about that."

"Bull."

His grimace was unamused. "Your crudeness doesn't impress me," he stated baldly.

"I don't give a damn. Nothing about me impresses you."

He lunged to his feet. Mandy felt strength returning to her own limbs. Her cheeks reddened warmly. Nothing she could say would change anything. Stiffly, she stalked to her bedroom. She left Russell brooding over the bar, his hands stuffed helplessly in his pockets.

Throwing her suitcase onto a chair, Mandy began emptying drawers and half-folding, half-cramming the contents into it. When Russell filled the space of the doorway, he cast a gray shadow across the carpet. She shot him a hostile glance and continued packing.

He was so very male standing there. Everything about the evening drew attention to his maleness—his strength over hers. Mandy glanced upward to watch him absently unbutton his vest. His browned fingers moved slowly, unconsciously. She had no idea, as she observed this ritual, what was going on in his head. Was he planning what he would do once he reached Zurich? Was he worrying about Opal and her?

Russell unbuttoned his cuffs. And when he began working

on the front of his shirt, Mandy jerked around to face him
squarely. None of the boy existed in his stubbled beard, his
tousled hair that grew a little too long. The muscles in his
neck were tense. His chest rose and fell raggedly. His gaze,
when it fastened on her, scrutinized her own discomposure.

Mandy met his eyes briefly, then looked at her busy hands.
His stare was dark and intense, searching for more than
Mandy was allowing him to see.

"Are you going to be all right?" Russell's forehead fur-
rowed. "I'll keep in touch."

The worry in his voice made Mandy wince. She turned her
face away, so he would not see her blinking back the tears.

"I'll be all right," she said huskily. "Go . . . change your
clothes. Whatever."

She threw open the closet with a louder crash than she
intended and pushed all the hangers tightly together. The
awkward stiffness of her shoulders was intentional, for he
knew her well. Russell would see them shaking otherwise.
Her tears would draw his response, and she couldn't bear to
back him into a corner one more time.

"Mandy?"

She refused to answer. She listened to his determined
intake of breath and prayed he would let it out. Her clothes
were heavy. She moved quickly toward the bed, keeping her
head averted.

"Answer me. Are you crying?"

"No," she lied, her voice breaking as she spoke.

At first Mandy fought him. When his arms enfolded her,
sending her clothes into a disorderly confusion to the floor,
she thrashed at him. She pushed against his chest and
muttered an incoherent stream of distraught objections.

Russell could not understand why she ached. He could not
know that her feelings for him were not remotely related to
friendship anymore. And Mandy didn't think she could ever
tell him how much she loved him. Love because of obligation
was no good. Obligation would always be between them, like
trapping a man with an unplanned baby.

"Don't cry," he murmured. His mouth was buried in her
hair, and he rocked her gently in his arms. "Shhh, don't cry."

It was a ridiculous thing for him to say, she thought. She
couldn't stop crying. Mandy slipped her arms beneath his
strong ones, up and over the hard curve of his shoulders. She

clung tightly, as if he were ballast in a storm, and let him comfort her.

But the need gradually changed, and it was more his need than hers. Mandy felt the difference first in Russell's hands. They moved experimentally . . . over the smooth planes of her back—stroking, testing her resistance, sliding lower to gently fill themselves with her hips.

As Mandy moaned softly, attempting to turn her head away while she could still think, Russell twisted his face and sought her mouth with a burning urgency which shocked them both. Once his lips fastened to hers, parting them, she stilled. The poignant search of her mouth was neither gentle nor bruising; it was an acceptance of what they had become to each other without remembering how it had begun or how it would end—only the hunger of it now.

Russell whispered hoarsely into her mouth. She couldn't understand what he said, but the words didn't matter. Like a spirited filly resisting the first tether, Mandy struggled. She knew exactly what he meant to do.

He was too big for her resistance, his weight more than she could withstand. They tumbled to the bed. With his body pinning hers, his mouth groped for the kiss she tried to refuse him at first. But his tongue insisted—telling her, then pleading with her to not fight. She knew he felt her surrender. Mandy melted beneath him and opened her mouth. The kiss deepened. They drifted in a limbo of tastes and smells. Long moments later, his large hand cradling her head, Russell reached to flick off the lamp. Then, only a faint sliver of light from the living room revealed the serious intentions darkening his face.

He braced a palm on each side of her. "I want you so much," he murmured.

No relationship of her past had progressed to this critical point. This was no time for coyness. A man's body pressed her back into the contours of the bed, a determined, virile body with hips which tightened to grind a hard masculine dimension against the bones of her body. Steadily. Rhythmically.

"Wait, Russell. Let's talk. Wait a minute."

But Russell had already shifted his body, his fingers had already begun to trespass below the silky barrier of her bodice. His hand closed about one soft, trembling breast. In the faint glow of light he watched it grow tight and responsive.

For a moment Mandy lay entranced with the traitorous sensations of her own body. Her mind screamed of danger, warned her to use her unique woman's ability to stop this before it rushed past the point of control. But she craved to know how it would be. She loved him, she rationalized. It was right that Russell should be the first man to make love to her.

Russell's knee forced her legs apart, and his thigh fit neatly between them. He was so urgent, so erect.

"Russell, don't!"

"You knew this would happen." He said it like an accusation, as if Mandy had planned it.

"Just kiss me," she begged and tried to stop his fingers from unzipping his pants. Her attempt to save them from the inevitable wavered. "Just kiss me. No more."

Slowly, unsmiling, Russell's mouth lowered to hers. "I can't just kiss you, Mandy. I'm breaking in two, and you know it."

With a tear in his breath, he adjusted his body between her legs. He drew her unskilled hand to touch the physical proof of what he said. His need shocked her, even as it filled her with a sense of power that she could inflame him so badly. When she attempted to recover her hand, he shook his head and trapped it.

"This isn't playtime now, Mandy. I'm not one of your little friends who'll flirt and go away."

She knew he was seducing her. She had imagined it happening a dozen times. She had pictured Russell a dozen ways standing naked before her even though she'd never seen a man naked before.

When she didn't argue, Russell arose to stand over her. He shrugged out of his vest, his eyes never leaving hers. Then his shirt with absent movements, dropping both without looking to see where they fell. Mandy grew acutely aware of her youth, of her ignorance. She lay dazed, unable to avert her eyes when he straightened from removing his pants. Then she squeezed them tightly shut.

He was beautiful, and he made her feel beautiful. When she finally did open them and found Russell smiling, she grew bold. Almost greedily her senses awakened. She was all flames and liquid and hardly able to keep still. He took her hand in his and taught her what she knew, yet did not know, of how to pleasure him.

Mandy still wore the gown she had danced in, and when Russell's knee lowered to the bed beside her she instinctively clutched it. "Please, let me keep the dress."

"Why, love? I want to look at you, too."

Her mouth formed the words without sound. "I'm afraid."

"Just a little, then," he urged gently.

Slowly, pushing her hand away, he slid the bodice of her gown over one shoulder. Mandy flushed, wanting him to look at her, to think she was desirable and half-fearing her ignorance would disappoint him. When his dark head bent, when he traced a line with his tongue between her breasts— postponing the moment when he would close his mouth over the yearning crest, she moaned. Turning her head from side to side in a final attempt to reconcile two instincts which refused to blend, Mandy grabbed his head roughly and held him to her breast.

As drugged as she became, Mandy fought his hands as Russell coaxed the hem of her dress up. With a heavy sigh then, Russell relented. But he stripped off her pantyhose with an expertise that abruptly made her despise him for the times he had done it to other women.

"Let me go!" She lashed out at him, pushing hard against his shoulders.

His head jerked up. "Are you still playing games?" When she would have thrown herself off the bed, he fell upon her.

"You act as if I can't refuse you," she accused bitterly. The glitter of his eyes frightened her a little, reminding her that, at this point, he was capable of force. "You don't control me, Russell."

His voice was hoarse and drawn with tension. "Refuse me, then," he challenged. "And mean it when you say it."

Trying to hide from him was hopeless. He caught her hands from covering her face. "I won't stand in line for you," she protested.

Mandy made her body limp and responseless. In a moment, as if Russell read through her frail objections, his wandering mouth lowered to brush against the nape of her neck. His laugh was knowing against its curve.

"Say it," he urged. "Tell me to stop, and I swear I will."

Her plea was not coy. "Russell, don't do this to me."

But they both knew the conflict was with herself, not with him.

"Say you don't want me."

"I—"

His knee forced its way between her own, and Mandy realized that her years of innocence had come to an end. The tightness slowly invading her was his own insistence to possess her. She tried to stop the trembling of her lips, but she couldn't.

"Say it, sweetheart," he whispered, his breath falling hotly upon her mouth. Mandy's lips parted. The arch of her body up to him was so slight that it scarcely happened, more like a gesture of her spirit to make it happen.

"I can't say it," she murmured into his open mouth before it hungrily captured hers.

The next thing she realized was the strength of her fingernails digging into the muscles of his back.

"I'm sorry, I'm sorry." Russell caught her face in his hands and stilled after his painful thrust. His voice shook as he kissed her over and over. "I didn't mean to hurt you."

He was vulnerable. She would never have imagined it, and she didn't know how to explain that it was all right, that it was a good hurt. She was different from the other women he had known. And though she couldn't possibly know the extent of it, that very difference drove Russell beyond his ability to restrain himself any longer.

Time, if they had had more, would have taught her how to seek release for herself. Now she only gave Russell the one priceless thing she had, and her satisfaction was in the giving of it. Now she was certain of what she had merely sensed before; no man could ever come after Russell. Filling the inside of her body was but a small part of it. He flooded over into her soul, branding himself into her brain and the way she would look at herself from now on.

She would like to have said, "I love you, Russell, for being gentle with my ignorance. For caring how I feel."

"I'm so tired," she breathed, hardly realizing there was no time for the words to tell him she had waited for him all her life.

The events of the day dimmed her mind. Mandy didn't know when Russell stood over her for long, thoughtful moments, watching her steady breaths rise and fall. She never knew when he sighed and stooped beside the bed.

"What did I do to you, my precious girl?" he whispered, wiping a hand across his eyes.

She stirred, snuggling deeper beneath the sheet. Russell drew the blanket under her chin, softly closed the door behind him and walked to the kitchen to make coffee. He would let her sleep one hour.

Chapter Eight

It was soon after daybreak when Mandy awakened. Only one hour of sleep had stuffed her head with cotton as gray as the shadows skulking about the corners of her room. Lying on her stomach, Mandy forced one eye open and blinked. Russell, disheveled and sexy, a cup of steaming coffee in his hand, gradually sharpened into focus.

Humiliation flooded through her immediately—the memory of the hours when she had been part of him. Though she had no doubts about her own love, he had only filled a need. She wasn't the first woman, and she wouldn't be the last.

"How do you feel?" he asked, placing the coffee on a table and nudging her into a sitting position.

His aftershave lingered on the pillow beneath her cheek, and her body ached with a vague tenderness. Becoming aware of the immodest gaping of her gown, Mandy clutched at it. With gentle amusement, Russell brushed her hand aside. The neckline fell away, and his slow inspection was unabashed, possessive. He didn't even touch her, and the pink nipples hardened tightly.

"I—"

He grinned.

Mandy sat with a jerk and crossed her arms over her

bosom. The room looked as if she had never seen it before— her pantyhose a pale film upon the carpet, Russell's vest and shirt in a crumpled heap beside the bed. Had she stupidly transformed her life into a long series of regrets?

"Drink this quickly," he said. "A fast shower, and that's all. I'll finish packing for you."

The grin tugging at the corner of his mouth was a mixture of indulgent father, teasing boy, uncertain guardian. Wandering in a maze of emotional confusion, Mandy didn't answer. She stumbled to the bathroom and reached for the shower spigot.

The hot water soothed the foreign soreness between her legs. Standing before the wide mirror, Mandy made a swift appraisal of herself, almost expecting to find something visibly changed. Her waist was just as small, her breasts as full and high. She was vacant-eyed, and her cheeks were still reddened from the stubble of Russell's unshaved jaw. But she was no taller, no fatter or thinner than usual. Only different.

She wasn't a child anymore. Hours earlier, anything she knew about sex she had read or guessed at. Russell hadn't touched her at all like a child. Her intuitions warned her: Russell would always be one step ahead of her. He had merely begun to teach her about the wonders of being a woman.

It was quite frightening, the power he exerted over her thoughts. When one took it all apart—sex and real love—a body touching another body meant very little. Not being able to stop living her life around him terrified her. The emptiness, the loss, the misery—those were things that only Russell's spiritual touch could soothe.

That was the unjust crux of it, she thought, leaning her wet curly head against the mirror in a gesture of submission. Her mind was a flesh-and-blood computer, irrevocably programmed with Russell Gregory. If she knew how to do it, she would make him fall in love with her as intensely as she was with him.

The darkness hovered thickly outside—that melancholy density just before dawn. Except for the muted preparations for breakfast by sleepy-eyed cooks, The Staad was majestically silent. Mattenaugst's hushed street outside only added the defeating touch to Mandy's unhappiness.

A week ago she had entered this hotel with flamboyant

girlish drama. Now she was leaving, creeping out in secret—a woman, older and wiser. A week ago she had begun a charade for a reason that now seemed empty and shallow. The play was over—leaving her more married to Russell in her heart than the illusion had been. She had come to make herself a name with a man she suspected of being a criminal. She was leaving feeling that *she* was, in some vague way, the criminal.

Simon leaned an anxious shoulder to open the glass lobby doors. With loose-jointed steps Russell stepped out into the chilly mist beside Reginald. Mandy and Opal followed and Allen, carrying Mandy's suitcase, glanced over his shoulder to see whether anyone took particular note of their departure. A cleaning man stooped to push a carpet sweeper back and forth over the lobby carpet.

"Call me the minute you girls land at Kennedy," Reggie gave his wife instructions and handed her into the back seat of the white Mercedes with old-fashioned courtesy.

As Reggie kissed his wife Mandy jerked her face away. She walked toward the rear of the car and stared at the taillights reflecting red pools in the water trapped on the ground. They looked like her life's blood puddling about her shoes.

When Russell's steps sounded softly behind her, Mandy lifted moist blue eyes to his. Seconds ticked away—all they had left between them. Worry clawed its lines down his features, making him look haggard. She didn't realize the anxiety staining her own face.

"Everything will be all right," he said dully. "You mustn't worry."

She wanted to scream that nothing would ever be right again. "I'm sure it will," she agreed levelly.

Polite, discreetly patient, Allen waited beside her door and Simon started the car with a spurting growl. Russell played his part to the bitter end. Opening his arms, he drew her curly head down to his hard shoulder and bent his lips until they touched her ear.

"Oh, Mandy," he breathed.

She knew, when he pressed his jaw to the smoothness of her cheek, that he was asking her to have mercy upon him and not cry. What a mistake, to have grown so accustomed to him that she knew what he was thinking!

A brilliant smile pasted on her face, Mandy lifted her head. "Be careful, Russell."

He grimaced an unhappy smile. "I will. Have a good flight home."

"Yes."

Mandy's nod was pathetically cheerful; her words were too brittle with optimism. She pretended not to notice the raggedness of Russell's breath.

"I hope everything works out for the best," she said, her thoughts weeping, *How can you let me walk out of your life like this?*

"And for you, too."

Then quickly averting his face, Russell blinked at the sky. The wind caught his hair and tossed it carelessly about his face. For one brief second the small boy was there.

"It's five-thirty, sir." Allen's voice forced them several steps apart.

Numb with misery, Mandy allowed herself to be guided into the back seat. This was so wrong. If she had only known of the pain, she would have erected a wall about her heart.

A panel of steel and chrome and glass separated them. Allen, after shaking Russell's hand and listening to a few last-minute instructions, climbed into the front seat beside Simon. The car ground into gear.

"See that Reggie doesn't do anything foolish, my dear," Opal ordered Russell with the dauntlessness that her years of unthreatened security could afford.

Russell leaned halfway through Mandy's open window and took one sidestep as the car moved. His eyes remained fixed upon Mandy's face. "I'll take good care of him, Opal."

Mandy's fingers twisted so tightly the circulation throbbed in complaint. With a wisdom born from the fear of loss, she saw the rest of her life without him. It was beginning this very moment, wasn't it—her loneliness?

As the car separated them by increasing inches, she thrust one hand frantically toward him. The tips of their fingers brushed. She felt her lungs bursting, her life draining away in this foreign country. The miraculous mystery of the hours that had passed between them earlier could not begin to compensate for the loss escaping her hands.

The expensive machine pulled farther forward. Her fingers reached pitifully outward, yearning to span the impossible. Then Russell was gone. The darkness covered him up like black paint on an artist's brush sweeping across a canvas.

Immediately, the groping began inside Mandy's head. Her

memory searched frenziedly for something to keep herself held together—the image of a firm jaw or the sound of a step, the sudden flushed awareness of being watched in an intimate moment. As the car nosed its way cleanly onto the road, she slumped against the open window. The misty wind washed her face. She felt like a woman in a World War II movie—straining for the last glimpse of a sweetheart while the train parted them.

Turning her head from Opal, Mandy wept soundlessly. Hot tears slid down her cheeks. In the muted silence over which the two men quietly conversed, the women instinctively grappled with the gulf of age and lifestyles between them. It was one of life's truly wonderful moments. Both were leaving men they would worry about. When Opal's thick hand reached out, closing slowly over Mandy's gently curled one, Mandy gripped it very hard, grateful for the demonstration of compassion.

"They'll be all right, dear," comforted Opal. "I've been forced to leave Mr. Patterson in a crisis more times than I like to remember."

Without any shame Mandy dabbed at her tears with her fingertips. "I always seem to be losing people I care about."

She didn't expect a sympathetic remark, or any comment at all. When Opal said how thankful she was that the pretense at marriage had worked as well as it had, Mandy neither agreed nor disagreed. She did not know if she were even glad that her life was ready to be picked up where she had left it.

She felt the car comfortably hugging the highway, skimming over the miles, and let out her breath. For long moments then, she dozed fitfully. Until something brought her wide awake.

Something was wrong. Mandy's subconscious grasped it before she fully awakened.

Her eyes, adjusting to the subdued light of dawn, caught Simon's disturbed reflection in the rearview mirror. At an odd angle, Allen's head positioned itself to observe his side mirror. Automatically, Mandy twisted in her seat to peer out the back window.

Behind them was a green Fiat. Its lights were extinguished, and its color blended into the shadows of trees like a moon passing behind thick clouds. With every break in the foliage, it flashed into threatening clarity.

Opal lolled against the seat with her mouth slackened in weary sleep. Mandy watched Simon deliberately grip the steering wheel with both hands. As his foot jammed hard on the accelerator, she braced her legs tightly against the forward seat. The Mercedes surged forward, and Opal tumbled sideways.

"What's the matter?" Her yelp was throaty and disoriented.

"Not much, Mrs. Patterson." Allen spoke without removing his sight from the side mirror. "An interested visitor—that's all."

"Oh, my God!" Opal turned to look out the back window with Mandy. Both of them imagined the worst.

Simon, clearly alarmed, drove magnificently, hugging closely to the inside of the curves, accelerating, dropping back in a squeal of rubber, unable to avoid throwing the women about like loose dice in a gambler's cup. In some crazy awareness, Mandy was shocked at the tissue-paper feel of Opal's flesh when the woman fell against Mandy's shoulders.

"They're after us. They'll take us," Opal said woodenly, as if announcing the time of day. "They'll hold us and demand a fortune from Reggie. Poor Reggie. Poor, poor Reggie."

"We don't know that, Mrs. Patterson," Mandy said, though she agreed completely. With a flash of adrenaline, she realized she had never conceived of her own death before.

"Anyone with money is a target. Like Patty Hearst's father, remember? Oh, Lord, have mercy. *Simon, can't you drive any faster?"*

"They caught us in the worst possible place, ma'am."

The women frantically gripped the arm rests, bracing themselves against the force of the propelling car, as Allen swore under his breath.

"How much further?" pleaded Opal, hardly aware of what she said. A series of miserable sounds bubbled from her throat.

"It's only four miles or so." Mandy was artificially cheerful. "I drove out here earlier tonight. Lots of switchbacks until we reach the valley. But then there're farmhouses. They won't try anything there."

Simon's face contorted with strain. His breath hissed between his teeth as he battled to keep the speeding car on the pavement.

"I haven't seen another car for a while," he said.

"No one will help us," Opal predicted bleakly toward her window.

Trees and grass blurred. Mandy's fingers closed about the older woman's wrist, not certain why. Until now Opal had had such an advantage. She had known about the silly charade. And she had obviously disapproved of Mandy's irresponsibility in ever following Russell to Switzerland. She could keep her comfort to herself, she thought: She could be petty and remember the condescending looks and let Opal survive the horror the best way she could.

But protecting Opal, comforting her as much as possible, was what Russell would do if he were here. Mandy was so much a part of him now, even separated, that she soothed Opal's fears.

"This could all be a silly mistake, you know," Mandy said brightly. "I think we've seen too many Charles Bronson movies."

"Do you really think so?" Opal glanced back at the green car as if she expected it to be gone because she wanted it to be.

Mandy continued to prattle. "Think how silly we're going to feel when that Fiat passes us and sails on down to the valley."

They smiled at her lies. Then the smiles faded. She and Opal quietly held hands. For every increase of speed the Mercedes took, the pursuing Fiat duplicated it. If Simon dropped back, the other car did too. After every curve it nosed into view again.

"Mr. Patterson's been had," Allen gritted his words through his teeth. "This is inside stuff. Probably some long-time client. Wouldn't that be the damned limit?"

No one debated his reasoning.

"Whoever it was had to be at the hotel," Simon mumbled.

The tires complained as he veered sharply to the right. Opal fought to keep upright.

"It's me they want!" she cried. "It's me, it's me."

"Shh!" hissed Mandy. But Opal could not swallow her panic.

"Someone tried to kidnap Reggie once. Anyone who knows Reggie knows he would pay anything to keep me alive."

Simon's oath was low and ugly. Mandy wondered if Russell

knew yet that his precautions had been all for nothing. Dear God, he would learn soon enough. She would do anything if she could spare him that agony. Now, because he cared about her, his suffering would only be compounded. She closed her eyes to the harshness of love.

"Stop the car, Simon," demanded Opal. Her words were slurred with fear. "There's no need getting us all killed. We'll talk to these people. Find out what's going on."

Her hand waved limply; then she simply ceased breathing. Alarmed, Mandy shook Opal's arm, then her shoulders. Hysteria prickled in Mandy's throat. Opal gasped loudly and crossed her arms over her heaving bosom as if she were praying.

Simon snorted at Mrs. Patterson's suggestion. "I'm afraid I can't do that," he said. He was right, of course. It wasn't simple theft if hostages were taken.

Daylight began spreading over everything. For a moment Mandy was grateful for it. But as the green car plunged over the crest of the last hill she wished for darkness. She could discern the Fiat plainly. Its left fender was crumpled. Three men occupied it—one with a handgun balanced upon the dashboard. Allen saw it, too. As Opal gripped the flesh of Mandy's upper arm, Mandy could smell her terror.

Allen muttered, half to himself. "He wouldn't be fool enough to shoot."

Horrified, Mandy watched him remove a pistol from the inside pocket of his sports jacket. He snapped the clip out to inspect it and slammed it back into place with the heel of his hand and placed it in his lap.

Once again the Mercedes screeched its tires. Simon sucked his breath loudly between his teeth. "Hold on!"

Both right tires slid into the gravel, spraying it everywhere like shattering crystal. The rear of the car swerved in a sickening fishtail. Opal screamed, then buried her face in her lap, rolling to her side like a listing ship.

The tires clawed into the pavement again, veered about to straighten, then lurched forward. Mandy twisted in the seat. The threat was still there, like a tenacious green leech. The Fiat had even managed to close the distance between them.

"Keep your heads down!" barked Allen, swiveling, balancing the pistol on the back of his seat with ugly hatred curling his lips.

Then, with perfect insight, Mandy realized what would

happen. Simon could not possibly win this chase. Why did he persist? Couldn't he see it was hopeless? They would all either be killed or injured or taken hostage; but they would not escape

Her journalist's eye glimpsed a mental panorama—her own name in the caption below a newspaper photograph of a smashed Mercedes. "The victims listed below are . . . "

When the car skidded off the pavement, Mandy knew they would crash into the cluster of spindly trees edging the road. Weeds scraped the fenders, whipping with sinister slapping sounds. The seconds spun out like hours, and though her body was frozen, incapable of reacting at all, she wished the impact would hurry up and get done. *It was taking so long to crash.*

Helplessly, Mandy squeezed her eyes tightly shut and was aware of being upside down, of her bag on the floor falling down on top of her, of glass breaking and a noise not unlike a crack of lightning.

Her last conscious thought was a fleeting prayer that it would not hurt much to be killed.

Chapter Nine

Mandy opened her eyes in dull surprise. The first thing she saw as she lay in a bruised heap against a tree was the car on its back like a beached whale. Oil drizzled over its chassis in slow, steady rivulets. Its tires whispered to a noiseless stop, one by one. She gathered she'd been thrown from the car and had been unconscious for only a few seconds.

Voices, one a rapid-fire French, swiftly grew louder. The slam of a door, running feet, a yell—the sounds converged upon her.

Blinking at the thin canopy of spruce above her, Mandy attempted to lift her head. Pain shot through it like a too-bright light. Gingerly, she probed the top of her head. A warm sticky fluid oozed from a cut on her scalp.

That Mandy was even alive was a miracle. And she was afraid to begin focusing her thoughts on her body for fear she would find herself shattered in pieces.

"Theo? She alive?" someone shouted in thick broken English.

Footsteps crunching through underbrush resolved into a man who bent over her. "Yeah," Theo answered in English. "How about that one?"

The eyes which peered down at Mandy were light gray, deceptively innocent and clear, set into a face that was as round as a dinner plate. On the back of his balding head perched a red ski cap. She guessed he was nearly fifty.

"She's okay," he called, squatting beside her.

"I'm bleeding," she contradicted, wanting to ask if Simon and Allen were alive.

Except for the grunting of the two other men as they dragged Opal out of the Mercedes, the car was silent. Perhaps the body guards were both dead. The whole purpose of the drive to Schauffhausen had been to prevent trouble. What was Russell doing at this very minute? Thinking she and Opal were safely boarded, on their way to connect with a 747 headed for the States?

Over the confusion of the men roughly trying to rouse Opal to consciousness she imagined a tableau of Russell being trapped in similar trouble—held at gunpoint, or caught in a building going up in flames from an explosion. "Oh, Lord," she moaned.

Stubby fingers fumbled with her curls, parting them without regard to the pain they caused. "Leave me alone," she yelped with a wince.

Theo sat back on his haunches. "Be smart, madame. Talk nicely to me. I can hurt you very much. If you are nice, you will see your husband again."

Before she could protest, he grasped her hands and pulled her to her feet. Debris clung to her clothes and some sifted to the ground. A hand upon her shoulder steered her toward the highway. Miraculously, her legs were not broken, but her hips ached fiercely as he prodded her toward the ugly green car.

"Opal," objected Mandy, turning back toward the woman on the ground. Theo, taking Mandy's outstretched arm, refused to let her stop. "What about Simon?" she cried. Her efforts to wrest herself free were wasted strength.

"Get in the car."

"But Allen and Simon. You have to—"

"Shut up!" Theo motioned his cohorts forward with impatient gestures. He rattled off a spurt of orders in French.

Mandy obeyed him exactly when he pushed her into the back seat. This was really happening; it was not a dream. When the three men clustered together, exchanging observations in French with an occasional gesture toward the tomb-like Mercedes, she made herself as small as possible. What were the chances of coming out of this alive?

Opal remained unconscious as the other two men dragged her limp hulk across the grass and dead leaves. For that Mandy was grateful. Opal's shoes had come off. Laddered runs spread up her stockings. As if she were a stubborn, uncooperative animal, the men handled her roughly.

As the last man squeezed his body into the Fiat, the door shut upon their lack of concern for Simon and Allen. Mandy started once to cry out in protest. One of the younger men in the front seat twisted about to scrutinize her with a face unbelievably free of emotion. He wasn't bad-looking, she thought, despising her cowardice for not fighting them to the death. After one false start, the car ground into gear.

The entire ordeal had taken less than five minutes. With Opal leaning heavily across her lap, Mandy dropped her head back against the seat and struggled to blink away the fuzzy grayness creeping into her vision. She must have a light concussion, for her body seemed to float somewhere separate from her mind. She began to shiver, aware of the sound of her teeth chattering. It seemed to fill her whole head. Before she could speak, she fainted.

When she awoke, the car had stopped. Opal groaned to consciousness. As well as Mandy could, for the woman's weight had numbed both her legs, she pushed Opal up into a sitting position. Large bruises purpled her face and she breathed with great effort. But other than that, she didn't appear to be seriously injured.

"Mrs. Patterson?" Mandy called softly, shaking her awake as the kidnappers busied themselves with getting out of the car. Opal's head turned from side to side before she opened her eyes.

"Reggie?" she said in a tiny voice.

"Wake up, Mrs. Patterson. They want us to get out of the car, I think."

Holding Opal's wrist, for just touching her seemed safer somehow, Mandy craned her neck. They were parked in a clearing of some sort, beside a small cabin. She had no idea how long she had been unconscious: It could have been five minutes or an hour. Her whole body was clammy with fear.

One of the men opened the rear door and jerked Opal's head back by her hair. Her eyes flared as she came to full consciousness. Tears spilled over their lashes, and Mandy knew that Opal must be suffering great pain. Still, the woman said nothing, not even a moan.

"Maybe they won't hurt us if we do what they say," Mandy whispered as Theo, the apparent commander of the trio of terrorists, stepped up behind the emotionless younger man.

"Let her go, Jules." Shrugging, Jules released Opal's hair. "You are correct, madame," Theo continued, addressing Mandy with something approaching approval in his voice. "We have no intentions of hurting anyone."

Except for Opal's warning hand closing over her own, Mandy would have shouted, "Liar, liar, liar!" at him. Leaving Simon and Allen was deliberate murder if by some miracle they were not already dead.

Theo jabbed a thumb back over his shoulder toward a wooded area. "Get out!" he ordered.

The third man, an anemic figure whose enormous hands were crisscrossed with prominent veins, led the way to a farmer's hut. Even at midmorning, the shadows of thick trees darkened the area. Perching on the side of a hill, which sloped down an incline for a quarter of a mile, the one-room cabin was approached by six steps. It was badly in need of repair, and a well hunched near the front door, a bucket dangling from a pulley above it.

As the women stumbled after Jules, Mandy congratulated herself. The sun was not too much higher than when she had last seen it after the wreck. She estimated she had been unconscious perhaps a half hour. Probably no more than twenty miles separated them from the crashed Mercedes.

"Can you make it?" Mandy asked, touching Opal's shoulder.

With grateful eyes, Opal nodded. Pain crossed her face like a scorching wind. She looked ghastly. As Mandy closed her hand over Opal's plump one, their eyes suddenly riveted with the other's. They stopped walking.

Opal's diamond rings were gone, and the wedding ring Russell had given Mandy had been removed. Holding her own hand outstretched, dumbfounded, she stared at the finger where it had been. She pressed her lips together; the ring was all she had had left of Russell. Then, her eyes hardening, she met the smirk of the third man with the large hands. She cursed herself for a fool. A piece of metal was only a piece of metal—quite meaningless now.

"*Allez!*" he said, motioning her forward toward the shed.

"*Je viens, je viens!*" she threw back at him, some of the few French words she knew. Mandy jerked her shoulder aside in a gesture of disgust. She was coming!

Only a couple of windows let in any light. No electricity ran to the hut, of course. A filthy table sat in the center of the slatted floor, a pair of ladderback chairs at either end. Near an old stone fireplace was a mattress on the floor, its seams bursting cotton.

Her feet stumbling on the wooden floor, Opal nearly collapsed against Theo. Not caring if one of the men knocked her down or not, Mandy moved to support Opal and thrust the man's arm away.

"Here, Mrs. Patterson," she said, pulling out a chair. "Come and sit down."

She led her, calling over her shoulder to Theo. "This woman is hurt. We need water. If anything happens to her, your plans won't be worth anything. You realize that, don't you?"

He gawked at her and removed his ski cap to rub his bald head as if smoothing disarrayed hair. "Watch your mouth," he said and turned to Jules. Jules returned his stare with a blank expression. "Well, get some water, stupid!"

Though behaving spitefully was a temptation, it was foolishly dangerous. Mandy didn't press her luck. She knelt at Opal's feet like a servant girl. Piece by piece she removed bits of debris from the bottom of the older woman's stockings. Loosening the waistband of her dress, Mandy eased Opal down from the chair to the mattress. Then Mandy searched about the unpainted room for something to prop Opal up with. Failing, Mandy grasped the chair and turned it upside-down, creating a support for Opal's back. When the man returned with water, Mandy proceeded to wash her newly found friend's face and arms, examining closely for any injuries.

"I'm so awfully thirsty, Amanda," said Opal.

"You don't dare drink this water. No telling what germs are in it. They have to give us food and water. Try to be patient."

Smoothing Opal's mussed hair into a semblance of order, Mandy dropped down beside her with a dreary hopelessness. Mandy rested her head upon her knees.

When the men stepped outside, the sound of the Fiat starting sounded almost immediately. The engine revved higher as it strained over the hill; then it faded in the distance. Opal clutched her forehead.

With anguished features she said, "Don't make them angry, Amanda." More alert now, the women watched Theo with calculating stares. Compared to the other men, Theo appeared less comfortable in his role as a holder of hostages. He moved his thickset body about the room with restless steps.

"Do you think the other one went to send a message to the bank?" questioned Mandy.

Opal lifted her shoulders as if it didn't really matter. "I don't know. We just mustn't panic. Reggie will send help. He'll find us. Somehow."

Giving what faintly resembled a smile, the older woman closed her eyes. They sank deeply into her face—discolored and swollen.

Mandy made a brave attempt at calmness. "Do you have any children, Mrs. Patterson?"

Though she studied the toes of her shoes, Mandy knew that Opal was surprised. When no answer came, Mandy repaired her clothing with meticulous care, picking debris from her pullover sweater and her hair. She didn't completely comprehend her desire to understand Reggie's wife, why such a common question was met with such a cold shoulder.

Opal finally spoke, hesitating between her words as if she were remembering. "Funny how something like this makes you see life as it really is. I hated being your age."

Mandy's gaze drifted to her companion. Opal's eyes remained closed as she went on. "I was a fat girl. I never did have any friends. No dreams. You wouldn't know what it's like to grow up poor and ugly. You couldn't understand how I felt when Reggie asked me to marry him."

Mandy shrugged, wondering what Opal was getting at. "I've been lonely. I can understand that."

"No, you couldn't. Not that kind of loneliness. You never had to degrade yourself just to get people to tolerate you."

Mandy didn't know how to respond to the quiet honesty of Opal's words. No one had ever said things like this to her before. She stopped picking litter from her clothes. Why was Opal revealing her heart? Did she believe they would both die here?

Theo stood in the open doorway, shutting off the small breeze, watching his French cohort as he walked over the hillside. Except for the faint roar of an airplane thousands of feet above them, the countryside was eerily silent. Snapping open a lighter, Theo lit a cigarette and lounged against the door frame as he smoked.

Thieves didn't leave witnesses these days, Mandy considered grimly. For ten dollars out of a cash drawer, an innocent observer could be gunned down in cold blood. To believe that these kidnappers would allow Opal and her to see their faces, to hear their voices and then release them was foolhardy. Opal did believe they would die here. She wanted to touch another human being before it happened.

"No," Mandy agreed gently, "I've never been that lonely. I always knew I had a future. I wasn't sure what it was, but I never doubted I had one."

Opal reached out a hand, her eyes brimming with tears. Taking it in hers, Mandy studied the puffy knuckles, the age spots on the top that no amount of cream could disguise, the impressions where her wedding rings had been for so many years.

"I haven't behaved very nicely to you, Amanda," the older woman confessed, unsmiling. "And yet you washed these hurt feet of mine."

"That's all right." Mandy cleared her throat awkwardly. "I mean, we don't need to talk about that now. I did a very stupid thing in ever coming to Switzerland. I deserved to be looked at as if I were crazy."

The silence drifted down upon them like silt, neither knowing how much Theo was listening to.

"You're not sorry you fell in love with . . . Ben, are you?"

Mandy's head twisted around, and Opal laughed softly at her surprise. "People's reaction is always the same. They think a woman who looks the way I do doesn't understand the finer aspects of love." She paused, her voice thick. "Reggie and I have something special."

For long moments Mandy tried to picture Opal and Reginald Patterson in the act of making love. But all Mandy could see was dinner parties with drooping chandeliers and receiving lines and formal clothes around bridge tables.

"How do you know what I feel about him?" Mandy honestly wanted to know. She hardly understood it herself.

Opal smiled. "I've known that man since he was a college student. I've seen him under some of the most frustrating pressures a person can bear. And never once have I seen him lose control. Not the way he did last night when we didn't know where you were."

The words felt like a skilled hand on an exposed wound. He *did* care: He might not love her like she loved him, with that aching need for satisfaction, but Russell did care. She urged Opal to continue with a lift of her brows.

Opal explained, "When he heard about the explosive device at the bank, and then you didn't come back, he was beside himself."

Leaning her head against the wall, Mandy let her eyes flutter shut. "Tell me about him. What's his family like?"

"They're the Establishment, I guess you'd say. But nice. Ben's father is independently wealthy, always has been as far as I know. There's an older daughter, spoiled rotten, but she adores Ben. She has two sons. Ben's very close to them."

"His mother?"

"Nice. Very beautiful and hard to please. Frankly, I've sometimes wondered if her husband hasn't been tempted to wander from the fold. If he has, he's been terribly discreet."

Mandy sniffed. "That wouldn't surprise me."

"Like father, like son."

Mandy's smile was faint, hardly there at all. "Maybe."

"Why are you so quick to assume that?" Opal's drooping eyelids opened a bit more. "What has your father done?"

"Mine? Nothing. Well, I say nothing. My mother died long before I was grown. My father remarried a couple of years ago—a woman much younger than he was. My aunts were scandalized, kept talking about his mid-life crisis."

Mandy folded her arms across her bosom and withdrew into her own thoughts and Opal changed the subject. "Do you think I'm the type of woman to be a good mother?" she asked. "Be honest."

Drawing up her knees, resting her cheek on them, Mandy thought for a moment. "Yes."

"Well, I'm not. Oh, for a while I thought I was. I couldn't believe it when my daughter nearly overdosed. It nearly killed Reggie and me both to learn the bitterness of that girl."

"I'm sorry, Opal."

"It was our own fault. She's married now and has a daughter of her own. She's as happy as she's capable of being."

"What happened?"

"I think it's what Reggie and I have between us. Dolores

always felt she couldn't get in, that I loved her father more than anything else. She never understood where I came from because she was never there."

Theo ground out his cigarette with his heel and watched them closely. Mandy lowered her voice to a whisper. "Could you believe me if I told you that I do understand?"

Opal studied her—a young, slender woman that, even in her disheveled state, was prettier than most women. As he leaned against the wall, the bulge of a pistol in his front pocket, Theo was obviously not unaware of her beauty, either. He moistened his upper lip.

"If you had said two hours ago that you understood, I would have answered no." Opal gestured to encompass the meanness of the room and the threatening man smoothing stubby fingers across his bald spot. "But now? Yes, Amanda, you'd understand."

When Theo's skinny companion reentered the room, the women stopped talking. Every horror story Mandy had ever read in the newspapers or seen on television flashed through her mind. She couldn't remember ever being so afraid. Not of Theo as much as she was of the passionless face which first scrutinized Opal, then her. Mandy recalled movies where prisoners of war made daring escapes. Now she understood why they would rather be killed than wait in terror.

"I need to go to the bathroom," Mandy said baldly to Theo.

Jules worked at a piece of food caught in his teeth without removing his eyes from her. After a grunted query to Theo, the paunchy man replied with a dry smirk. Jules motioned Mandy forward with his heavily veined hands.

"Don't go," Opal whispered.

But Mandy followed the gangling man, keeping her eyes veiled until they stepped out into the clearing. Could she and Opal hope to outwit the two men, to trick them with feminine games? Theo, perhaps. But to cherish visions of heroics with Jules was folly. His expressions were wild and erratic. He was capable of killing them both.

When Jules led Mandy into an area of trees and low shrubs, she tried to memorize the lay of the land. Though she couldn't understand a word he said, when he dug his fingers into her shoulder, jabbering a steady stream of French warnings, she needed no interpretation. Jules would break her neck if she attempted to run.

The angle of the sun was important, she guessed. As far as she could tell, Mattenaugst lay southeast of the cabin. When she began to dawdle, to take too long in her efforts to scour the land for marks and trails webbing over the slopes, Jules shouted at her.

Arranging her clothes, Mandy emerged from the undergrowth. Jules glanced over her body with disinterest. At least she had nothing to fear from him as a man. All he wanted was the three million dollars.

As the cabin door slammed behind her, making the room seem more like a dungeon than ever, Mandy was amazed to see Theo setting up a battery-operated tape recorder. Stubby fingers threaded a cassette tape, and after a few unsuccessful beginnings, he motioned her forward.

"Speak a message into this," he said. "Give your name and say that you have not been mistreated. When you do that, I will give you something to eat."

His clear eyes focused on Opal's exhaustion. "And," he added, "I will get some water for her."

Hesitating, then moistening her lips as if gathering her courage, Mandy stepped to the table. "After you feed us, will you kill us?" she spat her question rapidly. Sweat formed on her palms. She wiped them down the legs of her jeans.

Theo heaved an irritated sigh. "No one is going to kill anyone, madame. We're not stupid. Do as you're told."

"What about the men in the car?" Mandy felt Opal's silent pleading, begging her to cease arguing.

Theo, his index finger lifting as if he would threaten her, appeared surprised, then let it fall back to his side. "One was alive," he replied, as if he respected her nerve.

"I don't believe you."

His foul oath rippled through the room like the clatter of breaking glass. Opal gasped and Mandy cringed. She had gone too far.

"Don't press your luck, madame!" he shouted. Her shoulders slumped in submission. Jules, with a scornful laugh, made some remark Mandy was sure was obscene. She dropped into the chair.

"Push the botton," she said tonelessly.

As the button slid into the *record* position, the tape began its whispering path around the shaft. Russell would touch the cassette and sit in a chair to listen to her voice. Even that small contact was a comfort. Swallowing down the cotton in her mouth was difficult, but Mandy spoke clearly and seemingly without emotion.

"My name is Amanda . . . Hamilton. Opal Patterson is with me. We are both unhurt except for the wreck. Three men took us. They say they'll give us food and water. That's all I know."

Glaring, Theo snatched the microphone from her hand. "The women will be returned when we get the money, monsieur. Try to make any attempt to send in the police, and we will smuggle them out of the country. This is no empty threat, I assure you."

Theo stretched the microphone cord taut and thrust it beneath Opal's nose. "Say something!" he demanded.

Opal's courage appeared to have exceeded its limit, for at this tenuous contact with her husband she began sobbing. Several times she tried to steady her voice, but it persisted in breaking down.

"Reggie," she choked, "Amanda is taking good care of me. Please give them what they want. They say they won't kill us, but they will. I know—"

"That's enough." The button flipped into the *off* position, and Theo slipped the cassette into his pocket with the pistol.

There was nothing left now but to wait. It would be endless, Mandy thought.

Chapter Ten

Not until an hour before dusk of the third day did Mandy and Opal recognize their first real opportunity to escape. They had watched constantly, their exchanged glances sending messages to each other: The most frequent one was could we do it now? But with three men, two of whom were always present, the women might as well have been locked in a cage.

The kidnappers had fed them enough. Theo had even shown them a copy of a Zurich newspaper that had been picked up after the tape had been delivered. The newspaper was remarkably restrained concerning the ransom demand. More emphasis was placed on the bomb threat. But a search by a bomb squad had dispelled that fear quickly enough; there was no bomb.

Only Allen Zimmerman had survived the car crash, and his condition, reported his doctors to persistent detectives, was critical. He could not identify the extortionists. Simon's body was returned to the United States for burial. Mandy grieved for him. In a way, she had known him. He had spent hours outside her hotel door, trying to protect her from something he could not prevent.

Mandy scanned the paper for any mention of Russell—the

slightest hint that he was safe. But aside from Reginald Patterson's statement that he had no idea who could be behind such a criminal action, she learned nothing.

"Reggie keeps Russell's name out of print if it's at all possible," Opal whispered when Mandy worried. "Be thankful they have always been so careful."

"I thought he used another name to protect himself from violence like this."

Without makeup, Opal looked old and dreadfully tired. She rubbed her face with the palms of her hands. "We believe it has, many times. An extortionist can't hurt someone he can't find. And Benjamin Hamilton"—she lowered her voice —"doesn't exist in America."

"Perhaps Mr. Patterson has said he wouldn't pay the ransom." Mandy locked her hands about her knees and dropped her head back against the unpainted wall. Opal shook her head.

"Reggie will pay anything they ask."

"But Russell would try to bluff his way out." Mandy did not know why she was so certain. Living with a man, even for a week, could teach a woman a lot of things. Russell was a master at a battle of nerves—a gambler. He would take impossible chances.

"Oh, Lord!" breathed Opal, holding her abdomen as if it hurt. "Will this never end?"

Until Jules took some pills, Mandy wasn't sure that it would ever end. She almost missed seeing him do it, for the man turned sideways and his frail body was hardly more than a sliver of flesh in the shadows. He threw the pills down without water, thinking, she was sure, that no one saw. Particularly not Theo, who watched him like an old woman.

To Mandy's knowledge, Jules had not slept at all for the last twenty-four hours. Now he sprawled out, face down on the soiled mattress, and didn't move again. Mandy watched him almost constantly.

What kind of pills had he taken so covertly? Was it possible that one of their captors would prove to be a pill popper?

Theo chewed monotonously on some cold fried potatoes and read the paper. When Jules drifted off to sleep, Theo glanced once at his wristwatch and continued what he'd been doing.

Pretending to doze, Mandy glanced obliquely at Opal's

dark eyelids. If they were not released soon, the older woman would become really ill. Her breathing came roughly and her flesh was blotchy, besides the bruises.

Theo nodded over the newspaper, his bald head dipping toward his chest. Mandy could see clearly the lines of his skull beneath the tightly stretched skin. Experimentally, she cleared her throat, and his head lifted. When she remained perfectly still, after a few seconds, his lids fluttered closed once more. His head dropped forward.

Mandy hardly dared contemplate the possibility of escape. Even if Jules were drugged too much to rouse, it was ridiculous to think that she and Opal could outrun Theo. Mandy might do it herself, with a good head start, but Opal could never make it.

The room was deathly quiet. If Jules were actually out of it, perhaps it was not such an insane idea after all, Mandy decided after considering it for ten minutes. With the same bold nerve which had sent her following Russell in the first place, Mandy began inching across the floor on her backside. Soon she was so near the smelly mattress that she could touch Jules. Neither of the men had moved a muscle.

One of Jules's arms was folded over his chest, the other slung outward on the floor. Not pausing to decide what her excuse would be if she were caught, Mandy carefully freed the button of Jules's cuff. She knew they would be there even before she saw the red needle tracks on his arms. So, her enemy was a junkie. Now, she was positive he would pose no threat. Not for a few hours anyway.

As for Theo, the only possible chance was to slip up behind him and knock him unconscious. Impossible! She could never do it; that kind of thing only happened in the movies. Even if she worked up the nerve, how difficult was it to knock a man out? She might not strike him in the right place, *if* she could even find a weapon. Then what? He could kill them.

Scooting back to the wall, Mandy nudged Opal with the toe of her shoe.

As if Opal had been merely waiting, she opened her eyes alertly. Glancing quickly toward the drooping figure, then back, Mandy lifted her brows in a high arch, as if to say, "Do you think there's really a chance? Is this what we've been waiting for?"

With a slight shift of weight, Opal pulled herself up into a better sitting position. Theo's jaw slackened a bit more; then he chewed noisily in his sleep. They froze. Their breathing ceased. Jules flopped his arm back across his chest.

Opal mouthed a silent objection. "What about him?" She pointed hesitantly to the sleeping man. Mandy imitated Jules taking his pills. Considering for a moment, Opal smiled a weary glimmer of hope.

The older woman seemed to read her thoughts. Together their eyes scoured the room for anything heavy enough to use as a weapon. For a hysterical second, Mandy pictured herself hitting Theo with a chair. She swallowed down the jittery urge to laugh.

Mandy studied the fireplace, then looked at it a second time. Apparently, Opal had the same idea. There was no poker, of course; Theo had removed that immediately. But the sooty andirons squatted in the bricked recess like thoughtful little friends. Clumsily shaped, they were still slender enough to grasp. And heavy.

Slumping, Mandy took several breaths and attempted to reason herself out of it. There was no other way. And she would only get one chance. She had never even slapped a man's face before.

When their eyes met, Opal was trembling visibly, her breaths nearly choking her. They both knew what could happen if the attempt failed. Inch by inch, Mandy raised until she was standing. Theo did not rouse. Leaving Opal's open-mouthed stare glued to him, Mandy silently tiptoed toward the fireplace.

The instant she grasped the andiron, her hands were blackened. Thankfully, the piece was rather simply made, its only ornamentation being a giant brass knob on one end.

In the time Mandy took to position herself behind Theo's head, she lived a lifetime. Like some grisly surgeon poised over an unconscious body, scalpel in hand, she waited. Doubtful, she looked at Opal. Mandy's brows lifted in a question, and she made an imitation of a downward blow.

For all her propriety, Opal shook her head, pretended to grasp a baseball bat, and swung sideways. Mandy backed off from Theo almost a foot. Oh, Russell, she thought, I think I'm doing this as much for you as for us.

It was now or never. Clinching her jaw as tightly as she could, oblivious of black streaks down her jeans and one across her face, Mandy riveted her eyes to a spot slightly above Theo's ear. If he cried out, she didn't know what she would do. Wasn't that ridiculous? He had killed Simon. And here she was, terrified of hurting Theo!

She started, stopped, and Opal gasped. Mandy's hands were shaking horribly. Again she positioned the piece of iron. This time she positively would swing when she counted three. One! Two! *Three!*

Amazingly enough, the blow made almost no sound. Theo slammed forward onto the table. Both women stepped forward and stared dumbly at Jules. For an instant his eyes flared, then closed.

"Is he dead?" Mandy choked, bending over Theo, her face twisted with the violence of her own act. "Opal! I think I've killed him! Oh, God! I never hit anyone before."

They bent over the man cautiously, not daring to touch the flesh where the iron had laid it open. It bled profusely, running down into his collar, soaking it crimson and spreading onto the front of his throat to dribble off his Adam's apple.

Opal fumbled for his pulse, couldn't find it, then paused. "He's alive. Let's see, ah . . . well, I think we should hurry."

"But what about food? Water?"

"I can't get far, honey. My feet won't take it. Let's just get out of here."

Mandy stood quietly, pondering Theo's feet. The laced boots were heavy and too big, but that didn't matter now. She knelt to grapple with the thick laces.

"Please hurry," begged Opal. "Forget that."

"Go on, Opal. Get as far as you can. I'll be right behind you."

Realizing that she would move much more slowly, Opal didn't argue. She had not yet disappeared over the southeastern slope of the hill when Mandy caught up with her. Catching Opal's hand, Mandy pulled her into the underbrush for cover.

"Here," she panted, thrusting the boots forward. "Put 'em on!"

"Ugh!" gagged Opal. "Didn't that man ever wash his feet? I'll get leprosy or something."

In spite of the murderous danger, Mandy laughed. "We can treat leprosy, Opal. There's no antidote for dead. Hurry up!"

They stumbled along, sometimes half-jogging, sometimes pausing to breathe when their chests felt as if they would burst for air. Mandy's side ached so badly that she could hardly straighten, and Opal perspired until her hair was soaked and it drizzled into her eyes. By the time they reached the valley they were near to collapsing. And it was dark.

"Oh, Mandy," Opal sank to the ground, "I can't go on. I just can't."

"Yes, you can. We'll rest. Here, hold on to me."

Vineyards peppered the Swiss valley. Mandy recalled dusty pickup trucks speeding along a network of dirt roads. They had branched from the highway in a disorderly pattern. There was no way of estimating how far the nearest house was, much less a telephone.

"Do you think the other man has returned yet?" Mandy asked thoughtfully.

Opal moaned. "If he has, he'll be much more concerned about Theo's head than about us."

"You mean a normal person would be. None of those men are human." Mandy collapsed beside Opal and stretched out on the damp ground, ignoring the stones poking into her back. Every muscle in her body was screaming for rest.

"I'm so thirsty," Opal said with a sigh, licking her dry lips. "You were right. We should have brought some water. I had no idea it was so isolated out here. Do you think we went in the right direction?"

Mandy considered. "My sense of direction isn't the best but I figure the Mercedes was wrecked somewhere over there." She flopped a hand. "The highway must be over that way."

"Everything looks the same in the dark. Listen, Mandy, you must go on without me. You'll make good time by yourself. I'll be all right here. I swear I won't move. Find help and come back."

Threading her fingers through her untidy curls, unconsciously smearing soot across her forehead, Mandy disagreed. "No way. We stay together."

"Please. You must."

Mandy's forehead puckered deeply with self-doubt, thinking that it was a very bad idea to separate. She rotated—a slender axis in a gigantic circumference of strange dark countryside. The night sounds of insects seemed magnified ten times. The thought of walking alone, unable to see behind, becoming lost—It was best to act, not to reason, she decided.

"What if I can't find my way back?" she fretted.

"The local farmers won't have much trouble if you count the vineyards between here and the highway."

Mandy knelt beside the woman who had once resented her. Unused to such a surge of compassion for another woman, Mandy touched her face.

"Won't you be scared, Opal?"

During the silence their bond deepened.

"Yes," replied Opal, blinking rapidly. "Go on now."

Mandy made Opal as comfortable as she could beneath a heavy-boughed fir. Then she began trudging toward where the highway probably was. In another hour her feet throbbed, hardly able to take another step. But she forced herself forward. Mandy climbed over fences, scraping herself mercilessly. Stones tripped her, and roots. She wandered around acres of neatly laid vineyards. She guessed that she walked two hours more before the first headlights flashed in the distance. They dipped, disappeared, then glowed again. The highway!

Mandy thought she'd have to flag down a car, and the thought of doing so, after the last three days of terror, was too much. Fortunately, huddled in a distant cluster of beech trees lay a small farm. Dogs barked at her, sensing a stranger moving about in their midst. By the time Mandy reached the house, the dogs were in such a furious state that the sleepy Swiss occupant had turned on a light. She half-expected someone to step onto the porch, shotgun in hand, and yell, "Hold on there!"

As she stumbled toward the low stone fence, Mandy glimpsed the curtain moving. "Please help me!" she cried, then stood quite still. Fearing to go past the fence lest the dogs attack, she waited.

"Hello!" she called again. "Can you hear me?"

The man who came outside was no taller than Mandy was, but other than that she could distinguish nothing. At least it was another human being. He shouted a garble of German words she could not comprehend.

"Telephone," she called, gesturing to make him understand. "Do you have a *tel-e-phone?*"

He yelled at the dogs. When he stepped out into the darkness, they hushed immediately. His invitation to come into the house needed no interpretation.

The farmer and his stout frau fussed over Mandy, offering water, gesturing at her dreadful appearance with questioning eyes and messages telegraphed between each other. They probably thought she had been attacked. At two o'clock in the morning, Mandy let them think anything they pleased.

She pantomimed a telephone to the plump, gray-haired lady. Her eyes brightened, and she nodded vigorously, spouting a steady stream to her husband. She, too, pantomimed a telephone and looked to Mandy for confirmation. Extending a rough hand, which Mandy accepted gratefully, the woman drew her into a hallway and switched on a bare electric light. The black instrument was on a three-legged table.

Smiling, she nodded again, gesturing widely for Mandy to help herself.

Such was Mandy's relief at finding civilization again, discovering that Russell had not left a telephone number with Johann Gustave was almost the final defeat. Zurich was too large a tourist center; tracing Russell, especially if he did not wish to be found, was a hopeless task.

What now? Even if she took up the monumental task of locating Russell, his telephone could as easily be tapped as the bank's computer.

The longer Mandy stared at the phone, the more frantic she grew. She knew no one in this entire country. Except for The Staad's employees. And Richard Sanders!

Of course—the Englishman she had met on the highway. He'd said something about residing in the area. He had offered to drive her somewhere. Did she dare hope he lived near the farm?

She motioned the woman forward.

"Richard Sanders?" Mandy asked. "Do you know *Richard San-ders?*"

The housewife's face wrinkled with doubt. Glancing at her husband, her shoulders lifted in a shrug. *"Rich-ard San-ders,"* she mimicked. They conversed rapidly then lifted their hands helplessly.

"Forget it," said Mandy and jiggled the receiver for the operator.

By this time she had ceased believing in miracles, or even luck. But when the operator rattled off the number of Richard Sanders' home, she hardly believed her ears. She couldn't let herself hope it was the same man. As the

telephone buzzed she struggled, unsuccessfully, to force her
hands to stop shaking.

It rang eight times. A sleepy voice murmured "hello" in an
English accent. Mandy nearly wept with relief.

Every day that Russell flipped over a page of the desk
calendar in his Zurich office, he died a little. Time, he
thought, was like a hand grenade lying on the elegance of the
carpet: It was there and would go off. There was nothing he
could do but wait. And worry.

God in heaven, *where was she?* Mandy and Opal had been
gone three days. Perhaps they weren't even in Switzerland
any longer. The police should have come up with something.
Yet all they had was a cassette tape someone had mailed from
within the city. It was clean; no fingerprints, no clues.

So, three million dollars in marked bills waited in one of
the safes—the honeyed trap with no takers. So far.

Eva, who, in addition to her other duties, filled in as
Russell's secretary whenever he was in the country, tapped
gently on his door.

"Come in," he called, his voice thick from only twelve
hours sleep in the last seventy-two.

"Your coffee, Mr. Hamilton. Detective Barrot called. He's
coming by at eleven-thirty."

"Damn," Russell grumbled.

He accepted the black coffee gratefully and, with one
elbow braced upon the desk, threaded his fingers through his
hair and rubbed the back of his neck. He needed a haircut.
He needed a bath. He needed to know Mandy was all right!

After one glance at his stubbled beard, Eva Schmidt
rummaged through a drawer of his desk. She planted a
cordless electric razor in front of him like an unexpected gift.
Then she stepped briskly to his attaché case resting on a chair,
snapped it open, and removed the fresh gray dress shirt
Russell liked to keep on hand in case he couldn't get back to
his hotel to change.

"You need some sleep," Eva observed uselessly. "I'll send
your suit jacket out to be pressed."

"Need some sleep?" His laugh was short. "God, that's the
understatement of the century. See if the newspapers are on
the street yet. And phone Mr. Patterson's doctor. The shot he
gave Reginald yesterday could have killed an ox. Oh, Eva,"

he stopped her, framed in the doorway, "get my father on the phone, will you? Here's the number."

Russell scribbled some digits on a memo pad and ripped off the top sheet.

"Yes, sir," replied the secretary, her mouth pinched with anxiety for the passionless way he was driving himself.

After she left, Russell glanced about the small but luxurious office. Unless he or Reggie used it, it was rarely opened. But now, for the first time in days, it was empty of detectives, television and newspaper reporters, and Swiss Mercantile officials. Such a high profile unnerved Russell. Having his name constantly in the media was dangerous.

He would give this all up, he thought. All of it—the security of his anonymity, his job, his "place" in a shaky world economy. None of it had any value if anything happened to Mandy. *Where was she?*

His telephone buzzed as he scoured the razor over his jaws. Squeezing the receiver between his jaw and shoulder, he began unbuttoning his crumpled, slept-in shirt.

"I have your father on the line, Mr. Hamilton."

"Thanks, Eva. Dad? It's me. How's Mother?"

The deep familiar voice from Hartford, Connecticut caused the lines about Russell's eyes to relax slightly. He had no qualms about talking to his father, transatlantic. Discretion was a cultivated art with Robert Gregory.

"She's worried about you, naturally. Has anything changed over there?"

"No, Dad. The police still haven't a clue on the whereabouts of the women." Russell shrugged into the clean shirt and absently worked on the cuff buttons.

The senior Gregory's voice was hesitant. "I'm sorry to hear that. It must be rough for you. How's Reggie holding up?"

After tucking in his shirt, Russell poked through some stale sandwiches from the night before. Frowning, he sipped some coffee instead. "The doctor knocked him out. Are the newspapers still running the story?"

"Afraid so but no significant details . . . Ben. Fortunately, they only mentioned you a couple of times. Nothing big."

Russell nodded in relief. "Good. Listen, Dad, I have to go now. These phones may not be too safe. I just wanted you to know I was okay. We're certain everything will turn out fine. It may take a while, but things look good, considering."

After a pause, which strongly implied Russell was lying, Robert said with forced lightness, "Sure. Do you want to talk to your mother?"

"That's all right. Just tell her for me that she's not to worry, that . . . that I love her. Dad—" Russell broke off abruptly. He moistened his lips. In a moment of weakness he wanted to spill everything. He wanted to say he was half out of his mind with worry. That he had waited half his life to find someone like Mandy. That it wasn't fair that she should be snatched away before he had tried to make her love him.

"Nothing," he said dully, then forced a brisk politician's optimism. "Well, I'll see you when this is all wrapped up, Dad."

"Sure. Ahh, Ben—"

"Yes?"

"Please be careful. Don't try to take on things you aren't equipped to handle."

"I won't. I have to go now."

"Good-bye, son."

With bloodshot brown eyes, Russell stared at his hand trembling on the receiver. Slamming both hands down on the desk top, he relished the sharp sting to his palms.

"Yes, Eva. What is it?" He punched a flashing button on his phone.

The feminine voice paused, then spoke with practiced professionalism. "There's a gentleman out here who demands to see you, Mr. Hamilton. The security guards have him at the front door. What should I do?"

The main floor of the Swiss Mercantile was a disguised mass of electronic policing equipment. Telephone tracer systems had been attached to the incoming lines. Several plain clothes detectives tried their best to remain inconspicuous among the regular personnel. To the ordinary eye, it was banking as usual, but behind the scenes everyone's nerves were raw, from vice-presidents down to the window tellers.

Russell felt a shiver of anticipation tingle down his spine. "I'll take care of it," he said and twisted a necktie around his collar on the way out the door.

As he strode across the main floor with impatient steps Russell watched the small stir up front. He forced himself not to hurry. Jamming one fist deep into a trouser pocket, he clenched it until his knuckles hurt.

"What's the trouble, Herr Fischer?" he inquired tightly.

A tall, sandy-haired man turned to face him, his eyes tense behind thick glasses. Herr Fischer stood without answering as the two men assessed each other. Russell's instincts assured him the crumpled man with the face of a scholar was different from the dozen dead ends they had faced. This man was honest—tired, inexperienced and nervous, but definitely different.

"Mr. Hamilton?" the younger man inquired carefully.

"Yes."

"You want to talk to me, Mr. Hamilton." A promising smile curved his lips, and he cracked the knuckles of one hand.

"Ahh—" Catching his lip in his teeth, glancing about the expansive floor which already filled with the daily traffic of business, Russell gestured toward an empty office.

"Why don't we step over there?" he suggested. "It's all right, Herr Fischer. Send word up to Frau Schmidt where I'll be. And I don't want to be interrupted."

Herr Fischer frowned his disapproval at the impetuous risk the police had warned them to avoid. But at Russell's urging nod, he sighed imperceptibly and obeyed.

Stepping aside, ushering the young man into an office of understated richness, Russell closed the door and sank into the chair behind the desk as if he had all day. His hands were wet, and he casually wiped them on his trousers. The easy lacing of his fingers was a skilled lie; his mind was poised like a crouched cat ready to pounce.

"I feel better when people identify themselves," Russell said pleasantly.

"Oh, I'm sorry," the man apologized quickly, beginning to get up from his chair. Russell motioned him back down. "My name is Richard Sanders."

When Russell smiled at him again, Richard said plainly, "I have your wife, Mr. Hamilton. And Mrs. Patterson."

Before Sanders could explain, Russell was on his feet. In that moment the Englishman realized that the other man's control was only a mask, shielding a lethal violence.

"Wait!" the Englishman half-choked. "I'm her friend, sir."

His hand frozen in midair, Russell stared as he sank back

against the wall. He realized his pressure had reached the boiling point. "Explain," he snapped tensely.

"Mrs. Hamilton and I met accidentally a few evenings ago." He shakily waved down Russell's curiosity. "I'll explain all that later. Simply believe me. The women have escaped from the men who were holding them, Mr. Hamilton. Your wife managed to get to a telephone. How she did, God only knows. At any rate, she remembered my name and took a chance on finding me. It took us four hours to locate Mrs. Patterson. And another four to get them pulled together enough to drive down to Zurich."

"Why didn't you call me, Mr. Sanders?" Russell didn't mean to sound so threatening. He forced recklessness from his voice. "We've been in a nightmare down here."

"We knew that, sir. But Mrs. Hamilton said we couldn't risk calling. Someone might have tampered with your lines."

After considering for a few seconds, Russell nodded. Then he shrugged, grinning wearily. "Sounds like her. Where is she?"

Richard could see the other man was vastly relieved and believed him. Sanders slumped back in his chair. He fumbled for a cigarette and tried to light it. But his hands shook so badly he finally gave up and just held it in his fingers.

"I registered them in a hotel," he said. "Your wife insisted that I see you myself. Mrs. Patterson ought to see a physician. But she wouldn't call one until I told you where they are. They don't want to ruin the chances of catching the men who did this."

Pausing, Russell muttered absentmindedly to himself as he concentrated on the possibilities.

"Yes," he mused, "after all, they don't know that we have the women back. It's possible they could make a last-ditch effort to get the money, on the off chance that we still believe they are holding them." Russell jerked his head up and tugged his already loose tie. "No one followed you, did they?"

Turning his palm upward, Richard grimaced. "Not to Zurich, no. But walking through those front doors was like wearing a sign on my back. The whole police force knows by now."

"I'll take care of that."

Russell pushed buttons on the telephone. He waited irritably until the chief of detectives came on the line. After a heated discussion, the tired man slammed down the receiver. Russell smiled broadly and stepped to the door. He paused, his hand resting upon the knob.

"I won't insult you by offering you something for what you've done. You will stay, won't you?

"I really must leave. But it's quite all right. Really."

The two men exchanged an unspoken understanding. Each would have done the same, had the roles been reversed.

Russell swept open the door with an eager flourish.

"After you, Mr. Sanders," he laughed softly. "After you."

Mandy knew Russell would come as soon as he could get there. In less than an hour she would see his face again—that handsome face that she had sometimes despaired of ever seeing again. Still, it seemed like forever, and she paced the hotel room.

Dressed in dirty clothes over her freshly bathed body, because she had no others, Mandy stood before the window and fluffed her damp hair dry. It was growing longer. She wondered, if in all the confusion, he would even notice.

"What time is it, Amanda?" asked Opal from her enforced throne of pillows on the double bed.

Mandy had bathed Opal as carefully as an infant. She had wanted to call the doctor immediately, but Opal had been adamant. "Not until after I see Reggie. Then you can put me in the hospital for all I care."

"It's eleven o'clock," Mandy informed her, replacing the clock on the desk and pouring herself a glass of water she really did not want. "Do you suppose something has happened?"

"No, dear one. It takes time to get through all that security. Be patient."

She *had* been patient, Mandy complained to herself. She only wanted to put Russell's mind at ease now. His anxiety, in many ways, had been the worst of it. How like being in love—worrying about someone else's worry.

Below them, ten stories down, hundreds of small compact cars darted along the Bahnhofstrasse. With a vigorous tourist trade and a number of luxury hotels, the Bahnhofstrasse was one of the great shopping streets in Europe. Squinting,

Mandy wondered if she could possibly spot Richard Sanders's car in all that bustle.

Three times she picked up the clock. The hands read eleven-thirty before the soft tap sounded on the door. She had waited for it so long, something tightened in her throat. Almost dreading to open it, not daring to hope she would see the same need in his eyes that brimmed in her own, Mandy stood impotently as the rapping came again. Flicking the lock then, she finally drew open the door.

She was aware of Richard Sanders even before she saw Russell. Having no idea what her face looked like—stunned expressionless—Mandy simply remained rooted to the floor. For a second Russell took in Opal's relieved gasp, a wave of compassion sweeping across his gaunt features. Then his gaze locked with Mandy's. After what felt like a lifetime of standing, half in the hallway, Russell made a tiny sound of urgency in his throat.

Richard's cough broke the paralysis; Russell stepped forward and closed his arms about her. Mandy melted against him like wax to a flame. There was no passion to it, no exaggeration of exuberance. Just the deep satisfaction of seeing that all was safe again, the finding of something extremely precious that was thought to be lost. Mandy kept swallowing, and in her mind a voice kept repeating, "Thank you, God; thank you, God."

"Your hair is growing longer," Russell noted with the detached wonder of a boy.

Oblivious that Richard had shut the door and stepped to Opal's bedside, Russell cupped Mandy's face in both his large hands. He smiled, touching the deep center of her body with a curve of his lips. When Mandy closed her fingers tightly about the strength of his wrists, his mouth delicately brushed the corner of hers—blotting away the salt of her tears on one side, then the other. Slowly then, he bent his head until his face buried in the sweet-smelling curls. The steadiness of his chest faltered, and Mandy knew that in some private place inside him, that no one ever saw, he was weeping for her.

She could not hear what he said. She thought he said, "Thank you." It didn't matter. Mandy moved her palms over the hard expanse of his back, silently reveling in the fine sturdiness of his suit, the smooth circumference of buttons pressing into her breasts, the tiny catch in his breath as he lifted his head.

Russell could have felt everything; he was too complex and full of contradictions for her to be certain. But she was positive of one thing: He was happy. And in her own daze of gratitude, as he cradled her in the safe haven of his own body, it was enough.

Chapter Eleven

During the next hours, Mandy's life suddenly seemed to consist of a myriad of people asking questions about the details of what had happened to her. Russell had hardly brought her to his own hotel rooms in downtown Zurich, when the bombardment began.

Opal, in a state of near-exhaustion, had to be attended and Reggie notified. A clever Zurich newspaper reporter had gotten wind of the women's return through a contact at the bank. In less than an hour, the telephone was ringing off the hook. The police immediately requested that Mandy come to central headquarters and make a statement.

Barely able to control his temper, Russell tersely informed Detective Barrot that Mandy was not going anywhere and was not talking to anyone until she had been thoroughly examined by a doctor. Even before that could be done, however, he was forced to deliver half a dozen directives to the Swiss Mercantile.

In the same limousine which had whisked Russell from *Zürich-Kloten* to Mattenaugst—an eternity ago—his eyes met Mandy's. They were smiling eyes and, as intimately suggestive as a caress, they said, I'm glad you're back; I haven't forgotten how we touched each other.

When Reginald and Opal were taken to the hospital, Mandy was registered as an outpatient. Her first moment alone with Russell was in an examination cubicle. They took long, deep breaths and refolded their hands, trying to fill the tedious silence as they waited for the doctor.

"I didn't think we would make it," Mandy admitted as she studied Russell's hair feathering back over his ears. "If you had given them the money, I think they'd have killed us. I was so scared. I still can't believe I hit that man like I did."

Russell, concentrating first on her mouth, then on the whole length of her, hooked a hip on the side of the bed. Bracing a hand on either side of her, he leaned forward until his chest touched the curve of her breasts. Mandy flushed at the heady security of muscled arms trapping her. His face hovered only inches above hers, and he slowly moistened his lips.

"The past three days have been the worst I've ever lived through," he confessed.

His teeth were so white: She could smell the faint fragrance of shampoo when he tilted his head to gaze at her legs.

"My clothes are filthy," she said. "Quit staring at me."

"I can't help it."

With two fingers, he brazenly found the zipper of her jeans and opened and shut it several times. Mandy cast a stricken glance at the door as if it were transparent.

"Russell?" she said his name silently and grabbed his hand to stop him.

"You look like one of those heroines in a John Wayne movie who has just fought off an Indian raid or something," he observed pleasantly, his mouth dipping a fraction of an inch lower until his breath fell warmly on her cheek.

"You don't look so good yourself," she retorted breathlessly. "When was the last time you slept?"

The hours they had shared in Mattenaugst, the closeness of blended desires and bodies, somehow seemed far away—almost as if they had happened to someone else. It was as if she and Russell must begin again, as if they must retrace the path between two separate lifetimes.

Three days of terror had changed her. The prospect of death had a way of making small things important. She and Russell were different people now—seeing each other from new angles, with a fresh respect. They were cautious, not wanting to make the same mistakes this time.

Russell shrugged his shoulders at her attempt to distract him. "I don't remember sleeping. I know I did a little, somewhere in there." The brown of his eyes intensified. "Mandy, I want to ask you a question, and you mustn't be afraid to tell me the truth. None of those men . . . harmed you, did they? They didn't put their hands on you, or force you in any way?"

Finding her hand, he carefully fit her smooth palm to his. He studied the contrast of her small white one to his large tan one. She knew what he was asking. She shook her head no.

"They could have. I know they were capable of it. They . . . walked away from the Mercedes leaving Simon and Allen to die. It's only luck that Allen survived. I'm sure that hurting me wouldn't have bothered them. But no, they didn't—"

Thinking about what could have happened was too painful. Mandy focused upon the hard corded muscles of his neck. Russell wasn't a friend, yet he wasn't really a lover, either. Knowing her own love, she did not want to look into his eyes and find only protective concern. She twisted her face to the wall.

"I called your stepmother," he said. "I thought she'd want to know. I'm glad I did. The story got in the U.S. papers, and she was worried half out of her mind. Some editor . . . ah, Ken, I believe, had already told her the truth about why you followed me. I guess he knows you pretty well because he figured out Amanda Hamilton was also Amanda Phillips. Who's Ken?"

Staring at the textured ceiling, she replied absently: "Ken Hagan. An editor I've done some magazine features for. Newspaper stuff. You know."

Russell sat upright, rubbing the space between his nose and the curve of his upper lip. "He'll want you to write about this extortion-hostage thing, won't he?"

Acutely aware of his disapproval, Mandy propped herself on one elbow. His eyes fell to the gentle curve of her abdomen, but she thought he did not see her at all.

"Why does that bother you? What if he does?" she questioned.

Russell's features were veiled. "The less publicity, the better."

"Better for you?"

"Better for both of us. You forget that we say we're
married, yet we're not. If this thing gets laid open in the press
my cover will probably be blown. I might as well kiss
everything good-bye."

Mandy felt her mouth curling as options began solidifying
before her mind's eye. Ken smelled a good story. She smelled
it herself. "Well," she said presently, "that may not be what
he wants to talk about. But if he does want a piece, I'd do it. I
came for one, remember?"

When the muscles tightened in Russell's jaw, Mandy threw
herself on her side and glared at the wall. His breath was
determined, and his words made her flinch.

"And I'd stop you, any way I could," he promised.

She squeezed her eyes tightly shut. Russell Gregory never
made empty threats. She tried to keep the fear of loss from
choking her.

Russell grasped her face in his hand. His lips brushed her
ear with an almost shy persuasion.

"I don't want to fight with you," he whispered. "Look at
me."

He forced her face to his, and she thought he'd kiss her. He
hesitated as if it were a bad idea. Abruptly, surprising her, his
mouth dipped quickly and fastened on Mandy's lips with an
exhilarating hunger. Inhibitions made her resist for only a
moment before she melted.

Voices murmured, dangerously near on the opposite side of
the door. In spite of the intruding sounds, when Russell's
hand traced the curve of her throat, slipping lower across her
waist and fitting itself in the sloping crevice between her legs,
she whimpered. Mandy buried her fingers in the hair nestling
over his collar and pulled his head downward—possessively
forcing his kiss deeper into hers. Her searching for answers
without words seemed to inflame him. His hand moved across
the denim below her zipper—suggesting, making her remember when her knees had stopped refusing him, when she had
accepted and closed herself about him like a sheath about a
steel saber.

A strange sense of power made Mandy bold. But not bold
enough. Fearing that whoever was in the hall might hear what
they were doing, she pulled her face away. She caught her
lower lip in her teeth and shook her head.

She barely said the words: "Not here."

"Where, then? I've been through hell." His chest rose and fell rapidly, as if that were reason enough for lowering his face to the tempting arch of her throat.

"Listen to me," she gasped.

Reasoning with him was almost impossible when heat had begun to surge through her limbs. Mandy buried her fingers in the strength of his shoulders. But even that touch made him more determined. With a shift of his weight, Russell almost covered her body with his.

"Please understand," she objected. His weight was crushing her; circumstances were crushing her.

"Ask me anything," his words rumbled deep and intense, "but don't ask me to understand why I have to stop."

"Just because of what happened that night—"

Russell's head lifted. "What about that night?" He frowned at her complex morality. "It was something we both wanted. What's wrong with that?"

"Nothing, for you. But I don't look at things the way you do. I didn't mean for you to think I would . . . well, have an affair."

Russell stared in disbelief. A half-smile teased his lips. "What do you call what we did, sweetheart?"

Mandy's eyes narrowed. "I call it . . . something that happened."

Casting a ridiculous grimace toward the ceiling, Russell shook his head. "You have such uncomplicated female logic."

"If I'm logical, then you're egotistical, Russell."

With a soft laugh, Russell began undoing the buttons on her shirt. Mandy grabbed at his hands, her spine already triggering small throbs deep in her vitals. He only brushed her hands aside. Once the narrow valley between her breasts was bared his mouth curved into a grin. He studied the swells which peeped at him from beneath the lace edges of her bra. In a small movement he flicked a finger underneath and drew the nylon aside.

Russell adjusted his weight to an elbow and traced one of the pink circles. The nipple tightened beneath his fingertip. Mandy stared at the dark stain creeping up his neck. She thought she could not keep still, that she could devour him like some wild thing.

"I want a whole night with you," he mumbled hoarsely. "And no gown this time."

The rustle of the doctor entering the room drew Russell stiffly upward. He could not have disguised his arousal if he had known how to do it. Mandy fumbled with the buttons of her shirt, trying to fasten them before the doctor noticed. She couldn't.

A flood of red rushed into her cheeks as Russell slid easily off the bed. "Benjamin Hamilton, doctor," he introduced himself, and extended his hand. "I spoke with you earlier this morning."

"Ah, yes," nodded the physician, as he removed a stethoscope from his pocket without indulging in bedside chitchat. "Our little hostage, eh?" He fit the earpieces. "Well, let's see what we've got here. If you'll excuse us, Mr. Hamilton."

Russell left with a sardonic expression aimed at the back of the doctor's head.

"You're lucky young woman," the doctor told her when he finished.

Braced on her elbow, Mandy read as he wrote "Mrs. Amanda Hamilton" on her medical record. Detective Barrot thought she was Mrs. Amanda Hamilton. The newspapers thought she was Mrs. Amanda Hamilton. By now, Felice and Bergman thought she was Russell's wife. Everyone did except for the Pattersons and the woman who probably would have *been* Mrs. Hamilton, were it not for her—Carolyn Wrather.

Carolyn, much to Mandy's surprise was in Zurich. She and Mickey were staying in a suite adjoining Reginald Patterson's. While Mandy and Opal had been the captives of lunatic extortionists, Carolyn, to hear Russell explain it, had tended to Reggie like a daughter.

After the doctor dismissed Mandy with instructions to do nothing but rest for the next few days, Russell and Reginald talked banking while Mandy sat on the foot of Opal's hospital bed. Carolyn breezed in, demurely proficient. She offered to take Mandy's sizes and do some shopping to replace the clothes damaged in the wreck. Russell lifted dark brows in approval.

"We're all so relieved you're safe, Amanda," Carolyn remarked happily as she jotted down the statistics Mandy reluctantly gave her. "Russell and Reggie had been in such a state, poor darlings. I ordered food, but neither of them ate. Russell didn't remember to shower or shave unless someone turned on the water." She smiled.

"Russell is used to being a bachelor," Opal observed as she sipped water through a straw. The sight of her ringless hands made her pause, reflect a moment, and set the glass aside. She doubted if her jewelry would ever be recovered.

"What's the matter, honeybabe?" Reggie asked. He was celebrating by repeatedly putting the same cigar into his mouth, though the nurses wouldn't let him smoke it.

Opal held out her hands. "I'll never get used to my rings being gone, Mr. Patterson."

"I'll buy you bigger and better ones, sugar." Reggie removed his cigar and lifted her plump hand to his lips. Mandy thought, Opal was right; they did have something special. Could she and Russell ever have anything like that?

Seeing Russell staring at her own ringless fingers, Mandy self-consciously folded her hands. She made some flimsy excuse about needing to leave. Anxious to begin putting her life into some perspective, she started to walk toward the door.

"Well, I'll turn the job of Russell's caretaker over to you, Amanda, with my blessings," Carolyn commented. "I'll see you two later."

She wore a full-cut bias skirt with a smart zippered top. Carolyn was all shiny red hair and long feminine legs and outrageously high heels. Beside her, with soot-blackened jeans and boots scarred from wire fences and jagged rocks, Mandy felt like a street urchin. Carolyn was aware of this undercurrent; that did not surprise Mandy. It was Russell's incredible blindness where Carolyn was concerned that dumbfounded her. He appeared to accept everything about her at face value.

Waiting for the operator to complete a telephone call to Felice, Mandy was curled up in a brocaded chair in Russell's hotel suite, much like the one at The Staad. It was ten o'clock the same evening, and they had just finished eating sandwiches and soft drinks ordered from room service.

Unexpectedly, there was a rap on the door. Russell groaned, tossed a "not again" look over his shoulder and strode to answer it.

The contentment warming Mandy was much like that she had previously experienced with Russell in Mattenaugst—a gradual satisfaction at being in the right place. Padding in his socks, his shirttails flapping about his thighs, Russell unconsciously made Mandy want to cuddle him like a silky kitten.

Carolyn, her arms loaded with parcels, nearly fell into the room. Immediately, Mandy knew the feeling of well-being was not to last.

"I'm sorry to be so late, Russell, but Opal didn't have a stitch to her name, either. I just came from the hospital. Reggie is causing a commotion with the nurses. They've told him to leave three times, and he refuses." Her hands fluttered gaily. "Now you have something to wear besides those jeans, Amanda."

Carolyn glanced at Russell's robe which Mandy wore tightly belted about her. Carolyn was a well-bred woman when she wished to be. She could adapt easily to almost any situation.

She emptied three large shopping bags from the finest shops in Zurich. Out tumbled boxes of tissue-wrapped skirts, tops and pleated slacks. Slippers and an exquisite pearl-gray peignoir, and a large assortment of cosmetics.

"You bought everything!" exclaimed Mandy with delight.

Giving her belt a firm yank, Mandy rustled through the tissue and admired a three-piece knit suit. She turned to Carolyn, feeling guilty for nurturing such enmity since meeting her at the dance in Mattenaugst. Mandy was about to thank her, to force herself to behave in a sophisticated manner and stop being jealous of something that was in the past.

"Russell, this cost you a fortune," Carolyn interrupted Mandy's intentions. The auburn-haired beauty crammed a handful of receipts against Russell's chest as his lips curled into a smirk. "You'd better marry this girl for real," she allowed the words to fall distinctly, like marbles pinging on a sidewalk, "or I'm going to tell everyone you're a gigolo."

Mandy dropped the heather-tinted knit, her hands trembling. Her stomach knotted with dread. How could Carolyn say such a thing, even in jest?

"If you'll excuse me," Mandy choked. Carolyn's words had been no accident. But the woman was so secure with herself! She had a ten-year edge in knowing Russell which put Mandy at a terrible disadvantage.

"Oh, Amanda, come on," Carolyn chided. "And, Russell, quit frowning at me like that. Good Lord, you didn't really expect me to swallow that story, did you?"

To outward appearance, her smile was oblivious to the pain she was inflicting. Mandy thought she must surely know it.

"Carolyn," Russell growled his words, his brows were blunted, "I don't think this is the right time to talk about it."

As Mandy stumbled toward the bedroom, where the bathroom was, anywhere to escape those laughing eyes, Carolyn grasped Mandy's wrist. "Don't be so young, darling," she cooed. "I'm not criticizing you."

Carolyn's hand remained on her wrist even though Mandy resisted her touch. Mandy's eyes grew wide with wonder at Carolyn's ease.

"I'm sorry," Mandy said breathlessly.

For a moment neither of them spoke. Then with over-solicitous gentleness, Carolyn patted Mandy's cheek. Mandy closed her eyes, paralyzed.

"Carolyn," snapped Russell, "lay off." He stepped toward them, his face broodingly disagreeable.

Carolyn looked innocent. "She's very pretty, Russell."

Mandy thought if Russell had taken her own shoulder with as much physical display, she would have screamed at him.

Carolyn defended herself as he drew her away. "I was just being nice," she said with an impish pout.

Russell's glare warned her, and Carolyn searched about the room for her handbag. Reaching into his wallet, he withdrew several large Swiss franc notes, folded them, and pressed them into Carolyn's hand. "Thank you for shopping for Mandy," he said tersely. "And for Opal, too."

As if she were enumerating a list of objections without using words, Carolyn regally pulled herself up to Russell's height. A sick idea plummeted into Mandy's stomach: If she weren't here, would his intimate relationship with Carolyn have already resumed? *Had it been resumed during the past few days?* Mandy could never pry into such an area; she had no right. And it occurred to her that she really didn't want to know.

Wishing that she had the nerve to create a terrible scene and knowing that it was not in her to do it, Mandy walked to the bathroom. She shut the door and turned on both of the sink faucets. She stood woodenly, her palms braced on the vanity. If she could, she would disappear without a trace.

"Mandy," Russell called outside the door after ten minutes

of frustrating silence. "The operator has Felice on the phone."

Felice Phillips was already in bed when the operator connected her to Mandy. The blinds in the bedroom were drawn although it was only the late afternoon. The maid had been given the day off. When she lifted her head, her ash-hued hair was a shamble.

In the midst of the disordered bed, surrounded by strewn clothes, overflowing ashtrays and a half-empty bottle of bourbon, Felice yawned prettily. Bergman Reeves, with a muffled groan, dragged a pillow off his head.

In the Zurich hotel Mandy suspected Russell of deliberately eavesdropping. He stood before one of the sheerly draped windows, shirtless and moody, pretending to study the maze of car lights streaking along the Bahnhofstrasse below them. With an absentminded gesture, he smoothed the expanse of his chest with a spread hand.

For a moment Mandy studied the pattern of tanned muscles spanning Russell's back, marveling at his appeal. Old unwelcome longings stirred inside her and ignited a hunger which was all too familiar. Adoring him with her eyes was a dangerous pastime. She quickly averted her gaze.

"Mandy!" squeaked Felice when the operator monotoned the permission to go ahead. "I've been frantic about you. Where are you?"

Bergman dragged himself up against the headboard of the king-size bed, scoured over his dark stubble of beard and patted the tabletop in a search for cigarettes.

"Don't tell her I'm here, for God's sake," he muttered under his breath. Frowning, Felice covered the mouthpiece.

"I'm in Zurich," Mandy assured her stepmother with strained composure. "I got back early this morning. I'm all right. Really."

"It was all over the papers, honey. I didn't even know it was you until Ken Hagen told me. Then I was terrified until your husband called. But, sweetie, I didn't know whether to believe him or not. I told Bergman you wouldn't have gotten married without telling us."

Hating the increasing complexity of the deception, Mandy shifted her back toward Russell. He was hearing every word, and she lowered her voice until it was barely audible.

"Ah—" she groped for a decent evasion. There wasn't one.

"That's right," Mandy agreed cryptically. "It's all a bit confusing, I guess. I do apologize, Felice. Things have been so unreal lately, I hardly know what I'm doing."

"You mean you're actually married?" Mandy feared that Russell could hear Felice's shriek through the earpiece. "You know how disappointed your father would have been. He wanted you to have a good life with a kind man."

Mandy blinked, then closed her eyes. "I agree with all that, Felice."

"You should have told me. I would have understood."

"It was . . . quite sudden. And ah, well, I'll tell you everything when I get home."

Felice sniffed politely. "When will that be?"

As she talked, Mandy carried on a search in a desk drawer for a piece of paper and a pencil. She nervously dropped down to the carpet, clutched Russell's robe tightly about her bare legs and scratched random marks on the paper.

"The police have some questions for me, Felice," she explained. "If they catch those men, I'm going to interview them. That means several more days in Switzerland. And one of the newspapers wants an interview. I don't think I can escape that."

"Speaking of the press, honey," interrupted Felice, "Ken called again. He said some literary agent from New York is trying to locate you and wanted to come to Switzerland to meet you. You were still missing so I couldn't tell Ken anything. I have a phone number."

"Just a minute."

Scribbling, Mandy didn't realize Russell had moved from the window until he planted his foot beside her hip. She glanced up involuntarily, shrinking at the sight of him towering above her, and turned farther away.

"Go on," she told Felice and wrote down the name and number of Tony Schaeffer.

Curious, Russell dropped to one knee and lifted the paper from her hands. He scowled at the name. "Who is this?"

"Russell!" Mandy scolded, covering the mouthpiece. His quizzical brows did not match the muscle flexing in his jaw. "This is a private conversation," she said tightly. "It doesn't concern you."

"I doubt that very much," he drawled.

Mandy swiveled on her bottom, pointedly excluding him.

"Felice, Ken didn't tell you what this man wanted to see me about, did he?"

"It wasn't too clear. He was tact personified, of course, saying that he was sure you would return okay and that when you did you were sitting on a really saleable story. You know the line."

Mandy laughed softly. "He was more optimistic than I was, then. I wasn't sure until we got to Zurich that we were truly safe."

"You'll call him, won't you, Mandy? I promised my soul to the man."

"I will," she promised.

Russell resumed his disturbing position before the window. His legs bothered Mandy; they were spread in a purposeful stance. Without a doubt, if he knew who Tony Schaeffer actually was, he'd be angry. Not only would he be overly concerned about the Swiss Mercantile and his own image, he would have no sympathy with why she would feel compelled to do the story. If a story were what this was all about.

"Felice," Mandy said before they hung up, "I hate to sound mercenary, but did Bergman finish probating Daddy's will? I'm broke."

A surly sound of disapproval drifted from the vicinity of the window.

Felice's explanation lacked conviction. "It'll be soon, Mandy. At least more cash money is available now. Bergman has power of attorney, you remember, and he writes me a check anytime I want it. He's working hard on it, and I can have him wire you some of your trust if you want me to."

"He certainly is taking a long time."

"It's quite complicated, Mandy. He's doing the best he can. Doesn't your husband give you money?"

Not expecting such a question, Mandy blinked. "Certainly," she lied, "but this is special . . ." Her words dwindled to nothing.

"Oh."

"I have to hang up now, Felice," she said with nervous briskness. Mandy hated to deceive Felice, and she was anxious to escape Russell's silent objections to everything she said. "I'll call you before I catch my plane so you'll know when to expect me."

"Okay. Oh yes, Julie Deasy and Terry O'Connor got married the other day. I thought you'd like to know."

Mandy nodded and mumbled something about hoping they would be happy. She replaced the receiver with slow thoughtfulness. Scrutinizing it, she assumed a self-assurance that she wasn't sure she could maintain. She could probably no more escape Russell's razor-edged questions than she could leave the hotel without an explanation. Mandy was right.

"Who is Tony Schaeffer?" he demanded at once, his voice unyielding.

As Mandy toyed with a lock of her hair, he took a chair directly opposite her. He stretched his long legs until they nearly touched her crisscrossed legs. Then he steepled his fingers and waited like a devilish confessor.

"I don't have to tell you my business, Russell," Mandy began in fragile defense.

"Only if it affects *my* business," he agreed with cold professionalism. "And I have the feeling that it does. Directly."

Russell's inspection, when he was not guarding his manner out of courtesy, had always bordered on insult. And at this precise moment, his guard was either down or purposely discarded.

"Is Schaeffer a newspaper reporter?" he probed.

"No," she said brusquely.

"What then, a cop?"

"No, Russell! The man is not a cop. Or a reporter or a cousin or a lover. Damn, why does it bother you?"

"It bothers me if my name is going to be bandied around. Staying in Zurich to interview those criminals is dangerous, Mandy. Every time your name appears in print increases the chances that someone will find out I'm not who I say I am and that we're not married. I've gotten myself into a mess—"

"Because of me!" Mandy cried, moving to plop down onto the divan and twisting her head so she would not be forced to see the truth on his face.

"Yes, dammit, because of you!"

His eyes swept downward with a pointed expression of detachment. Mandy gaped at her half-bared breasts and clutched his robe tightly closed. Rising, she walked to the bedroom closet with defiant steps, assuring him that she did not wish to discuss Tony Schaeffer or anything else. After taking down a blanket and extra pillow, she returned. Briefly, almost longingly, she glanced at the beautiful peignoir draped across the end of the sofa. Denying herself, she fluffed the pillow and laid it against the arm of the divan.

"Are you planning to sleep in here because of me or because Carolyn offended you?" he asked. "Carolyn prides herself on shock tactics."

Frowning, Mandy tucked in the edges of the blanket. "Carolyn did not offend me. I'm not exactly a nun, Russell."

He grinned, saw that she was not amused, and uncrossed his ankles. Standing, he prowled restlessly about the room.

"I, of all people, am aware of that. Sleep on the bed," he offered with light generosity, gesturing at it through the open doorway. "I told you once before, I don't hassle women."

"Obviously!" Mandy snapped, whirling toward him in a futile attempt to hide her jealousy. "It's terribly convenient that Carolyn is so easy."

Mandy thought if he denied it, she would believe anything he said. She wanted dreadfully to believe him. She waited, giving him the chance to say she was wrong. He denied nothing.

His refusal angered her. Mandy dug through the cluttered assortment of clothes with furious movements. Grabbing a skirt and top and some underwear, she started for the bathroom. Russell roughly caught her shoulder and spun her about.

"We've had this fight before," he said angrily. "You're not leaving here. Every time anything comes up, you want to run."

Mandy lashed out at him. "I only want to leave where I have no business being in the first place. Just because we went to bed once doesn't give you the right to tell me when I can come and go." She could have added that just because she loved him did not mean she would bow to all his wishes, either. But she didn't say that.

"Going to bed is going to bed," Russell countered bitterly.

"Yes, to you it is precisely that. For your information, since you seem to be so obsessed with everything I do, Schaeffer is a literary agent. If he offers me a sale for a feature, I'm taking it."

Russell moved rapidly, pushing her against the wall with a force he would use on a man. Her head slammed painfully, and Mandy bit her lip, her face twisting. Russell did not apologize: He only curled the edge of his lip over his teeth

and glared down at her. Abruptly then, he pinned her with
his body, pressing her so hard against the wall she could feel
every muscle, every bone, every strength of his maleness.

"If *you're* taking it, then *I'm* taking it," he assured her, no
regret on his face, only dark intensity burning in his eyes. If
she could have, Mandy would have slapped him.

"Let me go," she said quietly. "You're making a fool of
yourself."

Russell's smile was harshly sarcastic. "Wrong. You've
already done that for me. And now you want to crucify me,
my little feminist." He shook his head. "No, no. I won't let
you do that."

She was trembling so badly that only the force of his body
was holding her up. She was a prisoner, her breasts crushed
flat to his bare chest, throbbing with a swollen reaction that
spread through her. He would use it against her if he knew:
He would say she wanted to remain in Zurich only for him.

Russell relaxed his entrapment for only the seconds he
needed to strip the belt of his robe from about her waist. The
robe parted, leaving her nakedness a prey to his touch. One
of his legs firmly invaded the space between hers. Keeping
her head down, Mandy could hardly avoid his chin as he bent
low. With a free hand he grasped her chin and forced her face
upward.

"Do you know what you are?" she accused him.

"Yes."

She gritted her words between her teeth. "I thought you
never hassled women."

"I've never had to."

"I'm not willing, Russell."

"You will be," he promised thickly.

Mandy struggled. And when he lowered his lips, she jerked
her face free. He tried a second time and finally resorted to
holding her face still with both hands. Escape was hopeless.
Russell captured her mouth and demanded that she yield.
Though she resisted, his tongue forced itself between her
teeth and plundered its way into the recesses of her mouth.

She cried out against his kiss. She could not bring herself to
surrender a conflict of principles, to reach upward and accept
the demands. And Russell refused to lessen the hungry power
of his mouth. He grew hard with driving need. The more she
resisted the more he wanted her—his body moving against
hers, pulsing, urging.

Only when he slipped his hands over her hips, filling them and lifting her upward against the stirred arousal, did Mandy realize he was no longer forcing her head still. The victory was not hers, but his. He reached between them for the zipper of his pants. Mandy flung herself away with a strangling sob.

"Leave me alone!" she groaned and threw herself face down onto the divan. Her words came distraughtly and muffled against the pillow. "I was nearly killed. I could have been killed, and all you can do is try to dominate me. I'm not a piece of property!"

Mandy did not realize that Russell had dropped his head into his hands, or that his eyes were blurred with remorse when he stood over her. She was exhausted, and the tears streaming from her eyes seemed to drug her. For long moments she did not move, complete in her own misery. She vaguely knew when Russell drew the blanket over her shoulders. He stooped to one knee beside her.

"You're right," he said gently. "I'm a rat."

Depleted, Mandy sniffed, her eyes swollen with crying. "It's all right," she murmured.

With a rueful grin, Russell combed his fingers through her curls. Moments later her breathing steadied and became a rhythmic slumber. With a heavy sigh, he stumbled to the bed and threw himself across it.

Amanda Phillips was one of the most headstrong women he had ever known. He must be spoiled because all his life women had made themselves available and eager to please him. And here she was, not only unwilling to compromise, but in a very real position to damage him.

His emotions were all tangled up with hers. He probably loved her. Oh God, he did love her, or he would have walked out tonight!

The problem was, he didn't know how to handle Mandy. He could not face losing her, and she was like a bottle of nitroglycerin held to his chest. That was the way he would handle her, he decided. Trying to force that woman to do anything was disastrous. So he would go along with her. He would deal with her as he would a dangerous explosive. And the first opportunity he saw to break her down, he would sure as hell take advantage of it. He was no fool, Russell congratulated himself.

Flipping himself to his back, he snapped off the lamp.

Through the open doorway she lay sleeping. By now he could have cajoled any other woman into his bed: Why was he lying here alone? Perhaps, after it was all said and done, Mandy was actually more clever than he was. Perhaps he was kidding himself; perhaps he really was a fool.

Chapter Twelve

Bergman Reeves was partial to blondes, though he didn't particularly care for them to be taller than he was. Felice Phillips exceeded his height by two inches. He would rather have had Mandy. Not only wasn't she as tall as Felice, her share of Preston's money was much larger. And something about her willful independence fascinated him. When he had first visualized himself controlling the vast Phillips fortune, he had relished the idea of breaking her down.

But Amanda had refused to be seduced, even after weeks of diligent effort. Then the Associated Press had run the story of Amanda Hamilton's being held hostage for three million dollars. The last thing he had expected was for Mandy to up and get married. He had to do something, so he had moved in with Felice.

"Well, what did the little twit have to say?" probed Bergman when Felice replaced the receiver with a thoughtful expression on her face.

He took a final drag off his cigarette and stubbed it out. He propped his dark head on a fist. Felice only lay flat on her back and stared at the ceiling. In the dimming light she was fragile and delicate, like her perfume which mingled with smells of sex and fine liquor.

She breathed a resigned sigh, plumped her pillow against the headboard and drew the sheet up to her waist. Her eyes, when they turned their gray wideness upon him, were astonished.

"She has really married that man." Felice touched her lips with her fingers. "I feel like I've failed Preston. He trusted me to be a good mother."

A fifteen-year gulf had separated Felice and the brilliant industrial designer she had met at a shopping mall. According to the grapevine, she had been standing in a telephone booth with mascara streaming down her face, taking a verbal beating from her ex-husband.

Preston, flipping through the yellow pages in the next compartment, had heard her crying. And when he asked if there was anything he could do, she had spilled her heart out. They had married two months later.

Not everyone accepted the shy, slender blonde as the new Mrs. Phillips. Some said she was ultra-clever and after his money. Others said Preston was suffering from a mid-life crisis and needed a harmless fling with a younger woman. But eventually the contentment on Preston's face convinced them all—even Bergman, who as a tough corporate lawyer never believed anything.

Preston Phillips's death left a complex jungle of business problems. Felice had accepted Bergman's authority without question. She welcomed it, for she was in way over her head and she knew it. What had surprised Bergman, even though women like her always knuckled under to a man in the end, was the ease with which he got her into bed.

"What the hell?" he said now. "Mandy'll land on her feet. That girl always does. When's she coming home?"

"In a few days she said," Felice mused. "But I guess she'll go wherever her husband lives."

"Are you going to tell her about us?" asked Bergman casually. His thick, square-tipped fingers teasingly crept up her arm. Bergman began pulling the shoulder straps of her tricot gown down to her elbows.

Felice was milky white all over—creamy and soft, like a Gibson girl on a calendar. And though he had undressed her many times, she still caught her breath and covered her breasts with both hands.

"Not now, Bergman," she protested gently with a shake of her head.

Bergman laughed softly, ignoring her objection. He pried several fingers away and lowered his mouth to close over the unaroused peak. His nibbling produced the desired effect; it swelled against his tongue.

But Felice pushed against him with her knee. "No," she whispered.

Bergman insisted. "I want to."

In spite of her wriggling, his hands worked the skirt of her gown into a knot about her waist. Giving the sheet a swift kick, he exposed her long, willowy legs and pale bonde curls. He knew she would not dare deny him, and he forced a hand into the down below her belly. As he groped for her mouth, his fingers drove deeply—violent and careless in their plunder.

"Stop!" Felice whimpered.

He slung the weight of a leg across her waist. "If you make me stop now I won't come back," he threatened. "Give it to me," he said, his voice hoarsening with desire.

She begged him, pleading against his kisses. But Bergman moved his legs between hers and braced his weight on his palms. He grinned down at the beautiful, imploring face.

"You know why I took the day off, what I'm in this bed for. If you want me to go, say so. But know the consequences."

When Felice went limp, he kissed her eyes and her cheeks, then her throat. And her mouth again. His hands roamed everywhere—kneading flesh and pulling her beneath him.

"You do it," he groaned, thrusting himself against her in a slow ritual. "Come on. Do it for me."

With mechanical response, an uncomplaining resignation drilled into her by a first husband who considered only his own desires, Felice obeyed Bergman. She grasped the part of his body which he took such pride in and guided it into her. Then she divorced her mind from his thrusts.

Bergman satisfied himself as long as it suited him. And when he was done, a film of sweat shimmered over his hairy chest and back. He ordered her to run him a bath. Felice did as he said without argument.

"Did you marry Preston Phillips because you loved him or because you couldn't stand to be alone?" he asked bluntly as he lowered himself into a tub of hot water.

Felice tossed over a washcloth. "Preston was a good man. He loved me," she said tonelessly.

"But you don't like being alone, do you? That's why you go to bed with me."

As Bergman lathered himself, she brushed her teeth. After combing through the fine gold wisps reaching to her shoulders, she began applying makeup. She paused only to reply, and she did not look at him.

"When a woman reaches her early forties, Bergman, a Preston Phillips doesn't come along every day of the week. No, I can't live by myself."

Bergman chuckled. "That's why you'll marry me."

Their eyes met—Bergman's cool and blue, Felice's timid and gray. "Why would you want to marry me?" she asked simply.

The attorney's first thought was how miraculously spineless she was. No wonder her first husband had left her! The edges of his mouth turned downward in a lighthearted smirk at himself.

"No reason," he shrugged off the question. "Generosity, if you want a name. I'll be good to you. You won't have to go places by yourself. You won't need to worry with running this house. I'm not hard to please, Felice. A little sex, decent food. You could do much worse."

Felice sighed and applied mascara. Blinking, she inspected a lovely face that had only begun to show its age. "Probably," she spoke to the mirror.

"It's settled, then," he said, satisfied with the result of only two weeks' work. "I'll do everything. If it bothers you to have people know you're remarried so soon, we can keep it quiet for a while. I think that's the best, anyway. We can get a J.P. to marry us. Then, after a year or so, it won't be any big deal."

Felice replaced her makeup and took a birth-control pill. The medicine cabinet shut with a calculated click.

"And then no one will say you married me for my money," she said with a dull rebuke. She left him drying himself.

Bergman never cooked, but he enjoyed the domestic sight of Felice moving about in the immense kitchen. His own kitchen in the condominium consisted of a formica bar and two vinyl-covered stools. The Phillips kitchen had every conceivable appliance and was connected to a large dining room where he could picture himself throwing huge, swinging dinner parties.

The house was an old colonial affair off St. Charles Avenue

which had been redecorated by an interior designer Preston had discovered in New York. As if she could care less that she was surrounded by thousands of dollars worth of glass and gadgets, Felice set coffee and food before him. She didn't try to make conversation—critical or otherwise—as he barricaded himself behind a newspaper. Only when she began loading the dishwasher with dirty pots did he voice an objection.

"Can you wait a minute?" He tried to dodge the trail of cigarette smoke drizzling into his eyes. "I gotta make a phone call before Tracy leaves the office."

"Your ex-wife?" she asked and made her face expressionless at his grimace. He dragged the telephone across the glass-topped table. As he dialed, Felice glanced through the mail and listened, only occassionally eating something.

"Hello, Alice," he said, keeping his voice low. "It's Bergman. Get Tracy on the phone."

"One moment, Mr. Reeves."

Bergman sipped his coffee as Tracy Reeves's secretary punched buttons on her telephone panel. Tracy owned a large real estate firm in New Orleans—successful, "in" with the right segment of the city's elite. While Bergman waited, he replaced Tracy's business card in his wallet and flicked ashes impatiently into a tray.

"Yes, Bergman," the realtor's voice came silkily, "what may I do for you?"

With an uncertain glance at Felice, Bergman answered. "Start the closing. I'm buying."

Standing quite still, Felice met Bergman's eyes. A refined perception lurked in her clear gray eyes. Bergman pretended, not difficult for him, that her malice was not there and assumed a hard-driving bravado.

"The Hartford property is the best," he raised his voice with cosmopolitan candor. "It's what I want. Nothing but the best."

The caution in Tracy's voice would have been deflating to anyone else. "Well," she hesitated, "I'll have to secure your down payment and talk to Wallace at the bank. You have the entire four hundred eighty thousand dollars?"

"If I tell you I do, I do. No problem," assured Bergman. He laughed dauntlessly.

Felice's eyes seemed to know everything, to guess motives that Bergman thought only *he* knew. He frowned—first at her, than at the silence hanging on Tracy's end of the line.

With business tact, Tracy set up an appointment for him to see the riverfront acreage.

"How long will this deal take to go through, Tracy?"

Tracy made a small sound of consideration. "Oh, a week should do it, Bergman. Is that too soon?"

He wiped a hand across his face and straightened his shoulders. "Hell, no!" he laughed. "Well, I might have to ask you to hold off a couple of days or so. But no more than that."

Again the silence. When Tracy spoke again, Bergman recognized the tone: Don't waste my time, you creep.

But Tracy said, "Sure, Bergman, I'll get things started. It's a good investment. You'll double your money in ten years."

"Don't I know it?" Bergman crowed. "Okay, good buddy. I'll see you."

"Yes," Tracy said and hung up.

The moment after Bergman dropped the receiver into its cradle was a condemning one.

"What was that all about?" Felice asked softly as she padded to the sink with their dishes.

"None of your damn business!" Bergman snapped.

Without replying, Felice ran water over the plates and placed them in the dishwasher. Bergman stepped up behind her and rammed his pelvis against her buttocks. Cupping her breasts with both hands, he nibbled her ear.

"Let's get married tonight," he wheedled. "There's no need to wait. Hell, we're not getting any younger."

He felt Felice's whole body stiffen. When she grasped both wrists and removed his hands from her, he almost slammed her against the sink.

"I'm meeting some friends," she said coolly. "Be gone when I get back."

"Sure," he chuckled, when he recovered from his surprise. He made a quick calculation of how long he would have to postpone buying the Hartford property if it took another two weeks to get Felice to the Justice of the Peace.

"See you later, baby," he called to her back.

When Felice shut the front door he still stood by the table, thinking.

"I could have met Mr. Schaeffer's plane myself, Russell," Mandy complained several days later as she struggled to match her strides to his long, deliberate ones.

They found themselves a few minutes late as they weaved through airport bustle. According to the computer, Tony Schaeffer's plane was due to arrive from America in five minutes. From their conversation on the phone, Mandy deduced that the agent was not only happy to have heard from her, he was extremely anxious to lay out his plans for a book.

"What book?" she had repeated, incredulous. "I can't write a *book!*"

"I've read what you did for *Today's World* and *The Reader's Digest,* and I think you can. This is a once-in-a-lifetime chance. You may never be held for ransom for three million dollars again," Schaeffer had advised.

"Oh, God!" was all she could say.

Now Russell took her hand and stepped behind her as traffic grew congested. "If everything I've worked for is getting sent down the tubes, I want to know it before the fact."

"You're putting the cart before the horse. The publisher he has in mind may reject my outline."

"They won't reject it," Russell returned. "They'll pay you a fortune in advance. I detest Schaeffer already."

Mandy stopped. College students bumped her with their backpacks and children, who clung to the hands of their mothers. She wore a linen skirt and a cranberry-colored crepe blouse. Three-inch heels added to the feminine impression of soft, fluid grace.

Dark and attractive in a pinstriped suit and vest, Russell glanced at masculine heads which turned back to take a second look at Mandy. She stood with a fist balanced on her hip, a slender gold bracelet dangling about her wrist. One good-looking man even had the nerve to catch Russell's eye and grin, as if to say, What's the matter, she got you stymied? Russell's brown eyes hardened with a warning, and the man moved on.

"I know I've done irresponsible things in the past," Mandy defended herself. "But that doesn't mean I'm going to this time. You'll just have to trust me, Russell."

"I wouldn't trust you, my darling, if you were bound and gagged. Here's his gate."

She grabbed at Russell's sleeve as he moved toward the roped area. "Do you realize that millions of people would give their arms and legs to be offered what I have been?" she arugued. "They beg people to publish their book, and here I've been *asked* to write one. You can't ask me to give it up."

Towering above her, frowning down into her pretty, upturned face, he softened for one moment. Then his words came with sober objectivity. "Do you realize how hard it is to keep a bank from collapsing? To coax people to invest in American goods, to keep millions of people employed?"

Mandy arched an accusing brow. "I doubt that my writing a book would compromise all that, Russell. Come on."

"You could put me completely out of commission, sweetheart," he said with a sigh.

"Perhaps you value your talents too highly."

She thought if they had not been standing in the middle of a crowd, he would have shaken her. A muscle leaped in his jaw, and he spoke through gritted teeth. "I value the years it's taken me to build the level of confidence I have. But it's not just me—Opal and Reggie have as much at stake. More."

Being placed in a position where nothing else except only two evils existed was a terrible way to make a choice. Mandy did not want to hurt Russell, and she didn't want to miss something which would probably never come again. Why was she so poorly prepared to make the right decision? Then it sharpened into focus. Her father would have looked five years in the future and said, "No decision affects solely one person, Amanda. One can't please just himself."

On the other hand, why should she consider Russell's future equally with her own? This interim "marriage" would end; they would both go their own ways. Then she would have jeopardized her career for nothing. She felt as if her feet were planted on two different moorings that were moving in opposite directions. The ever-widening gulf would tear her apart.

The computer screen above their heads printed the flight schedules. With a headache etching a groove in the center of her forehead, Mandy searched for Mr. Schaeffer's flight.

"He said he would wear a yellow tag attached to his suit pocket," she fretted as she studied disembarking passengers. "I don't see anyone who looks like that."

Russell growled his reply. "With any luck, he died yesterday."

"Russell!"

"Spare the tantrum, Amanda. I think I see your man."

Tony Schaeffer was a head shorter than Russell, and half

his hair was gone. A black moustache brushed the edge of his upper lip, and he virtually oozed sex appeal. He looked like something out of an Otto Preminger movie—sensual black eyes and a not-too-thick mouth. Wearing a suit somewhere between that of an avant-garde artist and a university professor, he was the type of man Mandy liked immediately. She extended her hand and said hello.

"You're exactly what I expected," he complimented her in round, soft-sell tones.

Aware of Russell's scowl over her shoulder, Mandy returned the agent's enthusiasm. "Well," she said in a slightly flirtatious voice, "you're not *anything* like I expected!" She laughed. "May I introduce Benjamin Hamilton, my . . . husband."

"I might have known he would be tall," Tony chuckled. "Well, Mr. Hamilton, you're quite lucky to have your new bride back in one piece. But I'm sure you know that. It could've easily become a tragedy."

Nodding in sober agreement, Russell strolled along beside them, one hand turning a franc piece over and over. He offered little to the conversation.

"Do you already have hotel reservations, Mr. Schaeffer?" he finally asked as they neared the crowded entrance.

"Call me Tony. And yes, I tended to that before I left. Would you two be my guests for dinner? Then we can discuss all the pros and cons of this venture."

Mandy met Russell's glance with an indecisive shrug. The Pattersons expected them at the hotel dining room for dinner to celebrate Opal's release from the hospital.

"I know a place where we can have a quiet drink," Russell suggested.

His pleasant smile directed at Tony Schaeffer was a complete surprise. Mandy wasn't sure why, but she didn't trust it. Another of Russell's facades? She understood why he didn't want her to write about the ransom. Why was he being nice? As he handed her into the back seat of the limousine, she leaned back into the seductive leather seat and brooded at the casual man-talk passing between them.

As the setting sun dipped to cast a brilliant glare on the windows, Mandy shielded her eyes. She wanted to be fair; she wanted to do the right thing; she wanted to write the book; she didn't know *what* to do!

Russell's driver deposited them before a small nightclub on

Lake Zurich. Following slightly behind the men, Mandy stepped into a dark, candlelit lounge. A fire blazed in a fireplace, though it wasn't really cold. The room's old, gracious charm had been preserved—original hardwood floors and hand-stained beams overhead. Leather groupings huddled in dark corners. Soft women's laughter rippled over the romantic clink of glassware.

The easy possessiveness of Russell's hand curved about her waist startled Mandy's thoughts from the important decision awaiting her. She was instantly aware of how his physical presence fit into the surroundings. A woman's head turned as they passed her table, and Mandy noticed the admiring glimpse of Russell's appeal.

They sat and Russell's thigh touched hers. He pointed to a couple dancing on a small floor and his hand brushed her shoulder. He ordered a white wine she liked with only a lift of his brows at her. He unbuttoned his suit coat and placed his arm across the back of her chair. From the bend of his head to the way he leaned across her to speak to Schaeffer, he announced that he was part of her life.

Oh, Russell, she thought as her manner adapted to his, you don't make this decision easy for me.

"What I'd like for you to do, Amanda," suggested Tony as she sipped her wine, "is work up an outline for me in the next couple of days. I want to be able to move while the news is hot. While your outline is being approved, see if you can rough in a couple of sample chapters about how you were taken by the kidnappers."

Russell's thumbnail gouged a jagged line into his napkin. He hates this, Mandy thought. Still, he said nothing.

"Two days isn't very long," she said thoughtfully. "Not for an outline of an eighty-thousand-word manuscript."

Tony smiled and turned to motion to the waitress to bring him another martini. "That's one of the cons I spoke of. You'd have to work quickly."

Excusing himself, Russell strolled toward the men's room. Mandy didn't know if he needed to disguise his anger or allow her to make a decision without his influence.

"Mr. Schaeffer," she began warily, staring at Russell's receding back.

"Tony," he corrected.

"Yes. Well, Tony," she looked at him directly across the

table. "There is one thing I'd have to be quite sure of before I agreed to do anything."

"And what is that?"

The agent sliced a small piece of cheese and offered it to her with a cracker. Mandy toyed with it and watched the way he held his glass. Tony Schaeffer was a perfectionist; not an unkind one, but a slave driver, nonetheless. Once she were committed, there would be no turning back. He would accept nothing but excellence and would make her do it over until she got it right.

"My husband's work is of a delicate nature," she said. "There have been threats on his life in the past. I could never place him in a position where he'd be exposed."

She waited for Tony's response, realizing that she might have just killed the greatest opportunity of her life.

His teeth gleamed beneath his moustache. "Mr. Hamilton would be willing to take the risks, I'm sure."

"*I* would not be willing," Mandy said quietly, meeting his eyes. "Definitely not willing."

He shrugged. "You mean to tell me that you'd turn your back on this opportunity on the basis of something that might never happen? After educating yourself and pounding out small feature stories?"

Love! Mandy thought with a mixture of anger and amazement. The sacrifice of what a person wanted for himself, the loyalty to another human being before oneself: that was what love was all about.

"Yes," she said at last. "I would"—she brushed her fingers aside in a gesture of finality—"I would let it all go."

The man across from her fished inside his suit coat for a cigarette. He lit it as he considered.

Schaeffer made his suggestion easily. "Change some of the names, then. Change the place if you must. It's done all the time."

Mandy slumped in relief. Taking a deep breath, she decided to go for broke. "Could I possibly print under my maiden name?" she asked. "That way, the other people involved would be shielded from things I can't foresee now. And, I could still get credit."

Tony braced his elbows on the table. "Anything you want. Just let me reemphasize the need for haste. Things like this have a tendency to cool off. You'd have to deliver a manuscript in only a few months. Otherwise, we can forget the whole thing."

Slightly deflated, Mandy covered her mouth with both hands. She nodded in agreement.

When Russell returned, he leaned back in his chair and stared at his drink for long, thoughtful moments. Condensation beaded, then slid down the surface of the glass to widen the puckered wet circle on the napkin. Without warning, his eyes locked with hers.

"Have you reached a decision, Amanda?" he asked tightly.

Mandy felt as if she were bracing herself in the Mercedes and waiting the interminable seconds until impact. "Yes," she said breathlessly, "I'm going to do the book."

God! she thought, watching the thinning of sensual lips, the hardening of a meaningful jaw. Oh, God, she had lost him!

Chapter Thirteen

During the trip back to the hotel, Mandy stared bleakly out the window of the limousine, and Russell intently studied the side of one shoe. His displeasure with her was a nagging, physical thing. It touched her like a cold clinging mist.

For one impulsive moment, she was tempted to strike out at Russell for his mistrust. Though not verbally, he was still accusing her of not being mature enough or sensitive enough to appreciate the delicate position he was in, that she was not skilled enough to protect him.

But to tell him that she had given his interests first priority, would be like begging him to believe in her. The man did not know what it was like to be in love—to consider someone else's needs over your own. He had not asked to talk about it. Russell had simply jumped to his own prejudiced conclusions.

So let him feel helpless for once! *He deserved to worry.* She would not explain.

The lobby of the hotel was busy with incoming guests and taxis blocking the entrance. French and German greetings and last-minute instructions blended with a potpourri of English and Italian. Bellboys swarmed among the crowd like blue-uniformed soldiers. Faces looked at her without seeing, and Mandy felt abysmally alone and confused.

If Russell had understood her, she could have slipped her smaller hand inside his and whispered that she was afraid she couldn't write the book after all. She could confess that she had probably made a colossal mistake by saying yes. And he would have stopped in his walk and towered above her in that marvelous way he had. He would have closed his hands over her shoulders and comforted her with his eyes. "Of course you can do it," he would've said. And she would have loved him for it.

"I beg your pardon, sir," interrupted a low, nasal voice immediately behind them.

Startled, Mandy's fingernails dug into her handbag, and she pivoted to see a huge man not three feet from them. He was not only tall, he was quite fat, and was mopping his thick jowls with a wilted handkerchief. When he stuffed it into his back pocket, the handkerchief conformed to the other rolls and bulges.

Russell's voice was his imperturbable one—the low, melodic one he reserved when he was irritated and didn't wish it to show. Protective fingers closed leanly about Mandy's arm, and the touch surprised her. When she covered the large hand with her softer one, it was as if she said, I hate the tension between us.

Russell's only reaction was the flicker of a muscle just below his temple. "Yes," he answered the man. "What is it?"

"I want a word with you, monsieur," the man said in an undisguised American twang that made his use of a French word absurd. His eyebrows, when they drew together, painted an anxious look on his face.

"What's on your mind?" prodded Russell, extremely controlled.

"A great deal, Mr. *Gregory*," he muttered.

All the sounds of the hotel lobby seemed to silence at once. Russell studied the man, and his grip tightened dangerously upon Mandy's wrist. Slightly inclining his dark head, as if congratulating the man for being so clever, Russell oozed cordiality.

"We're meeting friends for dinner, Mr. uh,—" he paused.

"Blalock," the obese man supplied, adjusting a tie which Mandy thought was remarkably unattractive.

"Ah, yes, Mr. Blalock," Russell agreed. He nodded and gestured toward the dining room with its steady flow of dinner guests. "Would you care to join us?"

Mr. Blalock's head jerked back in surprise, making the flesh on his neck quiver. "I thought maybe we could talk in private," he protested.

"I'm afraid not," drawled Russell. "I never discuss business without my immediate superior. He has a much better head for figures than I do."

The heavy man's mouth pursed like an irritated woman's. If Mandy hadn't been terrified of what the man knew, she would have laughed. Mr. Blalock hesitated. When Russell approached one step nearer, indicating that he fully intended for the man to precede them, Blalock took a few steps toward the double doors. Glancing back then, as if Russell could possibly have changed his mind, he shuffled forward.

The three of them entered the dining area to the musical sounds of glasses and silver, packaged melodies floating from recessed speakers. Clear across the room, sitting at a private table behind large potted plants, Mandy spotted Opal and Reggie.

"You look lovely, my dear," Reginald complimented Mandy as he rose to seat her. If silent messages passed between the two bankers, Mandy did not see them, for Opal leaned forward to catch her hand.

"Who is that creature?" she mumbled under her breath.

Mandy returned the whisper, her fingers unconsciously holding the soft crepe of her blouse as she bent forward. "I haven't the faintest idea. But he knows who Russell is."

"Oh, damn!"

Straightening, Mandy's astonished gaze darted toward Russell; Opal never swore. But the bankers seemed impervious to the curse. With an unreal sensation that she was watching some sort of rehearsed play, Mandy sat transfixed at their exchange. Russell made his announcement succinctly and with unruffled composure. He was the svelte executive she had first seen in New Orleans.

"May I present Mr. Blalock?" he said smoothly. "From the States, I presume. We haven't had time to become acquainted. In fact, I know absolutely nothing about him except that he is a very clever man and probably intends to bleed us for money."

Slamming a fist down upon the table until the water sloshed over the rims of the glasses, Reginald swore. He flailed behind himself and took his chair as if he were overcome.

Then he patted Opal's hand and assured her everything would be all right.

"Let's hear what the man has to say, darling," he comforted.

Opal, leveling her eyes at the newcomer, was a different woman from the hurt victim Mandy had cared for in the cabin. Opal drew up like an offended monarch. Under her wilting glare, Mr. Blalock's face assumed its worried expression more than ever.

Before anyone could speak the waiter stepped forward, pen in hand, and took their order. The look Mandy sent Russell said, What's going on here?

Slipping his hand around the back of her chair, Russell leaned closely and placed the menu between them. He lowered his face much nearer than was necessary and asked her which wine she wanted. His casual husbandly courtesies were for Mr. Blalock's benefit, of course, and Mandy fell back into her familiar role as his wife.

She murmured her selection and smiled at the subtle tilt of his head, the brush of a fingertip, the affectionate drop of his hand upon the slope of her shoulder. She wished he would stop playing this game; it wasn't an act with her anymore. Once she became involved she couldn't turn it off, and the reality of that was dangerous.

Agreeing to sole meunière, and salad, Mandy leaned back and discreetly attempted to remove his hand from her shoulder. She could no longer ignore his touch, even this small one.

"Thank you," she murmured, which meant, Get your hand off me.

His fingers tightened insistently. "You're welcome," he replied quietly, which meant, Don't cross me now.

Mandy felt herself blushing all over. As Russell stretched his legs lazily under the table, and cast a lethal smile at Blalock, his hand remained on her shoulder.

Seemingly as relaxed as a sunning cat, Russell continued to grin. "Well, say it all quickly, before I either call the police or throw you out of here myself."

Angry and confused by the charade of a man who should be wiping sweat off his upper lip, the heavy man drained his water glass and wiped his mouth. Then he pulled his suit coat together, buttoned it and twisted his neck against the bite of his collar.

"You fat cats at the top are all the same, Mr. Gregory," he said recklessly. "Guys like me don't have a chance against fat cats."

Reginald Patterson's words were like acid. "How much do you want, man?"

Mr. Blalock's green eyes narrowed. He resembled a shiny pink piglet. "A lot."

"How much is a lot?" snapped Russell's next question.

"Thirty thousand."

Russell's mouth curved in a handsomely comical grimace. He shrugged. Once again Mandy tingled with the impression that this was all some sort of bizarre stage comedy. Everyone seemed to know the punch line except the jowly figure and herself.

Blalock bubbled his demands. "And if you don't give it to me," he said with a twitch of his mouth, "I'm going to the newspapers with what I know. You won't look so good when Russell Gregory's name stretches across a few head-lines."

Mandy felt her pretended husband move, and it wasn't only the removal of his hand. Russell was threatened, and the primitive compulsion to protect himself rippled through his big body like an animal instinct. She started to speak once, to restrain him for she feared the violence in any man pressed this hard. She had already complicated his public image enough, so Mandy clamped her mouth shut.

"I won't even ask you how you found out, Mr. Blalock, or how long you worked at it." Russell was murderously polite. "I have a telephone call to make."

"Telephone call?" echoed Reggie.

"To the police," Russell said, squaring his broad shoulders with a movement of decision. Smiling, he pushed his chair back from the table."

"Then you'll give away your secret, Mr. Gregory." The object of all their stares grinned, his cheeks bulging. But his smile quickly faded when Russell stood.

"Yes," Russell agreed politely. "And so will you, Mr. Blalock."

The man's hand flashed upward, as if to prevent him. Almost comically, as some swiftly cautious cartoon character would pause and reconsider the wisdom of his actions, the fat man lowered his hand.

"Wait a minute!" Reginald's demand made them all pause.

As the old man leaned forward, stuffing a cigar into the corner of his mouth, his face grew dark and disgusted.

"You weasels make me so tired," he sneered. "You're a nuisance, all of you, I must have come across a dozen in my lifetime."

"Then you know I don't want trouble with the police," Blalock replied, wonder on his face, his manner slowly deflating.

"Which is why you've survived so long," interjected Russell. "Reggie, I'm for hauling the guy in."

"Well, I'm not," countered Reginald.

The drama at the table tensed, and Mandy stiffened along with it. As Russell waited, she realized that she was witnessing a game of wits. But what were the rules? Who was winning? How did she fit in?

"I understand what you feel, Ben." Reggie swept his cigar in a generous movement toward the unwelcome dinner guest. Then he pointed it at Russell's head. "When I was a young man," he continued, "I reacted like you, Ben. But now I think it's easier to pay the damn nuisance cost and forget it. Kind of like taxes."

"But he could go to the press!" interrupted Mandy, then she stilled, wishing she had not spoken. Her opinion wasn't important under the circumstances.

"No, he won't," replied Reginald. "Not unless we force him to. He doesn't want his name in the papers, either. It would cut off his income." The older man's eyes narrowed to stubborn slits. "I may be paying you off, Blalock, but I'm not thirty thousand dollars' worth of desperate. Ten thousand! Take it or leave it."

"I'll take it," Blalock choked without a second's pause.

Reggie slammed both palms flat on the table. "Agreed!" he barked.

"Be at the bank at nine o'clock in the morning," Russell instructed, amazingly quick to agree. But distaste curled the sensuality of his lips, and he aimed an index finger at Blalock's nose. The man flinched visibly. Slowly, a vague uncertainty began staining the round, shiny face.

He licked his lips. "At the *bank*?"

"Yes." Russell looked quite pleased. "We'll have it for you at the Swiss Mercantile. In twenty-dollar bills, unmarked. There'll be no problem."

Sweat glistened on the man's forehead. Russell, though he casually took his seat and draped his arm pleasantly around the back of Mandy's chair, watched Blalock flick the beads of moisture off with his fingers.

She saw the ruse then, and for a moment she pitied the fool. Russell was something of a confidence man himself—pretending to give the man what he wanted and removing it farther from his reach than ever. Mandy knew how he felt. And she knew also that Blalock would never walk into a bank equipped with cameras and alarms and pick up his blackmail money. In a grotesque way, it was all rather funny. And sad.

With his face flushing blood-red, the man realized he was an incompetent at his own scam. "Right," he gulped, nodding vigorously. "Nine o'clock. I'll be there. You just have it ready, you hear?"

Russell forced his face straight and nonchalantly replaced his hand upon Mandy's shoulder. "Sure, and let this be a lesson to you, Blalock. If it hadn't been for Mr. Patterson's understanding, you could have been in real trouble."

Opal coughed fastidiously into her napkin. As they watched the man weave his way out the entrance of the dining room without daring to look back, Mandy gave a sigh of relief.

That morning in John Dulick's office when Russell had strolled in so demandingly was laughable now. How young she had been then—nursing visions of herself as a successful literary personage waiting to be discovered. He had accused her of screwing up his life. Now she stared at the clean lines of his profile and thought it was a lie. He had screwed up *her* life, and she would give everything she owned to go back to the naïve days of wanting to be a renowned journalist.

Prepared to join in the witty remarks of congratulations, Mandy drew her gaze to their faces, her lips curved with the charm of a smile.

"I thought he was brilliant," she gestured toward Russell and smiled at Reggie. "You, too, Mr. Patterson." When their smiles did not respond, she glanced wonderingly. "What did I miss?"

Russell didn't look up when the waiter placed the fish before him. No one spoke until the wine had been poured, filling sparkling glasses. Awed by the eerie bleakness at the table, Mandy drew a continuous circle around the rim of her goblet. Without seeing Russell, she knew his face was turned toward her, that he was watching the curve of her cheek. And her fingers nervously smoothing her glass.

"I'm sorry, Opal," he said, and Mandy looked at him. Russell met her eyes without pretense of apology for the words which fell from his lips. "We won't put you through this anymore. We'll be married immediately. Tomorrow."

The words were spoken so easily. Mandy's head bowed because she could not believe how everything had happened. Somewhere she was alive; her breasts rose and fell beneath the crepe of her blouse. She could feel them rising and falling, and it didn't seem possible.

"Russ," Reggie began to object in a concerned fatherly voice.

Opal cut him off, and Mandy realized she had not said anything herself.

"It's best, Mr. Patterson," Opal told him. "I was really beginning to believe that this thing would run its course and no one would be hurt. But with the ransom and all the media exposure Amanda has gotten—people knowing so much, so much of our private lives available for anyone who cares to investigate—yes, I agree with Russell completely. At least we can all be spared that much embarrassment. It can all be undone quietly, when the time is right."

Strange things threatened inside Mandy's chest. The small pride she had just felt at Russell's swift logic now seemed ready to crush her. It wasn't fair that life should force all its disillusionment in the space of a few days.

"And now there's the book," Reggie considered thoughtfully.

"I'm writing it, Mr. Patterson." Mandy's head lifted, framing dangerous, glittering eyes which brimmed with tears. "And the *embarrassment* Opal mentioned," she continued, "was not all my doing."

"Oh, Amanda," Opal extended her hand. "I didn't mean to imply that—"

"I know what everyone meant!" Mandy bumped the table in her haste. White wine spread in a widening blot upon the cuff of her blouse. Mandy clutched her purse with trembling fingers and shot an unforgiving glare at Russell.

"If you will excuse me," she mumbled and traced the same path to the doorway as Blalock had, only a few minutes earlier. She guessed she did not feel any less defeated than he did.

Damn this entire affair! Mandy screamed in her mind. Love went only so far. She didn't have to lay herself down as a sacrificial offering for them. She had the right of pride!

Hitting the elevator button with her fist, she prayed that she could reach the suite before she began crying. "Fool!" she cursed herself. *"Don't you dare cry."*

As the doors opened, she whirled about, gaping at Russell as he covered the wide expanse of floor with determined strides. His features were angular with distress. When he took in the sight of her—so beautiful, even as anguish thinned her lips and drained her color—he hesitated.

Mandy slammed the button to the tenth floor with the ball of her hand and stood frozen as the doors groaned. Russell was less than ten feet away.

"Damn you!" she swore softly as the doors swished shut in his face.

When Russell returned to the table and glanced awkwardly at the faces of people who knew him far too well, he felt more exposed than he ever had in his life. Unwillingly, he battled with the sensation of being lost in an unknown land where thousands of roads all looked the same.

His past was composed of too few memories of open candor, of longings laid out to be scrutinized. Honest affection—that demonstrated caring, gentle touches and voiced love—rarely appeared in the large Gregory house in Hartford, Connecticut.

He loved his parents and his sister, and he appreciated all the advantages he had been given. But at the moment, he felt cheated. He needed someone to comfort him as if he were a boy and promise him that everything was going to be all right. There was no one who could do that, and he hated it!

Slumping down on his chair, Russell stared blindly at the cold fish shriveling on his plate. Finally he shoved it from his sight.

"She'll see things differently after she's had time to think," encouraged Opal, closing an optimistic hand about the lean fingers thrumming on the tablecloth. "It's by far the easiest way. I don't say that lightly, either."

Russell's smile was sad. "Not the easiest, Opal. That girl has enough pride for ten people, and I've trapped her."

"She's not a girl, my friend," Reggie corrected in a faraway voice. "Amanda Phillips is a woman. A beautiful, maturing woman. I figure she knows what she wants, whether you and I agree with it or not."

"Well, she sure as hell doesn't need anyone to help her get it." Russell's chest rose and fell with a deep, disheartened sigh. "God, how she despises me."

Opal shook her head. "No, she doesn't. Amanda cares deeply for you."

Russell questioned her bitterly. "Then why is she systematically destroying me?"

Running his fingers through the dark brown waves of his hair, Russell clapped a hand across the hard tense muscles in his neck. He could hardly believe the intimate question which came out of his mouth. He had never cried on anyone's shoulder, no matter how broad.

Opal again took his hand against his will and shook hard. "Don't shut yourself off from life any longer," she begged him. "You've done the work of more than one man all your life, Russell. Now, for the first time, you actually *need* someone. It isn't a weakness to need someone. Don't turn away from it. Let it happen."

Reggie shifted uncomfortably in his chair. "Opal," he frowned, "you can't advise him to shuck off his responsibilities that easily. This book of Amanda's—anything that lessens his ability to function—is a danger. Too many things depend on Russell."

"Do you know," Russell began in a vacant tone, wiping a hand across his face, "I really want her to write the damned book."

"That could ruin the work of many years," Reggie drawled.

"I'm nearly forty years old," the younger man replied. "I don't have to keep this job all my life."

Shaking his head in stunned disbelief, Reggie clucked to himself. "You surely can't be considering giving up a career just so one young woman can make a name for herself?"

"It might not come to that," argued Russell, the tone of his voice subduing the other man.

"It's risky," mumbled Reggie.

Russell stood, flipped over the check with cosmopolitan ease and slipped some bills from his wallet. When Reggie objected, Russell ignored him.

"I think you should tell Amanda the truth," Opal suggested.

Reaching to take a sip of his water before he left the table, Russell paused with his fingers curled about the stem of the goblet. "The truth?" he laughed and lifted the glass in a salute. "What truth? What makes you think she would believe anything I say at this point?"

"You forget I was with Amanda under terribly difficult circumstances." Opal smiled. "She's not a shallow woman. If you would tell her what you really feel, she could handle it. Tell her you love her."

For one brief second Russell's eyes flared with a blaze of resentment. Opal was practically like a mother, and his jaw still set with an irritable rigidity.

"Mandy would use the truth on me like a machete," he said finally and buttoned his suitcoat. "I'm sorry. I need to walk. I've got to think. I—"

He didn't finish. He only turned and walked loose-jointedly across the dining hall, his broad shoulders heavy with a problem he had never, in his entire life, dreamed he would carry.

"Look how people watch him," Opal remarked, her chin cupped in her hand. "You know," she added after Russell had been swallowed up by the hotel guests, "I suppose I love him as much as if he were my own son. His parents have never appreciated him as they should."

Reggie coughed with husky affection. "He really is hung up on that girl. I never thought I'd see the day Russell Gregory would actually be willing to turn his back on everything for a woman."

"He loves her, Reggie. What can the man do?"

Drawing back his gray head in disbelief, Reggie tilted it to the side. "Wanting to screw a woman, honeybabe, is much different than being in love with her."

Pursing her mouth at his crudeness, Opal disagreed. Her fingertip tapped knowingly on the back of his hand. "You can't bring it down to that level, Mr. Patterson. Those two need each other. I, for one, will do everything I can to open their eyes to that fact. Tell me, Reggie," she said, following him from the table and fitting her steps to his, "what is Russell beneath all that finesse and expertise? Since you know so much."

Oblivious after all this time that she was taller than he was,

Reginald chewed on an unlit cigar. "He's a man, honey," he said. "Russell is only a flesh-and-blood man who hurts when he's hit. And he's been hit, let me tell you that. Right in the heart, where it does the most damage."

Russell could not bear to go up to the suite just now. Too many emotions twisted inside him—emotions which he had never felt, which he knew existed yet vowed that he, the wizard of the banking world, would never be prey to. He was caught in the trap of a woman's honest blue eyes.

Wandering through the streets of Zurich, he was half-aware of its night life. He gazed up at the blinking lights of a jumbo jet as it traced its wide pattern to land and felt the evening chill on his face. In the west sprawled a chain of hills around Lake Zurich—high hills, rich and forested, yet enveloped in darkness they seemed as lonely as he was at this moment.

His shoes clicked on the sidewalk and became lost in the sound of other clicking heels. Music spilled from nightclubs and mingled with the laughter of strolling women as they clung to men's arms. Russell became another anonymous person, if only for the moment.

When he stumbled into the woman, he swore softly. He had not seen her at all, being so absorbed in his own misery.

"I'm sorry," he mumbled and was startled when her hand did not release the sleeve of his suit.

Looking first at her fingers with their long, glossy red nails and the smooth skin, Russell glanced at her face. She was quite young, as young as Mandy, he guessed. Yet age curved in the allure of her lips. They, too, were glossy red. Tossing back her head to swing auburn waves tumbling down a slender back, she laughed a throaty gurgle.

"Oh, I don't mind," she purred. Her tongue flicked over her lips. "I don't mind at all. Where're you going?"

Russell knew exactly what she was. He could even guess, almost to the dollar, what she would cost him. She wouldn't come cheap. One look at her shoes, at her jewelry, told him that. Her shoes were genuine, but her jewelry was not, though it was good. She had not bought it by working the streets.

"I'm not going anywhere in particular," he said, removing his arm from her grasp with an unoffensive movement.

Measuring him from the top of his stylish head to the flared cuffs of his trousers, she made a few quick mental calculations. She smiled, and Russell caught the intoxicating scent of perfume and good liquor. The total effect of her played havoc with his battered sensibilities, and he feared that it showed.

"We could have fun together," she breathed. "I know where we can go."

Assuming a silky grace that matched Russell's tall good looks, she fell into step beside him. Russell chuckled. He would not lie to himself and say that she didn't tempt him.

"I'm not having a good night," he said bluntly.

"I can make it better, darling," she promised, propositioning him with her eyes.

Russell met the look and smiled. "I'll bet you could," he replied, quirking a brow.

Stopping in the middle of the sidewalk, ignoring people who were forced to weave about them, the woman tilted up her pretty face beneath his.

"My name is Monique. I don't live far."

Russell glanced tiredly at the city about them—the ancient steeples, high-rise hotels, banks, life going on, Mandy up in the suite, hating him. He touched a bent knuckle to the center of the woman's lower lip.

"Thanks for the offer, doll. You're a beautiful girl. But no." He shook his head. "I guess you might say I'm spoken for."

Her lips turned downward in a fetching pout, and she turned her hands a fraction as if to ask what difference that made. "I would make it worth your while."

"I don't doubt it," he said with a laugh in his voice. "But not now."

After Monique traced the line of his jaw with a fingertip, she turned. Before Russell could say another word she slipped through passersby and disappeared. He felt as if something had drained from his body; he felt cold and alone.

One step came quickly after another, and he didn't know when he had flicked open the buttons on his suitjacket. Nor did he really realize when he began running. He simply came to himself and knew he was doing it—faster, down a dark side street, his shoes clipping briskly against the cement, his breath catching in hoarse, winded gasps. Still, he did not stop.

He ran on until his chest felt like it would burst. His clothes became drenched, and his eyes blurred. Arms churning, his heart pumping furiously, sweat streamed from his hair and down his waist.

Mandy. Mandy. Mandy. The persistent rhythm in his mind picked up his pace. When he slumped against the granite face of the hotel, he accepted the disapproving stare of the doorman with exhausted unconcern. The man held the door open, and Russell thought his legs would never make it to the elevator. Finally it shut him in, and Russell dropped his head forward against the wall.

Mandy had been such a girl when he had walked into John Dulick's office in New Orleans, he thought, gasping for each labored breath. He didn't know why he had zeroed in on her as he had. Her silly ruse on the plane had amused him; he liked her and enjoyed indulging her.

But Amanda had grown up. She had a splendid mind. Perhaps that was why he was so disturbed. Perhaps he could not stand the idea of being outdistanced by a woman.

But if she had been a girl, then he, after all these years, had still been a boy. He felt like a boy right now—exhausted, yet aware of a compelling drive pulsing through his body. It was unbelievable that just the curve of her cheek when she turned sometimes—soft, glowing and so innocent—could harden him until he was embarrassed at his own vulnerability.

She couldn't possibly guess the erotic fantasies she sent spinning through his head. At least he had done that well— hidden his love until Mandy thought he was a chauvinist who would lock her in a closet and refuse to let her use her talent.

Now he had backed her into a corner and suggested a marriage that would protect his friends. He was trying to play her exactly as he had played Blalock. And he was ashamed. Did he think that if he came right out and asked her to marry him she would say no? Probably. Definitely. She would say no. And who could really blame her? He hadn't exactly been Mr. Nice Guy through all of this. He had methodically seduced her, knowing exactly what he was doing. My God, why didn't he just offer her a million dollars to marry him? Once a man started behaving like a cad, why be squeamish?

Mandy was not asleep when Russell returned at midnight. The hours had dragged miserably. When the door whispered open and shut, she rolled onto her stomach on the divan and huddled beneath her blanket, pretending to be asleep. She listened to the shower in the bathroom, and to the silence, then to his soft footsteps as he walked through the living room as quietly as a cat burglar.

Instead of going to bed, Russell ran himself a glass of water in the kitchenette. He stood sipping it before the living-room window, much as he had done the night before. He remained still for so long that Mandy cautiously lifted her face from the pillow.

In the dim closeness of the room she could barely discern the dark outline of his height. A robe ended at his knees and his arms were loosely crossed in front of him. She tried to imagine what he was thinking about.

As if he felt her eyes drilling into his back, Russell took a breath and let it out in a long, slow sigh. His voice, when he spoke was low and edged with hoarseness.

"Are you asleep?"

At first she considered lying. "No."

"I'm—"

The silence was excruciating, and she imagined him figuring how long he had despised her for messing up his life.

"You're what?" she asked at last. Even if Russell hated her he was hurting, and she wanted to skim across the floor and wrap her arms about his waist and crush herself against his back.

"I'm sorry that I'm using you," he replied dully.

A quarrel was the last thing she wanted, yet she found herself saying, "Then don't do it!"

"Don't tell me what to do!" he raised his voice, spinning around. Mandy could not see the haggard lines of his features. "I do what I'm pushed into doing. Just as I've done ever since I've known you!"

Furious, Mandy flung herself off the sofa, her long pearl-gray peignoir sweeping against the carpet in a suggestive cloud he could discern despite the darkness. She was outraged that he could know what he was doing and still persist with it.

"Don't lie to me anymore!" she cried, as she drew before him. "You're not pushed into doing *anything*. I've seen you practically twist people around your finger. Just . . ." she thrust her hand outward, "don't pretend anymore."

They had grown accustomed to the dimness now. Extended high over the city, they were shut off in their own cubicle of turmoil. Eyes glittered and breaths fell unevenly.

"And what if I don't know what the truth is anymore?" he raged, moving so near he could have counted the lashes which blinked up at him.

Mandy answered with cold emphasis. "You know how guilty I feel about the 'Mrs. Hamilton' mess. You're offering to release me of that if I'll agree not to write the book. God only knows your real reason for demanding to marry me. *That's* the truth."

Russell's breath grew ragged. "Grow up, Amanda! How can you say such a thing?"

Raw now, much more than she had ever been with him, Mandy said what came to her mind. "Because I know you, Russell. I know men. You make us care, and you never give of yourselves. You never let us see what's really inside you, and then you use us. You said it yourself—you're using me. And that's called a relationship?" She laughed with bitter irony.

Russell was so angry that he stormed toward the wet bar. Remembering then, that there wasn't a drop of liquor in the place, he swore. Mandy did not turn. She pushed the sheer drapery aside and touched the coldness of the glass with trembling palms. Then she pressed them to her flaming cheeks.

His step, so quiet behind her, stiffened her whole body. The maleness of him worked on her—his scent of soap and cleanness, the knowledge that he was warm and strong, the virile life in his limbs which were so near she could touch them.

"Who hurt you, Mandy?" he asked softly, his breath caressing the back of her neck. "This can't all be because of me. Who hurt you?"

Mandy chewed at the tip of a fingernail. She had just accused him of keeping himself a secret, and yet she wanted to do the same thing.

"Everything," she began, then corrected herself. "No, a man. I was terribly young, and he turned out to be married. Nothing ever happened between us except that he . . . misrepresented everything. It was all so stupid."

Russell's hands took her shoulders, firm but not demanding. Slowly he turned her until her face was only inches below his. As if in a slow-motion dream, he fit a large hand to the back of her head, running his fingers deep into her curls, cradling her head. He made no attempt to draw her body to his.

"I'm sorry, Mandy. Those things hurt a long time."

She almost wished he didn't understand. She fit her cheek

into the nest of Russell's palm, moving her lips to brush his fingertips, kissing them with gentle, breathy caresses. And when she stopped, she felt him trembling.

When Russell had made love to her before, taking her virginity in a moment of fiery need, he had satisfied her powerful desire to give herself. But the womanly drive inside, the craving for completion, had never been sated. Fulfillment was a condition Mandy knew how to satisfy for herself. And she had often wondered if, in the end, it really mattered how it was reached.

Yet standing so near to his compelling male substance, she knew physical satisfaction did matter. One was a matter of mechanics; the other was a spiritual experience that she had never had. Demands awakened, and she flushed with warm, liquid yearnings. In a way she hated him, for these feeling would not subside. If she let them they would consume her.

Russell knew what she needed, as he seemed to know so many other things about her. And she could not bear for him to see her so exposed again, not when he gave so little of his own heart.

"Don't you ever need anyone, Russell?" she asked thickly. "Don't you have the same weaknesses as the rest of us?"

The room suddenly seemed too small, too full of erotic textures—the sensual roughness of the carpet beneath her bare feet, nylon moving upon her waist, her breasts beginning to throb against the sheerness which trapped them, the nubby lapels of his terrycloth robe which showed a deep slash of his chest, and dampness of hair curling about his ears.

"I have thought at times," he said, his low voice sounding remote, "that I would give everything I had to be able to just talk to a man without seeing fear in his eyes, that dread that I would somehow hurt him. I've laughed at men's jokes when I didn't want to, and talked about football and the weather. But if I had asked one of them what he thought about when he was alone, driving down the highway at night, he would have run from me."

The starkness of Russell's confession startled Mandy, and she closed her eyes in wonder at the loneliness which haunted him. With her cheek still resting against his palm, she opened to him.

"When I drive by myself," she said, "I wonder what people think about me. I wonder if I'll ever be able to make them like what I write. Sometimes I get scared that they only tolerate

me and gather in small groups behind my back and try to hide
their smiles so I won't know that I've failed."

Russell's stillness was such a contrast to his strength that
she stilled, also. She sensed him swallow, and sensed the
blinking of his eyes.

"I get afraid," Mandy finished in a whisper, wanting to
reveal everything now, "afraid that no one will care and that
I'll reach out and people will turn away and I'll look like a
fool."

She dropped her head then, and thought she could not bear
it if Russell said she should not feel that way. He had dropped
his hand from her head, but in her mind he still held her,
closer than a physical body was capable of holding. He did
not look at her when he spoke.

"I don't want to force you to do anything," he said
hoarsely, cutting through all her poorly erected defenses.

The steps she took away from him did not separate them
very much. She could not ever really separate herself from
Russell, Mandy thought.

"But you've forced me. You're forcing me now."

His nearness weakened her, when Russell stepped closer
behind her. She had heard of hearts that skipped a beat, and
hers did. She took a deep breath.

"Kiss me because I ask you to, then." His request was
gentle against her hair. "Kiss *me*. Then you can't say to
yourself, 'He forced me.'"

There seemed to be no place to run. Mandy spun about
because there was no choice but to face him. Her silence
seemed to splinter across the darkness in accusation.

"You push me into a meaningless marriage and have the
nerve to ask me that?"

"If I weren't pushing you into a meaningless marriage,
would you kiss me?"

Mandy had no sane reply for such a double-edged question.
As an unpremeditated measure of self-protection, she
stepped aside to the makeshift bed and jerked the blanket
free. She wrapped it about herself. He looked at the garb as
wryly as if she had encased herself in barbed wire.

"A typical move," Russell said, taunting her.

Never before had Mandy recognized the precise moment of
depression building up. Russell was playing some deadly
game that she wasn't familiar with. She was losing, and when
it was all over she'd hate herself.

"Are you afraid to kiss me?" Russell asked sharply. He appeared to see through everything—the blanket, the facade, the depression. "Are you afraid that if you say yes that I'll make you feel like a fool?"

Confronted with such honesty, Mandy walked away from him. Beneath the blanket, Mandy crushed her own breasts. She hurt for him. Before—in Mattenaugst—she had thought that she loved him. That had been a mistake. She was charmed with him, infatuated with him, caught up in a whirlwind of out-of-control passions for him. Giving herself had been an hypnotic response to his sexuality, though then she would have sworn it was more.

Now, she had lived through too much. She knew the man inside Russell Gregory—his insecurities, his failings, his tendency to manipulate people. And she loved everything about him, accepted all his faults. Any overture she made now, no matter how small, would be one of the intellect as well as one of the body. Those commitments would be permanent.

Russell was right. Mandy *was* afraid of offering that kind of love. Having an immature infatuation rejected would be devastating enough, but having her deepest emotions misinterpreted would kill her. Then, she really would be a fool.

How could she explain what she feared? Telling him would be more difficult than taking the physical step—the kiss. Who went first in exposing the inside of the human heart? Someone had to risk rejection. Was he suffering the same laceration of spirit? Was he waiting for her, as she was waiting for him?

Mandy felt his hands closing about her shoulders and shivered from the anticipation of being wounded. Immediately she sensed Russell's withdrawal, even though he did not remove his hands.

"What are you thinking?" he asked cautiously.

Mandy, turning, searched the depths of his brown eyes. But Russell was too careful. She could not find in him the same raw feelings she bore inside herself.

"What do you want of me?" she asked.

"Many things," he answered. His voice sounded as broken as hers. "But now I want to feel your mouth open under mine without having to seduce it from you. I want to feel you through that film of nothing you're wearing."

"Tomorrow we'll be married." Her words were toneless,

like a verdict, as if she wanted him to refute that it would happen.

Russell denied nothing. "Tomorrow is tomorrow. Get rid of the blanket."

"I can't be like you. I have to think of tomorrow."

"Get rid of the blanket," he softly repeated.

It was a test, not a moment of tantalizing seduction. A simple baring of the body before the baring of the soul.

Swirling the blanket from around her, holding it outstretched for a moment, Mandy dropped it in a heap upon the carpet. Her pulse quickened until it was hammering, and reasoning became increasingly difficult. Russell was so very near. She focused on the slow way he moistened his lips.

"Why is it so hard for you?" He was hoarse with mounting needs, and she thought what they were doing was cruel.

"You're wrong about getting married," she said. "Everything is wrong about it. I'm agreeing when I know it's wrong. I can't be any other way."

Russell shook his head. "A person can be any way he chooses."

Mandy's eyes fluttered shut. Her feet might as well have been sealed in cement, for all the strength she had to move. Will power began to evaporate dangerously; her body seemed to be sliding into a pit of warm velvet.

She whimpered. "How do you make me do things I don't believe in? It's so easy for you."

His voice shook. "Nothing is easy for me."

When she opened her eyes, the flush of restrained desire stained his cheeks. His lips were slightly parted, and the words Russell whispered were choked. She heard more with her heart than with her ears.

"Kiss me," he pleaded, and her feet were strangely mobile again.

Even as she stood before him, not touching but knowing he would hold her if she only showed him she wanted it, Mandy thought she could not bring herself to do it. It was so much more than a kiss. The spectrum of compromises was endless. Vividly aware of the current blistering her arms and legs, she lifted her face upward, despising her lack of self-restraint.

He bent, almost touching her mouth, and paused. Oh, God! she thought. Am I taking a step too far? Her arms—lifting, hesitating like fragile, uplifted wings of a butterfly—twined lightly about his neck. Finally, unable to bear the burning gaze of those eyes, Mandy reached on tiptoe for his parted mouth.

Russell went only as far as she did, brushing the moist lips with a feathery caress. Mandy reached again, gradually opening to him, gradually taking what she wanted, disbelieving that she really was, then ceasing to think at all.

"I'm weak right now," she managed to whisper into his mouth as it accepted hers. And as he touched the willingness of her tongue, he made a reply that was only a sound—lost in the staggering impact.

The contact was more devastating than lost virginity or the excitement of explored sexuality. She tried to explain everything by opening herself—her anxiety, her needs. And as they clung to each other, both of them so vulnerable, she wanted more. Much more. She yearned to take the risk, but she could not take it alone. Because Russell could not read her mind, only her urgency, he did not know what to offer her in return. He was only there. Waiting for what he hoped she would give him.

". . . too fast," she mumbled, yielding once again.

". . . if you listen, inside yourself . . ."

"I don't know, I don't know." She wanted to weep.

". . . trust. I won't hurt you."

They drifted endlessly. His hand slid hungrily down her body—touching her belly, moving lower, feeling so much through the sheerness that she made no gesture to remove it—yet nothing happened. Her trembling grew unbearable in his arms, and Russell crushed her to his strength until she stilled. He touched the warm lobe of her ear with the tip of his tongue.

"You want it," he whispered.

"Yes."

"Then take what you want."

Mandy knew she couldn't. She wasn't ready for such self-condemnation.

"I'd let you do it," she choked and felt scalding tears sliding down her cheeks. "I wouldn't blame you."

Shaking his head, Russell forced himself to lessen his hold on her. He was a big man, and he hurt terribly for her. This was not a moment of playful teasing; he understood that. Mandy was not flirting or being coy; she was wrestling with herself.

"I did that once," he said. "Not this time."

She could not believe it when he detached himself and walked away. The taste of his kiss lingered in her mouth, and her body ached for release from the tension of its arousal. Mandy's first impulse was to throw herself madly after him, to beg him to take her, even against her will, in spite of everything she had said. Tears of frustration streamed down her face. Russell had to know what he was doing to her!

With every obscene name she knew, she cursed him in her mind. Russell's door did not slam; it clicked softly, as if he scorned her feeble attempts to be a real woman. For several seconds, Mandy relished a true hatred for him. She wrenched the gown over her head. Standing naked and broken in the center of the room, she knew he would not come back.

Miserable then, and despising her own stubborn pride, Mandy jerked the blanket off the floor and fell headlong onto the divan. With her face buried in the cushion, her moaning muffling against it, she moved her hands between her legs and held tightly.

She could not stop the waves of draining climax—as if she were hurtling down some bottomless hole and could not prevent it. Head over heels she fell, over and over, until she couldn't feel anything. It was horrible and wonderful and terrifying at the same time. And when it was all over, she did not lift her face from the cushion.

Somewhere in the half-drugged limbo of approaching sleep, Mandy wondered, with delicious revenge, if Russell sought his own masculine relief of passion.

Chapter Fourteen

She had copped out. Mandy dragged herself to the shower. Standing beneath a jet of hot water seemed the perfect place to cleanse herself of the self-betrayals of the night before.

At least she could stop fooling herself. Today she'd marry Russell, for several different reasons that she could not begin to explain to herself. Today they'd create a legal union that would last . . . how long, three months? Six months?

Did she hope, somewhere in her confused thinking, that if she stayed with it, everything would miraculously fit into place in the end? Perhaps she was more deeply scarred from David Rutherman than she thought. Perhaps she could never bring herself to "reach out" again.

Dressing in a simple skirt and long-sleeved blouse, Mandy grimaced at her tired reflection and plodded to the kitchenette. She sloshed water into the coffeepot. The plug was stubborn, and she slammed it into the socket, pinching her finger. She welcomed the excuse to cry and tried not to hear the sounds coming from Russell's bedroom. He had awakened; the water was running. Soon he would walk through the door—the bridegroom.

Fishing through a bowl of fruit, Mandy selected an apple. She took down cups and saucers. As she bit an enormous piece out of the apple, she felt him behind her. Lifting bleak eyes, she found Russell slouching against the doorframe, frowning.

Slightly pale himself and apparently just as depressed, Russell had shaved and dressed in indecently tight denim pants with a soft, silky shirt unbuttoned halfway to his waist. The glances they exchanged were cursory, reflecting their reluctance to trust one another. Neither seemed to know where to begin. Mandy was thankful that her father would never know how she was compromising herself.

"You should let people know you're coming up behind them," she said stiffly, her mouth full of fruit.

Russell scowled and rubbed his temples, his eyelids still puffy. "I feel as if I've been beaten with a pipe."

Mandy swallowed. "I doubt that," she disagreed caustically, "since you've never been beaten with one."

The glare Russell shot her warned her to stop behaving like a child. Then he lazily allowed his gaze to soften, to roam over the slender curves as if her failure of the night before gave him the right.

Whirling, Mandy tossed her observations over her shoulder. "Your needs seem well under control this morning. I think I liked you better when you were battering away at my resistance."

"And you've replaced your battle armor, I see," he commented drily, rummaging in the fruit bowl. "It doesn't particularly become you—not a bride-to-be in less than twelve hours."

"You forget what you've so often reminded me of, Russell. As far as the world is concerned, I was blessed with that state weeks ago. The newness has worn off. The honeymoon is over!"

Russell's chuckle gave her the impression that, in spite of everything, he was pleased with himself. How very male! Here she was, hating herself, and he was happy at the prospects of getting a happy little housewife to the altar!

"If you want to fight," he suggested, his lips curving with irony, "we can find something more pertinent."

"I don't want to fight."

"Good." He smiled. "Let's pick up where we left off last night and go to bed and fool around."

Mandy challenged his teasing. "But I will if you keep that

up!" Then her voice dwindled. Her shoulders sagged. "Last night I . . ." she paused, "I . . . I know this sounds out-of-date to you, Russell, but I was raised to believe that a woman goes to bed with her husband. And that people get married because they . . . want to be married."

He selected an orange and began ripping off large chunks of peel. "Well," he drawled, a sleek section poised before his mouth, "you proved the first hypothesis to be incorrect several weeks ago. Today you'll disprove the second."

He popped the orange into his mouth and wiped his hands on a dish towel.

"Oh, Russell," she breathed with a weary shake of her head. "What a sorry human being you are." Mandy looked about, as if hoping for someone to agree with her. "I was indiscreet in Mattenaugst. I admit it."

He grinned. "But you commit your indiscretions with such a great deal of flair, my darling. At least in Mattenaugst you were honest."

Mandy found his levity in abominable taste. "Is that some sort of twisted compliment?"

Rubbing a lean finger over the edge of his mouth, Russell pondered. "Are you going ahead with Schaeffer and writing the book?" he questioned, all trace of joking gone.

"Yes," she replied as soberly.

"Then take it to mean anything you want it to."

Russell kicked out a chair, sat, laced his hands behind his head and leaned back. The injustice of the decisions he put before her made Mandy's hands tremble. An empty cup slipped from her fingers, shattering loudly. The broken pieces lay jaggedly about his feet.

Without a word, he knelt and she stooped, both their hands working to retrieve the slivers of porcelain. When he paused, still kneeling, Mandy slowly lifted her eyes to his.

"What's the matter, Mandy?" Russell asked, devouring her face with a gentleness that made her want to cry again.

"Everything."

"What's everything?"

She compressed her lips. "My father would never approve of what I'm going to do."

"You're a grown woman," he said, standing. "Some of the time."

Perhaps Mandy twisted his lightheartedness into arrogance. Whether she did or not, his words broke her down. He was so much more self-confident, so able to take responsibility for his own actions and then go on to something else. She had given this man her virginity; yet now they were so distinctly themselves—hopelessly separated. When she stood, her hands full of broken cup pieces, his height seemed to dwarf her more than ever.

After emptying the smashed dish in the wastebasket, Mandy sucked at a tiny spot of blood on her thumb. Grinning, Russell opened his palm to reveal his own wound. As if she were in a trance, she stood with her jaw slackened. Russell pulled her thumb from her mouth and placed it against his spot of blood.

"Now we're blood brothers," he said.

Returning his smile somehow seemed like a weakness, considering the seriousness of their circumstances. Mandy wet her lips, trying to prevent them from turning up. She wasn't entirely successful.

"Dracula, if you prefer," Russell laughed, taking her thumb into his mouth, sucking it. Then the tip of his tongue drew a slow line from her thumb to her wrist. Mandy's smile faded. Scalding heat swept up her throat and into her cheeks. A familiar tension feathered through her.

"You're under my spell, fair maiden." He imitated Bela Lugosi. "But then, Dracula preferred the throat, didn't he?"

With a wolfish growl Russell grabbed her, snapping her head back and gently burying his teeth into the delicious curve of her neck. Mandy, in her attempt to twist out of his grasp, shivered, and slumped against his length. The sound of her own soft moans horrified her. Already she was succumbing, she thought in panic. Her fingernails dug deeply into the biceps trapping her.

"Russell, please!" she choked.

"Aren't you under my power yet?" He held her in the loose curve of his arm and laughed down at Mandy in pretended amazement.

She pushed at his chest to free herself and nervously smoothed her hair. Her forced smile was a failure, for she had thought her self-loyalty would last more than ten minutes.

"Obviously I'm under your power, since I'm thinking about marrying you today."

The doubting ring of her words broke the magic spell.

Russell was silent as she poured two cups of black coffee. Shaken more than they would admit, they both sipped in preoccupied withdrawal. When she couldn't bear the intimidating quiet any longer, Mandy opened her mouth to make any irrelevant remark. Russell interrupted.

"You're not considering being difficult at this late hour, are you, Mandy? I thought that was all settled last night."

Why couldn't he have said "I love you, Mandy. I want this to be a real marriage"?

"Yes, I'm considering being difficult! You know exactly why we're going through with this. Can't we please sit down, like calm adults, and figure out a better solution?"

"You're not capable of being calm!" he lashed back. Regretting his hastiness, Russell wiped his mouth with the back of his hand. For a few minutes he sat, as if he were contemplating her point, but she knew he wasn't.

"No," he said. "You know there is no better solution."

Lacing her fingers like a judge about to deliver a verdict, Mandy presented her case.

"Look, Russell," she began sedately, "The police have already finished with me. You tricked that vile little man into keeping his mouth shut."

Russell anticipated her. "If you didn't insist on staying here until Jules and Theo are extradicted from Schauffhausen to Zurich, we might make it."

Though the set of Russell's mouth revealed no stubbornness, his fingers drummed on the table. Mandy glared at them.

"I need to interview them and their attorneys. You know that. The book depends on it."

"If you're staying in Zurich," he said, not the least affected, "I think we should do exactly what we said we would."

"*You* think? *You* think? What about what *I* think?" She made her voice low and intense. "And what if I refuse?"

Locking his brown eyes with her blue ones, Russell made her feel as if he had closed torturing fingers over her skull. He spoke his words with the carefulness of an ecclesiastic. "You have too much honor to harm innocent people."

Unable to begin all over again, to bear his mastery in such an important decision, Mandy shoved away from the table, jarring coffee from the cups. Storming from the kitchenette, she snatched open the living room draperies, flooding the room with sunshine. He was being unbelievably dominating, just because he chose to.

It was a simple power struggle. Last night had been a power struggle. Even the night they had slept together had been one. And yes, their kisses often were. If she trusted him, if she confessed that she really loved him, he would look at her with an expression which would say "I'm so sorry, Mandy."

When Russell's large hands closed about her shoulders, Mandy stiffened. "Don't touch me," she said tightly. "I can't take it."

"There have been times when I couldn't touch you enough," he murmured, bending his lips to the back of her neck.

She could have clung to him; she could have touched his face and drowned in his eyes. But he was making her choose—between him and the book—like being forced to answer, "Whom do you love most; your husband or your child?"

Jerking herself free, Mandy placed them apart by several yards and an interminable length of misunderstanding. His oath was pointed and quite audible.

"If I give you an inch, woman, you take a mile. You use my name, you eat my food, you accept the clothes I buy you, and you have slept in my bed!" His voice became insulting. "Well, my dear Amanda, in anyone's mind that constitutes consummation."

"You're very cruel."

He laughed. "I'm laid back, darling. If you leave me, I'll sue you for a six-million-dollar settlement for breach of contract."

Under her breath, as she swept from the room, Mandy called him an extremely ugly name.

"What did you say?" he called.

His laughter was unnatural, even for him. He was forcing himself to play another of his roles, and she hated when he did that.

"I said," she whirled to face him, practically shouting at him, "aren't you lucky, Russell? Instant wife, for as long as it's convenient for you. Everything's working out so nicely for you!"

His face darkened with anger. Mandy lowered helpless hands to her sides. Her fists balled tightly.

"Get dressed, Amanda," he ordered quietly.

When Russell was angry at her, her whole being slipped out of focus. It threw her into a limbo where she wasn't doing anything or going anywhere. Concentrating with a quarrel hanging between them was almost impossible. She was tempted to apologize, to take the blame upon herself even though she didn't believe she was wrong. He would not apologize, though, so why should she?

Mandy threw open the closet with a thundering crash. It seemed ironic that she should be married in a three-piece suit that Carolyn had selected. An expertly made suit, it probably cost a fortune, yet she tossed it to the bed as if it were a rag. She gathered everything she needed and stamped into the bathroom, leaving the bedroom for him.

The simple collar of the oxford blouse, especially with her hair short, made the column of her neck long and slender—a look she usually enjoyed. But it didn't seem to matter. However, she did take extra care with her hair.

Everything, from her bone strap sandals to her tiny pearl earrings, depressed her. She finished dressing far too soon. Afterward, she wandered about the living room restlessly, fearing to knock on Russell's door lest she become the target of his temper again.

Mandy browsed through her notes for the book, not meaning to become absorbed in it. But her pencil flew, changing large chunks of narrative into chapters, labeling the events to be included in each, jotting down remembered dialogue. Thirty minutes had passed completely unnoticed.

When Russell entered the room and she snapped up her head, he was wearing a black suit. The crisp gray shirt was austerely correct. Mandy could not remember ever knowing a man so good-looking that just the sight of him stirred her.

Russell's suntan could not disguise his paleness. And his hair, thickly waved, was brushed casually, curling low on his collar. Mandy could have touched the sensuality curving his mouth and say she wanted things to be peaceful between them.

"You look very nice, Russell," she said instead, with a discreet cough.

Masculine approval teased about the edges of his eyes, and

it gave her a tiny pang of pleasure. "So do you, ma'am," he drawled.

Mandy didn't thank him. She would even have turned her back, except for the knock on the outer door. His dark brows drew together as he wondered who it was. He strode across the living room and swept open the door. The sight of Carolyn with her son sent an icy shiver through Mandy.

"Oh, I'm sorry," Carolyn said, glancing at one, then the other. "Am I interrupting?"

She was wearing extremely tight jeans and a cotton knit shirt. Mandy's eyes narrowed as she saw, even from her side view, the fleeting inspection Russell gave Carolyn. How could he, when he was getting married in less than two hours? Mandy could have slapped his face.

"Not at all," Russell replied as he drew them inside and shut the door. "Come in."

"You were going somewhere."

"Nowhere important," he said absently, and Mandy clenched her jaw.

Now, she thought, she must assume a smiling mask and pretend she was not about to go to pieces. With a peculiar loneliness, she watched Russell drop to one knee and draw Mickey before him for a serious inspection.

He grinned at the boy. "You grew at least an inch last night. Let me feel that muscle."

Mickey proudly drew himself taller, his thin freckled face breaking into a gleeful smile. With an air of importance, he pushed up his sleeve and flexed his biceps vainly.

"I'm tall enough to reach Mamma's cabinet without a chair," he bragged, watching Russell's face intently for the slightest sign of affection.

"I'll bet you are."

Russell, with rarely witnessed indulgence, gave the boy a playful slap on the behind. And, gesturing for Carolyn to find a chair, drew Mickey towards Mandy.

"There's someone you've never met, Mickey," he said. "But she's heard a lot about you."

"Mamma told me you got married." Mickey looked up at Russell with an expression combining wonder and disappointment. Sympathy crinkling his eyes, Russell brushed Mickey's cheek with a hard knuckle.

"Yes. Isn't she pretty?"

Mickey's somber hazel eyes appraised Mandy. Stifling an

impulse to run her fingers through the gleaming red hair, Mandy smiled down at him. She found herself fearing that he wouldn't like her and would twist his head away in the tactless rejection children could inflict.

"My name's Amanda, Mickey," she said without looking at Carolyn. "But my friends call me Mandy."

"Oh," he said. After a long pause, he curled his mouth in a half-grin. "Did you know I have a new setter at home, Russell? She's red. She likes me. We go sailing together. She sits at the bow and sniffs the wind."

Mickey screwed his face into the imitation of a dog and sniffed loudly. Then he turned an unsettling gaze upon Mandy. "Do you have a dog?" he asked. Mandy got the distinct impression she was being evaluated.

"I'm afraid not, Mickey," she said.

"I have three." He frowned. "Don't you have a gerbil or anything?"

She shook her head. He ignored her then, and gave his attention to Russell.

"Mamma's teaching me to work the jib," he announced, walking to stand importantly by Russell's side.

Russell led him to the divan to sit beside his mother, and as they leaned back, conversing in low man-to-man tones, Mandy felt excluded. Over their heads, Carolyn met her eyes.

As much as Mandy hated to admit it, Carolyn Wrather was truly a stunning woman. Mandy shrank into insignificance beside her. Today her auburn hair was brushed until it gleamed like burnished copper. Everything about her was sexy—her hands, her height, the way she tilted her head.

"Don't try to take Russell," her look telegraphed. "Get out of his life and leave him alone."

Stiffly, almost hostilely, they smiled at each other. Wanting to leave the room and not daring to call attention to her discomposure, Mandy pretended to rummage in her handbag for a tissue.

The bonds between Carolyn and Mickey and Russell were years older than anything she and Russell shared. Jealousy made her skin crawl. Mandy wanted to say Russell belonged to her, to tell Carolyn to keep *her* hands off. But the fact was, Russell wasn't Mandy's. Carolyn was as incredibly attuned to that as if she were psychic.

"When are you going back to the States, Russell?" Carolyn inquired intimately, arranging her arm gracefully over the back of the divan, purposely exposing the thrust of her breasts.

He shrugged and turned his mouth down in a curve. "Three days. Two, perhaps. Are you going back with Reggie and Opal?"

The glance Mandy received from Carolyn warned her never to disregard Carolyn's influence in Russell's life. "No. I thought Mickey and I might stay a bit longer. Mickey hasn't seen you in so long. Could you squeeze in a few hours for him one day?"

Russell tousled Mickey's hair and the boy giggled, tucking his small chin against his chest.

"Of course I can. But I'm afraid you'll have to excuse us right now, Carolyn. Mandy and I are driving out to the country with Reggie. I'll give you a call this evening."

Mandy stood by the windows, watched Russell walk Carolyn to the door, and saw her link an arm through his. The manner in which he stooped to retuck Mickey's shirt into his pants wrenched Mandy's heart. Russell was so damnably wonderful at times!

Mandy had the wildest desire to yell at Carolyn: "He's mine! We'll be married today. If he needs children, I'll give them to him. I'll take his suits to the cleaners and put his shaving things away. Leave him alone!"

But, of course, she only said how nice it was to see Carolyn again.

The opened door drew Mickey's attention as if it were a barricade about to shut him off from the man he adored. Impulsively Russell swung the boy into his arms, hugging Mickey closely. Small thin arms wound about Russell's neck, placing the unhappy face directly before Mandy's own. The little mouth twisted in frustrated bravery, and he squeezed his eyes to force back the tears.

"It's okay, Mick," murmured Russell. He turned the tear-stained face around to his and blotted at the wet cheeks with remarkable tenderness. "The next time I go to visit Mother and Dad, I'll have you up. You can ride the horses and everything. How about that?"

Mickey snuffled. "All right," he said and hugged Russell's neck one more time.

Unable to watch the scene any longer, Mandy turned toward the windows as he shut the door. A guilt she did not comprehend seemed to be bursting her lungs. Somehow, in her ignorance, she had stolen something from the child.

Though no one said so, Mandy had the feeling Opal had been the one to locate a clergyman and made the preliminary arrangements for the marriage ceremony. Then she had probably crossed her fingers that the entire ordeal would not burst into flames. Mandy and Russell arrived at a small village outside of Zurich at precisely one o'clock.

The aging seventeenth-century cathedral was gray, and almost entirely covered with ivy. Its solemn history was written in added wings and repaired arches, in half-broken relics of the Reformation. Doves sunned themselves in peaceful disregard of Mandy's nervousness. The external serenity of the building itself cast a long shadow over the wedding. It chafed Mandy bitterly.

Reggie's and Opal's gravity, as they walked silently beside them, was nothing compared to Russell Gregory's stiffness. The sidewalk was narrow and wound between pungent, low-hanging firs as it led to the rank of offices at the eastern wing. The gardens were formal, revealing more care and planning than Mandy's own marriage ceremony.

Pausing, she took one last look at the Albishorn thrusting over three thousand feet into the sky. A beautiful lie, she thought; she should not be in such a splendid place.

"I dread this," Opal murmured.

Mandy wanted to scream, "Then why did you approve of it?"

Reggie consoled his wife. "One does the best one can." The look he gave Mandy was one of pity, and she got the impression that if Reggie had had his way, he would have taken his chances with a scandal.

"I mean," persisted Opal, "I want this done decently. Even if it is . . . well, you know, for appearances." She gave Mandy's hand an optimistic pat. "Who knows, my dear? Good things have come of much worse beginnings."

Mandy, knowing that Opal was quite aware of her love for Russell, almost spoke her mind. Opal, realizing her tactless blunder, apologized. "I didn't mean to be so thoughtless, dear."

"Russell," Reginald interrupted, "I hate to bring up mundane matters, but I need you at the bank this afternoon.

Belgium's considering a merger on that computer project. I'm sorry."

Russell, his mask well in place, revealed no emotion one way or another. "Sure, Reg."

The oak door beyond them, tucked into an arbor, swung open. A sandy-haired man with a clerical collar cutting into his neck stepped out, looked at the possible omen of clouds gathering overhead, and waved them inside.

"You're Mr. . . ." he paused to consult a card from his pocket, "Gregory?"

Russell inclined his dark head.

"Everything is ready," the cleric assured them in a thin tenor voice. "This must be the future Mrs. Gregory."

The smile he beamed at Mandy was completely free of any preconceived opinions. If he connected her to the woman who had been held for a three-million-dollar ransom, he was discreet. Mandy accepted his handshake generously. His wide gesture lead them into a short gallery lined with stained-glass windows. This would be, she predicted, a quick and relatively painless procedure.

And it was, almost. A man in a business suit, appeared seemingly from nowhere and opened a large carved door to a small chapel with only four pews lining each wall. The altar was a beautifully simple affair, lighted by ceiling floodlights bathing everything else in a soft glow.

As if he were used to hurried marriages, the clergyman stepped to a small table without preamble, gathered his books and some notes on a scrap of blue paper, and positioned the bride and groom before the kneeling rail. Mandy's distracted thoughts whirled in misery.

The tall disheartening form of her husband towered beside her. Russell did not look at her. She knew he hated it. And before this was all straightened out, he would wind up hating her, too. When they were told to clasp hands, Mandy was amazed at the dry warmth of his because hers were so cold. She haltingly repeated what was told her, wondering what her mother had felt when she had married Preston Phillips. Suddenly Mandy realized how unfeeling she had been. Never once had she thought to ask Felice about the details of her second marriage.

Mandy was jerked back to the present as Russell slipped a ring on her finger—an expensive but unelaborate gold band.

He looked down at her, but she could not force her eyes upward, staring dumbly at her shaking hand.

They were legally married! After all this! Russell's kiss was as impersonal as bumping a stranger on a subway or touching hands over a cash register. Oh, God, how had it ended so badly?

Wanting to scream, to run, to grab the clergyman and confess that the whole deed was fraudulent, Mandy walked solemnly beside her new husband toward the limousine. Surprisingly, Russell said good-bye to the Pattersons in a strained voice and politely accepted their mumbled congratulations.

Mandy shivered. The air was much cooler now; it was about to rain. Catching her sleeve, for she kept her head bowed low, refusing to look either right or left, Russell steered her toward a low-slung black Lamborghini. When he unlocked the door on her side with sophisticated ease, she finally lifted her head.

His mouth was hard and barely able to hide its contempt. He waved a hand toward the plush interior.

"Where did this come from?" Mandy asked incredulously. Then sarcasm tightened her words. "Is this yours, too?"

For the first time since they had repeated their vows, Mandy searched his face. Deep lines accentuated its leanness. Dark eyes were veiled behind drooping lashes, and she could not begin to guess his thoughts. When Russell pushed her down onto the seat, Mandy leaned her head back against the marvelous luxury and closed her eyes.

"I had it driven over," he said as he climbed in on the driver's side. "Yes, it's mine. We've got to talk."

Flaring wide, her eyes glittered a brilliant blue. "It's a little late for talk, Russell."

"It's never too late for talk."

His door shut with an emphatic click. With a flick of his wrist, he brought the powerful engine snarling to life. As usual, his manner was level, in control, but Russell was not the slightest bit amused with his facade now. Apprehension chilled her as she studied the thrust of his jaw. He backed the car skillfully, and his brows knitted with concentration as he swung it smoothly onto the highway.

"Where are we going?" Her voice was shrill.

The first raindrops splattered in broken stars against the

windshield. Russell turned on the wipers. "I'm hungry," he announced flatly.

When Russell wanted to be—even now when brooding, almost sullen—he was irresistibly magnetic. His work—the power it involved—had lent him, over the years, a certain mystery which women found intriguing. Even men admired and respected it. As she hid behind the furled curtain of her lashes, listening to the seductive rhythm of the windshield wipers, Mandy realized that if this marriage were a real one she would be hard pressed to keep Russell from the talons of designing women.

Once she had also been in awe of Russell's brilliance, his charms. But now? Now she had lived with him. Even if a certain part of her was still charmed, she saw too many of his faults along with his strong points. Now she was not mystified; now she only loved him.

He drove too fast. Sinewy brown fingers circled the leather-wrapped steering wheel. Russell was absorbed in negotiating the curves of the Swiss road, consoling himself, Mandy figured, for her uncomplimentary reservation during the ceremony. His hands held enough power to kill them both.

"You didn't pick the most opportune time to pout," he broke the silence abruptly.

Her reply was as caustic. She refused to look at him. "I was not pouting," she said through her teeth. "I was trying to convince myself that I should not be struck dead for what I was doing."

"There's a strong streak of Garbo in you, Amanda."

Mandy threw her eyes to the plush roof of the car. "I don't think I was the only one taking a guilt trip."

His jaw knotted angrily. A sudden twist of his fingers sent rock music bursting loudly through the multiple speakers surrounding them. The kilometers sped by beneath the engine's might. Russell still gave no indication where they were going. He began to frighten her.

As he took a hill recklessly, whipping past another car in their lane with what seemed like only inches to spare, Mandy stifled a scream. The tires screeched against the pavement, and she gripped the door handle until her knuckles whitened. Shutting her eyes, she grew aware of the sweaty warmth of the handle under her palm.

Hunching down beside the door, horrified at this side of Russell, she prayed he would not kill them both. When he finally glanced at her, recognizing her terror, he gently touched the brake. As the car slowed to a tolerable speed, Mandy slowly opened her eyes. He did not apologize or attempt to soothe her.

"I'll be ready to leave Zurich in three days," he offered after a moment, lowering the volume on the radio.

"That's good," she replied edgily.

"I want to take you to upstate New York to visit my parents."

"Russell—"

"Will you be finished with Theo and Jules or not?"

Mandy sighed dismally. "I'll try to make a point of it."

For the first time in hours, as if he had won some victory, Russell smiled. Loosening his tie, he tossed it over his head into the back seat. He grimaced against his collar and twisted it open. As he shrugged one arm out of his suit coat then, unable to keep the wheel steady, Mandy moved to help him. She tugged the jacket free of his arm, unnervingly aware of her hands upon his shoulders.

Thankful for something to do to keep from looking at the angles of his jaw and the smooth roundness of his Adam's apple, she turned the jacket wrong-side-out and placed it on the back seat.

As she leaned over to lift his tie from the floorboard where he had tossed it, she gasped as a large hand slid beneath her skirt, up the back of her leg to shape about the fullness of one hip.

Every minute of the last twenty-four hours should have sent her spinning around in a flurry of fighting hands and wrenched-down skirt. Instead Mandy knelt, almost incapable of moving, half-up, half-down, and stared with wide eyes at the sheets of rain pelting against the rear window.

She couldn't groan! she swore to herself as his fingers skillfully traveled over the sheen of her pantyhose, up to the low bones of her spine, retracing the contours of her backside by careful, exploring degrees. He could have been searching through her body for the center of her thoughts. She could not function when he touched her like that.

"Please don't!" Mandy said, and balanced her forehead upon the velour seat back. "Please don't."

Russell did not remove his hand. "Why?"

"I don't know, and that's why I want you to stop."

The honesty which strangled her words apparently touched

him. Russell removed his hand and did not look at her when she crept back into a sitting position. She smoothed down her skirt. Her hands were trembling. She threaded them tightly and waited for the inevitable argument.

"Is a divorce what you want?" he asked abruptly, betraying his calm exterior by chewing at the inside of his cheek. "After this is all over, do you want a divorce?"

"I—" A divorce was the last thing she wanted. "Do you want one?" she demanded.

"I don't want to be at the mercy of your feminine wiles, Amanda."

She groped for her handbag between the seats. "You're never at the mercy of anything, Russell."

He shot her an angry glance. "What do you think I'm made of?"

Mandy glared back at him as angrily. "Iron!"

He swore, and she leaned her face against her window. Heaven was crying for her, she thought.

"I asked you a question," Russell said, his voice level once again. "Answer it."

"Yes, yes!" she practically shouted. "I want a divorce! What do you think I am? A masochist?"

And as her mouth spoke the words, she stared at the monotonous sweep of the wiper blades and silently screamed, No! No, I don't want it. Please realize I'm lying!

"You're a fool if you think I'll give you a divorce," Russell muttered.

The brakes grabbed, and Russell swerved the car, skidding into the gravel of the shoulder. The engine whined down to a rich purr. Behind them a horn blared loudly and passed, fading swiftly into the distance.

His arms closed about Mandy so tightly that her resistance forced her head backward. Heavy with emotion, his oath growled against the rigid arch of her throat. Yielding limply to his resilience, she waited, almost counting the interminable stretch of seconds until he took the kiss he desired. She wanted him to take it—frantically. When Russell paused the space of a breath, wonder filled her face.

Her eyes fluttered open. "Well, go ahead," she said, dazed, confused.

"Go ahead and what?" The faint outline of mockery drew one side of his mouth in a lopsided smirk.

Fighting up through the traitorous heat, Mandy realized

immediately that she was trapped in some kind of subtle contest. She wriggled. He refused to release her and laughed softly—handsome, sensual, taunting.

"Kiss you, Mrs. Gregory?" he said, pausing for several seconds as if savoring it. "I would like to. I'd like to kiss you and make love to you like any other husband would his wife."

She frowned. "What are you hinting at? Marital privileges."

"Marital privileges?" His laughter rumbled deep in his chest. "Nobody says 'marital privileges' anymore."

Leaning as far away as possible, Mandy eyed him sternly. "Explain it to me then."

"What's the use of explaining anything? You'll dissect it with that journalist's brain of yours, and ask yourself, 'What kind of a game is he playing? Is he trying to trick me like David did? Is he trying to hurt me?'"

His words hurt. "David has nothing to do with us."

"David has everything to do with us!" Russell struggled to control his voice.

Mandy listened to him breathe, listened to the rain, the car, the turmoil ringing in her ears. "I don't even know what being married is," she finally admitted. "It all seems like a mistake. It's not even real."

"It probably feels unreal when you've planned to do it for years," he said, casting a vacant stare toward the rain. "There aren't any guarantees in marriage—replacement of defective parts for ninety days."

"A person needs time," she insisted.

"You don't know what time is." Russell shifted his body away from her. Absently, he adjusted a knob on the dash. "When you're thirty-nine, then you'll know what time is."

For a moment, Mandy studied the bigness of him, the power so carefully hidden beneath his proper black suit. "You planned this, didn't you?" she accused over the purr of the engine. "The wedding, breaking me down, everything."

"I didn't plan anything!" he clipped out the words. "But since it has happened, I think we should be sensible about it."

Mandy's eyes cut sharply to the side. She laughed. "Sensible!"

For the seconds that he faced her, he was vexed. Gradually his features softened until he smiled. "You've got the hots for me clear down to the marrow of your bones. It's only a matter of time until you do something about it."

"Oh!" she cried, jerking her face away. "You're disgusting, Russell! Crude and vulgar and—"

"Accurate," he supplied.

"No, not accurate. *Not accurate.* You're wrong!" She began adjusting her clothes in an overcareful, almost desperate way. "Don't ever again accuse me of playing games!" she flung at him.

Swinging himself about, fitting his long legs beneath the dashboard, Russell waited for a moment with his hand resting upon the gearshift. The silence became swallowed up in the rain. Outside a peal of thunder grumbled across the sky.

"Marriage," he said softly, his eyes fastened on some distant place—the future perhaps, or the past. "Marriage is enjoying something only because she is there to laugh with you. Or fight with you. It's knowing that you're alive with someone else, being able to reach out and touch in the dark or say things across a room with your eyes that only she can understand. It's not being able to rest until she has sympathized. It's being afraid to lose her or fearing that she'll die and your life will be over."

Mandy stared at his hand opening and closing about the stickshift. She touched it, timidly covering her small one over the brown hardness. His smile, when he turned it to her, held no frustration.

"You make me so mad sometimes I could break your neck," he said pleasantly.

"I know."

Mandy blinked rapidly. Now was the time to say the words . . . I love you. She tried. She wanted so badly to shape her mouth about them. He was right; David was very much involved here. She had once said the words to David, and he had hurt her. She couldn't bring herself to say them again. The moment was gone.

Giving her a fond pat, Russell sighed, as if he had read her thoughts. He pulled onto the highway then, and she leaned back in the seat, hating herself. Deep inside she was a coward. She was afraid to give that much. And she had been needing to face that for a very long time.

Chapter Fifteen

Both attempts to interview Jules and Theo were disastrous failures. By the time Mandy finally got through the red tape of the Swiss law-enforcement system, she was so jumpy that she could do little more than sit opposite the kidnappers and try not to shiver. Jules leaned across the partition separating them and yelled that she was a bitch. Theo leered at her with wild eyes, as if she had been unfair to hit him in the back of the head. He didn't bother to swear.

Both attorneys did their best to fill in gaps of background. And with their meticulous answers a voice in her head filtered through everything: *It has happened. Russell has grown distant. You have refused him once too often. He has hardly spoken a dozen words in two days. He will never want you again. You did it to yourself.*

So Mandy asked the wrong questions of the lawyers and had to contradict herself. The well-educated men in their business suits and classic ties looked at her as if she were unbalanced. She felt unbalanced. What the hell! Mandy thought; she *was* unbalanced. She could not put Russell Gregory out of her mind!

The prospect of writing a book was losing its challenge. Now it seemed a monumental task that would be of little value to anyone once it was completed. Slowly, after organizing the notes she had, she began some typing. For two nights Russell had been out until very late, and Mandy had brooded at the typewriter until past midnight. Presently, however, her outline and roughed chapters began to assume the appearance of a legitimate manuscript instead of a collage of unfinished sentences and isolated ramblings.

Russell's withdrawal was so marked that she was tempted at one point to see if he actually went to the bank or not. The Swiss Mercantile was busily engaged in switching to a new computer system. Or so he said.

Sikes Dalton, the computer expert who had tapped into the common communications system, proved to be a college student with a gift for electronics. For the entire morning, at Russell's request, she had been allowed to talk to Mr. Dalton. He described his "unauthorized penetration" of the computer terminal in technical detail.

By the end of the day, after spending the afternoon in the library researching statistics on computer thefts, Mandy stepped out of her cab at five o'clock—tired and discouraged. She wanted to blame Russell's opposition to the book as the reason why it was beginning to be so difficult. But that would paint her to be more dependent upon him than ever. Russell Gregory! Should she try to talk to him? Should she tell him she knew what he was trying to do by switching himself out of her life?

Let well enough alone, Mandy cautioned herself. After today, tomorrow perhaps, she would be returning to New Orleans, anyway. Out of sight, out of mind, as they said.

Her resolutions were firm when she tossed her new attaché case on the divan in the suite. These three days would end; her marriage would end; her misery would, in time, end.

Her feet were tired, and she kicked off her shoes. Placing the lightweight jacket of her summer suit over the back of a chair, she stepped eagerly toward Russell's bedroom. While he was gone she would indulge herself with a hot soak in the bathtub.

"I'm sorry!" she gasped, grabbing at the door frame to steady herself. At first she started to inch backward, but her gaze collided with Russell's.

He was stretched on the floor doing sit-ups, wearing the scantiest brief Mandy had ever seen. He could hardly have been more naked if he had discarded it altogether. And he had obviously been working on his tan during the afternoon, for the enticing scent of suntan lotion drifted through the room. His legs were richly bronze. A faint pink highlighted the chiseled planes of his cheekbones.

"Hello," he puffed between bends. "Didn't expect you back so early."

With his hands clasped behind his head, all his muscles were pulled into prominence. Mandy felt the burn of her cheeks flooding embarrassingly down the sides of her neck.

"Ah . . ." she searched for an excuse to leave, feeling like an afflicted child.

Russell stood and grabbed for the towel tossed across the foot of his bed. When he began rubbing himself down, Mandy was no more successful in wresting her stare from the tight leanness of his buttocks than she had been in leaving the room.

"I didn't know you were here, either," she mumbled. "I mean, I was going to take a hot bath. Or something."

"Be my guest," he returned with the most maddening grace she had ever seen him assume.

Facing her without the slightest hesitation, unable to miss her ridiculous attempts to avoid looking at the swell of his crotch, Russell smiled. She returned the smile stiffly, glanced about the room at his clothes draped casually over a hassock, and caught a quick breath. Then she laced her fingers so they would stop shaking, and smiled again.

"Was there anything else?" Russell inquired pleasantly.

"No! Oh, no!" she amended hurriedly. "Well! I think I'll just, uh . . . I believe I forgot to check the mail on my way up. If you'll—" Mandy backed into the door frame with a painful thump. "Oh, Lord," she breathed, horrified that she was being so obvious. *Why couldn't she stop blushing?*

Mandy could not remember with any degree of accuracy how she managed to stumble out of the room. For thirty minutes afterward, she sat in the coffee shop and tried to understand what had happened to her. She ran the gamut of emotions—from horror to panic to annoyance to anger. When she finally returned to the tenth floor, entering the suite with much more caution than before, Russell had gone again.

She did not take a bath. She hardly removed her clothes.

She could not concentrate on anything. Skipping dinner altogether, she went to bed early and tossed until one o'clock. Even after she heard Russell return from his final conference, she could not rest.

Usually the roles were different, Mandy thought irritably. The woman generally played the temptress and paraded around before the man until he was panting. How brilliant of Russell to reverse the order! How clever of him to flaunt his beautiful body before her when she was engaging in the most difficult task of her life! How knowing of him to invade her fantasies until she had imagined them doing every erotic act she had ever heard of!

"Are Carolyn and Mickey still in Zurich?" Mandy asked cautiously during breakfast the next morning. "I haven't seen them for a while."

Russell, carefully dressed now, and unmistakably aware of the bleakness of her color and the droop of her eyes, snapped his case shut. Mandy tried to ignore his stylishness and endlessly stirred her third cup of coffee.

"She's leaving tomorrow afternoon," he said quietly. "Are you getting everything packed?"

"Yes."

"Thank you for doing mine, too."

"You're welcome," Mandy said stiltedly, keeping her eyes averted.

His voice grew tighter. They were both careful not to look at the same things. "Have you made any plans for when you get home?"

The tension in Russell's words reached over the space between them and hurled itself against her. She felt him listening for the slightest vibration from her, like a pursuer attuned to the rustle of a footstep. She could hardly stay still. Her head began to hurt.

"My only plans are to finish the book."

He cleared his throat. "How's it going?"

Mandy replaced her coffee cup with exaggerated care. "Pretty well."

"You're awfully pale. Are you catching a cold?"

Before she could react, Russell's hand touched her forehead—coolly, in charge of things. She thought if she didn't move, he would do more, caress her or make some inane excuse to go on touching her. Mandy wished she could lean her head against his chest and say, "Please hold me." But of course she could not do that.

'I'm fine," she said brusquely, feeling rejected.

"I don't think so."

"I don't give a damn what you think, Russell!"

"I never thought you did!" he shot back.

Russell snatched up his denim jacket and slung it over his shoulder with athletic flair. He adjusted his belt, which was completely unnecessary, for his pants were indecently tight. Then he left. And the emptiness of the room was very bitter.

Mandy swore. Then she paced the room. How dare he invade her so? Dare to make her love him, to take such pride at the respect he generated, to make her delight in his smile and the way his eyes crinkled when he laughed? She repeated the same obscenity over and over as she stamped about the kitchenette.

Tomorrow, the next day, it would all be over. She had done what he asked; she had married him and protected the peace of mind of people he cared about. She didn't owe him anything now.

Mandy had tried so hard to not get hurt; yet here she was—awake in the middle of the night, hurting. She had lost control of her life, which made her feel like a complete failure.

Mandy leaned off the divan and squinted at the clock on the coffee table. She couldn't read it. Getting up, she knelt, and the soft peignoir slithered into a shimmering film about her knees.

Two-thirty. Russell was asleep. Russell always seemed to sleep when she roamed during the early-morning hours— achingly lonely, hungry to be held, needing to talk.

Packing his personal things earlier had developed into a slow torture. The intimacy of his clean handkerchiefs, his underwear, his socks, the scattered contents of his pockets, nearly drove her mad. His suits had a familiar scent about them which triggered memories she would rather have forgotten—their laughter when they had danced together, even the disaster of their wedding ceremony.

Declaring that she was a fool, Mandy had rushed through the remainder of the packing. Then, in a moment of complete discouragement, she had stolen one of his ties and hidden it in her suitcase, along with a crumpled piece of paper where he had scrawled figures as he concentrated. Such a girlishly infatuated thing to do, Mandy told herself. When she stopped loving him, she would throw them both away. Then she would smile at herself and gloss everything over with the excuse: "But loving Russell did make me a better person."

Still holding the tiny travel clock, Mandy stared at the door to Russell's bedroom as if it were an enemy. She tore her eyes away. Silently, refusing to even think about waking him up, she stepped to the window and pulled open the draperies. Moonlight flooded into the room. Below her the Bahnhofstrasse was busy, even at this hour. Mandy tried to concentrate on the parade of blinking red lights and found herself staring at Russell's door again. Perhaps she should work on the book.

Was one hurt any worse than another? Was the risk she took with David worse than walking into Russell's room, snapping on the light and saying, "Russell, I want to talk to you?"

She imagined herself dropping something, making some loud noise, and Russell awakening and coming into the living room. Not the way he had been behaving lately—testing her, starving her of friendship so she would admit that he was right. He was solving her, the way he would solve an economics problem that thwarted him.

So she stood smoothing the facing of his door, feeling every small crevice. Nudging the door open, knowing what she was doing and no more able to stop than a bird taking to its nest, Mandy drew into the shadows. She felt like a thief.

Moonlight filtered peacefully across Russell's features. The pressures of his work were soothed in slumber, and an innocence bathed away the firmness about his eyes and his shoulders. Even his hands, as they relinquished their control. Mandy unconsciously matched her breathing to his. The shame she would feel if she woke him would be as unbearable as her longing, but she knew now that shame would not stop her.

When she moved to his side, standing above the length of him—powerful even in repose—the risk took her breath away. As he lay flat on his back, his head slightly turned, the fingers of one large hand nestled in the waves of his hair, Mandy lowered herself and balanced on the edge of the bed beside him. For a second Russell stirred. He blinked as his consciousness returned, and he stilled.

He knew immediately, and she knew. Yet honor compelled her to say something, to explain what coming to him was doing to her. "Russell," she whispered pleadingly, "I—"

"Shh," he said, pulling himself up on one elbow and placing a finger across her lips. "There's no need to be ashamed. You're a lady, a beautiful lady."

"I never thought I'd ever do this," she began her defense. "I don't know quite—"

Swinging his feet off the bed with an easy grace, Russell purposely refrained from taking her in his arms. Mandy was disarmed, for she had thought that he would initiate things now. He did not.

"This is dangerous," she breathed as he stood.

He smiled. "Very dangerous."

A smooth-muscled abdomen branched up from the low cut of his briefs, swelling into the span of his chest. Mandy's breasts strained against her gown, aching to be touched. Yet Russell did not fill his hands with them. He caressed her hair. She understood then. He would not do everything; she must meet him halfway or not at all. Her whole body burned in preparation for being a woman. She wondered if he knew.

"I'm warm, too," he grinned down at her, and his eyes touched what his hands did not—everything. "Let's take a swim."

Laughing, Mandy pressed her lips. "Now?"

"Yes. It's very late. No one will be in the pool. I've never been swimming with you, Mandy."

Shrugging, growing more bold, Mandy forced herself to not hurry. They had all night—endless time to explore, to learn. "I'll put on a suit," she said and caressed the gracefulness of his collarbone with her fingertips.

Russell returned the touch with excruciating slowness. She could feel his own heat, and he traced the shape of her lips with a gentle thumb. They both fought the need—understanding, man and woman, both wanting it now and letting it bank like hot coals hidden beneath ashes, ready to burst into flames.

As Mandy walked behind Russell to the elevator, she adored the leanness of his hips flexing beneath tight jeans. She had pulled on a worn cotton shirt and tennis shoes. Yet

even that pleased him, for he kept looking at her, allowing his
gaze to drink her at his leisure. The elevator lights blinked
through the numbers. She flushed.

"I'm wet," she said abruptly and slumped back against the
wall, astonished at her own nerve.

Russell groaned. "God, don't tell me that now!"

He caught her hand and drew her out a side exit, through
tall shrubbery toward the heated pool in the back of the
hotel.

"I should steal a bottle of wine from the kitchen," he
chuckled.

"No," Mandy said, shaking her head. "I'm fine. Do you
know where you're going?"

"Yes."

The pool was quiet. The distant swish of traffic almost
drowned the faint hum of the filtering system. About the edge
of the pool deserted chaise lounges mingled with parasoled
tables to create looming, monster-shadows. Only the lights
along the walkway from the main entrance to the hotel cast a
subdued glow—making a public place private in its own
special way.

"Do you think anyone will hear us?" she whispered.

"Would you care if they did?" he retorted, glancing over
her head at the partition of wooden fencing. "Does the
possibility of getting caught frighten you too much?"

Scrutinizing his profile—the narrow nose, the curved
mouth which grinned at her, the high, proud cheekbones—
she matched him with her own beauty. "No," Mandy said and
grasped one of his hands.

She slowly lifted it to her lips. When she kissed his fingers,
touching one with her tongue, drawing the tip of it into her
mouth, nibbling, sucking with a shattering suggestion, Russell
slipped his other hand behind her head.

"I could stand here and look at you," he said. His words
were hoarse and ragged. "I could kiss you all over. Forever."

"I know."

His leg moved closer, muscular and hard, touching hers
from the waist down. "I've been wanting you to come to me
for such a long time, sweet lady."

"I've been hating you for days."

"Because I was forcing you to open your eyes? To admit
what you feel?"

Mandy freed the top button on his shirt with swift fingers.

And when she hesitated, Russell tugged the shirt from the waist of his jeans and unbuttoned it himself. Because he wanted her to, and because she could not deny herself any longer, Mandy closed her eyes and languorously smoothed the flat of both palms across the expanse of his chest. Sighing, she moistened the dryness of her lips.

"I've never been an aggressive woman," she said, wishing he would stop prolonging the agony of it and just crush her against him.

"I like you just the way you are," he whispered. "You're my smile, Mandy. All the good things I feel inside."

"Do you want me, Russell?"

"Do you need the words? I've wanted you so badly that even when I forced the tension from my body, I still desired you. You're the center of every fantasy. No woman ever looks as good, no pleasure as tempting. I've risked a lot for this moment."

Their minds were locked together. So she played the temptress for him, tingling with strange new energy. She emerged from her jeans and shirt like a fragilely clad butterfly from a cocoon. Certain that he was already aching for her, she bent low, deliberately drawing his eyes into the shadowy valley between her breasts. Presenting the curve of her back then, she flicked at the stretch of her bikini panties below the curve of her buttocks. Her legs were smooth and firm and, lifting her chin, she flaunted herself in a sultry walk. Mandy's dive into the pool was fluid and broke the water with only a whisper of foam.

When her face lifted through the shimmering surface she blinked away the water. Russell was not ten feet away, drawing an arm through the ripples in a slow, powerful stroke. Her toes reached for the bottom of the pool and barely touched it.

"You found me," she whispered, her eyes glistening with arousal. She moved her arms trimly through the water to balance herself.

Russell, ducking below the surface, emerged before her, gleaming and dripping. Slick wet hair clung to his neck. Mandy ruffled it. As he pulled her toward him by her wrist, an intent smile only teasing at his lips, her feet left the bottom of the pool, and she grabbed for his neck. Only when she let him fit the length of her body to his did she realize he was completely naked. And very hard.

"Russell!"

"What?"

"You're . . . *you are—*"

"Yes," he grinned. "I am."

And with one skillful twist of his fingers at the back of her bikini halter, the skimpy piece of knit slipped free. Before Mandy could do more than gasp and splash for a footing on the pool floor, Russell tossed the bra over his head. In the faint light she gaped at the fragment of blue fabric which floated for a moment, then lazily disappeared to the bottom of the pool.

"And now you are, too," he said, satisfied.

In the seconds it took for him to stretch his legs in a driving scissors kick, Russell balanced himself in front of her. His hands threaded through the water as he studied her arms crossing protectively over her bosom. His eyebrows disapproved and arched in a mocking tease.

Mandy shivered as his eyes branded her, but she didn't want him to stop looking. With a provocation she did not dream she was capable of, she lowered her arms until Russell could see all of her. She inflamed him, knowingly, as she sensually lifted her hands to trace the circles of her pink-tipped breasts. Deliberately, insolently, she tortured him with the suggestion of her fingers, hoping as she did that he would break with desire of her. Her nipples responded, shrinking with tight readiness. And when Mandy smiled, Russell's deep, prolonged breath warned her that she had succeeded more than she knew.

"I will ask you just this one time," he promised huskily. "Be very sure."

She spoke with drugged difficulty. "You're driving me crazy."

"I want to drive you crazy," he murmured and mingled his tongue with the eagerness of her own.

His fingers teased at the soft knit of her panties—slipping beneath, moving back, roaming, going nowhere, then returning. He was persecuting her, and Mandy was shocked that she was much more urgent than he. In the timeless command of woman, she impatiently thrust her hips forward.

He found her with his fingers. Everything about them seemed liquid, a melting current that swirled and blurred, making them one, not two.

"Don't be afraid," he murmured, finding the shell of her ear. "Don't be afraid to touch me."

And when she did, curving her fingers about him in gentle wonder, Russell trapped her face between his hands. For breathless moments he fell into the intensity of her blue eyes. They touched with frightening warmth and wondered how much longer they could sustain the moment.

He had to love her, Mandy thought. No man could devour a woman with his eyes as Russell did without loving her. Moving her hands, pressing hard against the firmness of his buttocks, trying to tell him she had reached the limit of endurance, Mandy gave one low moan.

"Please?" she whimpered. Her whole body was climbing now—building to the point of explosion. She feared her legs would not carry her back to their room.

Wetting his lips and clasping her tightly to his chest, Russell paddled them to the rim of the pool. She clung to the edge as a burning urgency crept up her body. For several seconds Russell disappeared, only to burst through the surface. She let him replace her top and lift her out. Her world was narrowing dangerously, consisting of his hands touching her as he dressed her.

Walking beside the pool, feeling her legs flex and straighten, carrying her shoes with their tied laces, Mandy grew dizzy with the sensuality of his jeans, the wet flapping of his shirt. As they left, ducking through the momentary darkness of the shrubbery, Mandy closed her fingers into the damp cotton of his shirt. Swallowing hard, she attempted to read his features in the dense shadows as he turned.

"You made me this way," she tried to explain, pulling against him, stopping him. "Please."

Without hesitation Russell moved against her. Her tense demand, driving her beyond caution, excited him. Heat spilled over her body, and he grinned down at her.

"Here?"

Her head dropped backward as he crushed her maddeningly against him. "Here. Anywhere. Now."

Throwing a quick glance over his shoulders, Russell took two steps forward and pinned her gently against the ivy-covered fence. The thick canopy almost wrapped them invisibly in its arms. Furry evergreen shrubbery whispered shut behind them, promising to keep their secret.

"Mandy?"

He was uncertain now. She was more than ready, and he wanted to help her. Adeptly, in contrasting tenderness to Mandy's increasing tension, he stroked her through her panties, then beneath.

"Damn!" Russell breathed. He seemed not to have enough hands.

Helping him, Mandy flicked his zipper downward. Finding her as she stood, rigidly arched on the tips of her toes, taut as a strung bow, was completely instinctive. It felt as if her bones locked around him. And no sooner than they did, the pent-up sensations of weeks forced her over the brink of conscious control. She felt it coming, but she could not stop it. She did not want to stop it. She only buried her fingers into the muscles of his back. She wrapped her legs around his hips and hungrily focused on the one part of herself that mattered. Russell let her direct him—learning, adapting as she clutched him to her, ever closer, closer. She clung fiercely at first, for it did not let her down quickly. Russell trembled with a satisfaction because she was so. He kept her pinned securely, never relaxing his tension until her head dropped forward into the curve of his neck. Gradually her heart slowed its frantic pace, and her breaths steadied.

"Oh!" She tried to talk, embarrassed now.

"Shh," he murmured into her ear, kissing her wet hair and presently tipping up her face. Smiling drowsily, she attempted to turn her face away. Her legs were still clamped around his hips. She was still drugged and sated.

"I can't hold you up all night," he teased tenderly.

"I can walk," Mandy said, though she hardly realized that she did until they held each other in the dark center of their room. The unspoken needs of the other were understood, and she knew he would be the most gentle he could be.

Not so thirstily impatient now, secure because he had thought only of her, only of her completion, Mandy languidly explored him. She undressed him with exquisite leisure and returned some of the pleasure he had given her. With unhurried care, she learned all the parts and facets of Russell Gregory. She kissed every swell of muscle, every smooth surface, his fingers and toes and ears, the inside of his mouth.

And he—trapped in a masculine readiness that tightened and hardened with each increasing skill of her mouth and hands—yielded up to the demands she made. Mandy was marvelously attuned to his moves, to the ability of his knowing hands, his subtle teaching, his urging. And when her tension broke into waves of pure sensation, he drew his weight upon her and filled her quickly.

"I want to see you," he whispered, bracing himself. She said his name in a low, hoarse sound and buried her fingernails into the taut muscles, lifting herself upward to accept and lock him to her.

Covered with a moist, gleaming sheen, Russell came only after she was floating down to the solemn center of herself. He was strong and driving and took her even farther, again and again, until she begged him to stop.

"No more," she whimpered.

"No more," he said and gave himself up to the oldest instincts of time itself.

Later Mandy aroused him again, dragging him back from the hinterlands of slumber. Placing herself above him, she guided him into her. She took without asking. She took and he took. They both wanted and they both gave.

Finally, emptied and exhausted, they entwined themselves and slept again.

Sometime before dawn the purr of the telephone probed annoyingly into Russell's slumber. Goggily he opened one eye to observe Mandy nestled in the crook of his arm, her face crinkling prettily at the persistent ringing. He groped for the receiver.

"Hello," he mumbled and blinked at his wristwatch.

"Mr. Hamilton, this is Philip. We have an emergency on our hands."

Russell kicked at the sheet, instantly awake. Pinching the receiver between his jaw and shoulder, he automatically felt the floor for his jeans. He stood and began pulling them on as he talked.

"Okay, give it to me," he said tensely.

"Orban. Turn on the radio. An earthquake has just destroyed half the capital."

Russell swore. "What about the bank?"

"It's holding at about half security. Fires are everywhere, sir. That's our main concern right now."

"Vandalism high?"

"It's pretty bad. Five thousand government troops have just been brought in."

"Well," Russell's face was drawn with dread, "they'll need assistance from the United States, that's certain. Get Reginald. Tell him I'm on my way."

Russell knew only too well how much Reginald would lose if his bank did not continue to support the crippled country of Orban. Heavy loans had already been negotiated from Reginald's firm. With the economy threatened by a natural catastrophe, they would be forced to borrow even more.

Russell located his shoes as he gave Philip Graves his instructions. Mandy, also awake now, propped on her elbow and frowned at the one-sided exchange. As he sat on the bed to pull on his socks, she smoothed the familiar symmetry of his backbone.

"I'll charter a plane to Egypt immediately," Russell stated, making his good-byes swiftly and replacing the receiver with a vexed pause.

When he offered no explanation but gathered a dress suit and some items from a suitcase, Mandy hugged the sheet about her bosom and began inching off her side of the bed. Her clothes were nowhere to be seen, and she snatched the sheet completely off the bed in a flurry.

Rubbing the stubble on his jaws, Russell began striding toward the bathroom.

"Wait," she demanded. "What's happened? What's the matter?"

"I've got to go," he said flatly. "There's trouble."

He explained then, as if he were unaccustomed to having someone be more than a casual bystander to his affairs. "In Orban. An earthquake has nearly destroyed it."

Mandy was horrified. "You're not flying into that, Russell!"

Following in the path of his long steps, she argued to his back as he flicked on hot water and patted shaving foam on his jaw. When she persisted, repeating her ineffectual arguments that he could get someone else to go into the disaster zone, Russell finally whirled and grasped her shoulders painfully.

Blond wisps furled about her face, framing the sleepy blue eyes and making her look like an adorable child. Despite the tension of an unexpected emergency, he kissed her mouth lightly, and the tip of her nose. Then he blotted flecks of foam off her cheek.

"I have to go, Mandy. It's my job. Now, be a sweet baby and make some coffee. And call the service desk about chartering me a plane from Zurich to Cairo. I'll do the rest after I get dressed."

"Charter *us* a plane, you mean," she corrected and swung her hips at him as she left the room swathed in the sheet.

"Just a minute!" Russell called after her. She pivoted. He shook his head from side to side in slow deliberation. "Uh-huh. Not this time. Orban is no place for civilians."

Mandy tugged the sheet more securely beneath her arms until her curves were unconsciously outlined. "You're a civilian."

"I'm a man, too, dammit! I can't argue with you now."

"Well, I'm a woman then, dammit! And a journalist besides. This is a hot story." Her features softened. "Please," she wheedled.

"No."

"You always fight me about writing. I wouldn't even mention your name, Russell, I swear."

"That has nothing to do with it, my lady." His eyes narrowed beneath their brows. "You cannot go to Orban."

Mandy drew herself tall and set her jaw in the typical Phillips fashion. "Are you afraid I *would* get a story? Of course," she half-turned, as if reasoning with herself. "That's why you didn't want me to do the book. I would have something of my own that you couldn't control. No wonder you don't want me in Orban. If you had your way, women would be chained to the kitchen and have a baby every year."

Throwing his eyes to the ceiling, Russell started to ignore her prattle as nonsense. But, glancing back at her a second time, he realized it was not entirely foolish talk. He stepped to the doorway and braced one arm as Mandy talked to the service desk.

"Your mind, my dear wife," he observed when she finished, "is an amazing thing. All right, I'll make a bargain with you. You stay here, and as soon as I think it's safe, I'll send for you. When *I* think it's safe, not before. Take it or leave it."

"You're very free with your wifely considerations," Mandy retorted with a small triumphant smile. "I'll take it. In the meantime, I'll have a few days of peace and quiet to work on the book. You promise you'll send for me?"

"On my honor."

She frowned. "Insufficient collateral, I think. The coffee's nearly ready."

By the time she poured coffee and made toast, Russell entered, immaculately dressed in a pinstriped business suit, his image one of briskness and unstudied efficiency. He brushed back his hair with an absent gesture.

"You forgot to get a haircut," she said fondly, placing a steaming cup on the table before him. She reached to his forehead and arranged a lock into place. She traced the arch of one brow. At that small touch, the wanting began again.

He grinned and sighed. "You forgot to put on your clothes." Russell caught her in a possessive trap of steely arms. Pulling her close, he tipped her head back. Without words, they were caught in remembering the closeness of the night, the opening to the other, the kisses, the murmured urgings, the heat, the intensity, the warmth of satisfaction, the goodness.

"I don't want to say good-bye to you," he murmured hoarsely, his smile fading as his mouth slowly lowered to hers. "God, I don't want to leave you."

"Then don't," she whispered, her lips parted. Her lashes fluttered to her flushed cheeks.

Their kiss deepened swiftly and throbbed far past the point of a casual caress. Russell's hands eagerly reacquainted themselves with the curves and secret softness of her. He forced his head up with a low groan.

"If I don't stop now, I'll wish I had later," he predicted with a resigned sigh. "Get dressed? Walk me down?"

Feeling very much as if she would cry, Mandy only nodded. A lean inquisitive finger tipped up her chin. Blinking vigorously, she began once more to memorize the face she would not see for a while. Russell's features were sobered, not masking his emotions as skillfully as before.

He hesitated. "Mandy, about this arrangement we call a marriage . . . We'll work it all out when the mess in Orban is cleared up. I know we're leaving things up in the air, pretty tangled up, to tell the truth. But we can't make any decision until we have time to sit down and talk."

"What's there to talk about?" Mandy asked dully, wondering if he was thinking what she hoped he was, that it could be a real marriage with a little work, that it could last.

"Well," he shifted his weight, "people need other people.

I've always liked to think I didn't need anyone. Now I don't know what I think. I know sex between us is good. We probably ought to give the rest a chance before we end something simply because we said we would."

Again Mandy was tempted to be completely honest. She should go first; she should say the words out loud. But what if he could not say them, too? She would embarrass him and make herself look stupid.

Tears brimmed in her eyes, frustrated tears, and Russell misinterpreted them. "There's no hurry," he said, breaking the spell.

There's no hurry! she thought as she dressed. He was walking into another dangerous situation. And she didn't know how to act; she only knew what she wanted—him. When she returned, Russell was studying his wristwatch and taking a last hurried sip of coffee. At the sight of her, all graceful and feminine in a skirt and shimmery blouse, Russell tightened the knot of his tie uneasily. He stepped beside his suitcases, and she followed him mutely like a distraught child.

Pausing, placing his luggage outside the door, he opened an arm to her once more. Mandy went willingly and dropped her forehead against the protection of his chest. His fingers absently threaded into the curls at the back of her hair, and his lips pressed against a spot above her temple. Then he smiled down at her for a long minute.

"Don't worry," he said.

Mandy almost laughed. Already she was ill with worry. Why were the women left behind? She wanted to indulge in a temper at the unfairness. Instead she tiptoed to place a gentle kiss upon his cheek. He smelled good, she thought. But she would forget his smell and the feel of him beneath her hands.

"Last night you would never have settled for a kiss like that." He grinned. "My Mandy was a hungry tiger. My, my."

He bent, intending to kiss her again. She placed her fingers to his lips in a gentle protest.

"Don't kiss me again, Russell. I honestly can't bear it."

In the elevator, they sent wordless messages behind the back of a faceless passenger—messages about parting and missing and waiting. She did not want to be courageous; Mandy wanted to be petted and consoled in her misery. This loneliness would not be like before, when Theo had separated them. That parting had served a purpose. She had been consoled with the burning outrage of being forced to endure it. She had been a modern heroine—brave enough to escape and have people say how clever she was, smart enough to be asked to write a book.

This loneliness would not make their hearts grow fonder because she was too much of a coward to ask Russell what his heart held. She would not be thought clever; no one would care that she had fallen in love and joined the human race.

So Mandy nursed a small needlelike hatred that Russell did nothing to make it go away. As the doors swished open she grabbed for the 'hold' button. "I don't want to go to the lobby with you."

She did not say she was afraid. Russell looked, for once, to be the thirty-nine years he was. Mandy suffered visions of never seeing him again, of never smiling again.

In the seconds that Russell paused to check the inner pockets of his suit, she knew she should be grateful that she had known even this much of love. Some people were not so blessed. She could not be generous, nor could she be grateful.

"Am I supposed to say at this point that it's been nice knowing you?" Mandy asked dully.

Russell stiffened. At a loss to cope with a strange new pain, he said nothing. He only placed a hard kiss upon her lips. Then he quickly turned his back. Mandy bit the lips he had kissed and, bracing weakly against the door, watched him until the very last second.

Russell disappeared before the sound of Mickey's shout rang across the expanse of the lobby. "Russell, wait!"

Mandy saw the boy then, skimming across the floor in brown corduroys and tennis shoes, his mother gliding smoothly behind him as they returned from an early breakfast. Even if Mandy had had time to realize she was eavesdropping, it wouldn't have stopped her. The possessiveness of her love attracted her like a powerful magnet, and she stepped from the elevator.

Frozen, she watched Mickey grab the tall man about the thighs. In a halfhearted attempt to detain her son, Carolyn reached outward. Over Mickey's head their eyes met, and Mandy would have given much to see Russell's face.

Mickey detached himself enough to take in the sight of Russell's suit, his luggage waiting beside his legs. "Where're you goin', Russell?" His freckled face screwed into a question mark. "You goin' somewhere?"

"Hold on, Mick," he tried to sooth, the rising agitation in

the child's voice. Russell placed a large hand upon the shock of red hair. "I'm going away for a few days, yes. You know I always go on trips. What are you doing up so early?"

The boy ignored the effort at sidetracking him. "Can't I go? Couldn't you take me, just this once?"

Again the two adults locked eyes. Carolyn plucked at Mickey's collar. "Honey, please. Russell is in a hurry, can't you see? Now be a brave boy and say good-bye. He promised you could come and visit when he got home."

"I want to go with him now!"

The child straightened himself stiffly, struggling into his pretense of bravery like shrugging into an overcoat several sizes too big.

"Please, Russell. I'd be real good. I promise I'd mind you and not get in the way."

"Mickey!" insisted his mother.

"It's all right, Carolyn." Russell bent his head lower and wiped Mickey's tears with a tenderness that sent Mandy pressing against the wall behind her. There was something slightly obscene about spying on an innocent child's grief.

"I'd like to take you, Mick, I really would. But I can't. I'll call you the minute I get back. I promise."

"I don't believe you," Mickey blurted, rubbing one eye with the hand that still held the remnants of a breakfast roll. Unconsciously, Russell brushed crumbs from a trouser leg.

"Why?" the man asked. "Have I ever lied to you before?"

"You said you'd be my daddy, Russell. I told people and everything. And you're not my daddy. Now you'll never be my daddy."

Mandy couldn't have torn her eyes away if she had tried. Only one other time had Russell looked that stricken. And that was when he stood beside her in the chapel at their wedding. Mandy could've struck him she was so hurt. Why hadn't he told her how Mickey felt?

Russell glanced at a bellboy and lowered his voice. Whatever he said obviously comforted the child. Looking distraught, Carolyn was caught in an awkward dilemma she did not create. She moistened her lips. When Russell smiled at her, she shrugged. Bending over Mickey's head, she murmured something in his ear. Like conspirators, the two adults talked softly. Russell reached to touch Carolyn's arm. When she closed her hand about the larger one, nausea surged in Mandy's stomach. Truth was so cruel. It was more encompassing than words, than legal mumbo-jumbo, than money, than anything.

Horrified then, that one of them would accidentally glimpse her, that they would know she had seen everything, Mandy held her breath and moved toward the stairway. She did not want to view the final parting, the kiss that could not be given because of the observers, words that could not be said over the head of a seven-year-old boy. One did not have to see a falling boulder to believe it would gouge a crater in the earth.

Mandy got into the elevator on the next floor and took it the rest of the way up. As she groped for the door to the suite, closed it and leaned against it, she laughed scornfully at herself. She'd been a girl when she had met Russell. Now she had grown up; she had become an old woman in the space of a few weeks. For some moments, she stared at the telephone. Then she stepped into the bedroom and stared at her packed suitcases.

It took her over an hour before she could control her voice enough to call for a bellboy. Mandy stepped out onto the Swiss street that was already beginning to get busy. The taxi driver shut her into the back seat and inclined his head.

"The airport, please."

Chapter Sixteen

Mandy deftly headed her Datsun south on Canal Street but noontime traffic in New Orleans was heavy. She hit nearly every red light. After discovering a parking space on a side street, she clicked off the ignition and sat fanning herself. It was hot for October. Heat radiated off the street in waves, like her nausea. She had been home nearly two months.

Locking her car, she weaved through windowshopping tourists on her way toward the Mississippi River. The river smelled bad, and she loved it. She had learned to walk on these streets along the river, holding onto one of her father's fingers and dragging her wooden ladybug toy. She knew, for Preston had taken her picture once—a round-faced toddler dressed in corduroy overalls with white hightop shoes, clutching the cord to her ladybug on wheels.

How easily the past twenty-odd years had managed to pass into another lifetime. Would her father have approved of Russell? That was not the issue; Russell was a courageous man, and Preston would have adored him. Would Preston have criticized her for not following Russell to Orban as she had agreed to do? Undoubtedly.

Wind flirted with the hem of her peasant skirt and whipped it out gracefully, like a floral cotton balloon. The short-sleeved jersey blouse tucked into the waistband grew moist and alluringly clinging. She did not notice. Shading her eyes from the glare of the sun, Mandy squinted behind enormous sunglasses.

Two barges, one behind the other, moved up the Mississippi against the current; their horns wailing like melancholy groans from some wounded river dragon.

She was like a tugboat, Mandy thought, fighting everything against the current, trying to carry things many times her size. Progress on the book was better. She guessed she would meet the month to her deadline with no difficulty. Doubleday had accepted her outline with an advance of ten thousand dollars.

"Not much of an advance," grumbled Tony Schaeffer, who had been more than a little disappointed. "Not for a story like this."

"I don't care," she had told him. "At this point, having any book published is an accomplishment. I'm a nobody."

"Hardly that," he disagreed. "We'll make it up on subsidiary rights. I'm seeing an agent in Los Angeles next week. This would be a helluva TV movie."

Mandy could not conceive of a TV movie. To her, the kidnapping had been a nightmare of blurring days, days of being frantic for her life. Reconstructing that time was emotionally devastating. She felt horrible anyway. She had just come from the gynecologist. She was pregnant, and she was stupidly, incoherently dumbfounded.

She had to untangle everything all over again now. On the flight home from Zurich Mandy had, at a dreadful cost to her self-esteem, accepted the fact that she had overreacted. She was foolish, though infatuated, and she could not change her status as Mrs. Russell Gregory. Not easily. In spite of her hurt over Mickey, she really wanted her marriage to work if it could.

Practicality was a learned habit anyway, and she was very strong. She could learn to do anything. Hadn't she proved that? She could survive her own love for Russell Gregory if she had to—scarred yes, but intact.

Russell had called her from Orban one week after she had returned to New Orleans. Attempts to reach her in Zurich, to tell her that conditions were too serious for her to come, had failed. Why hadn't she waited? he had demanded. Their words had traveled half a world over annoying crackling cables. Communications in and out of the small devastated country were bad and limited to emergencies. Russell was rushed and under pressure.

Mandy could not help but reach for hidden meanings in what he said—the slightest intimation he would ignore the fact that she had broken her word. He did not protest; he did not say he understood. She had hung up the telephone empty and disappointed. His cruelty would be completely different from David Rutherman's. If she did not face Russell in a refined divorce, they would continue on a civilized see-you-every-few-years basis, with each of them living quietly successful lives.

What was a failure at a marriage? Everyone suffered these days, and almost everyone made at least one bad attempt at marriage. Nothing seemed permanent . . . except babies. And she had a choice even about the baby, the gynecologist reminded her. Mandy had refused to talk about it. She could not even consider it. At that precise moment—the prospect of going through a pregnancy alone, rearing a child alone—dying looking like an inviting alternative.

So, for the past several days she had alternately wept and typed on her manuscript for twelve hours at a stretch. Between every line the word "baby" emblazoned itself. She and Russell had created a small speck of human life that would change the remaining days of her life. Not if they divorced and remarried a dozen times would they be completely separated.

When Mandy pulled her tiny car up to the black wrought-iron gates on St. Charles Avenue, they creaked open like giant pages of a book. The Phillips' white-brick mansion looked like a fairytale castle. Yew hedges and magnolia trees were interspersed across the wide lawn. Even now, as hot as the summer had been, everything gleamed a lush emerald green.

Mandy steered along the long curved driveway to a four-car garage on the end of the west wing. It was ridiculous that she and Felice should be rattling around in this huge place. Skirting the terrace, Mandy took a sidewalk bordered with a riot of white mums. This path allowed her to avoid Felice in the back of the house. Mandy needed some time to herself to gather her courage before telling Felice about the baby.

Pushing open the door to her combination sitting room and

bedroom, Mandy tossed her handbag to the bed. She barely glanced at the pale reflection of herself in a full-length mirror. Her palor would go away in time, or so she had heard; pregnant women were supposed to glow. The circles beneath her eyes would disappear when she stopped waiting for the telephone to ring and ceased waking up at odd hours to remember things she wanted very much to forget. Once she settled into a pattern of living without Russell and learned to hate him a little, she would gain back some weight. And by the time the book was completed she should be back to her normal, stable self, ready to build her life around a child.

"Mandy?" called Felice, tapping gently at her door.

"Damn!" breathed Mandy. She hoped for a few more minutes of respite. "Come in, Felice."

Entering, pale and timidly beautiful in a lavender slack suit, Mandy's stepmother glanced about the orderly yellow room. Mandy often thought their relationship was more like that of sisters separated by almost twenty years. But today she was ages older than Felice.

"I thought I heard you," Felice said, hesitantly sitting on the foot of the bed, an is-there-anything-I-can-do look drawn on her face. "Are you all right?"

Mandy discreetly rose, switched on the stereo to softly fill the awkwardness, and pretended to inspect her mascara. She waved one hand haphazardly at her typewriter surrounded by stacks of notes and open books and loose paper scattered upon the floor.

"Take a look at that and ask me again," she replied, applying a light shade of lipstick. She turned, smiled, then glanced away aimlessly.

"Well, you're always strung out with your manuscript these days. I even hear the typewriter in the middle of the night."

The time would never be any more advantageous. Felice would be affected; she had to know. Mandy moved to her desk and peered blindly at a typed page with its red pen marks crossing out lines and substituting words.

She swallowed down her last shred of isolation from the world and began. "I haven't been feeling well lately," she explained wanly.

"I know that. You went to the doctor, didn't you?"

Mandy spun about, a bit incredulous at the sympathetic eyes. Neither of them moved for a while.

"You know, don't you?" Mandy's head tilted to one side in disbelief.

"That you're pregnant?" Felice laughed softly, an understanding laugh that Mandy thought was the most wonderful sound she had ever heard. "A lucky guess, that's all."

Mandy's face fell, and the arch of her brows knit with practical sobriety. "Lucky? No, not lucky."

"But—"

"If you're so intuitive, Felice, surely you must have guessed how it is between Russell and me. I've been home for weeks and he has called me exactly once!"

"But honey, you know the reason for that."

"Are you pleading Russell's case, Felice?"

"I'm reminding you that he can't get out of that country. There's no telling what it's like over there."

Mandy remembered how Russell had fought bitterly for his own independence, too, yet had cradled her in his arms and pleaded with her not to cry.

"I can't start hoping again," she said and turned her back, as if it would make it easier to explain. "There was never enough time for us. What happened, happened too fast. Maybe the love was never there. Maybe I dreamed everything. Oh, damn!" she sighed, drooping, "I don't know what I mean."

Felice chose her words carefully; Mandy sensed her reluctance to interfere, to give unwanted advice. "It'll be different when Russell finds out about the baby, honey. A baby does things to men—it changes them. When he finds out, nothing could keep him from you."

Her mouth curving from frustration to scorn, Mandy pointed a slender finger at Felice. "Do you think I'd use that to lure him? I have no intention of telling Russell about the baby. I can raise it all by myself."

Felice choked, all caution gone now. "Mandy, you can't do a thing like that! A man has to know about his own child!"

"Says who?" Mandy answered hotly. "I don't need Russell Gregory to have my baby. God, he has a built-in son already if he wants a child. Carolyn Wrather has drilled into Mickey's head for years that Russell was going to be his father. Well, let him play daddy with *her* son!"

Mandy's hand sliced through the air as if making a permanent separation between Russell and herself.

"You're jealous now. That's normal when a woman's not secure about a love affair. But believe me, when you come down to the concrete level, you may be very grateful for Russell."

Mandy's cheeks burned with stubborn pride. Her head lifted with independence. With an absent palm, she smoothed back soft swirls of hair which fell gently about her face.

"I may be jealous," she said. "Yes, I admit it, but I mean what I say. I wouldn't beg him before, and I won't beg him now."

The expression of horror widening Felice's eyes did not soften Mandy's attitude. She despised Felice's reliance upon a man's comfort for her happiness.

"Oh, Mandy," Felice breathed, "I had no idea you were so angry. Don't do this. I know we're different . . . You're so strong, and I'm . . . well, sort of clinging and all. But you're legally married. And you're going to have a baby. It's not a failure to bend a little, to . . . ask for a little consideration."

The look Mandy shot her could have melted cast iron. "I'm not asking for anything!"

"Ask for your baby, then!"

Slumping, Mandy shook her head. "You're right, Felice. We are different. Russell knows that I love him. He's not that insensitive. If he wanted—"

Her voice dwindled to nothing, and she stacked manuscript pages noisily, one after another, thumping their edges together. She could not share with anyone the needs gnawing inside her . . . or the long hours she stood looking out the window at night, trying to sort out the masses of confusion banking in her mind. And when she threw up in the bathroom every morning nothing needed sorting out . . . she hated Russell because he was not there, holding her, whispering to her.

"I can't open myself up like that again, Felice. I let David Rutherman nearly kill me. Now, I'm doing the same thing with Russell, only ten times worse. I don't know what's wrong with me that I keep letting men hurt me."

Felice felt helplessly in the way. "What are you going to do?"

"Nothing," Mandy answered. "Absolutely nothing. Except finish my book. Look, Felice, I feel like a rag. I think I'll lie down for a few minutes."

As Felice moved toward Mandy, intuitively sensing the

right thing to do, the two women clung to each other, each needing consolation in her own private way.

"I just hope you won't be sorry, honey," Felice whispered into the sweet-smelling blond hair. "A good man is a rare thing."

Scalding tears slid down Mandy's cheeks onto the curve of Felice's neck. "I'm sorry already," Mandy whispered.

The door closed behind Felice like a lid on a box, penning Mandy in and shutting out Russell's advocate. She thought, as she paced back and forth on the cream-colored carpet, that now it was just her, the typewriter and the unborn baby.

That was what she had always wanted, wasn't it? To write, to express herself, to show what she could do? Like she had told Ken Hagan so often? Well, now she had it—the pattern of her life: up at seven, breakfast, and work for three hours; lunch break, retype what she had done and work for another three hours. When the baby came, she would never want for anything to fill her evenings. She would be happy, Mandy reflected, and wiped the mascara off her cheeks.

One sentence at a time. That was all writing was—one sentence after another. Her fingers felt for the keys, and she detached her mind from the rest of the world, slipping back in time to the moment she was so afraid and so panicky to escape. Visually, she picked up the andiron again and stood studying the best way to break open Theo's head.

From Russell's quarters at the home of Orban's prime minister, the streets of the capital looked like a war zone: a shambled network of half-standing buildings and damaged property amounting to hundreds of thousands of American dollars.

Between the cement factory and the oil refinery which kept the town alive, work-weary nationals labored round the clock to restore order. On each side of the street were mounted machine guns, their sights trained on potential looters. Donkeys burdened with bundles of firewood trod beside four-wheel Land Rovers. Telephone and telegraph lines were restored but grossly overburdened with relief efforts from all over the world.

Many of Russell's days were spent in the capital itself, working with city officials. They examined damaged building sites and twisted railroads: estimating, juggling costs and wrestling with figures which refused to be optimistic. Some days, grimy and exhausted from hours in a jeep, he despaired of ever talking to Mandy again, much less leaving the country.

Orban could not have survived without American money. Loans of millions were extended every year from American banks to small countries. All this to maintain a needed balance of power, the government reasoned. When the independent countries found themselves in trouble, as Orban had, the only solution was to lend them more and more money or lose everything. Once a country was dependent upon American banks, cutting off the money flow would destroy the entire nation. It could not be avoided, and it could not be stopped.

So here he sat, doing what he could week after week, easing the strain where possible, and wishing to God that he had never heard of Orban.

It was in the middle of the seventh week that Russell realized he could not work. People talked to him, and he let them walk out of the room and then wondered what he'd said to them. He would come to himself and realize that he had sat for some indeterminable time tracing her name over and over. God, how Amanda Phillips Gregory had taken root in his mind! Russell forced down a consuming need to destroy something, to dislodge something stable to prove to himself that he still commanded *something* in his life.

Rain had fallen during the night, and had settled the dust, lending a sweet pungency to the air. Standing before the window in khaki pants and rolled-up shirt sleeves, he absently smoothed the backs of his arms.

Overlooking a flagstone courtyard, he listened to the last drops of rain drizzling down from the tile on the roof and slithering through the gutters below. He was worried about her. Was she well? Was she happy?

During the darkness Russell had lain between damp sheets and remembered things that had happened between them— the times he had held her, had marveled at the soft, eager yearning, had begun cherishing hopes for the future. He recognized many mistakes he'd made and wished for them back, for a chance to do things differently.

He had thought when he finally contacted Zurich, only to find Amanda was gone, that he could kill her if he had the chance. She'd been a complication in his life ever since the first day he'd seen her. Swearing he could forget her now, he thought of everything about her he disliked. It didn't work. He missed her so badly that he could forgive her anything, he thought.

He shouldn't have fought with her so mercilessly. He should have cared more about her work. He had blamed her for not looking through thirty-nine-year-old hindsight when she was only a girl. Jesus, he was in love with a girl—a willful, brilliant, talented *girl!*

The sun licked at the rain. In another hour, he would hardly know it had fallen. A jeep whined and Russell watched it swing into the semi circle of the drive.

Wearily, he turned to face the starkness of the neat white-walled room. It was all so clean and undisturbed, completely unlike the inside of his head. As he closed the door and listened to the softness of his own footsteps echoing down the hall, Russell wondered if he could find it in himself to let go. Could he pick up his life and go on as before? The marriage was a ridiculous joke, and he was as much to blame as she. He suffered the same doubts.

No, he decided as he heard the garble of foreign words floating up the stairway toward him. No way. He could never forget her, even if it made the rest of his life miserable. He wanted to go home.

Chapter Seventeen

It was eleven-thirty at night when the telephone rang. Mandy was restlessly puttering about the kitchen, rifling through the refrigerator searching for cheese. Felice, having just shampooed her hair, was watching television with her hair wound up in heated rollers.

"Will you get that, Felice?" Mandy yelled over the commercial. "Who in the world, at this hour?"

Despairing of finding something that tasted good, Mandy decided to settle for a bowl of cereal. She was pouring milk when Felice filled the doorway, pointing speechlessly toward the yellow kitchen phone.

"Answer it," she said breathlessly. "It's for you."

Mandy froze, the milk poised in midair. Anticipation sent a blend of hope and dread spurting through her. Part of her prayed desperately that it would be Russell; another part cursed him for not having called before.

"Who is it?" she asked with a cracked voice.

"It's Russell."

Swallowing the compulsion to dart for the phone, Mandy bent, burying her elbows in her abdomen, holding herself intact for several seconds. She thought she had settled everything in her mind. How dare Russell shatter it? Wrenching up her face, shocking Felice with the haggard drain of her strength, Mandy shook her head.

"I can't talk to him." She waved her hand before her then clapped it across her mouth as nausea raged in her stomach. "I can't go through that again," she choked and headed for the bathroom.

Once she left, the nausea oddly receded. Felice's footstep caused her to wonder if she didn't really want Felice to argue with her. Her stepmother caught Mandy's wrist and drew her back with amazing strength.

"At least you can stay with me," Felice insisted through her teeth.

The unexpected display of authority quieted Mandy, and she obediently retraced her steps. When Felice spoke into the yellow instrument, Mandy felt a small part of herself die. She could picture Russell—shirtless, leaning against a wall, his legs slightly spread in those tight trousers he wore.

"Mr. Gregory?" Felice ventured a bit too loudly, "are you still there?"

"Yes," his voice came from a distance, tense and waiting. "Where's Amanda? What's the matter?"

Felice hesitated, and Mandy flushed for trapping her in the position of arbitrator. Mandy stared at her feet and unconsciously held her abdomen.

"She . . . she can't come to the phone just now, Mr. Gregory. I'm sorry."

Russell's oath was blurted before he could check it. He stood in an office of the prime minister and drew perturbed triangles on a piece of paper. His knit shirt opened at the throat, and the trousers bloused above steel-toed boots. He apologized.

"It's taken me four weeks to get this call through, Mrs. Phillips," he said with frowning distaste that he must explain himself. "You tell Amanda to damn well put herself on the telephone."

His quiet anger hacked through the words and into Felice's ear. Curling her thin fingers about the mouthpiece of the receiver, Felice arched her eyebrows and pleaded with Mandy to talk to her husband. "The man is desperate, Mandy."

"Russell is never desperate." Her face was ashen, and her nerves felt as if they had been mutilated with dull shears.

Felice whimpered at what she considered the most flagrant kind of waste. "You're making a terrible mistake, dear. You can't toss a good man aside like this. Please—listen to me. Please."

"I can't, Felice. Not now." Mandy felt her heart breaking, hurting the whole center of her, her most vulnerable being. "Tell him . . . tell him to call back later. Maybe later. I—"

When Felice turned back to Russell with her unconvincing apologies, Mandy ran from the room, her bare feet skimming across the carpet. Up the stairs and into her room. She had to get away, for if she didn't she would snatch the phone from Felice and begin pouring all her miseries into Russell's ear. Mandy would tell him everything; she would damn her pride and plead with him to come to her.

There were times she thought she had toughened enough to stand up to Russell if Russell burst through the front door. She had their child to think about, and what would happen to them when Russell came and went again. And, went again.

Seating herself at the typewriter, she began copying draft furiously, making dozens of typographical errors, not seeing them, and not caring. When Felice tapped softly on the door she yelled, "Come in!"

Mandy typed as fast as she could. Felice seated herself on the foot of the bed without interrupting. Mandy could feel her gray eyes penetrating. They would not accuse, but they would not understand. Mandy's fingers hesitated upon the keys.

"He sounded very nice," Felice said lamely. "We talked for a few minutes after you left."

Felice wanted her to ask, "What did you say?" Felice wanted to spill everything and scold Mandy for being so stubborn. But Mandy didn't give her the chance. She continued typing blindly. Her fingers fumbled, and the keys jammed, clattering their distorted staccato until Mandy, hovering upon the brink of hysteria, slumped over the machine.

Stepping beside her, Felice snapped off the typewriter. The room hushed in an abrupt silence. Except for the whisper of Mandy's labored breathing. Felice covered Mandy's hand with hers.

"It's my time to control my life, Felice," she whimpered. "I have to. I have to."

"What are you afraid of?"

Mandy shook her head. "I don't know. Me. David Rutherman. Russell. The baby. Mickey, maybe. I don't know."

"Russell said he's coming back to the States in a week. Things are finally settling down over there. He'll call when he gets back. I told him you'd be feeling better by then."

"You didn't tell him I'm pregnant, did you?" cried Mandy, wrenching up her face.

Felice's grimness assured Mandy that she had not been betrayed, though Felice would have liked to. Suddenly the house seemed to threaten Mandy; Felice threatened her; New Orleans threatened her.

"He may come here," Mandy mumbled, half to herself. "He'll undoubtedly come here."

"Not without being asked," Felice disagreed.

Mandy grimaced. "You don't know Russell." She stumbled to a window opening onto the terrace. Drawing the drapery aside, she studied the shadows of dark trees and beyond, to the glow on the horizon that was New Orleans. The city had a colorful history. It was the largest city in Louisiana, and one of the most important ports of the nation. Its side streets were lined with art galleries, sidewalk cafés, perfume shops and tearooms. It boasted of its Mardi Gras, the Vieux Carré—its city within a city—the French Market, Royal Street, Bourbon Street and the International Trade Mart. Mandy felt like a tiny speck that would never be noticed.

Mandy did not turn when she reminisced. "I'll never forget watching them drag Lake Pontchartrain for a seventeen-year-old boy. There was a crowd watching the boat and the grappling hooks. I asked Daddy to stop the car. We got out and stood with everyone for a few minutes. Kind of a quiet ceremony."

Turning, Mandy met Felice's sympathetic eyes. "The worst thing of all," Mandy went on, "was what I pictured in my mind. Somewhere at home his mother was going about her work, not even knowing that people were searching for the body of her son." She dropped her head. "It broke my heart. I cried for a woman I didn't know."

Felice waited patiently for Mandy's explanation.

Mandy sighed. She shook her curls. "Life is short. I don't want to deliberately hurt Russell. This isn't the way I want it to be."

She moved listlessly about the room—touching the typewriter, the back of the winged chair as if it were a trusted friend. Then the stereo her father had given her for Christmas, the portable television.

"I think I should go somewhere," she said quietly. "I must finish my book. I can't let even Russell keep me from that. Perhaps an apartment—I don't know. I'll get some money from Bergman and look for something."

At the mention of Bergman Reeves, Felice shifted her weight and fidgeted with a strand of her hair. The whole atmosphere in the room changed, adjusted to concern of another sort. Alertly sensitive to her vibrations, Mandy stilled in her process of taking a nightgown from a drawer. Tossing it on the bed, she pondered Felice's abrupt change of mood.

"What's the matter?" she asked. "I don't mean I'm unhappy when I say I'd like to get an apartment. It has nothing to do with you."

"I know what you mean."

One of Felice's hair rollers slipped free, and Mandy stooped to pick it up. When she replaced it, the older woman was disturbed, almost shaking. Sensing that she should say something, she spoke at the same moment as Mandy did.

"Go on. You first," prompted Mandy.

"Well, I was just going to say . . . ah, what if, I mean what would you think if I got married?"

"Felice! What do you mean, married? What're you talking about?"

Not replying, Felice walked to Mandy's mirror and began pulling rollers from her hair with increasing agitation. Before Mandy could say anything, Felice was tangling her hair, yanking the rollers roughly, her eyes smarting with tears of pain. Amazed, Mandy removed Felice's shaking hands and began removing the rollers herself, gently.

"What is it, Felice?" she repeated.

When her stepmother spoke, Mandy kept her eyes riveted on her own pale reflection, staring at it with a mixture of fear, embarrassment and repulsion.

"Bergman said something about getting married a couple of months ago," she confessed. "Before you came back from Switzerland."

"Bergman?" Mandy dropped several rollers and bent to retrieve them. Her rudeness made Felice choke, and Mandy knelt beside Felice's thigh, placing a hand upon it in an effort to calm her stepmother.

"I didn't mean to be offensive. But *Bergman?* How on earth—Bergman is a jerk, Felice. I know he's brilliant at his work or my father would never have retained him. But as a human being, he's an incompetent. And I'm beginning to wonder about his legal expertise, if you want the truth. He's taking forever to probate the will. Anyone else could've finished long ago."

Gathering up her hair rollers in a distracted heap, not realizing what she was doing, Felice realized she had nothing to carry them in. She glanced about in a daze, and Mandy brought a towel from the bathroom. Together they placed them in it, each wanting to say much more but not wanting to hurt the other.

Finally Mandy braved the risk of offense. "Tell me, Felice. It's all over you. Something has happened."

Felice slumped to the vanity stool before Mandy's dresser and braced her elbows on the smooth surface. She didn't like Bergman but she needed him. When her head dropped down into her hands, the uncombed ringlets fell about her face like a welcome curtain.

In a gesture of compassion—almost one of maternal comfort—Mandy picked up a hairbrush and began running it through the tresses.

Looking up gratefully, her cheeks damp and pale, Felice confessed. "Bergman spent some time here while you were gone. I wanted to tell you before, but I was embarrassed. You're so strong. You would never have done anything like that."

Mandy grimaced. "Don't give me any halos I don't deserve," she said drily.

Felice had a real weakness about men; she feared being alone as much as some people feared cancer. And if Mandy knew Felice's weakness, Bergman did, too—the rat. For a few minutes Mandy's sense of justice was so wounded, she forgot her own problems.

"I think I'll pay Bergman a visit about Daddy's will," she said lightly, fluffing Felice's shimmering hair. "It's time my money was mine, and your money was yours."

She might as well have thrown it in Felice's face that Bergman was only interested in her for her share of Preston Phillips's money. The other woman drew in upon herself so completely that she scarcely seemed to move, to even be sitting there.

Mandy gave her shoulder a gentle shake, and Felice peered deep into her eyes, craving to be understood. "Your affairs are your own business," Mandy said. "If Bergman is what you truly want, okay. But if not, don't let him move in on you."

Mandy almost confided that Bergman had attempted to put the moves on her several times. But, on the chance that Felice could actually find some sort of lasting relationship with the wretch, Mandy withheld her criticism.

"It's late," she told Felice. "I think we're both exhausted. Let's forget our troubles with our men until tomorrow."

They smiled at each other, and Mandy was awed at the trust Felice bestowed upon everyone. Was Felice the smarter of the two? Was she better off blindly trusting Bergman than Mandy was in being suspicious of Russell?

Having one's eyes wide open only brought added sorrow, she decided as her hand smoothed the flatness of her abdomen. It suddenly struck her that she was asking much of a child to grow up with one parent. She had missed a great deal by not knowing her mother. Now she was considering rearing a child without a father. Was she thinking of the child or herself? Was it selfishness when her child could know its father with a little swallowed pride on her part?

Mandy's anger, when she stepped off the elevator and faced Bergman's suite of offices, was as much for Felice as for herself. Bergman Reeves and David Rutherman were two of a kind—womanizers. Yet, to be fair, she and Felice had been willing victims. They had feared confronting the world alone, had dreaded the insecurity of not "belonging" to someone. So they had tolerated the lies and the pressures. But no more!

Tossing her head back lightly, praying that her nausea for the morning had run its course, Mandy forced a cheerful smile for Bergman's secretary.

"I need to see Bergman, Miss Lambe," she announced brightly.

Miss Lambe's eyebrows shot upward. "I wish you had telephoned you were coming, Miss, ahh . . . Mrs.—"

"Gregory," Mandy supplied. "Well, I didn't know until the last minute. Is someone in there with him?"

The secretary shook her head and inspected the flashing

buttons on her panel. She offered no apology. "He's on the phone."

Mandy beamed a cunning smile upon the woman, dispelling her objections before she could voice them. "He won't mind if I go in."

Despite Miss Lambe's squawk of indignation, Mandy breezed through the offices and swept open Bergman's door without knocking. She found him facing the window with his feet perched on the sill. He leaned so far back in his chair he was nearly prone. At her entering, his body snapped upward. Focusing a glare upon poor Miss Lambe in the doorway, he gestured his secretary out. The woman would probably meet with repercussions later.

Pausing for a curious moment, Bergman measured Mandy's stance. Without looking at the telephone, he spoke into it. "Look, Tracy," he began with a stern voice. He paused pointedly, and Mandy immediately walked toward the bookshelves. "Tell those jerks they don't have to keep so much in that escrow account. Their interest rate is extortion. Hey, I've got someone in the office. I'll get back to you."

Apparently not waiting for a reply, the attorney hung up and rearranged his facial expression to one of congeniality.

Mandy cut off the pretended amenities she knew were coming. "You could have finished your conversation."

As if it all amounted to nothing, Bergman shrugged at the receiver. "It'll keep. Now, my sweet, what brings you into the lion's den?"

Mandy's queasy stomach put her in no mood for inane pleasantries. She sidestepped Bergman's casual attempt to kiss her cheek and positioned herself in front of his wall of windows looking down on Carondelet Street.

The suit she wore had been a gift from her father. Bergdorf's. Preston could never resist buying her clothes when he took a trip to New York. A green two-piece, so dark it was almost black, complimented her blond hair, lending her an ethereal air which was in laughable contrast to her behavior. The coral lipstick and soft blusher partially disguised the fact that she could not keep her breakfast down.

"You look great," complimented Bergman as he nervously adjusted the clasp on his belt. "Switzerland was good for you. Marriage too, obviously. Well," he threw out his hand in a question, "where's the lucky man?"

Hedging, Mandy began to browse through the office in the

pretense of lightheartedness. "Russell? He's in Orban. An earthquake. He's closely associated with the economy over there. He called last night. He'll be coming back soon."

Bergman's sigh left her wondering if he believed anything she said. Poising one hand upon her hip, Mandy met his noncommittal stance with a vigorous frontal attack.

"You're finished with Daddy's will now, aren't you, Bergman? I need to go to the bank and put my accounts in order."

Bergman pulled his vest into place, paused, then spoke with a quick smile. "What's the rush? You're not doing without anything, are you? How much money do you need? I'll write you a check. Anyway, several more things have to be adjusted now that you're married."

Mandy shook her head, more suspicious of Bergman's ethics than ever. "No more adjusting, Bergman. No more writing checks for me. I want my money without any middleman."

He laughed, then moved closer to her. Mandy braced herself for one of his tirades, absently smoothing the edge of a law book in the floor-to-ceiling bookcase. Confronting Bergman was never easy; he always intimidated her. And she had always come out the loser.

"No problem," he said pleasantly, running his gaze over her. "Anything you say, honey. You really are looking extraordinarily good, Amanda. When did you say your husband was coming home?"

Removing a book and letting it fall open, looking blindly at its pages, considering the calculation in Bergman's chuckle, Mandy shut it with a noisy clap. "What's the great interest in Russell?" she met his flank attack.

"You don't have to put on that act with me," Bergman said softly.

Her eyes widened, and she measured him then—levelly, hostilely.

"You're . . . different, Amanda," he said smoothly. "Marriage has changed you, I must say." Straightening his tie, he continued. "I find it absolutely intriguing. You're so—"

"Grown up?" Mandy prompted. "Not so gullible now, Bergman? You forget, I was held hostage by barbarians for three days. That has a way of putting things in perspective."

"Perhaps." Bergman ran his tongue around his lips and drew himself as tall as possible.

Mandy's alarm crawled up her spine. If she were different,

Bergman was different, too—harder, more obvious, maybe even a little desperate.

Antagonism laced through the silence. "You're right," she agreed at last. "Marriage has been good for me."

"Come off that, Mandy," he said tersely, flipping open a cigarette case and thumping one upon the desktop. "Felice told me everything. Oh, she didn't mean to go telling tales out of school. Don't go jumping on her case. She didn't think it was any big secret that you two got married just to keep from embarrassing a couple of old prudes."

Mandy spoke through her teeth. "They were not prudes, Bergman. And you're interfering where you have no business."

"Bull!"

When Mandy began backing away from him, Bergman took one step for every one she retreated. He almost had her pinned against the wall. Mandy was so astonished at his next words that she hardly realized it.

"Those things happen all the time," he said. "Hell, I can whip you out a suit for divorce in a few hours. You don't have to be saddled with that kind of arrangement. We can soak the boy on community property if we play it right."

"But—" She stared at the tenacity in his eyes and the smirk curling his lips. Nausea rippled through her.

"You're not a little virgin anymore, are you, Mandy girl? Now that you're all gown up, maybe we—"

In some respects Mandy suffered more fear now than she had felt from Theo. "Let—me—go, Bergman. I won't listen to this." She stood stiffly, pinched and drawn from his shocking proposition.

"You could have all the freedom you want, Mandy. Forget the community property if you want to. Think about it—no chains, no demands."

Mandy's lips thinned. "Your gall amazes me, Bergman," she said tightly. "Felice is under the impression that you want to marry her."

Turning up his hand, as if by waving it he could dispense with Felice and her emotions like some fairy godmother, Bergman grimaced. "Felice and I spent a few nights together. Hell, so she jumped to a few conclusions. She wanted it." The attorney cocked his head in a chiding mannerism. "*She* happens to dig men."

If she didn't finish this quickly, Mandy thought, he would

drive her to hysteria. She stopped him with the one weapon he could not avoid.

"I'm pregnant, Bergman," she dared him to continue. "I haven't the slightest intentions of filing for divorce."

"Really?" he sneered. "You should've been more careful."

His lack of surprise at her announcement startled Mandy. After a moment's pause, she sighed. "Loose tongues should be illegal—especially Felice's."

"Felice means well," he chuckled. "And what does the big guy say to becoming a father under these circumstances?"

Mandy knew she could not remain silent to such a question. And, not knowing how much he actually knew, she spoke the truth.

"Don't be my protector," she said and pulled herself tall. "Russell is unaware that I'm pregnant. If and when I tell him will be *my* decision."

"Okay, okay!" Reeves waved his hands in an indication of truce. "So you're married to a man whose interests are . . . elsewhere. Where's that going to get you? I'm available." His shoulders lifted, and he watched her closely. "I'd be generous, save you from embarrassment. I would be an easily explained father to your child. Face it, sweetheart, you need one."

Mandy trembled with outrage that he would force her into the position of refusing such a gesture. The limits to which he would go were farther than she had first thought, and she had no desire to anger such a man. How dare he put her in the role of rejector!

She grabbed her purse. And as she placed her fingers on the doorknob, Bergman protested, spinning to answer the unwelcome buzz of the phone.

"Wait a minute!" he yelled at Mandy, pointing a meaningful finger. He snapped his hello into the receiver. Pausing, glancing at her from time to time as if he feared she would sneak away, he lowered his voice.

"I have to take this call in the other room," he said pushing the hold button. "Don't you move an inch, Amanda," he demanded as he slipped through a side door.

Mandy watched the stocky shoulders with distaste as they disappeared through the door. And then with trepidation, for unless her instincts were failing her, she had made some dangerous mistakes with Bergman.

Even though she loved Russell desperately, she had never

accepted the role as his shadow. At least Russell had respected that. But Bergman did not respect her, even as a human being. What was he doing with her money?

Mandy was so angry she stepped to his filing cabinet and yanked open a drawer. Flipping through the yellow tabs, she searched until she found Phillips, Preston. The folder was fat and clumsy. She removed it and spread it upon Bergman's desk. Most of it pertained to affairs before her father's death, but toward the back she flipped over the pages much more slowly.

Records revealed her father's procedure of changing his will and reorganizing many of his stocks and shareholdings. They showed his death, and the correspondence regarding the beneficiaries. The authorizations she had signed were dated and in order. Bergman's power of attorney was signed and dated, several copies paper-clipped together.

Each transaction he had made with a bank was stapled to his signature on its proper form. Mandy browsed through them, musing if her nagging sense of doom were uncalled-for. Most of the transactions meant nothing to her—monies transferred from one company to another, money to Felice, money to her.

When Mandy lifted out the draft of four hundred eighty thousand dollars, she placed it on top of the file and stared at it for long, disbelieving moments. "Payable to Summit Realty" it said. Ordinarily she would have thought nothing about it. If it had not been dated only one week earlier, she probably would have passed it over with all the rest of Bergman's professional duties.

She searched for Felice's name on the attached warranty deed. Had Felice purchased property? Evidently not, and the deed was issued to Bergman Reeves—not Felice Phillips. And it was cosigned by Amanda Phillips Gregory!

Alarm bells shrilled through her head, and she bent to examine the forgery more closely. A good likeness, she thought grimly. Even though she was the loser here, Mandy felt oddly like a witness to a crime who hesitates to become involved.

Something at a loss, uncertain whether it was best to stay or go, Mandy folded her arms across her bosom and studied the traffic on the street below. Russell would never run from something like this. And though she might question her motives later and try to convince herself that the thoughts had

252 AN INNOCENT DECEPTION

never really come, she knew that she wanted Russell to approve of her. She felt herself strengthening.

When the door opened, she spun to face Bergman with both fists planted on her hips, her features pale, the inside of her knotting.

"Sorry to keep you, sweetheart," he said, smiling. "Where were we? Oh, yes, your suit for divorce. As I see it—"

"I don't give a damn how you see anything, Bergman," she said quietly.

Lifting the draft carefully, and its attached paperwork, she held it high enough that the drop sent it spinning across the top of the desk like something from outer space. Bergman bent to retrieve it, glanced at it for several tense seconds, and met her mute accusation with glittering eyes.

"What do you thing you're doing?" he asked, his face ugly. Mandy realized what she was doing; she was backing him into a corner like an angry animal. She was stupid to do it.

"I think that's my question, don't you?" Mandy felt the thrill of fear rippling up her spine. "Why don't you explain this to me?"

"You had no right to go through my files," he said righteously. He stepped in front of her and scooped up the file, slammed it shut and crammed it back into the cabinet.

"Doctors don't like for you to ask what's in the hypodermic either, Bergman," she clipped off the words more emphatically than she felt, "but I always do. I have a nasty habit of asking questions."

"And sometimes you jump to the wrong conclusions, Miss Mickey Spillane," he snarled, giving her a small shove from the front of his desk. "Like you did about one Russell Gregory?"

Reeves pushed her shoulder again, and she stepped backward attempting to brush away his hand. He did it again, and again she stumbled back. "There happen to be a few things in this world that you can't control, Amanda," he warned her, striking her shoulder again.

He could hit her quite hard if he really wanted to. To threaten him openly would be madness.

"I don't recall telling you I wanted to buy river property, Bergman. Has Felice decided to play the real estate game? Or are you playing a game of your own?"

He opened his mouth to answer, but she cut him off with acid words. "Well, since I'm a landowner now, I might as well pay Summit Realty a visit. I'll take over my property, Bergman."

Bergman whitened threateningly. "I can't stop you. *But*"—he clenched his teeth—"your father entrusted me with power of attorney for you. I can do what I feel is in the best interests for your financial affairs. You can't touch me, not with the law."

The rage Mandy felt whirled tiny white spots into the sides of her vision. "That, I'm afraid, is one of the privileges of being married to Russell Gregory, Bergman. I can engage a whole battery of lawyers to investigate you if I want to. Don't force me to do it."

Bergman's oath was filthy. He showed no sign of nervousness, yet she knew he was. He had to be. In a way she felt sorry for him. His bluster, his big talk—and now he was at the mercy of a woman.

"Don't be stupid, Amanda," he warned, his skin a mottled color.

Her temper flared. "And don't you threaten me! I laid open a man's head with an andiron once, Bergman. And I can lay yours open if I have to. I'll expose you. I can ruin you for the rest of your life. Don't underestimate the power of the pen."

"You bitch!"

"Yes," she agreed. Bluffing, gathering her purse with a shaky caution she hoped was not obvious, she paused in the doorway. "And Bergman, leave Felice alone. She doesn't need you. I don't think she even wants you."

"Get out of here!" he shouted.

"I'm going."

Mandy passed Miss Lambe with a stiff back. The secretary's eyebrows were stunned, and Mandy did not look at them again as she pushed the elevator button and waited.

As the elevator swallowed up Amanda, Jessica Lambe slumped at her desk. She could not imagine what had gone on in that office, but she had never seen Amanda leave this way before. She stepped to the doorway of Bergman's office and waited to be acknowledged. The thickset man leaned over his desk, both palms bearing his weight.

She finally urged, "Sir?"

He looked up, and crimson distress stained his neck and face. "Get my realtor on the phone, Jessica. Cancel my

damned appointment." He waved a disturbed hand outward
as if trying to clear his head of insects. "And hold all my
calls."

"But sir—"

"Do it, dammit! Now get out of here and leave me alone!
Just—" He took several steps toward her, his eyes wild and
disoriented. Miss Lambe retreated. "Just, *get out.*"

Pausing for only one prudent second, Jessica Lambe
touched her throat in an unconscious, protective gesture.
Nodding dumbly, wondering if she would be required to find
herself another job as the result of today's incident, whatever
it had been, she softly closed the door on Bergman Reeves.

Chapter Eighteen

Mandy left Bergman's office on an emotional high which lasted for days. Between the bouts of nausea and the long hours of work, she gradually fashioned her life into a pattern that she could cope with. Mandy accepted the future with more confidence than she ever remembered having. If a part of her life was missing—her husband—she was glad to have what she did: a child to be born, an outlet in which to create, the knowledge that she was becoming her own person.

Her editor pressed her for any draft she could deliver. Every fifty-page segment was mailed to be edited immediately. Four months to prepare a manuscript, to have it copyedited and readied for the printer, was a monumental task. The cover art had been commissioned, he said. She should be prepared, however, to spend three days in New York for one grueling work-through when she delivered the final draft.

Everything seemed to be going well for her, she decided, so she ignored her insomnia because Russell haunted her nights. As long as she drove herself through the hours of the day, just getting through them, she considered herself to be successful. It was the nights! She had hurt Russell badly. He had never called again. And when she found her excuses wearing thin, Mandy buried herself in exhausting work so she could not think.

When Russell did call again, Mandy was so shocked that she could hardly collect her wits.

"Russell!" she breathed, her eyes oddly out of focus, her thoughts skating off track. She sat in the middle of the floor in her room, wearing jeans and a smock, surrounded by stacks of drafts, a pencil in her hand. "Where are you?"

"New York," he replied evenly. If he were angry, he hid it. She swore his tone held disinterest more than exasperation. "I'll arrive in New Orleans at eight o'clock tonight."

Her sting of pleasure blurred with hurt feelings. He should have said, "Why didn't you wait for me? I can bear anything if you'll stay married to me. I'm dying to see you." But nothing in his voice even hinted at such a concession. His pride was equal to hers.

"You—you're coming here?" she stammered.

Russell audibly forced down the malice in his voice. "A man usually wants to see his wife, Amanda. Does that surprise you so much? Obviously not, since you didn't even wait for me to send for you."

"You couldn't have sent for me, even if you had wanted to, Russell!" she defended herself hotly.

"You didn't know that when you left."

He wanted her to say she was sorry, Mandy knew. In many ways she was. Rubbing at the space between her brows, she hedged. "I'm very busy," she began, then realized what an exaggeration it was.

"I won't take up too much of your time then, *darling.*"

His sarcasm was stabbing. She winced and shaped the next lie with difficulty. "I'll meet your plane, then."

"That won't be necessary," he said carefully. "Give me the address. I'll find you."

Not unless he had an extraordinary sense of detection, Mandy promised herself. Was it more the book that placed her at such odds with him, or the guilt that she was hiding a pregnancy?

"Is your family well?" she inquired politely just to hear his answering voice.

"My family is fine. They want to meet you. Are you all right?"

Images of what he looked like at this moment flashed

through her mind—that dazzling smile when he chose to bless someone with it; that big, easy grace. She kicked papers everywhere.

"I'm doing quite well, thank you," she mumbled.

"Oh."

He knew she was lying. The tension drifted over the distance separating them. She didn't want to talk, yet she didn't dare hang up.

"Are the Pattersons still in Europe?" she clutched at conversation. She gritted her teeth.

"No. Are you sure you're all right, Amanda?"

"Yes, yes! I'm fine, Russell! Well, it's so good to hear from you again. I'll . . . uh, get ready to see you."

His sound of disrespect made her flush, as if he could see her cringing. Her greatest talent seemed to be in making him angry. She would not detail her regrets or explain her refusal to be swallowed up in the dynamism of his personality. After slamming down the phone she raced for the bathroom to lean her head over the sink. She vomited until she could hardly stand up.

Oh, Lord! she thought, hanging onto the sink with both hands. She wanted to see Russell more than anything in the world. Must she run so scared?

"You can't leave here!" cried Felice when Mandy told her she was packing. "Where will you go? What will I do when Russell gets here? What will I tell him? He'll be furious, and he'll have a perfect right to be."

"Undoubtedly," Mandy agreed, as pale as a sheet and as limp. "I talked to Julie. She's going to let me spend the night with Terry and her. Several days, if I have to."

Felice shook her head disapprovingly and pushed Mandy down into a chair at the kitchen table. "I'll make you some tea. You look terrible."

Draping her head upon her arms on the table, Mandy winced at the truth. "I feel terrible. I was never so shocked at anything in my life as when he called. I can't see him yet. I'm too confused right now. Maybe after the book is published."

Water boiled cheerfully, and Mandy listened to the comforting sound of tea being brewed.

"Why after the book is published?" asked Felice as she spooned tea.

Mandy lifted her shoulders. "It's hard to explain—like I

could say, 'This is what I am. I've done something by myself that's successful.' "

"Because Russell is a success?"

Mandy's face opened at her stepmother's surprising insight. "Yes, I guess so. I need to at least be equal with him. How can I stand up for what I want if he overpowers me so? He always thinks in such large terms. His concepts are the world and tens of thousands of people. Mine are a few lines on a piece of paper." She leaned her forehead on her laced hands.

Felice sniffed. "You have to admit you got in your licks, honey. You injured his ego pretty badly when you refused to accept that call from Orban. No man would let that go."

"I know it." Lifting her head, Mandy brushed at tumbling wisps of hair. She would be mature. This was no time to weaken, not when she was within touching distance of achievement. "I'm—"

"You're what?" Felice finished pouring hot water.

"Afraid of him, I guess," Mandy replied thoughtfully. "He's the only person I know who can make me end up doing something I said I'd never do. And when he gets mad at me?" She turned her palm upward.

"You're married to the man now, Mandy. You owe him a few things as his wife."

"Marriage is a state of being, Felice. Not just a piece of paper. Our differences are pretty basic. I think I expected his next move to be a polite letter from his attorney."

"I don't know what to say."

Mandy's eyes apologized, and she shook her head. "I'll work it all out. I don't expect you to solve this mess. Just give me some time to put it in perspective. I'll have a long talk with Julie."

Felice made a sound of impatience. "You should be talking it over with Russell."

"I'm pregnant, Felice! All Russell would want to do is play the big father role. I don't want him that way. I'm selfish. I don't want him any way except that he loves *me*. Not because he's responsible for embarrassing Opal and Reginald Patterson. Or because he fathered my baby. It sounds egotistical and impractical to say it out loud, but it has to be for *me*. Me!"

As Felice poured her own cup of tea, she carefully kept her back to her stepdaughter. Mandy didn't notice. "You ask a lot," she said. "Perhaps too much. Take it from one who knows. Get your man when you can, even if the reason is not the best. Careers and all that can come later."

It was what Mandy would have expected of Felice. And many of the women she knew. Catching Russell was something many women would sell their soul for. *Catching?* She didn t want to *catch* a man.

Rising, Mandy stopped in the doorway, beautifully flushed and stubbornly resolute. "I can't settle for that. That may work for you, but I happen to want it all—husband, baby, career. And respect. Especially respect."

Felice met her with sad, disillusioned eyes. "You're making a mistake."

Mandy shook her head. "I can't help it. If I were any other way, I would be having a shabby little affair with David Rutherman."

Mandy left to pack her suitcases. Could a marriage exist between true equals? Must one partner live for the other? Many had tried mixing two careers and two forceful, demanding personalities. It seldom worked. Yet, she had proved with Tony Schaeffer that her needs would never transcend Russell's. Her love would always consider his rights equally with her own, perhaps before her own. But the choice had to be hers!

Terry's and Julie's off-campus apartment was a cramped two-room box, two flights up. The only thing that saved it from being dreadful was Julie's cleverness with posters and plants. Though Julie had reassured Mandy in a stream of garbled questions and answers that she would positively not be in the way, Mandy knew she was.

Her friend had dashed over during her lunch break from classes. Piling Mandy into her car, she had moved her into the apartment. Now Mandy threw one doubtful glance about the place, settled her shoulder bag on top of her suitcases, and realized she would be a burden.

"I'll only be here a couple of days," she promised.

"Nonsense, stay as long as you need to. How're you feeling?"

Julie, leaning against the kitchen sink, munched a peanut butter sandwich. Mandy's stomach began rebelling at the smell of it.

She imitated a gag. "I'm beginning to disbelieve that 'morning sickness' bull. I'm sick twenty-four hours a day. Do you think it'll ever go away?"

"All this business with Russell Gregory has you too nervous," Julie diagnosed. Her authoritative expression behind her glasses made her look like an impish wise owl. "The books say, if an expectant mother is contented, her nausea is little or none at all."

Mandy's eyes narrowed threateningly. "You know what you can do do with the books, don't you?"

Laughing, Julie grabbed up her tote bag. "I'm late. Do you want me to cut class and help you organize your things?"

Debating which of the three suitcases she would place behind the door, Mandy shook her head. Her Selectric was on the floor with the box containing the original of her prized manuscript.

"I'll be neat," she assured lamely and walked Julie to the door.

And Mandy tried to be. When Terry returned from work, she had disposed of the suitcases, worked for several hours on the book and had dinner in the oven. The three of them suppered on broiled ground beef patties, salad with baked potato and English peas.

"Delicious," approved Terry, swallowing. "Julie doesn't have time to cook. We eat a lot of cornflakes around here." Glancing at his wristwatch, he announced what everyone was thinking about. "Mr. Gregory's plane has arrived at International by now."

Terry had made no bones about disapproving of Mandy's refusal to talk to Russell. His loyalty for the man's rescue, which probably saved him from losing his arm, ran much deeper than sympathy for Mandy's state of confusion. He and Julie had argued for half an hour before he even agreed to let Mandy come.

"She'll go to a motel if we don't let her!" Julie had protested hotly. "She's too sick to be in some room by herself, Terry. That apartment is half mine, you know!"

Terry yelled back that he didn't like being a party to thwarting a man from seeing his wife. Mandy should be given a hard shake and told to wise up. Julie had countered by calling him a redneck, and at the table they hardly spoke ten words to each other. Mandy drooped and memorized the tines of her fork.

"Maybe it would be best if I went to a motel," she suggested tonelessly, poking at her baked potato which already looked as if it had been through an artillery practice.

"No!" snapped Julie.

"Yes!" Terry drowned out his wife's disagreement.

Realizing that Mandy was suffering from their constant bickering, Terry grabbed up plates and carried them to the sink. Mandy watched him—slender, wearing fraying jeans and a plaid shirt, his light-brown beard hiding most of his face. He and Julie were the epitome of a generation who could care less about external appearances.

"Stay out of it, Terry," warned Julie.

"I'm in it!" Terry slammed a palm down on the edge of the sink. "There's no way I can be out of it. The man has the right. They're married, and she's pregnant. My God, the world's being overrun with the rights of women. You're not the only ones on this planet!"

"Terry!" Julie's blush was furious. It would have changed into a flood of angry retorts, but the telephone shrilled beside the refrigerator. All of them froze and exchanged wordless glances. Mandy didn't breathe until it had rung four times.

"I'll bet a hundred dollars that's Felice," Mandy said darkly.

"I'll get it." Terry snatched up the receiver. "Hello!"

As he listened, his eyes measured Mandy closely. She felt as if she were on display, under a microscope. Terry nodded without commenting, then said, "I don't think I should, Mrs. Phillips."

Rapidly nearing the screaming point, Mandy chewed on her lip until it began bleeding. Then she blotted it on her napkin. She felt like a delinquent hiding from authorities.

Terry kept agreeing but saying nothing more.

"What—is—she—saying?" hissed Julie.

Mandy simply covered her face with her palms and steeled herself.

"I really would like to, Mrs. Phillips," Terry replied politely. "Tell Mr. Gregory I sympathize with him whole-heartedly. But Mandy is adamant that she won't see him tonight. Maybe she'll change her mind by tomorrow."

Shaking her head, Mandy rose and stepped swiftly toward the door where her suitcases were hidden. When Terry said, "Yessir," she stiffened as if someone held her trapped at gunpoint. Her heartbeats thudded in her ears.

Russell was in New Orleans! He was talking to Terry. The father of her child was standing in her own home, and she could almost feel his anger throbbing across the miles that separated them. She clamped her teeth to keep them from chattering.

"You know I'd like to tell you where she is, sir," Terry choked out the words. A fine line of perspiration beaded across his forehead. "But she has rights, too, Mr. Gregory. I'm caught—"

Silence.

"I'll tell her, sir," replied Terry anxiously as he slumped. He soberly replaced the receiver. Mandy hated herself, for she was quite familiar with the intimidating drive of Russell's personality. Julie, pouncing on her husband, demanded to know every word which had passed between them. Terry ignored her curiosity.

"He said he'll find you if he has to tear the city apart," Terry warned Mandy with knitted brows. "He will, too. Even though he doesn't know my name, I give that man twenty-four hours before he knows who I am and where this apartment is."

"Screw the drama, Terry," Julie made a caustic suggestion.

"Russell never makes empty threats," Mandy said in a different tone altogether. "I'd better go."

She pulled one suitcase from behind the door, then another before Julie caught both her arms. With a hostility born out of panic, Mandy jerked from her friend. The anguish of rejection swept across Julie's face, and Mandy immediately grabbed the other girl in her arms.

"I'm sorry," she said into the curve of Julie's neck. "See the things he makes me do? I know it's not fair, dragging you two into all this. Anything between Russell and me should be worked out in private. But I'm not used to this. I don't know what to do. I'm running scared, and I can't help it."

With a gesture more like that of a father, Terry wrapped his arms around them both. Mandy lifted her face to her friends. "Please forgive me," she begged.

"We love you, Mandy," he said tenderly. "It's always been the three of us, you know that. We've cried all over each other for so long, I'd be offended if you didn't. But I can't help it if I believe he's right."

"Ter—" began Julie.

Mandy held up her hand. "It's all right, Julie. I understand Terry's point. In the morning I'll get a room at a motel and think everything out." She leaned back on Terry's arm, taking comfort from the feel of his long, lanky body pressed against them. "Please don't tell Felice where I am. Russell's not like you, Terry. He's used to having his way. He'll wangle the truth out of Felice in five minutes. Once he finds me, I'll be saying things I don't mean and agreeing to terms I can't live with."

Shaking his head, Terry replaced her suitcases behind the door. "Tomorrow then. He can't do much damage tonight. Let's go to bed. It's late."

Mandy smiled at the two of them with their arms twined about each other. With their jeans and shirts and flowing hair, they looked like Raggedy Ann and Raggedy Andy.

"You're my dearest, dearest friend," she said and kissed Julie's cheek. "Don't take Russell's side too much, Terry. I'm the one who needs your sympathy."

"Frankly, I think you're nuts about the guy." Terry winked. "Why don't you admit it?"

Mandy twisted her mouth out of shape prettily. "Oh, I've never had trouble admitting that. But I'm kind of nuts about my book, too. And Russell hates it. I can't let anything keep me from finishing it, not even him."

But in spite of her words, as she drowsily curled herself into a knot that night, Mandy wondered if it wouldn't be much simpler to give in to her husband and try to make a go of it. Perhaps she should find some other niche in life besides her controversial writing. Life, after all, was not a series of self-fulfillments; it was more a pattern of self-sacrifices. That was why so few people were truly successful at it. Was she making the same selfish mistakes that she condemned Bergman for?

Julie's cuckoo popped out of his hand-carved clock and tipped his musical head ten times the next morning. The apartment was empty. Terry and Julie had left hours earlier after a breakfast of cornflakes. Mandy had been typing steadily for over two hours.

Yawning, she stretched in a weary attempt to clear her head. Her eyes felt as if they were filled with sand, and she bent over her Selectric for several minutes, critically reading the draft. With an immense sense of accomplishment then, she ripped the page from the typewriter and leaned back to stare at it in near disbelief.

It was done. Some editing, a final typing, and she would make her rigid deadline after all. The relief was all-encompassing—tired, happy, lonely. Before she rested, Mandy would place a call to her editor. Then she'd allow herself the luxury of congratulations.

Caught in the backlash of pregnancy drowsiness and nervous exhaustion, Mandy folded her arms over the carriage of the machine and dropped her head upon them. She meant to close her eyes for only a moment.

Insistent knocking on the door roused her from the oblivion of sleep. Lifting her tousled head, she nearly collapsed with a sudden flood of nausea. She sat very still. Julie must have decided to cut a class and come checking on her.

"Just a minute," Mandy called groggily.

It occurred to her, somewhere in the hazy shadows of her mind, as her reflexes automatically turned the knob, that Julie would not be knocking; she would be using her key. But it was too late. The panel already creaked on its aging hinges, leaving Mandy exposed to the unflinching impatience of her husband.

"How did you—" she began and pressed timorous fingers against the paleness of her lips.

"Very easily," he replied between his teeth. "You look terrible."

Without benefit of any explanations, the tall man stalked Mandy back into the room. She did not need to hear his reasons. His outraged pride was all over him, and she felt a terrible impulse to fly at him with defenses of her side. But nature betrayed her. Nausea bubbled into her throat, and she clapped her mouth hard, dashing for the bathroom.

The slam of the door shattered between them, and Mandy wrenched on the spigot of the claw-footed tub. The sound of running water protected her, and she tried to retch as silently as possible. Burying her face in a towel, she thought that she hated Russell quite as much as she loved him. His virile manhood had made her pregnant yet he towered over her in perfect health.

As the door swung open behind her, Mandy splashed cold water on her face.

"Russell?" she faltered, whirling about, her face half hidden by the towel.

She found no comfort in the depths of his brilliant brown eyes. The impending battle could not be prevented. It would consume them like an ugly virus, and they would both sicken from it. "I was going to call you today," she explained lamely, thinking it was not entirely a lie, for she truly had longed to hear his voice.

"Were you now?" he bit the clear words dangerously. "Like you were going to wait in Zurich until I sent for you?"

Mandy's face twisted with a fresh guilt. Her excuses for deceiving Russell now seemed completely inexcusable. Her feminine pride, even her professional pride, felt like a hollow illusion. Her independence felt like a folly. Now he would despise her and never trust her again. And she could not blame him. What had she expected?

Carefully, she inched past him and paused in the center of the small living room, looking like a slender boy in her tight pants and blouse. She faced Russell then and struggled not to crumble at the sight of the hard chiseled features and the angular intolerance of his mouth.

His voice slashed through her defenses like a knife. "Don't you ever put me in this position again, Amanda."

She stiffened. "I didn't hurt you intentionally, Russell. I'll admit that I left Zurich in haste, but—"

"How cool we are," he mocked. "Suppose you explain Zurich to me, then. I've spent considerable time wondering about your hasty exit, as you call it. Tell me some lies, my loyal little wife."

Mandy drooped in defeat. "What good would it do to explain? Your mind is made up. You're always so sure you know everything, Russell. You see nothing but my faults anyway. Think what you please."

"Tell me!" he commanded. Russell took one deliberate step toward her, his whole body tensed with repressed violence. She could not stand up to the force of his contempt. Her well-rehearsed plans began to sink into the same cement her feet felt embedded in.

"I was going to stay," she said shakenly, "exactly as we agreed. But I saw you and Mickey in the lobby as you were leaving."

"So?"

"I kept telling myself that your behavior was only a gesture to comfort a distraught child, but it didn't help. I was insulted."

Russell's dark eyes narrowed in puzzled concentration. When he did not counterattack, Mandy chewed at her lip. "I don't even remember what I said," he mused softly.

"It wasn't so much what you said, Russell. But you practically apologized to Carolyn for marrying me. What would you have me feel? If our positions were reversed—if I made excuses to Bergman Reeves—you would strangle us both. I came home and kept my accusations to myself."

Mandy did not know if Russell believed her or not. His face was an unreadable mask. He turned with chilling abruptness and walked about the room without speaking. Pausing over her typewriter, he studied the stack of typescript. When he reached to lift the final page resting on top, Mandy darted for it like a panicked adolescent. Grabbing it from his fingers, she scooped up the remainder of the manuscript and clutched it tightly to her chest. Russell's eyebrows lifted, as if her protective instincts amused him.

He chuckled. "Do you think I'd destroy it simply because it may cost me my career?"

"I don't want you to mock it." She challenged him with the flushed zeal of a mother defending a misjudged child. "Do you think you're the only moral person in the world, Russell Gregory?" she cried. "From the beginning you've mistrusted my judgment. Did it ever occur to you—*just once*—to consider my discretion?"

"You could have corrected any misconceptions if you had wanted to," he snapped hotly. "You didn't have to always let me think the worst."

Her eyes sparkled angrily, plunging into his brooding ones. "A person doesn't want to build a case for something like *trust*. What do you think trust is, Russell? It's belief when there're no reasons to believe. If you must have a reason, I told Tony Schaeffer the first day that I wouldn't even consider writing the book if it would hurt you. He thought I was crazy, but at least he believed me. He had more faith in my responsibility than you did."

Mandy's words had the desired impact. For a long moment Russell's hand rubbed across his jaw, a blank vacancy lurking behind his eyes. They were opposite chesspieces on the same board—motionless, with no logical move left to make. In a reaction bordering on shock, Mandy watched the handsome man grasp her typewriter beneath one arm and remove a suitcase from behind the door.

"What are you doing?" she whispered.

"Taking a chance on my heart instead of my head," he answered with a slight grimace. "You're coming home."

"You haven't asked me if I wanted to!" she blurted.

"I'm not taking that big a chance," he returned, flinging open the apartment door and disappearing.

When he returned empty-handed, Mandy still had not moved from the center of the apartment. She was incapable of moving. All the late-night reasoning and self-examinations seemed for nothing. She observed his possessive movements with a helpless loss. She wanted him to take her back home. She wanted to be cuddled and understood. But she could not bring herself to ask anything from him.

"Would you believe me if I said I'd rather stay here a while longer?" she got out the question.

"No." He paused. "I won't even discuss it. Have you seen a doctor?"

Leaning against a chair, Russell unconsciously hooked a foot upon its rung and braced his forearm across his knee. He was alarmingly attractive in that position. She was no more equipped to ignore the muscular thighs and tightly pulled corduroy pants than before. The sexual part of her flinched at the outline of his crotch. She jerked her eyes away.

"I . . . I don't need a doctor. I've picked up a virus. I'll be all right in a few days."

He was silent for so long that her eyes darted to his face, only to find him brooding upon the outline of her legs. Her fingers warily smoothed the edge of her manuscript as the curve of her cheeks blazed hotly.

Russell took two quick steps toward her, and their eyes collided again. A sweet pain shot through her. Her dread blurred with her craving to be held, and her heart beat too quickly, for she didn't know if she could bear it.

"You'll catch the virus," she said in a foolish, small voice.

"I'll take *that* risk," he said quietly. He grasped one trembling wrist and slowly pulled her toward him.

Flicking her tongue over dry lips, Mandy wriggled against the demand of his fingers. "Don't," she pleaded.

"I've come a long way for you, Mandy. And I think I've been patient. Now I want the truth about how you really feel, and I don't want it in pieces. You and I had an understanding."

"Understanding?" She taunted his assumption. "A good sexual relationship was what we had."

"That's part of any understanding."

Her grimace was not flattering. "To an uncomplicated male ego, perhaps. I need more. Much more."

"Tell me what you want then, wise one." He grinned maddeningly.

"You accuse me of half-truths and deceptions, Russell, but that's all you've ever given me. I've never known where I stand with you!" Mandy jerked her hand free and hugged herself to keep from shivering. As she whirled away, she visualized the gaunt tension curling the sensuality of his mouth. She heard his swift intake of breath and shivered beneath his wounded stare.

"Come here, Mandy," his voice drifted huskily from behind her. She refused. Her head moved slowly from side to side.

"I . . . I can't think when you're like this. You make me feel like a fool when I know I'm not."

"Think all you want to," he said. "Or feel like a fool. I don't care. Just come here."

Mandy's nails cut grooves into the smooth flesh of her palms. Russell didn't miss the small sign of desperation. He had waited so many weeks for this moment; now he feared that in his anxiety he would ruin it. His gaze inched upward to the brave slenderness of her shoulders. And to the distraught rise and fall of her breaths.

"After we talk, maybe," she protested. "After we understand—"

"Now."

She could not argue with him anymore, and if Russell guessed that she was incapable of taking the step herself, he did not show it. He touched her shoulders with comforting, wandering fingers. Then he carefully turned her until she faced him. His body seemed to fit itself about her, taking her completely into himself. She groaned as her strength drained away. Touching his tongue to her ear, he caught the tiny lobe in his teeth.

Russell knew she was on the brink of relenting. Mandy knew it, too. She felt the fragile threads of resistance snapping. And when his big body bent over her vulnerable one she could not cherish her list of grievances. Her blue eyes filled with the liquid need to understand his affections.

"But I had everything . . . all planned out," she choked. "I knew what I must do."

"Damn your plans," he murmured, as if he consciously sensed the boundary over which he was stepping. "I love you."

Pressing his cheek against hers, he let his eyes flutter closed. Mandy slumped against him. After all this time she hardly believed that he had said the words.

"Oh!" she said.

"Don't give it away, Mandy," he whispered and moved his lips over her mouth. "Not for the sake of a dream that might never come true." Russell opened his eyes, and they told her almost more than the wistfulness of his voice. "Meet me in the middle, sweetheart."

His kiss was infinitely tender—not dazzling, not shattering, but warm—like the earth. Mandy opened to him, accepting as a rose welcomes gentle, life-giving rain. She smiled into his kiss. And then she grew light-headed from the fierce pulse of heat flaming between them.

Without releasing her lips, Russell drew her toward the beckoning haven of the adjoining bedroom. Mandy had no doubts about what he wanted for she wanted it, too. But she could not yield; not like this, not with a lie hanging between them. It would be wrong; it would leave them disappointed and unhappy. She tore her lips away.

When he lifted his dark head, his eyes glowing with a desire to see a responding passion, she touched her fingers to his lips before he could object.

"I'll let you take me home," she said. "I won't fight you. But I . . . I can't make love, Russell. I want to. You know me far too well for me to pretend. But words have to be said. They're important."

"Say the words to me, then." He kissed her softly. Then again. And again. "Tell me what I already know. Say the words."

Mandy's head draped back over the strong curve of his arm as he held her up. As she slipped into the warm current of his need, the words came easily.

"I wanted to say them before," she said. "I've loved you for a long time. I've loved you all my life."

"Hold me," he whispered. "Don't let go."

"Are you afraid to love?"

"Yes. Very afraid."

Mandy lowered her head to the hardness of his chest. "What will happen to us?"

"Nothing," he said, deliberately misinterpreting. "Nothing will happen that you don't want to."

One hand held her up, and Russell's other slipped beneath the bottom of her blouse. His hand closed about the firmness of her breast and paused as it tightened beneath his fingers. She thought she should tell him about their baby. But he was crushing her with such urgency—kissing her, drugging her with his tongue, smoothing her waist, her back, her buttocks which flexed against his palm.

"You always know how to touch me," Mandy whimpered, knowing that her secret would be told when the time was right. Now he would make love to her. He would touch the center of her soul, and she would not refuse him again.

Through the daze of Russell's hands which hungrily roved over her, Mandy only half heard the bantering voices in the hallway. She struggled to clear herself of euphoria. Russell's sound of complaint groaned against her mouth, forcing them both back to the present. The key scraped in the lock.

"Oh!" Julie's hand flew to her open mouth. "I'm terribly sorry! I . . . ah, oh dear."

Russell, coming to his senses, slowly steadied Mandy upon her feet. She stumbled against his legs, and he caught her with a steady arm about her waist.

Clearing his throat, wetting his lips, Terry let out his breath. He was completely at a loss and stood in the open doorway, stroking his beard. Extending his hand then, he finally stepped forward.

"We've never formally met, have we?" he grinned. "I wasn't in much of a condition to converse the last time. Or thank you either, Mr. Gregory. Which I do now, sir, with more gratitude than I can tell you."

"You've already paid me back more than it was worth, Terry," Russell said, innocently creating a roomful of instant tension.

Mandy's quick intuitions, completely recovered now, flashed across her face. "What—" she began and darted a question toward Julie. Then toward Terry.

Terry, bearing the swift disapproval of his wife, flushed. "Well," he shrugged, trying to remain angelically unruffled,

"I did give Mr. Gregory a short call this morning. Now, before you hit the ceiling, Julie," he indicated Mandy with a wave of his hand, "you can see it didn't do any damage."

"But after all we said last night?" Julie cried.

Terry pulled at his beard and shot a glance toward Russell. "I think I'm in trouble, sir."

"Undoubtedly," Russell chuckled, picking up Mandy's remaining suitcases. He had no intentions of being trapped in any domestic scraps beside his own.

He didn't give Julie time to do more than sputter, "You haven't heard the last of this, Terry O'Connor."

"Go easy, Mrs. O'Connor," he said, giving Mandy a gentle shove out of the apartment. "We men are forced to use the best weapons at hand. That's only good self-defense."

He might have said more if Terry had not given him a tiny salute and shut the door.

Chapter Nineteen

"I have to call my editor," Mandy said with a worried sigh. Russell swung the rented car up the curved driveway off St. Charles Avenue as the wrought-iron gates creaked shut behind them. Terraced steps gleamed invitingly, stretching upward, welcoming Mandy home.

So many things in her life had changed during the last twenty-four hours, Mandy felt she had been gone a month. As she slid across the car seat and reached for her door, Russell grabbed her free hand. Holding it with unflinching determination, he flicked off the ignition and rolled down the windows with a touch of a button. Settling back, he lazily stretched his long legs beneath the dashboard.

"I should call right away," she added. Beyond the fence, cars passed and their sounds mingled with an occasional horn and the muted activity of the long tree-studded street.

"A few more minutes won't make any difference," Russell said.

"But I told him I'd come to New York the minute I finished the manuscript. A film agent in California is waiting for my final draft right now."

"You'll get to New York in plenty of time," he assured her.

"I'm taking you myself. My parents are coming to meet you the end of the week."

The fall breeze was warm, and it blended the discreet scent of his aftershave with the fragrance of fallen leaves. Mandy struggled to adapt to his possessive decisions as she watched amber leaves tumbling over the lawn, scuttling on the asphalt with happy, scratching noises, flinging themselves against the impasse of the car.

Crossing her legs, Mandy picked at a thread of her jeans. "I feel as if I'm trying to stand up with the weight of the whole world on my shoulders," she confessed. "Indecision does this to me."

Russell, threading his hands behind his head, shot her a curious glance. "You're exhausted. You have absolutely no sense of your limits, Mandy. If your color doesn't improve drastically in the next few hours, I'm calling a halt to everything—agent or no agent."

"I want to walk," Mandy changed the conversation hastily and shoved open her door.

Without looking to see if he followed, for she knew he would, she swiftly stepped across the manicured lawns. The more she postponed telling Russell about the baby, the more complex the deception grew. It had been a terrible mistake not to tell him at the very beginning. Now, the longer she put it off, the more like a liar she would look when she did explain.

How could he keep from guessing? Human nature was so funny, she thought; it was incredibly blind to something it wasn't expecting to see. If she did not want to wreck every hard-won shred of trust between them, she must choose her moment with great care. Kicking at a drift of leaves, Mandy sent them cascading in a flurry. Russell's footsteps crunched behind her.

"I love fall, don't you?" she asked without turning. "The smell of it, I guess."

His head lowered to the exposed nape of her neck. "I love you," he said softly, brushing his lips gently along its curve.

She whirled about, not knowing what to say. "Did you stay here last night?"

The silence was deadly until he answered.

"Felice made me quite at home," he finally replied. "In fact, we had a lovely dinner and frittered away the evening going through all your old photograph albums. Your step-mother likes me. She thinks you're out of your mind by letting a prize like me . . . dangle."

"Did she say that?"

"I figured it out," he grinned. Gesturing at the huge, two-story brick estate, he asked, "What are you going to do with this house?"

"What d'you mean?"

Russell swept his gaze over the huge property. "We'll have to live in New York, of course." When she made a small sound he met her eyes. "Don't give me any of your arguments, Mandy. You'll be closer to your work."

"I just can't—"

"Let Felice have it. Bergman can look after her. This place is more than you can handle right now."

Mandy braced both fists on her hips. Her hair tumbled wildly about her face. "How do you do this to me? *I* don't even know what I'm going to do yet, and you have my life all mapped out. For one thing, Bergman is not in my employ anymore. He misappropriated some of my money, and he's lucky I don't have him disbarred. In the second place, I have property besides this, thanks to Bergman. I can't go packing off to New York on a permanent basis."

Russell took her by the shoulders more roughly than he realized. Studying the oval beauty of Mandy's face, scowling at its uncustomary paleness, he drew her to a wrought-iron bench and pushed her down onto it. When he took her hand and spread it over his braced knee—smoothing it, studying the soft shape of it—Mandy swallowed down her tempest of objections. High overhead, squirrels darted, chattering as they went about their business. She suffered a horrible need to vomit.

"Look, Mandy," Russell said, "you might as well accept the fact that I want my wife to be with me. I'll do anything I have to. And I'm thinking of your career as much as my own. I'm not trying to take anything away from you. Why can't you believe that?"

"Since when have you taken an interest in my work? You've fought me ever since I began this book!"

"So we're back to that." He gave a soft sigh and closed his eyes for a moment. "You might as well come off that paranoia. I'm not against you. I've never been against you, only what you could do to me if you weren't careful. If you'll be halfway fair, you'll admit that I had good reason to be worried."

"I haven't forgotten some of the things you said," she said, trying unsuccessfully to remove her hand.

Bending over her head, placing a soft kiss in the disheveled locks, Russell said thickly, "And I remember some of the things *you* said. If I could have forgotten, I swear to heaven I wouldn't be here now."

He was remembering the last night in Switzerland—her reaching out to him, her taking, her changing concepts of herself.

She whimpered. "I don't want to lose that. I mean it."

"There's no need to lose it. Let me help you. Do you feel like walking again?"

Nodding, she sent him a tiny smile. "Yes. I'll show you the potting shed."

Pulling her up, Russell supported her with a strong arm about her waist. Chuckling, he matched his steps to hers. "I'm excited. I've never toured a potting shed before."

"Clown," she scolded laughingly. "I was a strange child."

"I can believe that."

Mandy poked him in the ribs with a fist, and he stopped to lift her hand to his lips. For a moment she was awed by the tender eroticism. Dizzy, she closed her eyes and gave herself up to the chain of electrifying sensations chasing through her body. As he kissed her wrist, her fingers, she finally lifted dazed eyes to his.

"Oh, Russell," she breathed. "You do the most frightening things to me sometimes."

"I don't want you to ever be frightened . . . of anything."

The moment drifted away and became lost in time. Unconsciously, her hand moved below her waist to the imperceptible swell. The desire to lean against his chest and cry nearly overcame her. Tipping up her chin, Russell smiled.

"About your childhood," he urged and inclined his head toward the small stone building huddling at the rear of the property.

Swallowing, Mandy let out her breath slowly. "I don't know how I ever grasped the concept of things growing in the ground," she began her explanation. "It just came to me. Maybe I followed the gardener around, I don't know. Anyway, I somehow figured out that life did go on down there—in the ground. I think the greatest disappointment in my life was over the tricycle."

Russell frowned. "The tricycle?"

"It broke. Right below the handlebars. I didn't tell Daddy."

"Oh, I wouldn't have, either."

Mandy pointedly glared at his interruption. "Anyway, I dragged the tricycle out to the potting shed and worked for hours filling a box with dirt. I buried it. The tricycle. In the dirt."

She gazed into his eyes with the open wonder of a child. Russell's mouth twisted downward in an attempt to not laugh.

"A logical move," he nodded, sobering instantly.

Mandy's mouth pursed. "That's not the whole story."

"Oh."

"I wasn't able to cover the entire tricycle, of course. But I was careful to cover the broken part. I fitted it back together exactly right. And patted the dirt over it just so." She frowned. "I don't remember watering it."

"God, I hope not."

"Russell!"

"Sorry."

She went on. "I let it stay there for at least a week. If the gardener found it, he never said a word. Later, when I went out to look at it, I uncovered it with such confidence. It never occurred to me that it wouldn't have grown back together. You can't imagine how I felt when it came apart. I thought the earth healed everything."

Russell wet his lips. "Of course I can understand."

"I remember sitting there in my corduroy overalls. I just looked at it. I didn't tell anyone what I had done. Not for years."

Reaching over her head, Russell shoved open a stubborn, creaking door. The shed smelled of potting soil and rank, stale air. He squinted into the dimness.

"Was this where the miracle did not occur?" he asked quietly.

"I don't suppose you've ever done anything stupid," she smirked at him then lifted her shoulders in a slender shrug.

"Many times," he chuckled. "But this is not one of them."

His arms went around Mandy, and her face lifted to his naturally. He kissed her for a very long time. And when he cradled her to his chest his voice was thick. "Why can't you trust, sweetheart?"

"I'm trying to, Russell," she whispered. "Sometimes I feel like we're strangers, that we've just met."

"That feeling will go away. I'm not going to change my mind about you, Mandy."

"When you didn't call me from Orban, I thought you had. I wouldn't have blamed you if you had. I was unforgiveable."

"I was hurt, honey. You made me expose myself to you, and then you turned away. If I could have, I would have put you out of my life for keeps, right then."

"Give me a little time, Russell," she begged him, holding him tightly, a bit frantically. "Just a little time."

"How could I refuse to indulge a lady who grows tricycles?" he asked, kissing her again.

Mandy sensed Russell's strength all through the evening. It radiated to her from across the dinner table. Later, it wrapped her in its warmth like the music they listened to while stretched on the carpet in the living room. Occasionally he touched her—her cheek, her hair, her knee—simply to touch her. And, their eyes met in a silent exploration, putting their times of physical love into a perspective with a deeper oneness.

"I'm tired," she murmured at last.

Russell led her upstairs. She did not debate sleeping with him. It seemed the right thing to do. Fighting down the nagging persistence of nausea, she showered and prayed it would soothe some of the feverish ache. When she emerged from the bathroom, not finding him, she ducked into the hall.

Russell was hunched on the top of the carpeted stairway, his chin balanced on his knees, reading her manuscript.

An unexplainable horror flashed through her, and Mandy stepped toward him with trembling steps. And when he lifted his eyes to her, and then continued reading without a single comment, Mandy felt like she was dying. Yielding to the need to know his opinion of her writing, she carefully knelt down beside him.

She could hardly ask the question knotting in her throat. She thought if he said he didn't like it, or even if he looked like it, she would shatter into a thousand pieces. Please let him like it, she prayed. Please let him like it.

"Russell?" Her voice squeaked.

"Hm?"

Shrinking inside herself, she squeezed down beside him. She could hardly breathe.

"Where are you?" He turned the manuscript page toward her. Her eyes scanned down the page. "Oh." Then, unable to stand it, she covered the page with her hand. "What do you think?" she whispered.

Russell rubbed his jaw. "I didn't expect this," he said after a thoughtful pause.

"Expect . . . what! *What?*"

"You write with a good clean technique, Mandy. I guess I expected some dramatized, maudlin account. But it's not. It's beautifully constructed." His brows lifted. "I'm impressed. It's quite good, I think. Of course, I'm no expert. But—"

"You like it?"

"Yes."

"Are you sure?"

"Yes. I'm sure," he said.

"You're not being nice because you love me, are you?"

Russell laughed, his head tilted to one side. Placing the manuscript aside, he reached for her and drew her almost beneath him. Positioned at a crazy angle, he ground himself against her, smiling into the anguished eyes.

"Yes, yes. I like it. I really do. You should be proud of it."

Mandy's face twisted. "But it's not *really* good. I mean, compared to—"

A large hand clapped over her mouth and garbled her protests. "What does it take to convince you?" he chuckled.

"I—"

The kiss grew out of control like a flashing spark in dry tinder. Mandy's hands eagerly touched him everywhere. Her body strained to his, unable to get close enough.

"Oh, Mandy," Russell moaned and began undoing her robe.

When she grabbed her mouth and began fighting him, stumbling upward to disappear into her bedroom, he didn't know what to think. Slowly, Russell dragged himself up and followed her. Puzzled, dazed, trying to fit pieces together that he was unequipped to handle, he slumped down on the edge of her bed and waited for her to return.

Mandy did not come back right away. Russell sighed and braced his elbows upon his knees, worrying about her.

Coming to a decision then, he frowned and reached for the phone book on the table beside the bed. He ran a long finger down the penned list of numbers in the front. Emergency numbers. When he came to her physician, Dr. Wes Baker, Russell stopped. He memorized the number, considered a moment, then dialed.

The telephone rang three times before a feminine voice answered. The doctor's wife, he presumed.

"Dr. Baker, please," he said.

"One moment. Could I say who's calling?"

"Russell Gregory. I'm calling about Amanda Phillips Gregory. Dr. Baker is her physician, I believe."

"Just a minute."

Russell waited, drumming his fingers on the bedside table. When the masculine voice spoke he was not surprised at the gruff professionalism. "Yes, Mr. Gregory. What can I do for you?"

"It's about Amanda. I'm her husband. She's not at all well, Dr. Baker. And I'm getting rather worried."

"Is she still nauseous? Perhaps I'd better prescribe something. I told her if that stomach didn't settle down in a few weeks to give me a call."

"Oh?"

"It should confine itself to simple morning sickness in a week or so. If this prescription I'm ordering doesn't control it, she should move up her next appointment."

Russell felt as if he had walked out of a dark room. Bleak bitterness drained the color from his face. For several seconds he sat like a dead man—a lifetime, it seemed to him—and the calmness in his own voice shocked him.

"I'll see to that," he agreed smoothly. "I'm flying to New York tomorrow, however. She wants to come with me. Flying won't be any risk, will it?"

"Oh, I don't think so, Mr. Gregory. Not at this stage. But I don't want this nausea lingering too long. Amanda's in good health, and I don't want any iron deficiency or for her to lose too much weight. Make sure she takes her vitamins."

"Of course. And I'll get the medication immediately."

"Good. Don't hesitate to call if you need to."

"Thank you," Russell answered numbly and replaced the receiver without conscious effort.

Mandy stepped from the bath with the unknowing ignorance of a hit-and-run victim. Wanly, she smiled at him—pale, yet warmly happy because he understood her work at last, approved of it.

Russell arose and blocked her path with one long step. The flesh over his cheekbones was colorless and drawn tightly. Her eyes flared wide.

"I ought to wring your neck," he said unexpectedly, and the cutting words seemed to slap full across her face.

She drew back in surprise, gasping a little, her blue eyes searching for an explanation to his white-hot fury. Her mind barely grasped the rumpled bed, the open directory, the telephone spilled over the bed. But her guilt comprehended it instantly. No lie in the world could protect her now, Mandy thought dumbly.

"Oh, Russell!" she breathed, wishing for a thousand ways to correct her mistake—for at least one way.

"Don't 'Russell' me!" he thundered at her, unable to control his hurt. "You're the most selfish person I've ever known! What were you waiting for, my love, to have an abortion before I could find out? Did I happen upon the scene before you could get the evil little act done? Hm? I spill my guts to you and tell you I love you, and *you do this to me?* What kind of woman are you, for God's sake?"

His fingers crushed her shoulders, and he jerked her, snapping her head backward. Wounded tears welled in his eyes, and when they wet his cheeks Mandy wished she could disappear. Never, in her wildest resentments of Russell, would she have willed this pain upon him.

"I'm sorry," she whispered, and the words sounded more like a lie than the other.

For one eternal second a large hand poised beside her head. Mandy closed her eyes and dropped her chin, thinking he would hit her and not caring if he did. She deserved to be hit.

And when he slowly dropped his hand, standing stricken and beaten before her, she shook her head and gradually bent until her face almost rested upon her knees. She heard him pacing and swearing under his breath.

"Damn you, Amanda!" he yelled at last, spinning about. "Don't you care about anything?"

"Yes," she choked and kept her head down. "The baby. You. Me."

Stumbling toward to the hall door in a daze, instinctively

craving to escape the force of his wrath, she snatched it open.
It suddenly wrenched from her hands and slammed furiously
before her face.

"No!" Russell choked, positioning himself before her until
she was compelled to lift her tearstained face. "You're not
running this time. Not this time."

She was too tired to figure it out, too sick, too weary of
counting her mistakes. Her head slowly pivoted from side to
side.

"I wanted the baby," she said dully. Her distraught words
were a monotone. She did not focus her eyes. "From the
moment I knew, I wanted it. It's mine. You can't take it. It's
mine. It's mine."

Russell hardly recognized the sound of his own voice when
he spoke again. "What about us, Mandy? You and me,
together—the people who made this baby? What about us?"

She could not bear his anguish any longer so she turned
from it and groped blindly for the door. Mandy's answer was
the most honest she could give him.

"I swear to God, Russell, I don't know."

To look back upon a mistake, to know it was caused by
circumstances run amuck, was one thing. But to know that
someone else's pain could have been avoided was another.
They had loved blindly and with passion. But they had hurt
each other, almost beyond repair. The blame was equally
shared, compelling them to be cautious.

So, Amanda Devon Phillips Gregory arrived at Kennedy
International Airport with a new respect of her responsibilities to people besides herself. The agreement between them
was mutual; they would back off. They would not scrap a
marriage in haste, nor would they force one that was a
mistake. They would give time a chance.

The handsome, brooding man who now seemed to be
constantly at Mandy's side never ceased surprising her. Since
Russell had discovered his impending fatherhood, she had
glimpsed an entirely new side of his personality. He possessed, tucked deeply away inside him, a large streak of
patience that she had never suspected.

He did not gush and hover over her like a fussy, over-
zealous hen. Russell moved her into a quiet, peaceful bedroom of his New York town house, all to herself. He followed
her to the bathroom and refused to turn his head like a

gentleman. He knelt beside her when she vomited and bathed her face with cool water. He rubbed her feet and brushed her hair and brought her ginger ale to drink with her medication.

Never once did he pressure her about taking her place in his bed. At the end of the day, he left her at the door of the bedroom adjoining his. He kissed her tenderly, then climbed into the big double bed in his room.

But though the open door between them did not threaten her, Mandy knew the day of reckoning would invariably come. The sun always rose; spring always bloomed. Russell wouldn't wait forever. He would want his answer. Was she his wife or not?

Mandy swore vehemently, the day after they arrived, that she could never drag herself into the office on Park Avenue to meet with her editor. Russell would have none of it. He compelled her to shower and laid out a slack suit of beige gabardine and a floral jersey blouse.

During lunch he drove over from his office at Security Federal and sat quietly while she and Adam Johnson talked and ate Reuben sandwiches. The deli was a posh affair, attracting the publishing industry's elite with its antique hanging lamps over tables surrounded with wicker chairs, beveled mirrors and drooping ferns.

When the subject of the screenplay came up, Mandy held up protesting palms.

"I just can't, Mr. Johnson," she said.

The stocky man peered over the top of his gold-rimmed glasses. "There's not much involved besides a trip to the West Coast. The man who's been asked to adapt the book wants to have a few informal conferences, that's all. You have such a straightforward piece of work here, Amanda, it would be a shame to wind up with a soapy, trivial adaptation."

"But I feel so bad," she said, slumping, pasting a hard little smile on her mouth.

More than anything, she wanted to pacify the frown etching a groove between her husband's brows but she felt incapable of it. Absently, Russell adjusted snowy white cuffs before he spoke. They could have been alone, for the subtle intimacy lacing his words.

"You won't always feel bad, Mandy," he said with gentle authority. "And you'll look back upon this opportunity and hate yourself that you didn't get through it somehow."

She sighed and poked at her lunch with a toothpick.

Sensing that they needed to be alone, Johnson discreetly excused himself and joined a neighboring table of friends.

Mandy stared dully at her hands, folded them, then sighed. "I would have thought that taking a trip to California was the last thing you would want me to do."

"The image of a chauvinist is something you forced on me, Mandy."

"But they don't need me to do the screenplay," she insisted, her head wrenching up swiftly at his accusation. "My contribution would be exactly zero."

When Russell looked away, staring at nothing, his jaw bunching tightly, she studied the beginnings of silver hair feathering back from his temples. Had she put that gray there? Yes, she supposed she had. She frustrated him endlessly. And Mandy knew, instantly, when he narrowed his brown eyes, that his intensity had nothing at all to do with California and screenplays. Or careers, or books.

"You undersell yourself, Amanda. I won't stand by and watch you do it," Russell said softly.

A tremor plunged through her limbs. "Oh, Russ, you—"

"You can make it," he said, his voice growing hoarse. "I'll go with you . . . all the way."

For a moment she fumbled with a button on her blouse, then stilled. She hadn't expected this demand for an answer to come so quickly!

A slow, coaxing smile caught the corners of his mouth. Yet his gaze remained thoughtful, solemnly lingering upon her lips, then moving higher to her brimming eyes. The yearning in his own reminded Mandy of every precious moment they had shared.

"I never knew a man like you. How can you be so understanding?" she questioned him, breathless.

"Because I love you," he answered simply. "And we're working at a partnership here, not a dictatorship."

"But you keep on waiting. I complicate your life. I inconvenience you. I—"

She stopped protesting. His ability to compliment her inner self was incredible. The muscle in Russell's temple leaped as his eyes increased the tenacity of their hold. He meant to have it now, all of it.

"I'll inconvenience myself anytime I choose, Amanda. And

I won't pretend it's easy or that it's not a worry. But it will be what *I* choose. And I'll expect you to do the same for me. That's the way a marriage works."

Mandy could hardly breathe, so naked were her weaknesses. And for once, she did not try to shield them.

"I'd depend on you too much, Russell. I'd wear you out with my insecurities. I'm in way over my head. . . . Half the time I'm bluffing—learning as I go and hoping no one can tell."

"You're dreaming, my darling, if you think I'm not. Don't put me on any pedestals simply because I can bluff, too. I'm a mass of needs, like anyone else."

Mandy pressed her palms together as if she were praying and held them against her lips to still their violent quivering. Her eyes closed, for she feared she would cry.

"Do you think there's a chance for us?" she whispered brokenly.

"Look at me," he said. For long moments he waited until she could compose herself enough to lift her eyes. She blinked rapidly with tear-spiked lashes. He touched her flushed cheek with a slow-moving fingertip. "Do *you* think there's a chance for us? You—" and he brushed across her nose with a knuckle, "—you still keep so much of yourself out of my reach."

Her editor could not have chosen a more inopportune time to return to the table. Russell breathed a particularly unpleasant oath and inclined his head toward Johnson. Mandy groped for the fleeting shreds of her facade.

"I've got to know, little one, Russell murmured, covering her hands with his large one. For a moment he toyed with the symbolic band of gold circling her finger. "I'm playing my high cards. I'm going for broke, Mandy."

The great knot of respect lodging in Mandy's throat refused to swallow down. Her words came with choked difficulty. "You're a good man, Russell Gregory."

"Well!" said Adam with a pleased interruption. "Everything must be decided." He thrust out his chest energetically and smiled without being seated, his hands resting on the back of his chair.

Mandy paused, a glass of water lifted halfway to her lips. Without tasting it, she put it down. It clattered against the table.

"Yes, she's going," Russell said gravely.

Russell's breaths came hard and roughened. From across the table, Mandy's eyes locked forcibly with his. Both men waited for her answer, for two drastically varied reasons. Every muscle in Russell's body seemed rigid. He ignored Adam and everything else around them.

"Aren't you, Amanda?" he repeated so quietly that she hardly heard him.

"Very good," congratulated Adam.

"She'll go," Russell said evenly.

Mandy sank back in her chair, washed with gratitude. He had known what she needed—someone to take things out of her hands, give her the push. If she had had to do it for herself, she would have shrunk from it. But for him? She'd kill herself trying.

"I told you, you'd feel better once you'd met 'em," Russell said, yanking off his tie and draping it across the arm of a piece of ultramodern furniture. "My mother doesn't *adore* many people," he added and rolled up the sleeves of a silk shirt.

"Oh come on," protested Mandy. Rather violently she threw herself onto a recliner. Layers of sheer apricot knit swirled about her knees in a graceful flurry. "Let's not get carried away, Russell."

With unhurried care Russell inspected the curve of her legs as she folded them beneath her. Lifting his brows then, he chuckled. He crossed his heart with the devilment of a boy.

"I swear." Then he imitated a feminine falsetto: "She's just adorable, Russell. Robert is simply taken with her."

"Well, he really was, you know," Mandy smirked. "He tweaked my ear."

"Dad tweaks every woman's ear. It's his favorite pass."

Mandy flung a pillow at his head. "Pessimist!" He laughed and ducked.

They had just returned from Sunday brunch with his parents who had come down to Manhattan just to meet Mandy. Though Mandy had been a shamble of nerves, her debut into the family was a small triumph.

For the last two weeks Russell had played the courteous, thoughtful father-to-be. He was her comfort, her constant friend, the guardian of her health. He vigorously supported her career. He made her the mistress of his luxurious town house.

Russell's conservative taste spilled over into the decor of his home—*their* home now. Muted shades of coral and gray lent a quiet background for spaciousness. His furnishings tended to Oriental simplicity. But it was a man's home, he said, and gave her free rein to change anything she wanted to. Long evening hours were spent planning changes that the baby's birth would necessitate. Sometimes they simply studied each other in silence as they read or watched television or lounged and listened to a Mahler symphony.

She was growing toward him. Her tastes were inseparably blending with his. Mandy did not question it any longer or resist it. He rarely disguised his masculine desire for her, nor the fact that he considered their marriage a permanent fixture. She hoped it would last. At times she glimpsed a vision of their future together. But she was still uncertain of it.

"If you still want to go sailing, you'd better change your clothes," he interrupted her musings.

Starting, she realized he had been studying her. His brows lifted at her preoccupation. "The lake is a good drive from here," he said. "This may be the last good day we'll have this year."

"I'm not a very good sailor," she offered, only half-hearing her own words. She stared at his easy grace as he lounged in the doorway, flipping a quarter with absent skill.

"You will be," he said softly and lifted warm brown eyes. Then he slapped the coin to the back of his wrist. "Heads says you will."

"Heads says I'll be a good sailor?" She shook her golden head in pretended doubt, for she knew what he meant.

"That you will be my wife, not just in my bed," he answered without hesitation and voiced what she had just been thinking. "People get married, but they don't have a marriage. Eventually it comes out—in a year, in five years, sometimes in twenty."

"I knew we'd face this," she said, growing suddenly warm as if she had drunk too much. "I've never kidded myself about it. But I don't know how."

He could always make her feel like a little girl, Mandy thought. He was always so many steps beyond her.

"I want to keep up with you, but you take large steps. I feel myself growing more in love with you every day. You'll have to admit I've come a long way," she said.

Russell, his wide shoulders slumping a fraction, accepted his failure. He sighed, then grinned wickedly.

"I know you have. Sometimes you've shocked me with your contradictions. But I've felt your reservations, too."

"Everyone has reservations," she protested, wishing it were not true.

"And lots of marriages never make it. I don't want just your surrender, darling. Almost any man, if he's patient enough, can make a woman surrender to her natural instincts. I want more from you. And I need to know what *you* want, everything you feel. What you think—*especially* what you think."

"I want what you want," Mandy said, something at a loss now, for she did not dare to think of giving that much. She had not said what he wanted to hear. She was not sure any person could say that much.

The lake was filled with small sailing craft; boats out for the last warm breezes of fall. As Russell helped her onto the *Gentle Lady,* Mandy found herself quickly becoming absorbed in his movements. The detachment from the bustle of the world, the only sounds being those of the boat and the water slapping against the hull, thrust her into a special world where his voice was a lifeline.

The *Gentle Lady* was a tightly made boat. Its brass fittings gleamed, and the cabin was just large enough for two people to squeeze past each other in comfort. Lines seemed neatly coiled everywhere, but Mandy had not the slightest notion of what any of them were for. Russell paused often to smile at her, to explain things he suspected she had no interest in. But talking kept pulling them together, gave them a reason to touch. Her looks of admiration exhilarated him. He enjoyed his own virile sex appeal because she enjoyed it.

Since Russell seemed to know everything, Mandy gradually relaxed. When he placed a rope in her hand and told her to pull hard, she gasped as the jib went up. Imitating him, becoming caught up in the ritual, she fastened her line and stared in rapt amazement as the mainsail flapped noisily and billowed, full and white. Soon they were skimming across open water.

"Nervous?" he asked after several minutes of relaxed silence.

"I was. At first," she admitted.

When he began explaining the principles of how they could sail against the wind, Mandy arranged some deck pillows and stretched like a sunning cat, enjoying his authority.

Though they sailed for an hour, they never lost sight of distant dots of other boats. Adjusting the mainsail so that they barely drifted, he slumped down beside her, stretched full length and clasped his hands behind his head.

Everything was so different on the water—the smell of the wind, the noise of the bow slicing through the water, and now the idle seduction of the harnessed swell and fall. The total absence of tension between them almost made her jittery. But they giggled and told corny jokes and watched the sun amble over the sky until it shot red blurs of color across the clouds.

"Hungry?" he asked.

Mandy nodded. "I'm growing perpetually hungry."

"We'd better start back," he said and made no move to go. Mandy flipped onto her stomach and searched for a station on the portable radio. She found Kenny Rogers and propped on her fists to listen.

Russell's fingers silkily drew up the hem of her shirt. Mandy stilled instantly, almost choking with sensations of exquisite delight. His lips lazily roamed over the small of her back, and she was incapable of moving, even if she had wanted to, which she did not. She only gave him a tiny whimpering encouragement and slumped over her arms as he curved his hand over the soft swell inside her thigh.

"Would you fight to keep me?" he whispered as he explored the smooth planes of her back with the tip of his tongue. "You would never leave me, would you?"

Stunned, her own pleasure forgotten, Mandy rolled over beneath the gentle play of his caress. She pulled up her head to stare at him, amazed that he would ask such a question. She had thought worry of this sort was hers, not his. He was the one who was always so sure of himself, of his appeal to other women, of his personality which could seduce anything from anyone.

"Well?" he countered the question brimming in her eyes. "You think I'm so macho that I don't suffer insecurities like that?"

"I think I'm not the only one who has kept secrets," she said wonderingly, deeply moved.

Leaning back on her elbows, she watched him toy with the

zipper of her jeans. And because she so wanted their marriage to work, her thoughts began to grasp one of the secrets of commitment.

It did not matter, she realized, if two people looked at a thing the way everyone else did: At nature, at God, at education, or children. But they had to be united in what they believed. They must know what the other thought and compliment it with their own thoughts.

"We have to go home, sweetheart," he said and kissed her nose.

"Yes," she said and smiled happily. "Home."

He rose and began letting out sail. Though she did not know as much, Mandy helped him. Together they were a team, working for the same thing. He had met her halfway about her book, hadn't he? She would do no less for his needs, all of them. And she would go the extra distance if she had to. She was astonished she had not seen it all before.

By the time Russell slipped the *Gentle Lady* into her mooring he was working in the dark. Clutching their paraphernalia, Mandy waited patiently as he skillfully secured canvas and lines of rope.

The roof of the boathouse was high, cutting off the chill of the wind. Standing inside it was like standing in a tunnel; the water slapped with hollow echoes and voices ricocheted back and forth.

Mandy waited on a narrow platform of planks forming a slender "U" around the boat. Wearying of the wait, Mandy fumbled about in the darkness for a low stack of folded canvas.

"I'm just about finished now," Russell called encouragingly.

The boat bumped lazily against its cushions of old tires anchored around the edge of planking. She squinted at the shadow of Russell's movement as he leaped lightly from the boat deck to the walkway. His deck shoes squeaked, and she walked toward the sound of his voice.

"Where are you, woman?" he called.

"I'm here," squeaked Mandy, inching nearer. "Don't you have a flashlight?"

"In a locker somewhere around here," he answered, his voice nearer now. Like a blind woman, Mandy reached for the sound of his voice. When her hand suddenly encountered the hardness of his chest, she gasped.

"I can't see anything in here," she giggled. "Let's go."

"Wait a minute. I'll get the flashlight. Don't want you to break your lovely little neck getting to the car."

As he stepped past her, Mandy stood stone still and smiled as he stubbed something and choked a blistering oath.

"Temper," she laughed. "Be still. Where's the silly locker? *I'll* find the flashlight."

Russell growled his complaint amid sounds of irritated rummaging.

Intending to help him, stumbling forward, Mandy collided headlong into him. His elbow struck the radio she held and, to her dismay, she dropped it. The Panasonic struck the planks with a thump, and she suffered visions of Russell kicking it into the water.

"Oh, darn!" she wailed.

"Don't move, babe," he ordered. "You'll kick it into the lake."

"I'm not moving, Russell! I'm standing perfectly still. And be careful, or you'll kick it over yourself. I swear this boathouse is moving. It's making me seasick," she yelped.

Cautiously she continued to flail about for the elusive stack of canvas. She inched forward. She had to sit or she'd throw up.

When her head smashed into Russell's, he gave a small grunt of pained surprise and grabbed her shoulders tightly. Holding her, he toppled to the side. They landed on the canvas with a heavy thud.

"I told you not to budge," he said.

"I was going to upchuck in your boathouse!"

Their legs were a tangled confusion, and Russell, half up, half down, began reaching outward for a bearing on their proximity to the water. In an attempt to escape from beneath his crushing weight, Mandy wriggled. The rubbing, the moving, the flaming awareness took their breath away. And both of them steadied their huffing and puffing.

"Now you will be still, I think," he said softly and positioned his body above hers.

Breathless, Mandy shoved against his chest. "I think the radio is beside my foot."

"Damn the radio," he said hoarsely and found her mouth with a hungry fierceness.

It was almost as if all their life's energies were focused upon this moment, like a blinding ray of the sun splintering through glass to burst into flames. Mandy felt herself turning to liquid, and Russell grew hard with denied wanting.

"What we have is good," he whispered and lost himself in the deep searching of another kiss.

Water whispered.

Breaths drew—slow and poignant.

Darkness sparkled with shifted weight and half-coherent murmurings.

"Russell, you're mad," she gasped after a moment.

"I'm horny," he said.

Mandy fumbled with buttons, and so did he. Nothing worked quickly enough. His hands seemed everywhere, and he drew her nearer, deeper into himself.

"I'm in your mind," he whispered, his hands full of her hair, holding her face up to his.

"What do you see?"

"I don't know. That you're burning. That you love me."

Mandy opened her mouth willingly and felt the smooth edge of his teeth. The kiss was intensely giving, not taking. The low sound in her throat was a yearning to share, not demanding.

He stood, pulling her up with him.

"It's forever, Mandy," he said and dropped her shirt at her feet. He spoke with his mouth against the bare curve of her shoulder. "No secret provisions anymore. No bailing out in case it gets rough."

"No bailing out," she repeated breathlessly, for his hands never stopped moving.

His fingers found the button to her jeans, her zipper, and then the silkiness of her naked hips, the backs of her legs. And the wet readiness she did not expect so quickly.

"But you—"she protested weakly as he dropped to one knee. She was thinking of his needs, and he was only aware of hers.

Her voice spun out, melting into submission when his lips moved across the trembling muscles of her waist, the smooth shelf of her pelvis. She sighed. And then she groaned, for he knew what to do. His fingers sank into her, and it was suddenly, almost savagely, upon her.

"No," he whispered. "Let me."

She held his head tightly and moved against his mouth, teaching him more. Then she was at his mercy and gave herself up to him, to the shattering point where he took her.

He took her beyond—again, and again—until she slumped against him, shivering, collapsing. It was like the setting of a seal which would not break, for he knew her that well now.

She could hardly see his face. She did not need to see his face. She carried his face inside her, burned into her.

When it was over, when she could walk, Russell found the radio and held her hand. They walked to the car in silence. They didn't need words, and they didn't need promises.

For a moment the clouds parted, and the moon winked at them. Mandy smiled at it and tried unsuccessfully to fit her steps to the longer ones of her husband. Pausing, glancing down at her, Russell automatically made his steps smaller to fit hers. And she lengthened hers to fit his.

It would always be that way, she thought. He would adapt. She would adapt. They would, for the rest of their lives, meet somewhere in the middle.

Dear Reader:

Would you take a few moments to fill out this questionnaire and mail it to:

Richard Gallen Books/Questionnaire
8-10 West 36th St., New York, N.Y. 10018

1. What rating would you give *An Innocent Deception?*
   ☐ excellent ☐ very good ☐ fair ☐ poor

2. What prompted you to buy this book? ☐ title
   ☐ front cover ☐ back cover ☐ friend's recommendation ☐ other (please specify) _____

3. Check off the elements you liked best:
   ☐ hero ☐ heroine ☐ other characters ☐ story
   ☐ setting ☐ ending ☐ love scenes

4. Were the love scenes ☐ too explicit
   ☐ not explicit enough ☐ just right

5. Any additional comments about the book?

   _____

6. Would you recommend this book to friends?
   ☐ yes ☐ no

7. Have you read other Richard Gallen romances? ☐ yes ☐ no

8. Do you plan to buy other Richard Gallen romances? ☐ yes ☐ no

9. What kind of romances do you enjoy reading?
   ☐ historical romance ☐ contemporary romance
   ☐ Regency romance ☐ light modern romance
   ☐ Gothic romance

10. Please check your general age group:
    ☐ under 25 ☐ 25-35 ☐ 35-45 ☐ 45-55 ☐ over 55

11. If you would like to receive a romance
    newsletter please fill in your name and
    address:

    _____

    _____

    _____

...the door swung shut behind her, Blanche snatched out...
...her tattered hat.